Nichole Severn writes explosive romantic suspense with strong heroines, heroes who dare challenge them and a hell of a lot of guns. She resides with her very supportive and patient husband, as well as her demon spawn, in Utah. When she's not writing, she's constantly injuring herself running, rock climbing, practising yoga and snowboarding. She loves hearing from readers through her website, www.nicholesevern.com, and on Facebook, @nicholesevern

Juno Rushdan is the award-winning author of steamy, action-packed romantic thrillers that keep readers on the edge of their seats. She writes about kick-ass heroes and strong heroines fighting for their lives as well as their happily-ever-afters. As a veteran air force intelligence officer, she uses her background supporting Special Forces to craft realistic stories that make readers sweat and swoon. Juno currently lives in the DC area with her patient husband, two rambunctious kids and a spoiled rescue dog. To receive a free book from Juno, sign up for her newsletter at junorushdan.com/mailing-list. Also be sure to follow Juno on BookBub for the latest on sales at bit.ly/bookbubjuno

Discover more at millsandboon.co.uk

GRAVE DANGER

NICHOLE SEVERN

AN OPERATIVE'S
LAST STAND

JUNO RUSHDAN

MILLS & BOON

First Published in Great Britain 2022
by Mills & Boon, an imprint of HarperCollins*Publishers* Ltd
1 London Bridge Street, London, SE1 9GF

www.harpercollins.co.uk

HarperCollins*Publishers*
1st Floor, Watermarque Building,
Ringsend Road, Dublin 4, Ireland

Grave Danger © 2022 Natascha Jaffa
An Operative's Last Stand © 2022 Juno Rushdan

ISBN: 978-0-263-30326-1

0122

MIX
Paper from
responsible sources
FSC™ C007454

GRAVE DANGER

NICHOLE SEVERN

For my babes: You drive me nuts, but I wouldn't
have it any other way.

Chapter One

Three months ago...

"When I'm done, you're going to beg me for the pain."

Chloe Pascale struggled to open her eyes. She blinked against the brightness of the sky. Trees. Snow. Cold. Her head pounded in rhythm to her racing heartbeat. Shuffling reached her ears as her last memories lightninged across her mind like a half-remembered dream. She'd gone out for a run on the trail near her house. Then... Fear clawed at her insides, her hands curling into fists. He'd come out of the woods. He'd... She licked her lips, her mouth dry. He'd drugged her, but with what and how many milliliters, she wasn't sure. The haze of unconsciousness slipped from her mind, and a new terrorizing reality forced her from ignorance. "Where am I?"

Dead leaves crunched off to her left. Her attacker's dark outline shifted in her peripheral vision. Black ski mask. Lean build. Tall. Well over six feet. Unfamiliar voice. Black jeans. His knees popped as he crouched beside her, the long shovel in his left hand digging into the soil near her head. The tip of the tool was coated in mud. Reaching a gloved hand toward her, he stroked the left side of her jawline, ear to chin, and a shiver chased down her spine against her wishes. "Don't worry, Dr. Miles. It'll all be over soon."

His voice… It sounded…off. Disguised?

"How do you know my name? What do you want?" She blinked to clear her head. The injection site at the base of her neck itched, then burned, and she brought her hands up to assess the damage. Ropes encircled her wrists, and she lifted her head from the ground. Her ankles had been bound, too. She pulled against the strands, but she couldn't break through. Then, almost as though demanding her attention, she caught sight of the refrigerator. Old. Light blue. Something out of the '50s with curves and heavy steel doors.

"I know everything about you, Chloe. Can I call you Chloe?" he asked. "I know where you live. I know where you work, and I know your running route and how many hours you spend at the clinic. You really should change up your routine. Who knows who could be out there watching you? As for what I want, well, I'm going to let you figure that part out once you're inside."

Pressure built in her chest. She dug her heels into the ground, but the soil only gave way. No. No, no, no, no. This wasn't happening. Not to her. Darkness closed in around the edges of her vision, her breath coming in short bursts. Pulling at the ropes again, she locked her jaw against the scream working up her throat. She wasn't going in that refrigerator like the other victim she'd heard about on the news. Dr. Roberta Ellis. Buried alive, killed by asphyxiation. Tears burned in her eyes as he straightened and turned his back to her to finish the work he'd started with the shovel.

"Don't bother trying to break the ropes. Dr. Ellis learned that the hard way when she dislocated her elbow trying to escape. She suffered for hours before she ran out of air. Needlessly, I might add. If she'd just followed the rules, she would've died peacefully like she was supposed to." *Peacefully.* He said the word as though he'd been doing her colleague a favor when he buried her inside a fridge just like this one. The scrape of metal on rock grated against her nerves. A pile of dirt landed beside her. He was digging a hole, large enough for the refrigerator to fit.

Her grave.

Chloe forced herself to take a deep breath, a combination of chemical cleaner and staleness burning her nostrils. He'd cleaned her makeshift coffin. Police hadn't been able to recover any forensic evidence from inside Dr. Ellis's tomb. It'd been wiped down with bleach before her killer had placed her inside.

She memorized the interior shape of the refrigerator, imagined the door closing on her forever. She had to stall for time. She had to find a way to get free. Scanning the trees and ground around her, Chloe fought to clear her head. Dr. Ellis's body had been buried within the city limits. If the man above her had kept to the same MO, she still had to be in Denver. "If you're going to kill me, why hide behind the mask? Why disguise your voice?"

A combination of dirt and ice froze her from the outside in. Her fingers stiffened. Depending on weather conditions, it took two hours to freeze a body solid. She could still move. They hadn't been out here long. She closed her eyes. She had to focus, listen. Yes, there. A breath of relief rushed from her lungs. Brakes on asphalt, but not a vehicle. Something heavier. A plane? Had her attacker intended to bury her by the airport? If she escaped—

"Oh, I'm not going to kill you, Dr. Miles." The man in the mask rounded back into her vision. Rough hands wrenched her to her feet, and the surrounding forest tilted on its axis. A hint of peppermint dove into her lungs. Gum? "I'm going to let the refrigerator do the job for me. Don't worry. The police will have your location by this time tomorrow, but, one way or another, the truth will come out."

The truth?

"Please, please don't do this. You don't have to do this!" Chloe fought to pull free of his gloved grip, but the ropes around her ankles only unbalanced her. She hit the ground hard. A few inches of soggy foliage softened the blow, but a sharp sliver of rock lodged in her side. A scream escaped her chapped lips. Blood spread across her long-sleeved shirt and jacket as her heart pumped faster.

"Hmm. Well, I don't like that." He stood over her, hands curling into fists. He'd discarded the shovel next to the hole meant to become her grave. "While any injuries inflicted will only make your last moments far more unbearable, that one is going to bleed you dry before I've had a chance to have my fun. But you know that better than anyone, don't you?" Digging into his black cargo pants, he knelt beside her. He produced a small orange plastic box. "Good thing I brought my first-aid kit."

"Go to hell." Covering her wound with both hands, still bound, Chloe locked her jaw against the scream. The rock hadn't gone in too deeply as far as she could tell, but he wasn't getting anywhere near her. Two tugs was all it took to dislodge it from her side, and another moan escaped her control. She quickly set the rock against the ropes around her wrists as he riffled through his small kit.

He laughed. "Every second you waste is another second you're likely to bleed out, Doctor."

The bloodied rock cut through the rope around her wrists faster than she'd expected. Kicking with every ounce of strength she had left, she connected with soft tissue protecting his digestive tract. Pain exploded down her side and across her back, but she shoved it to the back of her mind. Her attacker fell, and she swiped the rock underneath the rope around her ankles before he had a chance to rebalance. She didn't wait to see if he'd gotten up and forced herself to her feet. Chloe pumped her legs hard and ran, her heart in her throat. The main road had to be close. It had to be close.

A growl reached her ears, and she pushed herself harder. Puffs of crystalized air formed in front of her lips. Tears froze in their tracks down her cheeks, the dropping temperatures working to slow her down. She was a runner, but the laceration from her fall on the rock shot agony through her side. Barreling footsteps echoed from behind.

"Help!" she screamed as loud as she could, branches cutting the skin across her neck and face as she raced toward the sound of the road. Her breathing filled her ears. Was that a car passing? "Help!"

The trees started to thin, the light brighter here. Or was that the desperation playing tricks on her mind? Blood seeped through her fingers, but she didn't dare stop. Didn't dare look back. She had to keep going. She had to get to the road.

A wall of muscle slammed her into the icy dirt.

"You're faster than I gave you credit for." His lips pressed into her ear, his breath hot against her over sensitized skin. A shiver raked down her spine, intensifying everything around her. The trees. The roots. He wrapped both hands around one ankle and pulled. "Even when you're bleeding to death. That's why I've always admired you. Your determination. The quality of your work."

All too easily, she imagined Denver police heaving that light blue refrigerator out of the ground after her attacker's anonymous tip and finding her body inside.

"No!" Clamping onto the nearest root, Chloe heaved herself closer to the base of the large pine. The root broke away clean, and her attacker dragged her backward. She couldn't think—couldn't breathe—but she swung as hard as she could.

A groan filled the clearing. His hold on her ankle loosened. She clawed across the foliage. A whooshing sound reached her ears, and she exhaled hard, her tears stinging her cheeks. A car.

Chloe dug her fingernails into the nearest tree and

lifted herself to her feet. Run. No looking back. She stumbled forward, gaining strength with every step before she was finally able to jog. Every muscle in her body protested.

Another car drove past. Louder. Closer. Her heart threatened to beat straight out of her chest, but... slower than before. She gasped for air—she was losing too much blood. She could do this. Pressing her hand into her side, she pushed forward. Couldn't stop. He'd catch up any minute. He'd find her. She just had to flag down—

The ground dropped out from under her feet. She rolled end over end. Branches and bushes scratched at her skin as darkness closed in at the edges of her vision. Sliding down the last few feet before the road, Chloe closed her eyes as oxygen crushed from her lungs.

A rumbling tore down the road, growing louder, and she forced her eyes open. No. This wasn't the end. Pain tore through her as she flipped onto her side. She couldn't scream. Couldn't let him find her. "Move, damn it."

A red pickup truck barreled down the road. Chloe struggled to her feet. One step. Two. Asphalt solidified her balance as she raised her hand for the driver to stop. Tires screeched loud in her ears a split second before the darkness swallowed her whole.

Three months later...

THE CALL ABOUT the body had come in a little more than an hour ago.

Police Chief Weston Ford shoved his truck into Park,

the entrance to Contention Mine a soft outline through
the windshield. He pulled the flashlight from the glove
box and holstered his pistol. It was probably nothing.
Teenagers liked to come out here at night. Dare each
other to go inside the abandoned mines. It was a rite of
passage, proof they weren't kids anymore.

Straw weeds and bushes bent at the wind's whim
as he shouldered out of the vehicle. Snow had started
melting over the past few weeks, but low temperatures
still solidified the dirt under his boots as he surveyed
the area. Pressed right into the San Juan Mountains,
Battle Mountain, Colorado, and its twenty-eight hundred residents were stuck in the chaotic season shift
where the weather couldn't make up its damn mind. It
warmed above freezing during the day, but right now,
with the sun ducking behind the mountains, ice worked
under Weston's thick sheepskin, wool-lined jacket and
jeans. He reached back into the vehicle and collected his
cream-colored ten-gallon hat, centering it on his head.

He swept his flashlight around the edges of the mine.
Up until a few years ago, Contention Mine had been
the main source of income for the town and most of the
families who lived in it. The owners had been forced to
file for Chapter 11 bankruptcy when it became too hard
to even purchase toilet paper on credit, but the promise
of a fresh start had been enough for town residents to
hope. Until things got worse. Battle Mountain coal had
supported the economies of two states for decades and
fueled a shrinking number of power plants across the
country. Now more than six hundred families were out

of jobs while the entire town waited for a new company to take over operations.

They'd been waiting six years.

Weston surveyed the footprints in the dirt leading straight into the mouth of darkness. Too many sets to count. The wind rustled through thick pines on either side of the short incline leading into the mine. A low whistle reached his ears from inside. It'd been over a decade since he'd shoveled coal, but the layout had been engrained in his brain a long time ago. He crossed the threshold into pitch-blackness.

Thick supports braced up along either wall and crossed the ceiling above him in expertly measured intervals. The familiar scent of gravel and must dived into his lungs as he searched along the tunnel. His footsteps echoed off the walls the deeper he walked into the mountain. His heart thudded steadily at the base of his skull. None of the kids had waited around for him to show up, most likely terrified of what their parents would think of them crawling around in the deserted mine. But as Battle Mountain's only law enforcement officer, he was duty bound to check it out. In a dying town this small, most of the calls he responded to were domestic violence–related. The unemployment rate had skyrocketed into mid–double digits, stress was higher than ever, tempers raged, and he didn't have time for prank callers.

The ground sloped down. He followed the cart tracks at least three hundred feet. The tension bled from his shoulders, and Weston pulled up short of the slight decline. The flashlight beam vanished about ten feet in front of him. No sign of a body. No sign anyone had come this far into the mine.

"If anyone's down here, I think this is when you're supposed to jump out of the shadows and kill me. No takers? Great." His words tumbled one over the other as they echoed down the length of shaft. He'd wasted an hour climbing up the mountain and another twenty minutes getting dust and the smell of coal lodged into the fibers of his clothes. "Won't stop me from finding which one of you called in a false report."

He turned back toward the entrance, and a glint of something metallic caught in his flashlight beam. His nerve endings shot into awareness as he maneuvered the beam back. This was a coal mine. Nothing in this mountain should reflect light back like that. Weston closed in on the abnormality. He crouched over a dark patch of dirt. Loose. Disturbed. That didn't make sense. The mine had been shut down six years ago, and he doubted any of the teens in town would spend more time in here than they had to.

The pool of light spread over the patch as he set the flashlight between his teeth and reached for a pen he kept in his jeans. He scooped the metal from the dirt with the end of his pen. It looked like some kind of silver handle, fitting the shape of his hand. Scratches and a couple of dents gouged the worn surface. Mine workers were deliberate about bringing personal effects into the tunnels in case of an accident of the explosive or cave-in variety. Watches, photographs, rings, wallets—anything they could use to be identified in the aftermath.

But this length of stainless steel didn't seem to fit the bill. "Now what are you doing down here?"

Weston stepped back, gauging the width and height of the disturbed dirt. Approximately five feet by three feet. Who the hell would come out here to bury something? The hairs on the back of his neck stood on end, and the piece of steel slipped from the end of his pen. He positioned the flashlight near the wall, angling the beam down across the patch of dirt. Unpocketing his phone, he tapped the flashlight button and set his device screen down to cast a wider circle of light. Collapsing, he clawed through the first couple of inches of dirt and scooped it out onto either side of his knees.

He hit something solid.

He hesitated, feeling out the shape of what he'd found with both hands. Following the curve of cold steel, Weston pushed dried, packed dirt out of the way. The smooth surface of the container transformed into a ripple of lettering in the upper right-hand corner. He reached for the flashlight, brushing away as much dirt as he could to read the letters. "Galanz."

A refrigerator?

Warning knotted his gut tighter as he pushed back onto his heels. Something wasn't right. Shoving to his feet, he raced back to the entrance of the cave and out into the frigid temperatures seizing his muscles. He rounded the bed of his pickup and pulled a shovel from the back. Sweat built in his hairline despite the freezing temperatures. His legs protested the exertion as he worked his way back through the tunnel and started digging.

Friction burned his bare hands as he dug out the shape of the rest of the container. There was only one reason someone would come all the way out here to an abandoned mine and bury a refrigerator. No. He couldn't think like that. The call that'd come into the station had to be from one of the teens in town. This was a prank. Battle Mountain was safe. Plunging the end of the shovel into the crevice between the retrostyle refrigerator and the wall of dirt around it, he tore his jacket from his shoulders. Something broke away from the door, and Weston angled the flashlight into the shadowed hole.

A padlock.

Swiping his dirt-caked hands under his nose, he shook his head. Not a prank. Minutes passed. Hell, maybe an hour, but he wasn't going to stop. An ache set up residence in his shoulders as he discarded the last shovel of dirt off to his left. The refrigerator had been set perfectly level within the cocoon of dirt and gravel, the door and freezer box angled straight up toward the ceiling. One foot in the moat he'd shoveled around the container, Weston wedged his fingers between into the rubber seal and pulled.

The gray refrigerator door ripped open and slammed into the earth. Sickening odors escaped, penetrating through the mustiness of the mine as he stepped back. He covered his nose and mouth, but it'd be impossible to forget a smell like that. Decomposition.

He collected his phone from the ground and pointed the flashlight into the container. Air crushed from his lungs as the dust settled around him. Long brown hair coiled around the woman's thin shoulders, dark lashes sweeping across her colorless cheeks as though she were sleeping. Her blue pinstriped shirt and dark jeans followed the contorted shape of her body. The padlock. The burial. The evidence of cracked lips and broken fingernails that had been crusted with blood. A shot of nausea exploded up Weston's throat. It was impossible to get an identification from the swelling around her face and neck, but there was no doubt in his mind. The woman inside the refrigerator had been buried alive. "Holy hell."

He lunged away from the scene and braced himself against one wall as he emptied three cups of coffee from his stomach into the dirt. This wasn't happening. Not in his town. Not like this. Son of a bitch. He had to radio the station. His hands scraped along the walls as Weston stumbled back along the tunnel. The call hadn't been a prank, but his gut said the teens who hung around the mine hadn't been the ones to report the body. They wouldn't have even known it'd been there without unearthing the damn container used to suffocate her.

The killer had made the call.

Weston wrenched open the driver's side door and reached in for the radio strapped to his dashboard. Compressing the push-to-talk button, he tried to force the images he'd seen in that tunnel from his mind. In vain. "Macie, do you copy?"

The radio crackled before the sound clipped short. "Hey, Chief. How's the body hunt going?"

Ignoring the sarcasm in his dispatcher/receptionist's voice, he skimmed the back of his hand across his chin. The soft outline of Contention Mine stared back at him through the windshield, just as it had before. Only this time, a shiver chased down his spine. He'd taken over as police chief three years ago when Charlie Frasier had retired after forty years of protecting Battle Mountain. Nothing like this had ever happened in their town. He didn't have the resources or the officers for an investigation of this caliber, but he couldn't ignore the evidence he'd uncovered in that refrigerator. He had a dead woman on his hands, and he sure as hell was going to find out who put her there. "I need you to get that new coroner up here, the one who just moved here. You know whom I'm talking about. Dr. Pascale."

"Sure, Chief," Macie said. "Did those teens give you trouble, and you need help getting rid of their bodies?"

"No." Weston set his forehead against the steering wheel and closed his eyes. "The call wasn't a prank."

Chapter Two

She was living a lie.

A knot of tension set up residence in her stomach as Chloe hiked the short distance from her vehicle toward the mine's entrance. She wasn't sure why, other than the fact the call that'd pulled her out of bed obviously hadn't been because of natural causes. And she wasn't really a coroner.

She'd gone to medical school, but the license currently hanging in an ornate frame in the smallest back office of the town's funeral home didn't belong to her. Not really. Dr. Chloe Pascale, graduate of University of Colorado's School of Medicine, didn't exist. She'd searched for a graduate name, requested an official copy of their diploma, paid the fee, used her apartment address for the delivery and replaced their name with her assumed identity with the help of some videos online. Chief Ford hadn't questioned her credentials when she'd inquired about the job. She looked every bit the woman she intended him to see.

The police chief's pickup truck took shape off to her right, the headlights illuminating the dark mouth leading deeper into the mountain. She clutched her medical kit a bit tighter. Macie—Battle Mountain's dispatcher— hadn't been able to tell her much over the phone, but the tone in the woman's voice had revealed the urgency. Chief Weston Ford had discovered a body, and it was her job to investigate the cause of death.

Chloe's boots wobbled on the rough terrain. The small remote mining town was the opposite of everything she'd come to love about Denver. There, she'd had a salary, a support staff, an assistant, an office, family and grocery stores that stayed open past eight o'clock and on Sundays. She hadn't been prepared for the ruggedness of Battle Mountain—the isolation—but escaping to the last place anyone would think to look for her had been her only option. Goose pimples rose along her arms as she stepped into pitch-darkness. "Chief Ford? It's Chloe M—It's Dr. Pascale."

Her voice echoed down the long tunnel. Twice. Three times. Pinpricks of light filtered through the dark, and she put everything she had into shutting out the doubt clawing through her. She buried herself inside her thick coat and fisted the faux-fur collar together with one hand. She'd never been inside a mine before, let alone investigated a body dump. Her nerves shook like the leaves swirling around the entrance to the mine.

"I'm down here, Doc!" The chief's voice hooked into her, tugging her forward.

Chloe took a single step forward, then another. The walls seemed to close in on her all at once, but it was nothing compared to what she'd faced three months ago. She could still envision the exact light blue color of the refrigerator when she closed her eyes. No. She couldn't think about that right now. The chief needed her to ascertain the cause of death on a body left here in the mine. She needed to do the job she'd convinced him she was qualified for when he'd appointed her to the position the first week she'd come to town.

Her fingers tingled as cold set in. She'd been a cardiothoracic surgeon in Denver. She and her team had saved hundreds of lives through life-saving heart transplants, bypasses, stent placements and pacemakers. She could do this. The light at the end of the tunnel separated into two sources. A flashlight and what looked like the light from a smartphone, but she couldn't see much else other than the chief's muscular outline blocking the rest of the scene. Her eyes adjusted slowly. "Macie said you needed me. That you found a body?"

"Yeah. I appreciate you coming all the way out here. I know you haven't been in town long, but I wasn't sure who else to call." Weston craned his head over his shoulder. A few days' worth of beard growth intensified the sharp angles of his face. Dirt stained the waistband of his jeans and the damp white T-shirt clinging to his muscular frame, and she swallowed to counter the punch of attraction coiling through her. Sweat trickled from his short dark hair as he sidestepped around a large hole, giving her a perfect view of what he'd uncovered. "I didn't want to move her."

Everything inside of her went numb.

Blood drained from her face and neck, her entire body heavier than a moment before. She traced the outline of the light gray refrigerator with her gaze, memorized the damage along the edges. Most likely brought on by the shovel in the chief's grip. The dull shape of a padlock—so stark against the darkness of the dirt around the container—claimed her attention. Weston had ripped the door open, exposing the body within, but Chloe couldn't convince herself any of it was real. It couldn't be. She'd escaped. She'd disappeared. This wasn't happening again.

"Doc? You okay? You're looking a little pale." The chief reached out, settling his hand beneath her elbow as though to steady her. His concern battled to counter the ice crystalizing in her veins, but it wasn't enough. It would never be enough. "I have some water in my truck. I'll get it for you."

She didn't want to be left alone with the victim staring back at her.

"No. I'm okay, but thank you." Chloe forced herself to study the woman trapped inside the container, her hands shaking. Long brown hair framed a diamond-shaped face. Warm-toned skin had been drained of warmth upon death and highlighted high-arched eyebrows expertly manicured above the victim's eyes. Lacerations cut through a full bottom lip with the slight hint of bruising along one side of the woman's face. But it was the broken fingernails, painted dark blue and crusted with blood, that stole her voice now. Corresponding scratches were gouged into the interior of the refrigerator door. Chloe motioned to the victim. "Do you... Do you know who she is?"

"I searched her pockets. I didn't find any ID, but in a town this small it's hard not to know everyone who lives here." Weston cleared his throat. "I'll wait for your official report, but I'm almost positive this is Whitney Avgerpoulos. Her family owns the Greek restaurant on Silver Street."

"Did they report her missing?" she asked.

Weston shook his head, grief evident in his expression, in the sinking of his shoulders. "Whitney goes to Colorado Mesa University. She's supposed to be at school right now. She's getting her degree in psychology."

Her heart jerked in her chest as the weight of losing one of his own settled between them.

"I promise to be gentle with her." She'd lived with that same feeling the moment she'd heard of her colleague's murder back in Denver, and she wouldn't wish it on anyone. Chloe unpocketed her phone and tapped the flashlight button. She set down her medical bag. "I'm going to need help removing her from the refrigerator, but before we do that, I need to document the scene."

The chief nodded, a line of determination cutting through his expression. Coming out of his trance, he set the shovel against the nearest wall. "Tell me what you need me to do."

"Can you move your flashlights over her? It'll help with the photos." He did as she asked, and Chloe documented the scene as best she could. Every tap of her phone's camera button echoed around them and punctured through her nerves. She'd gone to medical school, became a surgeon, to help people, to give them a chance. Whoever had put Whitney Avgerpoulos inside the fridge had taken away that chance.

She ensured she'd photographed every inch of the hole Weston had dug around the refrigerator, the container itself and as much detail from the victim as she could. Advancing technology had the capability of seeing more than the human eye. There was a chance her phone had captured something neither she nor Weston could see right now. Crouching, she angled her phone's flashlight to beam from the other side of Weston's, then pulled a tarp from her medical kit. She unfurled the plastic—so loud against the thready pulse throbbing behind her ears—and laid it out flat. "We need to take her out of the refrigerator now."

Weston moved without answering.

Chloe stepped down into the space between the sidewall of the hole and the container, fitting her hands under the victim's right leg and shoulder, as the chief did the same on the other side of the body. They hefted the victim free from the refrigerator and set her gently on the tarp. "I'll collect as much as I can from her hair, fingernails and clothing, but I won't be able to run the tests myself. I have to send it to the Unified Metropolitan Forensic Lab in Denver."

Extracting the sterile cuticle sticks, she ran one each under the victim's broken fingernails and secured them in evidence bags. The weight of Weston's attention pressurized the air in her lungs as he watched from a few feet away. There wasn't anything more she could tell him, nothing she could say that would make the situation easier to process. No matter how much she wanted to. She collected as much evidence from the victim as she could, including a swab of what looked like blood from Whitney's collar. There was a high possibility the sample belonged to the victim given the state of her lip and fingernails, but she'd have the lab run it anyway.

"I'm finished." She secured the evidence inside her medical bag and raised her gaze to the chief's. "We'll need to get her to my SUV so I can perform the autopsy back at my office. I should be able to give you and her family an official cause of death in the next couple of days." Her "office" was nothing more than a generous description for the town's funeral home exam room, but it was all she had to offer.

"Thanks, Doc." Weston didn't move, didn't even seem to breathe. "I'm not sure I could've done this without you."

Her gaze wandered to the gray '50s-style refrigerator still half-buried in the earth a few feet away, and a strike of remembered soreness shot through her. The mostly healed wound in her side caught fire as though aware of the thoughts in her head. She'd survived her attacker, made it out of those woods with some of the same injuries as the woman in front of her. Her fingers curled into the centers of her palms as the memory of clawing free from her killer's hold flashed to the front of her mind. She couldn't ignore the striking similarities between Whitney Avgerpoulos and herself. The same shade of hair color, the wide nose and full lips. Based on her heritage, Chloe could imagine the same color of light green in the victim's eyes as hers if she were able to see them. Their skin tones differed, but not enough to set them widely apart. Had the killer come looking for Chloe, only to mistake this woman's identity? She tore her gaze from the scene and fisted both hands in the tarp under the body. "I'm glad I could help."

They moved as one, hauling the victim free from her mountain grave. The chief might not have been able to do this without her, but Chloe couldn't help but wonder if this woman had been killed because of her.

HE'D NEVER HANDLED a homicide investigation before.

In the three years he'd taken over as police chief for Battle Mountain, there hadn't been a single case that'd ended in murder. The preliminary results from the coroner hadn't come back yet, but there was no other way to look at it. Whitney Avgerpoulos hadn't locked herself inside that refrigerator on her own. She wouldn't have destroyed her fingernails trying to claw free if she'd had some part in her own disappearance. No. One of his town's residents had been murdered, and he was going to find out who was responsible.

Weston hiked the short set of stairs leading to the cabin-like home at the end of Bluff Street. The Avgerpouloses's red-brown vertical planking contrasted with the minimalist rock design of the yard. A set of antler horns stood guard over the front door and screen. Despite the desertlike landscaping, the air had a bite to it this early in the morning. He hadn't slept—hadn't eaten—since helping Dr. Pascale get the victim's remains to the funeral home. Not just a victim. Whitney. He'd known Gregory and Delphine Avgerpoulos since they'd arrived in town nearly twenty years ago. Hell, he'd eaten at their restaurant a couple blocks away more times than he could count. He knew these people, but today wouldn't be a social call.

Old hinges protested as he swung the screen wide and rapped on the front door three times. Hints of vanilla and fresh bread in the air filled his lungs from the bakery two streets over. Tall pines and uneven landscape hid his view of the gulch on the other side of the trees surrounding the property on three sides. What the hell was he supposed to say when they answered?

Footsteps shuffled louder from the other side of the wooden door a split second before Gregory Avgerpoulos opened it wide, his dark gaze brightening with an equally matched smile. Aluminum gray hair, peppered with hints of brown, receded halfway down the back of Gregory's shiny head. Thick eyebrows and tanned skin testified to his heritage, but it was the laugh lines branching from either side of his wide nose that caught Weston's attention now. "Chief, to what do we owe the pleasure? Come in, come in." The midsixties father, husband and restaurateur turned back into the house as he cleared the entryway to make room for Weston. "Del! Weston's here."

"Oh, my boy!" Delphine's voice filled the entire house as Weston crossed the threshold just before the woman herself stepped into sight, arms wide. Dark brown hair, coiled in a football helmet of curls, surrounded the woman's head. At nearly six-feet tall, the matriarch of the Avgerpoulos family towered over her husband, but her loud, buoyant personality was what put her over the top. A bright red button-down shirt with geometric patterns in equally bright colors was all he saw just before she wrapped him in one of the most lung-crushing hugs he'd ever experienced. "So good to see you, honey." Pulling back slightly, she pinched his jaw in a strong grip and studied him with deep-set eyes highlighted with bright blue eyeshadow. "It's early. You look like you could use something to eat. Let me get you something."

Weston managed only a few words of protest with his lips squeezed together, but Del ignored every single one of them with two slaps to his cheek. She shuffled into the kitchen as Gregory collapsed into a beat-up recliner as old as he was. The couple had most likely been up for hours.

"No use in fighting her, boy." Gregory's graveled voice reverberated through his chest and rattled slightly. "I think that's how she's gotten me to stay for so long. She just keeps feeding me so I'm too slow to run away."

"I'd take that deal." Weston shut down the urge to relax and removed his hat, pinching the brim between his thumb and index finger. Photographs of the family stared back at him from over the old brick fireplace with brass fixtures. Pictures of Gregory and Del on their wedding day, surrounded by smiling faces. One with Del covered head to toe in the same maroon paint clinging to the walls in this room. The day they opened their Greek restaurant here in Battle Mountain twenty years ago. Baby pictures of Whitney, all the way through elementary school to high school graduation. Weston picked one from the collection. The twenty-two-year-old had an entire life ahead of her after she graduated college. She'd planned on becoming the town's first therapist and helping with the restaurant when her parents needed her. Pressure built under his sternum, and he replaced the photo on the mantel. He wasn't here for lunch. "Have either of you heard from Whitney lately?"

Del danced back into the living room with a plate filled with pita bread, white clumps of cheese, some kind of meat and a whole lot of onion and vegetables. "Not since she visited two days ago. She should be home again on Friday to help with things at the restaurant. We are just so proud of her. Our college girl. Maybe when she is done with her studies, you two can finally go on a date. Neither of you are getting any younger." She set the plate on the small round table separating the living room from the kitchen at the back of the house and pulled out a chair. "Come, sit. You look like death."

"That's very kind of you, but I'm not here for breakfast, Del. I'm here on official business. About Whitney." Weston didn't know how to do this, but he couldn't keep the truth from them. Their daughter—their only child—wasn't coming home.

"Why would you be here about Whitney? She's at school." Gregory locked those small dark eyes on him as Del closed the distance between her and her husband. The old man struggled to his feet, his expression set in hard stone, and gone was the welcoming atmosphere of the family's home. "Spit it out, boy. Tell us what is happening."

"Did something happen to our Whitney?" Del pressed a hand to her chest as though preparing for the worst. She would need the fortification.

"A call came last night around eleven. Someone reported finding a body in the mine. I responded, positive it was just teenagers messing around." Weston dropped his gaze to his hat, unable to face their pain. "But that wasn't the case. I found Whitney."

"No, you're wrong." Anger filled the old man's expression as he shook his head. Gregory shucked off his wife's hand and stepped forward. "That's impossible. Whitney's at school. She went back two days ago. She wouldn't have any reason to be in that mine. You're lying."

"I'm sorry. The coroner and I were able to collect evidence, take photographs and have her remains removed from the container we found her in." A knot of shared grief tightened behind his rib cage, strangling his own breath. "But her dental records from Dr. Corsey confirm it. Whitney is dead."

A high-pitched sob punctured through the living room and set his nerve endings on fire. Delphine Avgerpoulos collapsed, one hand out as though reaching for support, but Weston couldn't force himself to move. Her husband wrapped her in his arms, setting his withered cheek against her mountain of hair.

"I'm very sorry for your loss, Mr. and Mrs. Avgerpoulos." He stepped to the mantel, to the box of tissues, and grabbed the box. After offering each of them a tissue, he took a seat on the edge of a matching recliner next to Gregory's. "I give you my word we're doing everything we can to find out what happened to her, but I need to ask you some questions."

Del nodded, her eyes still closed. "Anything."

"Did Whitney mention any new people in her life, possibly a man you hadn't met yet?" As much as women were capable of murder, it was highly unlikely the person who'd held Whitney down in order to seal her inside the fridge was female. The inclusion of the refrigerator told him the girl's murder had been premeditated. The son of a bitch who'd done this would've had to have been strong enough to haul the damn thing into place before killing his victim.

"No," Gregory said. "No men. Just her friends from school. She has a roommate. We have her phone number on the fridge. Why wouldn't she have called us if Whitney never made it back to school?"

"I'll take her number if you don't mind. I'll be sure to get an account of the last time she saw Whitney." Replacing his hat on his head, Weston unpocketed his notebook and a pen from his coat. "I'll also need the make, model and license plate of her car if you have it and permission to pull her cell phone records."

"What did you mean, you and the coroner removed her from a container?" Del clung to her husband. The gut-wracking sobs were gone now, and a fresh wave of clarity and controlled rage hardened the woman's face. "You ask about new men in her life. You found her in a mine. You collected evidence, you need her car information, you want her cell phone records. Why is all of this necessary?" Del climbed to her feet, staring down at him with promised fire in her eyes. "You tell me the truth, Weston Ford. What happened to our little girl?"

He'd hoped to avoid the details, but they deserved

to know. Meeting her at her level, Weston stood. "The evidence suggests Whitney was murdered."

Del stumbled back a step but refused to go down as Gregory settled back into his recliner behind her. "Who? Who did this to my Whitney? Tell me so I can kill them myself."

"We're not sure yet. I have the coroner examining her now. I'll keep you updated as soon as I have any news. Until then, I need you to call me if you think of any changes in Whitney's life. No matter how small. Understand?" He curled his fingers tighter around his pen. Grief affected people in different ways, and Weston had no doubt in that moment this mother would do as she threatened if given the chance. Hell, he would've done the same if there'd been anyone to punish after his wife had passed, but this wasn't about him. "I'm going to find who did this to her, Del. I'm going to make them pay. I give you my word." He sighed. "Is there someone I can call for you? Your priest or a friend?"

They both shook their heads.

His phone chirped with an incoming call. "I have to take this, but I'll be in touch soon."

Weston left the Avgerpoulos home, kicking up dirt as he headed for his truck. He answered the unidentified number on the fourth ring. "Yeah, this is Ford."

"Chief, it's Dr. Pascale, the...coroner." Her voice wavered with nervousness as she spoke, and he couldn't help but smile at her assumption he'd forgotten her so quickly. "I've just finished Whitney Avgerpoulos's autopsy. There's something you need to see."

Chapter Three

Chloe tore the latex gloves from her hands and deposited them into the hazardous waste basket on the other side of the room. The back room of Jacob Family Funeral Home filled with the chemical odor of a variety of preservatives, sanitizing and disinfectant agents. White upper and lower cabinetry wrapped around two walls of the small space. It wasn't much, but considering there were too few businesses in Battle Mountain willing to handle remains for free, it was all a town this size had to offer.

The steel examination table supporting the remains intensified the colorless pallor of the victim's face and neck exposed by the sheet she'd draped over the body. Chloe studied the sutures holding a perfect Y incision together from shoulder to sternum. Whitney Avgerpoulos hadn't died quietly. While it would take a few days for the samples she'd sent on to the Unified Metropolitan Forensic Lab to render any results, perimortem bruising didn't lie. The victim had fought back. Maybe enough that the killer's identity was somewhere in these samples. Maybe enough to end the nightmare she slipped into every night when she closed her eyes.

"Doc?" The chief centered himself in the doorway, and Chloe stepped back into the corner near one of the cabinets, her heart shooting into her throat. Glass jars stocked with Q-tips, cotton balls and tongue depressors rattled from the impact. Weston raised two sets of coffees as though preparing to approach a wild animal with an offering. The florescent light tubes overhead reflected off the large oval belt buckle at his waist, instantly drawing her gaze down his body. Light stains of dirt dusted the thighs of his jeans and creased his white T-shirt, revealing he hadn't gone home to change since they'd removed the victim's remains from the mine. "Sorry. I didn't mean to startle you. You said you had something for me?"

She shook her head in an attempt to force herself back into the moment and crossed the small preparation room to collect her notes from the other set of cabinets. "Yes. Please, come in, Chief Ford. I just…wasn't expecting you to get here so quickly."

"Not sure if you know this, but it's a small town. It takes me less than five minutes to get anywhere, and you can call me Weston." He stretched one of the coffees toward her. The to-go cup featured the logo of the coffee shop she'd recently discovered on one of her trips through town. Caffeine and Carbs, a combination bakery-and-coffee shop that rivaled the major chain she'd visited in her previous life. "Figured you could use some caffeine. I wasn't sure what you liked, but Reagan assured me your last order was black with two sugars."

"Thank you." Surprise rocketed through her as she took the promise of energy and happiness rolled into one. Her finger interlaced with the chief's for the barest of moments, and a curl of warmth slid through her. Weston had been right. She definitely needed the pick-me-up, considering she hadn't slept since bringing the body back here to the funeral home. The heaviness she'd noted in his body language, the grief that'd contorted his expression in that mine—it'd given her motivation to complete the autopsy as quickly as possible. To give him and the victim's family some kind of answer, but she couldn't ignore the truth. Whoever had attacked Whitney, whoever had buried her in that mine inside a refrigerator, knew Chloe was here.

This victim had been a message.

She wrapped both hands around the cup to chase back the permanent ice of the room. "He remembered my coffee order?"

She read her name written in slanted masculine marker. *Chloe*. Reagan had even spelled it right.

"He remembers everyone's coffee order. I think he keeps notes." Weston pointed to the victim, rounding the other side of the exam table. He worked that chiseled jawline with the press of his back teeth as he studied the young woman's face. "I just had to tell her parents she wasn't coming home from school this weekend. They didn't believe me. Thought I'd made a mistake. She was their only child. Studying to become a psychologist. She was a good kid. Never got into trouble with the law. Parents said she kept to herself, roommate said there hadn't been any major changes in her behavior or

schedule recently. She figured Whitney had decided
to stay in town to help her parents, which happened a
few times now that they're getting older. Didn't mention anyone new in her life, but there has to be a reason
someone did this to her."

That same heaviness she'd noted in Weston's voice
inside the mine's shaft settled behind her rib cage.

There *was* a reason Whitney Avgerpoulos had been
targeted. Because of Chloe.

Fear and shame lodged in her throat. The evidence
they'd encountered suggested this murder and the attempt on her life three months ago had to be linked,
but detailing her past for a stranger she'd just met shut
down the part of her that craved to share her secret. She
handed off the file folder with her handwritten notes
she'd recorded during the autopsy. "This is everything
I was able to determine during the examination, but the
main thing I wanted you to see is the puncture wound
at the base of her neck."

Setting her coffee on the counter, Chloe tugged a
new set of gloves from the flimsy cardboard box and
snapped them into place. She motioned Weston around
to her side of the table and pressed her index finger just
below the puncture mark. "I sent a sample of her blood
along with the evidence we collected at the scene for
a toxicology screen. There is evidence of a struggle
in the perimortem bruising across her face and down
her arms, which means it was caused in or around the
time of her death. I'm almost positive whoever attacked
Whitney sedated her before putting her into that refrigerator, but she fought him." Images of a ring of trees,

of the wind on her skin, of lethargy and fear battled to the front of her mind. She straightened, reaching for the coffee cup as though its contents could fortify her against the oncoming storm. "He would've sedated her to get her into the refrigerator. When it wore off—"

"She tried to claw her way out," Weston said.

"Yes." Chloe nodded. "Based on the dimensions of the refrigerator, the victim's size and the evidence of her desperation to get free, I calculated she died of asphyxiation within an hour of waking. The lab can determine what kind of sedative her attacker injected her with. From there, you should be able to trace the drug's purchase to a potential buyer."

"I'm the one who's supposed to protect this town. How could I have let something like this happen?" Weston turned away from the examination table, his head sinking.

"You know as well as I do this isn't something you could've predicted." Her gut clenched at the assumed guilt lining the tendons between his neck and shoulders. Chloe pressed her lower back into the cabinet behind her for support.

"Is there any way to get a rush on those results?" he asked.

"I've already put in the request, but the lab is backed up. They handle over seventy-five percent of the forensic evidence for criminal cases throughout the state. It could be a few days, even a few weeks before we see anything, but I will let you know as soon as I hear something. The only thing we can do now is wait." There wasn't much else she could do. Not here. Her gaze wandered back to the victim. She'd lost patients before, but there'd always been a sense of hope before she'd operated. This... There'd been no hope in this. "Can I ask how you knew she was out there? According to town gossip, Contention Mine has been closed for nearly six years."

He didn't turn to face her, his head low.

"Macie took a call at eleven, but the caller wouldn't give his name. He said there was a body in the mine. When I got there, I figured it'd just been kids playing a prank. She's tried calling the number back, but there's no answer and no record of anyone registered to that number. I'm working on a warrant for the local usage details. I have a feeling whoever placed the call used a burner." Weston shucked the guilt-ridden exterior and straightened, every ounce the police chief she'd met her first day in town. "Have you ever seen anything like this in all your time as a coroner?"

All of her time as a coroner consisted of two months on the job. In those short few weeks, she'd autopsied one resident who'd died of natural causes. But personally? She had more experience than he would know what to do with. She decided to answer honestly. "No. I haven't."

Weston shook his head. "How are you holding up? Can't imagine you've gotten much sleep or anything to eat since last night."

The question knocked her control off balance. One of his town's residents had been murdered, but he wanted to know how she was holding up? Terrified, isolated, helpless—all the same emotions she'd experienced when she'd woken in the hospital after her attack. Only tenfold. This wasn't just about her anymore. Another victim had been killed. One tied to the new town she'd run to hide in. Chloe tossed her unfinished coffee in the trash and ripped the latex gloves from her hands before shoving them in her lab coat pocket. "I was going to go home and catch a couple hours of sleep after I finished here. I won't be able to release her remains to her family until the investigation is concluded, but I'll make sure Mr. Jacob takes good care of her while she's here."

"You're good at dodging personal questions, Doc, but considering you look as beat as I feel, I'll let it slide." Weston tossed his to-go cup into the same trash can, a hint of aftershave and dirt cutting through the smell of embalming fluid, which was a permanent part of this establishment. "Have you at least eaten anything?"

"I'm fine." She pointed toward the door, every nerve ending she owned frantic to end the personal conversation between them. The more questions he asked, the more she had to lie, and lying to him could get her removed from this investigation. There had to be a connection between her attack and this murder, but she wouldn't put anyone else's life at risk to find it. "I grabbed a bag of chips from the vending machine at the front a couple hours ago. There are still a few left in the bag if you're interested."

"Breakfast of champions." He headed for the door and into the hallway. "There's a diner down the block. Greta's on Main. Great food. I'll be there eating my bodyweight in waffles and bacon for the foreseeable future if you're still hungry."

Chloe followed him through the building, past the casket showroom and to the front door. She had to stay detached from the people here. From him. It was the only way to make sure nobody else would get hurt. As soon as she handled the details of Whitney Avgerpoulos's remains, she'd get out of town. Move on to the next place. She'd start over. "Thank you, but I'm—"

The glass door exploded around her, and she hit the floor.

HER SOFT EXHALE brushed against the underside of his jaw.

Weston tried to keep his weight off her, but the force with which he'd tackled her to the floor had pinned her beneath him. A waterfall of brown hair tangled in his hands as he searched her face for the slightest sign of distress. The edge of her thick dark eyebrows met over the bridge of her nose and deepened the small vertical line between them. Pale green eyes searched their surroundings as she set her hands against his chest, and an explosion of adrenaline and concern combined into a vicious tornado of emotion. Someone had just shot at them. "Tell me you're okay."

"Kind of hard to breathe." Full pink lips parted as she pressed against him.

"Oh, sorry." Weston rolled off her and shoved to his feet. He offered her a hand, locking his jaw against the comfort of her soft gold skin, and tugged her to her feet. Their breaths mixed in the small space between them before he forced himself to release her. Glass crunched under his boots as he surveyed the damage. A frigid burst of air raised the hairs on the back of his neck. "Stay here."

He wrenched what was left of the glass door open and stepped out onto Main Street. A few parked vehicles. Little movement. Fragments of startled conversation and worried faces filtered in from his peripheral senses as he jogged into the middle of the road. No sign of the shooter. No vehicle leaving the scene. His heart caught in his throat. Whoever had shot at them was already gone. He twisted around, facing the residents hugging against the walls of the fly shop and the small internet café on either side of the funeral home. "Is everybody okay? Is anyone injured?"

Terror contorted the faces of the townsfolk, but no sign of injuries. He'd gather statements as soon as he determined they were all safe.

Footsteps echoed from behind as Frank Jacob Sr., the funeral home director himself, lurched to a stop on the sidewalk outside the property. "Chief, I heard the shot from the back room. What's going on? Is there anything I can do?"

Details raced through his mind. Less than eight hours ago, he'd uncovered the remains of a young woman. Now this. It couldn't be a coincidence. Whitney Avgerpoulos's murder and the shooting had to be connected. Whoever had targeted the funeral home obviously hadn't wanted an investigation into her death. They would've known he'd brought the victim's remains here, where the coroner worked. The bastard must've followed him from the mine, which meant... "Chloe."

She brushed pieces of broken glass from her white

lab coat and stumbled from the shattered remains of the front door.

The homicide investigations he'd studied over the years had all had a similar theme. Murderers would do whatever it took to ensure they weren't caught. If Whitney Avgerpoulos's killer had gotten word Weston had taken the case, there was a chance the perp would target anyone involved. Including the coroner who'd collected evidence from the remains. He charged back onto the sidewalk. "Mr. Jacob, I need you to secure Whitney Avgerpoulos's remains as soon as possible. Move them to another location if you have to, but I want them under lock and key."

"I don't understand." The thin aging director's hollowed cheeks sank a bit deeper as confusion set in. "What's going on?"

"I don't have time to explain. Please, make sure nobody but you has access to her or any evidence Dr. Pascale hasn't forwarded to the lab until we figure out who took that shot," he said. "I'll have someone from Hopper's start working on your door as soon as I can. Until then, make sure everyone here is okay, and send them to the station to give a statement to Macie."

"I'll do what I can." Frank Jacob strode back into the funeral home.

Frantic questions penetrated through the ringing in his ears as he closed the distance between him and Chloe. *Chief, what happened? Who would do this? Are we in danger?* Damn it. He didn't have answers, but it was only a matter of time before the town learned of Whitney's murder and the wildfire of rumors would spread. This was already getting out of control. He slid his hand between the doc's rib cage and arm, directing her to his pickup parked down the street. "Come on. I need to get you out of here."

"You think this is related to Whitney Avgerpoulos's murder." She quickened her step to keep up with him as he pulled her down the street past Hopper's Hardware. "That whoever killed her might be targeting us to keep us from solving the case." Her voice remained even despite the fact they'd just survived a shooting. How the hell was that possible under the circumstances when it took everything in him not to panic? "You can drop me off at my apartment. I'll pack a bag and check in to the hotel."

Weston wrenched open the passenger side door of his truck and deposited her inside. Townspeople called after him as he rounded the front of the pickup and collapsed behind the wheel. The twenty-year-old engine growled to life, and he ripped away from the curve, heading straight out of town. His position required him to gather statements from witnesses and collect evidence, but all he could think about was Chloe's safety. "You can't go back to your apartment or to the funeral home. Whoever pulled the trigger might already know where you live. As of this moment, you're officially under Battle Mountain PD protection."

Main Street shops bricked in various shades of red and thick clusters of winter-stripped trees blurred in his peripheral vision as they left the town limits. Snow-capped peaks demanded attention as they headed west.

His heart pounded behind his ears as he fought the onslaught of adrenaline.

"And by Battle Mountain PD, you mean you. Alone," she said.

"Not alone, really. Macie has her concealed carry permit." The weight of her attention told him adding Macie into the mix hadn't helped his case, and she was right. Battle Mountain didn't have the resources of Grand Junction, where she'd come from, or any of the bigger cities across the state, but this small mining town was all he had. As much as he wanted the truth to be different, there was no changing their reality. He wasn't real law enforcement. He'd taken the role of police chief after no one else in town had been willing to step up when Charlie Frasier suffered a heart attack on the job. In the eyes of the town, he was the one responsible for protecting every man, woman and child in and out of these town limits. Hell of a job he was doing so far, but just because he hadn't gone to the academy, didn't mean he wasn't capable of keeping Chloe safe.

"Okay, so you and your dispatcher." That sense of calm he'd noted earlier cracked on her last word and sucker punched him straight to the gut as though she'd physically hit him. "No offense, Chief, but have you or Macie worked an active shooter or homicide investigation before?"

"No." He took his eyes off the road ahead to glance in her direction. "Have you?"

The doc pulled her shoulders back, sitting a bit straighter in her seat. Sun cut through the back windshield of the pickup and highlighted the barely evident birthmark on her chin. "No. The people I work with are usually victims of those two scenarios."

"I guess that makes us even." Weston gripped the steering wheel tighter. "You and I are the only two people who know what really happened to Whitney Avgerpoulos, and we're the only two who can bring her killer to justice. Her parents deserve to know what happened to their little girl. I can't do this without you, Doc."

Chloe directed her attention out the passenger side window and up the jagged peaks of the San Juan mountains. Hints of her perfume still clung to his T-shirt and jacket and filled the cabin of the truck. Something complex, mysterious even. Bright citrus notes and a smooth touch of bourbon that caught in his throat. Hell, he'd never smelled anything like it and wanted to drown in it. A crushing wall of apprehension slammed into him as she turned in her seat to face him. "I was able to ship the samples I collected from the mine and the victim's remains to the forensic lab just before you arrived. Lucky for us, I got everything I could from her before the shooting, but we won't be able to get a conviction if her remains are compromised. I heard you tell Mr. Jacob to move her to a secure location. As long as he follows instructions, you'll have a case. I've done my job. You don't need me."

Instinct raised goose bumps on the back of his arms, and Weston pulled the truck to the side of the road. Dirt kicked up alongside both doors and clouded the view behind them. Draping one hand over the steering wheel, he faced her, memorized her expression, the slight changes in her breathing.

"What are you doing?" she asked.

"I've been working under the impression that bullet was meant for me. Tell me I'm wrong." Something was off. He might not have been officially trained in law enforcement, but he trusted his gut plenty of times to get him out of trouble. And right now, his instincts were screaming she hadn't been honest with him all this time, that she was hiding something. In all the times he'd asked her a personal question or tried to get to know her these past few weeks, she'd given him a sarcastic answer or changed the subject entirely.

She didn't move, didn't even seen to breathe.

Her reaction in the mine flashed through his memory. According to the degrees hanging at the back of the funeral home, she was a coroner. She dealt in death, but he'd watched the blood drain from her face when she'd gotten a good look at Whitney Avgerpoulos's body in that refrigerator, noted the tremor in her hands. At the time, he'd pushed it off as nothing more than exhaustion, but now... "I was so worried that I might've put you in danger by dragging you into this investigation, I didn't stop to think why this was happening in the first place. Battle Mountain hasn't seen a homicide investigation in over thirty years, but within weeks of you coming to town, I've had to pull a body out of a mine and nearly got shot for my trouble. You know something."

"You're wrong. I don't know who's doing this or why someone shot at us." She shook her head, gazed out the windshield as though working out a way to escape. "I don't know why this keeps happening to me."

Air stalled in his chest. "What do you mean?"

She curled her lips between her teeth and visibly bit down, drawing a bead of blood. "I think whoever killed Whitney is the same person who tried to kill me."

Chapter Four

She hadn't said the words before. Not out loud.

The weight of Weston's attention pressurized the air in her lungs. She didn't know what else to say, what to do. Whoever'd abducted and buried Whitney Avgerpoulos in that refrigerator had followed her from Denver. It would be too much of a coincidence otherwise.

"We need to get off the main road." After sending a text on his phone, Weston slid his grip to the bottom of the pickup's steering wheel and put the truck in Drive. A blanket of dust kicked up behind them in her passenger side mirror, blocking her view of Battle Mountain, and the hollowness in her chest expanded. "I know a place. Once we're out of town, you're going to tell me everything."

Chloe nodded.

They turned onto an unpaved road a little outside town and wound through a combination of mountainous ridges and family-owned ranches. Dropping temperatures seeped through the vehicle's windows, and she burrowed inside her coat. She hadn't come out this way before, too aware of the openness, the exposure of leaving the town limits, but she couldn't help soak it all in. In all her years in Denver, she'd rarely left the comfort of the city, with its skyscrapers, clean lines and detachment from nature. But this… Her fingers tingled with the urge to brush her hands through the dense pines climbing higher along the ridge steps of the mountain, to breathe in their fresh scent, to forget.

Serrated peaks fought to pierce the bright blue sky. A gaggle of geese called over rocky canyons and high valley floors. A crystalline river flowed alongside the dirt road, promising adventure and endless exploration, before it widened into an impossibly green-blue lake nestled in a small valley. No matter where she looked, the magic captivated her all over again, and a sense of belonging solidified in her stomach. "It's stunning."

"It's home," Weston said.

Time distorted into a warm, wondrous fluid as they climbed higher, but just when she didn't think they could go any farther, another valley spread out in front of them. She wasn't sure how long they'd been driving, didn't care. She couldn't remember the last time the world had been this beautiful.

Momentum pushed her forward in her seat as Weston turned once more up a long dirt drive. They passed beneath the behemoth logs supporting the large sign over the entrance to the fenced property reading Whispering Pines Ranch. The pickup rocked back and forth as they headed toward a large log cabin surrounded by a ring of massive trees. A herd of deer raised their heads at their approach up the driveway. A bright green roof and trim set the structure apart from the smaller satellite cabins located less than a few hundred yards in each direction, but Chloe didn't understand. He'd told her he was taking her out of town, somewhere safe. "What is this place?"

"Welcome to Whispering Pines. Nine hundred acres of wilderness, lakes, wildlife and…" Weston pointed out the windshield as a white-haired woman stepped down from the front porch of the main cabin. Another outline, a man equal in age to his counterpart, left the shade provided by the wraparound porch and secured a hand on the woman's shoulder with a wave of his own. The chief raised two fingers from the steering wheel in greeting. "…them."

"I don't understand. Who are they?" Hesitation tightened the tendons between her shoulders and neck as the truck pulled to a stop.

"My parents, Karie and James Ford." Weston cut the engine, and a bite of nervous energy skittered down her spine. "Come on. If I don't introduce you, they'll pull you out of the truck themselves."

Chloe gripped the passenger door handle and forced herself from the vehicle. A finger of cold worked under her coat as Weston rounded the front of the truck and met the older couple halfway. He secured his mother in a tight hold, and Chloe's stomach flipped at the obvious warmth between them. James Ford shook his son's hand before bringing him in for a one-armed hug, and a responding smile creased her lips. Nervous energy spun in a chaotic funnel behind her sternum as she suddenly realized she was intruding on an intimate reunion. This was the chief's family, his home, his land. Why would he bring her here?

"Mom, Dad, this is Dr. Pascale. She's the new coroner in town." Weston extended an arm toward her, a renewed brightness in his gaze. "Doc, these are my parents. They'll be doing everything in their power to get the two of us to settle down and give them grandchildren."

"Someone has to." Karie Ford hit her son with the back of her hand against his chest, and he feigned injury. The Ford matriarch closed the distance between them, extending one hand. Callouses scraped against Chloe's palms as the woman studied her up and down. Ear-length white-gray hair turned out at the ends effortlessly, framing a delicate jaw and piercing brown eyes, but there wasn't much else delicate about Karie Ford. Dark jeans and a flannel shirt with a fitted T-shirt underneath highlighted lean muscle that could only come from decades of working the land around them. Her laugh lines deepened around her eyes and mouth as she smiled. Dirt stained unpolished short nails, but the contact of this woman's hand in hers settled Chloe's nerves faster than a straight black cup of coffee. "It's so nice to meet you, Dr. Pascale. Weston has told us a little bit about you since you came to town, but he didn't tell me how beautiful you are."

Her gaze cut to Weston. He had? A series of internal tremors rocked through her at the thought. The chief had been discussing her with his parents. "Chloe is fine, and thank you for letting me visit. It's nice to meet you."

"Visit? No, dear. Weston messaged us and said your

apartment wasn't safe until you two figure out who killed that poor girl. You're staying with us. After what happened at the funeral home, I imagine you could use a good meal and some sleep." Karie released her hand and called over her shoulder. "You got it all set up, right, James?"

"Yes, ma'am. You're welcome to stay as long as you need in Weston's old cabin." The head of the Ford family stepped into her peripheral vision. Unkempt gray hair swung into James Ford's eyes. Similarly dressed as his wife, Weston's father nodded at her with a finality in his voice, a grumble that could soothe the most terrifying situations. Thick beard growth worked to mask the ranch owner's age, but the set of forehead wrinkles put him somewhere in his sixties as far as Chloe could tell.

"Then it's settled. As long as there is a psychopath in these parts, you're ours," Karie said. "And you're just in time. Lunch is almost ready. Hope you like corn chowder. It's Weston's favorite, and since he's too busy policing the entire town to visit his parents, I figured I'd try to lure him to come back more often."

The low rumble of James's laugh battled to penetrate through her panic.

Another bolt of hesitation flooded through her, but the Fords were already maneuvering her up the main cabin's front porch steps and into the warmth of the family home. A killer had followed her from Denver to Battle Mountain, and the first place Weston could think to take her was his family home? Chloe glanced back toward him for a sign of what she should do, but the police chief only smiled back with compliance. There would be no argument.

Heat enveloped her the moment she stepped over the threshold. A massive stone fireplace climbed two stories up the open main living space. Light grade wood, lighter than the exterior of the cabin, absorbed the sunlight penetrating through floor-to-ceiling windows on one end of the home. A frayed multicolored crocheted rug took up a majority of the hardwood floor. A small carved bear holding a bowl of fruit claimed her attention from the table stretching the back of the dark leather sofa. Similar carvings had been strategically positioned around the open kitchen and against the grand staircase leading to the second level. Handcrafted lamps, varying shades of animal fur and muted nature paintings finished the space in old-style hunter decor. It was perfect in every way. It was a home.

The scents of pepper, cream and potatoes filled her senses as Chloe took it all in, and her stomach revolted against the single bag of chips she'd gorged herself on hours ago. But as much as she wanted to sink into one of the leather sofas with a bowl full of soup and soak in all the warmth Karie and James Ford offered while she forgot the fact that Whitney Avgerpoulos's killer might've come to Battle Mountain for her, she couldn't. Not without putting the police chief and his family at risk. "If you don't mind, I'd like to use your restroom to freshen up."

"Follow that hallway, first door on the left." James vaguely motioned toward the stairs as he stirred the steaming pot of chowder.

Weston studied her from the end of the kitchen island as his mother handed over plates, spoons and bowls to set the massive wooden family table, but she couldn't focus on him right now. The longer she stayed here, the more danger she'd put him in.

Her boots echoed off the hardwood as she followed the hallway through the main level and stepped into the bathroom. She secured the door behind her and locked it, instantly relieved at the sight of the large square window over the Jacuzzi-style tub. Climbing into the tub, Chloe unlatched the window and slid the pane back on its tracks slower than she wanted to go to keep them from protesting. She knocked the screen out and hauled one leg through, then the other. A jolt of impact rocketed through her as she hit the ground. It would be a long and risky trek back to Battle Mountain, but she'd left her car at the funeral home and her go bag with supplies in her apartment. She had to take the chance. Chloe crept along the side of the house and rounded the corner to the front.

Weston crossed his arms over his muscular chest as he settled against the hood of his truck, and she froze. "Now where do you think you're going?"

"You and I weren't able to finish our earlier conversation." Weston shoved off the hood of his pickup, closing the distance between them. Chloe's gaze darted to the driveway off to his left, and amusement hooked into him. "If you're thinking about running again, I have to warn you. I know every inch of this land. You won't make it more than half a mile before I catch up to you."

Her throat flexed with a hard swallow. "I told you I believed the person who killed Whitney Avgerpoulos was the same man who attacked me, and you bring me straight to your parents' house. The longer I stay here, the more danger they are in, and they don't deserve to suffer because of me. Neither do you. I'm going back to town. I'm going to get as far from here as possible and give you an escape from this nightmare before more people end up hurt. Or worse, dead."

"First, my parents can take care of themselves. If you don't believe me, just wait until you see my mom peg a coyote from three hundred yards." He stepped toward her, cutting off her view of the driveway and forcing her to meet his gaze. "Second, whoever killed that girl did it in my town, and as police chief, it's my job to bring him to justice. Third, I brought you here because it was the safest place I knew. Every member of my family believes in the second amendment, and they are not afraid to exercise that right. Our killer might be smart enough to connect me to the investigation and this place, but he'd be an idiot to try to come here for you. You're safe here, Doc. I give you my word. But in order to protect you, I need to know what happened before you came to Battle Mountain."

Her lips thinned as she shifted her weight between both feet. She was beginning to break, the circles under her eyes darker than before. Hell, it seemed like a lifetime ago they'd pulled Whitney's remains from that mine. Not nine hours. Time flew when being shot at. Chloe lowered her chin to her chest and kicked at the dirt around her with one boot. "My name isn't Chloe

Pascale. It's Chloe Miles, and I'm not a coroner from Grand Junction. I lied after... I am—was—a cardio-thoracic surgeon out of the heart and vascular center in Denver. I was in the middle of a run in the woods near my house when he ambushed me." She shoved her hands in her coat pockets, still unwilling to meet his gaze. "Three months ago, I woke up in the middle of a clearing. He was there, digging a hole. I didn't rec-ognize him because of the ski mask, but I remember it was cold. I couldn't feel my toes or my fingers or pro-cess what was happening. Until I saw the light blue re-frigerator a few feet away."

A refrigerator. The same kind the killer had used to bury Whitney? Weston's instincts shot into awareness. The puncture wound on the victim's neck. Chloe had known to look for it because she'd been in Whitney's position. "He drugged you."

"I can't be sure with what, but my best guess is with propofol, yes." Chloe relaxed her shoulders away from her ears and finally lifted her attention to him. "The injection knocked me out almost immediately, but the sedative has a short half-life, and the effects don't last long. It doesn't show up in standard urine tests or toxi-cology results. I imagine he specifically chose propofol for those reasons. He had to work fast to get me into the refrigerator, but once I was inside, I'd know ex-actly what was happening. He wanted me to be aware of every second up until I ran out of air, and when my body was discovered, the medical examiner wouldn't be able to tell what I was sedated with." Chloe took a step back. "It was a good plan, one that would've worked if

I hadn't fought back, but now he's in Battle Mountain. He knows I'm here, and he killed that girl to make sure I got the message this isn't over."

Hell. He'd have to deal with her deception at some point. He'd appointed her under false pretenses, and his duty to the town meant he'd have to consider the consequences of her lies. Right now, though, he needed to focus on protecting her. Weston countered her escape and wrapped his grip around both of her arms. "He's not going to lay another hand on you, Doc. Not as long as I'm part of this investigation. Okay? We're going to figure out who killed Whitney. We're going to make him pay. Together."

"How? We don't have the resources to run the samples I took from the victim's remains ourselves. I'm a former surgeon, not police, and you're the only law enforcement officer in this town." She swiped at her face, a rattle of a sob entwining with her words. "He's killed two people now, including one of my colleagues. How are we supposed to do this alone?"

Whitney wasn't the first victim? Damn it. She was right. He didn't have the resources of a full-fledged department to connect all the spiraling pieces of this case, but there was a chance they'd get at least a description of their shooter from witness statements or some kind of lead from reviewing that first case. But the priority had to be Chloe for now. His gaze flickered to the satellite cabin farthest from the main house, and his gut knotted tighter. He hadn't spoken to the man on the other side of the door in months, but it was worth a shot. Chloe was right. They couldn't do this alone.

He slid one hand down her arm and cupped her hand in his. Weston tugged her after him. "I have someone who can help—my brother."

She fought to keep up with his steps.

He banged on the cabin's wood front door, removing his hat out of respect. Footsteps echoed from inside a split second before a wall of muscle and hostility filled the frame. Weston released Chloe's hand, standing a bit straighter, but even at six-one, his brother outranked him by more than three inches. "Easton."

Several days' worth of stubble softened the sharp, angular jaw underneath. Two distinct lines furrowed between Easton's eyebrows as the former Green Beret stared down at him for a fraction of a second before turning that detached gaze on the woman at his side. Unkempt hair and the odor of sweat and staleness revealed the soldier Weston had once admired wasn't taking care of himself here at home any better than he had been in the Middle East. Easton folded broad arms across his chest and leaned against the doorjamb. "Who's this?"

The muscles down Weston's spine hardened with battle-ready tension at the hint of disrespect in his younger brother's voice. "This is Chloe. She's the new coroner in town, and we need your help."

"I didn't realize Weston had a brother." Chloe rubbed her palm down her jeans before stretching it out in greeting. "Nice to meet you."

The hostility intensified as seconds distorted into silent minutes. The soldier pushed off the doorjamb and stepped back into the house. Shadows cut across his neutral expression as he slammed the door shut in their faces.

Disappointment and frustration tornadoed in his chest as Weston stepped off the cabin's small front porch. He replaced his hat on his head. He should've known six months back home wouldn't be enough to introduce Easton back into the real world, but he wasn't about to give up. Not on family.

"I take it your brother is more of the strong, silent type," Chloe said.

Weston retraced their steps back toward his pickup, then farther to the cabin his parents had cleaned out for Chloe. The rustic exterior matched the main house apart from the shade of trim framing the front door, a single window and the roof. With six satellite cabins, plus the main house, his parents had managed to raise a family and build a successful guest ranch for tourists looking to get the real experience of mountain living. Including the ill-tempered bear he'd called his brother all his life.

"Easton is former Special Forces. He and his unit were almost single-handedly responsible for rooting out terrorists and insurgents in Afghanistan and Iraq during the war." A note of sobriety tinted his voice as his frustration with Easton's behavior faded. "He doesn't like to talk about it, or talk in general, or leave his cabin, but from what the army has been able to tell us, he's the only one who made it home."

"I'm sorry to hear that," Chloe said. "I can't imagine how hard that must be."

Weston twisted the knob and shoved inside. The door swung back into the handmade shelves he'd installed years ago above the single-countered kitchen to the left. A small square dining table matching the same wood as the cabin floor angled off to one side, leaving room for him and Chloe to pass into the living room. A queen-size bed had been positioned under the second window at the back left corner, and exhaustion suddenly drained the last remnants of his energy dry. "It's not much, but you're welcome to stay here as long as you need."

Her gaze roamed over the small one-room space, and Weston suddenly found himself memorizing the small changes in her expression. She shucked her heavy coat and hung it on one of the three hooks beside the door at the same time as the heat from the fire hit him full force. His parents had taken good care of this place, wiping any and all surfaces clean of dust, but the memories were still engrained at the back of his mind. Her boots echoed off the hardwood as she moved through the kitchen, fingers brushing the sleek granite countertop on either side of the sink. "This was your cabin?"

"Up until about three years ago." He surveyed the room, hands on his hips, taking it all in again. "Once I took up as police chief, I figured I needed a place closer to town. Mom and Dad rent it and the other four available cabins out to tourists now. Keeps them busy and gives them something to focus their parental nagging on."

Her laugh drove into the spaces between the massive logs holding this place up and his nerve endings caught fire. "My parents both passed away when I was in med school, but I still remember their constant check-ins. Making sure I did my laundry, that I was staying on top of my studies, questioning me about any men I'd started dating. And I lived on campus. I couldn't imagine having them any closer than that until I found myself wishing I'd answered more of their calls before their car slid off the road one night." She moved to the kitchen drawers, pulling them out one by one, and lifted what looked like a framed photo from inside. She turned the frame toward him. "Now I can definitely tell this was your cabin, but who's the woman next to you?"

Air crushed from his lungs as recognition burned through him. He stood a bit taller without needing to see the photo to know exactly whom he'd been standing beside when it'd been taken. "Her name is Cynthia. She's my wife."

Chapter Five

His wife.

The words echoed in her head even as her gaze dipped to the bare ring finger of his left hand. Chloe forced herself to set the heavy frame back in the drawer where she'd discovered it and swiped her hands down her jeans. She hadn't expected the knot of disappointment to hit so hard, as though she'd physically taken a sucker punch to the stomach. The kindness Weston had shown her and the invitation to breakfast before a bullet had almost penetrated her skull hadn't been out of interest. He treated everyone with the same amount of respect and warmth. Wow. As much as she'd told herself personal connections would complicate her situation, the hollowness behind her sternum flared. How could she have been so stupid? "I… I didn't realize you were married."

"Would've been four years this past December." Weston closed the distance between them and reached past her into the drawer where she'd set the photo. He swiped a thin film of dust from the glass with the sleeve of his jacket, filling the space between them with a floating array of airborne glitter. Staring down at the blonde beauty in the photo, the police chief angled the photo toward her. "We'd only been married a few months when she was diagnosed. Lymphoma. Her dad had been diagnosed the year before. He managed to pull through, but Cynthia…"

Dread pooled at the base of her spine, and her heart jerked in her chest. "She didn't survive," she said on a whisper.

"No. Her doctors did everything they could. We all did, but the chemo and the cancer itself was too much for her to handle." Weston sniffed as he lowered the frame to his side. He turned, scanning the rest of the cabin as though willing to look at anything but her, and set the photo on the small dining table in the middle of the room. "I didn't realize this was still here. I'll check the rest of the place to make sure my parents didn't leave anything else like this around."

Chloe took a single step toward him. "I didn't know."

"It was a long time ago," he said.

But the scar still lingered in his mesmerizing brown eyes. Grief was frustrating like that, rising and falling in a flood of sadness and detachment before disappearing for a while. One trigger. That was all it could take to re-ignite the despair and widen the hole where the person you loved had carved out space in your heart. As much as she'd pushed off her parents' constant concerns and their pressure for her to succeed as a Latina woman in a male-dominated field, she'd loved them. She missed them. At least she'd had someone to worry about her, to love her. Now, she had no one.

"Before, you said Whitney Avgerpoulos isn't the only victim in this case, that whoever killed her killed one of your colleagues." Weston hooked both thumbs into his front pockets, exaggerating broad shoulders and muscled arms beneath his sheepskin coat. "From what I've studied from some other department case files, the more victims there are in a homicide investigation, the higher chance of recovering evidence that leads to the killer's identity. Sooner or later, they make a mistake."

The investigation. Right. Chloe swallowed past the dryness in her throat, forcing herself back into the moment. "I'm not sure how much help I can be. It was mostly on the news, but I knew the first victim. She was an anesthesiologist in the hospital where I worked. Dr. Roberta Ellis. She sedated a number of my patients during surgery up until about four months ago when she stopped showing up for her shifts."

"Was that like her?" Weston's voice dipped into neutral territory. No hint of the controlled grief cracking through his expression.

"No. She never missed a shift. She was interviewing at larger hospitals a few weeks before her disappearance. She loved working with us as far as I knew, but Roberta wanted to take on more shifts, and we didn't have the resources at the time. When she didn't show up for two of my surgeries, I assumed she'd moved on to another job. Until I recognized her photo on the news." Chloe folded her arms across her chest as the memories charged forward. "Police received an anonymous tip about a body in Washington Park. When they arrived, they found a handle from a refrigerator lying on top of a recently disturbed patch of soil. The reporters had gotten footage from the crime scene. There was a yellow refrigerator in the hole they'd excavated. Later, I learned she'd been buried alive inside of it."

"And when you woke up in that clearing three months ago and saw a similar refrigerator a few feet away, you believed you'd been targeted by the same killer." Weston's footsteps reverberated through the hardwood floor and up her legs as he closed the distance between them.

She hugged herself a bit tighter, a sting of awareness bristling from the mound of scar tissue under her clothing. "I didn't want to be his next victim. That's the only thing that kept me going."

"Did you go to the police? Were they able to find the scene where he intended to bury you?" Weston asked.

"I gave them everything I could remember. How he'd ambushed me, how I escaped, what his voice sounded like. The driver who nearly hit me with his truck was even able to pinpoint exactly where he picked me up, but the search teams didn't find anything. My doctors informed the detectives who took my statement that I'd been sedated." A bubble of renewed fear closed in, and her blood pressure spiked. "After that, they discounted me as a reliable witness, and anything I had to say wouldn't only be inadmissible in court, but a risk the district attorney wasn't willing to take. But he was still out there."

"They dropped the investigation, and you ran. You changed your name and came to Battle Mountain. Hell." Weston scrubbed a hand down his face. "I'll send my notes to the original detectives and request the investigation files from Denver PD. There are too many similarities between your colleague's and Whitney's murders for us to think these cases aren't connected. They might not have had the evidence to pursue your case, but they won't be able to ignore another body." He wrapped his hands around her arms, just as he'd done outside, and a flare of warmth penetrated through the permanent ice that'd set up residence since her attack. "I'll make sure of it."

She stared up at him, and time stretched from one minute to the next. A coil of appreciation tightened inside her the longer he held on to her. It'd been months since she'd had someone to talk to, someone to listen. While the nightmares and persistent fear of her attacker closing in had weakened her over the past three months, Chloe felt as though Weston stood as a wall of physical and mental protection in a killer's path. "Thank you."

His hands slid down her arms, and Weston stepped back. He narrowed his gaze on hers. "You said you and the first victim, Roberta Ellis, worked in the same clinic? A heart and vascular center in Denver."

"Yes," she said. "Roberta was an anesthesiologist, and I was in cardiothoracic, but we frequently worked together during surgery."

"Did you or Roberta ever hang out outside of work?" he asked. "Did she ever say anything to you about feeling like she was being followed, or did you notice anything out of the ordinary leading up to the attack?"

"No, nothing like that, but we weren't exactly friends. We just worked together." Chloe shook her head as the past threatened to collide with the present. She'd answered all these questions for the detectives who'd worked her case. "We'd go out to drinks with some of the other doctors on my team every once in a while to celebrate a successful week. The last time had been a couple weeks before Roberta disappeared. We were supposed to meet up again at our regular bar, all of us, but..."

His attention pressurized the air in her lungs. "But what?"

Tension teased the space between her eyebrows, and a rush of exhaustion slithered through her. She swept her tongue across suddenly dry lips. "We—my team and I—lost a patient after a routine mitral valve repair procedure. We were treating her for stenosis, which is a narrowing in the inflow valve of the heart. Everything went according to plan, but a few days after the surgery, the patient's discomfort was out of control. Not even morphine dulled her discomfort. I... I wanted to submit her to an angiogram and see what was causing her so much pain, but before I had the authorization, she died of cardiac arrest. It didn't make sense. She was a healthy woman in her thirties. Nothing about her medical history or health told me she wouldn't come out on the other side of surgery. Turns out, my instincts were right."

"What do you mean?" Weston asked.

"Her family didn't want an autopsy done. Her husband was grieving. He was in shock. He just wanted her buried so he and their children could move on with their lives, but I couldn't get her off my mind." Sweat trickled in a line down her back. "Before the clinic released her remains, I performed my own autopsy against the family's wishes. I found a clamp still in her chest, one we'd missed before suturing her up after the surgery was completed. It's never happened before, and I don't know how I missed it. The day I was attacked, I was going to inform the board of the mistake."

A striking of a loud cattle bell broke through the comfortable silence between them, and the present ripped her from the past.

"Lunch is ready." Weston cleared his throat before striding toward the door, collecting the photo of him and his wife from the table along the way. He reached for the old dented brass knob, hesitation clear in his rugged features. He twisted the knob and wrenched open the cabin's front door. "Did the patient's husband know the real reason his wife had died?"

Chloe couldn't hug herself any tighter. She shook her head. "No. Nobody knew. As soon as I saw the clamp in her chest, I panicked. I should've left it in as proof, but the more I ran through the procedure, the surer I was I hadn't been the one to leave it behind, that one of the other doctors on my team had. I removed it and stitched her back up so she could be released to her family."

"Where is it now?" he asked.

"Someplace safe." She couldn't tell him any more than that. Not without putting him in more danger than he already was. If the killer was tying up loose ends by coming after her and Roberta Ellis, there was a chance he'd turn his sights to Weston. Too many people had been hurt already.

"You and your team might've lost your medical licenses if you'd gotten the chance to tell the board what went wrong." The slight change in his expression said he was putting together the pieces, the ones she'd tried denying all these months. "How many other physicians were in the surgical suite with you that day?"

Her breath shuddered out of her chest. She'd known this day would come, when she'd have to face the truth, when hiding wouldn't be enough to keep her safe. "Apart from me and Roberta, three other doctors. The resident surgeon who assisted me, a scrub tech and a nurse."

Weston replaced his hat on his head. "Then that's where we start."

THREE SUSPECTS. Three potential killers.

After lunch, Weston filled out the incident report for the crime scene in Contention Mine from one of the other satellite cabins on the property. One void of memories. It was the same set up here as Chloe's and Easton's quarters, only this one had been decorated with soft flannels and darker woods. Perfect for tourists looking to experience the outdoors without leaving some comforts behind.

The end of his pen tapped against the glass of the frame Chloe had recovered from the kitchen drawer, and a knot of guilt set up residence in his gut. The photo had been taken before he and Cynthia had gotten married, the years of their on-again/off-again relationship barely evident in their smiles. He hadn't talked to anyone about his wife's diagnosis or her passing, not in years. But for some reason he'd found talking to Chloe comforting. Easy, even. There hadn't been an ounce of pity in her expression, no apologies for his loss, as if she knew expressions of condolence sometimes meant more to the giver than to the recipient. Just a simple understanding between them. They'd both lost people they cared about to unpreventable circumstances, but she stood there as a testament for life after loss. Strong, realistic, beautiful.

The past day had threatened to rip him and this town apart, but with her personal insight into the investigation, they actually had a chance of solving the case. He might not have any other deputies to share the weight of protecting Battle Mountain, but he had Chloe, which was more than he could ask for.

A flash of wide pale green eyes and a quick full smile filled his head in an instant, and his heart rate ticked up a notch. His scalp prickled as the nerve endings in his hand woke with remembered warmth when he'd tackled her to the floor inside of Jacob Family Funeral Home. Hints of her perfume still clung to his coat, but it was the feel of her pressed against him that'd engrained itself in his brain.

Weston forced himself to focus on the paperwork in front of him, and not on the kernel of attraction for the newest resident in town. He'd lost Cynthia to circumstances he couldn't prevent. His vow to protect her, to cherish and love her—it'd been everything to him, but it hadn't been enough to save her. Becoming police chief of this town was the only thing that'd saved him from locking himself behind one of these cabin doors and hiding from the world like his brother. Connections like the one stringing between him and Chloe led to emotions. Emotions led to vulnerability. He couldn't go through that kind of loss again. Wouldn't.

Weston finished filling out the incident report from Whitney Avgerpoulos's death scene and moved on to the paperwork for the shooting that'd occurred this morning. Lunch had been a rushed affair once his parents had started their interrogation, but Chloe had handled each and every question with humor and interest. In that short time, it'd been all too easy to imagine the coroner visiting his parents for future lunches, happily chatting with them when they came into town, getting to know every aspect of his family. As though she belonged. It'd been then the barrier he'd relied on against the grief determined to shred him from the inside seemed to crack. Because of her easy-going nature, her laugh, her sincerity. Because of her.

But as much as he'd wanted to pretend reality didn't apply out here at the ranch as he had so many times before, a killer had followed Chloe to Battle Mountain. Five physicians had been involved in the wrongful death of one of Chloe's patients. One had already been murdered with the same MO as Whitney Avgerpoulos. Roberta Ellis, the anesthesiologist. He was running gun ownership records on the others but doubted there'd be a hit. Whoever'd killed Whitney had gone as far as wiping down the refrigerator used to suffocate and bury her with a cleaning solution that smelled of bleach. Someone who took that much care not to leave behind DNA evidence wouldn't willingly register a weapon they'd planned on using for another attempt. But why the change in MO? Why try to bury Chloe three months ago, succeed with Whitney, then attack a second time with a gun? It didn't make sense.

His phone pinged with an incoming email. The background checks he'd requested for each doctor, including Chloe, filled the screen. No registered weapons, which meant the shooter had either purchased the weapon illegally or stolen the gun to do the job. No outstanding warrants, arrest records or parking tickets, either. The staff who assisted Chloe that day in surgery were clean. "Damn it."

Why else would Chloe and the anesthesiologist have been targeted if not for what happened during that patient's surgery? And what did that have to do with Whitney Avgerpoulos's death?

Weston sent an email to Denver PD's chief of police. Despite the lack of resources and support for police investigations in Battle Mountain, it'd been easy to request a warrant for all three suspects' records. Especially when granted by the only judge in town.

According to the background information he'd gathered on all five surgical team members, each lived within Denver's city limits up until Chloe fled three months ago. The resident surgeon who assisted Chloe during the surgery, Michael Kerr, had graduated at the top of his class from University of North Carolina–Chapel Hill, the best medical school in the country, in primary care before joining the staff at the heart and vascular center last year. His last name alone raised the hairs on the back of Weston's neck, and a cursory study of the man's lineage confirmed his instinct. Michael Kerr was the son of Senator Miranda Kerr out of Ohio, but that didn't mean he wasn't capable of murder. Being in the political spotlight from the time he'd been born was sure to have added pressure to succeed.

Luke McMillan, the scrub tech, had been working at the clinic for six years, never once having been promoted or awarded a raise in that time according to his financial records. No debt to speak of aside from the man's home and no large payments incoming or outgoing to suggest illicit activities. Married with two children with his salary as the single source of income. A mistake like the one Chloe had described could be the trigger to make a man like McMillan desperate to protect his family.

And Celeste Stanley, the nurse assigned to assist that day, still had over fifty thousand dollars in student loan debt to contend with for the next decade. Single, a fierce dog lover according to her social media accounts and an advocate for breaking down complicated medical practices and terminology for her masses of followers. From the collection of comments across her posts and the photos tagged by friends and family, she was generally well liked and the life of the party. No evidence of a connection to the patient who'd died from the clamp in her chest or anything other than a professional relationship with the physicians she worked with, but the records, the social media accounts, the background check—none of them went back further than four years ago, which meant Celeste had changed her name. Why?

Then again, Chloe distinctly remembered a male attacker, which could take Celeste out of the running.

Weston made a note to check public records before reviewing the shift schedules Chloe had given him access to through the clinic's employee portal. All five team members had operated together on half a dozen occasions over the years, but there were no other reports of malpractice or problems between doctors. At least not as far as he could tell. Chloe and Roberta Ellis only had one thing in common: they'd both been attacked by the same killer.

He moved onto the next background check and sat a bit straighter in his seat. Dr. Chloe Miles had been born in Denver, excelled through high school and had graduated from Harvard Medical School before completing her residency at Mount Sinai in New York City. She'd immediately returned to Colorado and taken up the head surgical position at the heart and vascular center, and a ping of understanding hit. Even with the world at her feet and a far brighter future ahead of her, she'd come home.

All three suspects had motive for wanting to stave off a malpractice suit. He just had to find the right one capable of murder. A gust of wind shifted the trees through the side window and rattled the screen. There was one other possibility, one that had nothing to do with the motives of the physicians who'd been in that surgical suite, and everything to do with the patient who'd died at the hands of one of her doctors.

He scanned through Chloe's schedule. She hadn't given him the patient's name, but he knew from talking with her the surgery had to have occurred a couple months prior to her police report. The months scrolled by until he landed on her calendar for that month. Whoever'd organized her calendar had done so by type of appointment and color-coded surgeries red to stand out from the rest of her appointments. There. Only three surgeries the entire month. Logging into the government's public access for lawsuits and court filings, Weston searched by Chloe's name. The results narrowed down to one. "Bingo."

Three light knocks penetrated through the haze he'd lost himself in for the past two hours. He shoved to his feet, his own footsteps overly loud in his ears, and wrenched open the door. An automatic smile turned up one corner of his mouth as Chloe centered herself in the door frame, and a lightness filled him that hadn't been there a minute ago. He hiked a thumb over his shoulder. Nervous energy skittered down his spine as he considered the information he'd uncovered. "Hey, I was just finishing up the paperwork from the shooting this morning. Everything okay?"

"Yeah. I couldn't sleep. I kept thinking about your mom's corn chowder and how I might be able to sneak back into the main house for more without being caught." Chloe raised her shoulders to block the wind ripping through the trees and sweeping her hair into her face. "Any luck on narrowing down a suspect?"

"Yeah. Why don't you come inside? Storm's going to be here soon." Weston reached out, curling one hand around her wrist wrapped securely against her chest, and helped her over the threshold. He secured the door behind him and shut out the cold. He rounded the small kitchen table and stared down at the court-issued paperwork filling the screen. "I've gone through financials and background checks on each of the physicians who were there with you during the surgery. Without interviewing them myself, there's not much to work on, but I can think of one person who might want to kill you and anyone else who was in that surgical suite that day." He spun the laptop toward her. "The patient's husband was suing you for the wrongful death of his wife."

Chapter Six

She couldn't think, couldn't breathe.

She'd been so tied to the idea her admission of malpractice had been the catalyst for getting Roberta Ellis and Whitney Avgerpoulos killed, she'd blinded herself to the motive right in front of her. "Jonathan Byrd is… suing me?"

Blood drained from her face and pooled in the throbbing recesses behind her ears. No. That wasn't possible.

"You didn't know?" The bite left Weston's voice, and the tension between his neck and broad shoulders drained. The fine lines around his eyes deepened, and suddenly he looked much older than midthirties. Raw, even. The past day had added a weight she'd never meant for him to shoulder. Clouds darkened the ridge protecting the Whispering Pines Ranch and cast a wide shadow across his exhausted features. He'd been running off adrenaline and little rest since he'd called her to that mine late last night. They both had. Weston bent to read through whatever he'd meant to show her on his laptop screen. Court documents? "The lawsuit was filed a week before your attack. Is it possible he learned of the mistake your surgical team made and tried to take things into his own hands instead of waiting for the courts?"

"You think he's the one who attacked me and Roberta, who followed me here and killed Whitney Avgerpoulos?" Chloe unclenched her fists and forced her knees to hold her upright. Confusion and desperation combined into a violent quake of emotion. She shook her head. "No. I know Jonathan Byrd. I talked to him for hours during the months leading up to his wife's surgery. He works as a handyman and likes to go to the movies on the weekends. He was grateful we were able to help his family. He wouldn't hurt anyone, least of all the physicians who saved her life."

"Even if he learned your team was the reason she died?" Weston's expression softened as he closed the distance between them, slowly, as though approaching a wild animal. "Grief changes people. Think about it, Chloe. Out of everyone who was in that surgical suite, out of everyone who had something to lose when your patient died, Jonathan Byrd lost the most. He lost the one person he counted on being with him for the rest of his life."

He was speaking from experience. She knew that, and logically his theory made sense, but her brain refused to superimpose Jonathan Byrd's face where the black ski mask silhouette haunted her dreams. Refused to acknowledge he would go out of his way to harm an innocent young woman who had nothing to do with his wife's death.

"Handymen have easy access to old refrigerators,"

he said. "You have to admit, he's worth looking into, even if it turns out we're wrong."

He was right. She knew that. She slid her hands into her coat, frostier than she'd been outside. "For not ever working a homicide investigation before, you sure seem to know what you're doing."

"I'm a fast learner," he said. "Besides, I'm just doing my job."

"It's more than that. You care about this town. You'll do whatever it takes to keep it safe." She shifted her weight to the back of her heels. So much violence, so much blood. When would it end? With her death? With Weston's? The thought of finding another body, of watching the police chief—the man in front of her— or his family pay the price for her mistake, churned a wall of nausea in her stomach. She hadn't been in Battle Mountain long, but the detachment she'd held on to these past couple of months had thinned in that time. In the way Reagan remembered her coffee order at Caffeine and Carbs, how Mr. Jacob invited her to accompany him and his son to lunch every day to make sure she got something to eat, how Weston had stopped her on the street to see how she was adjusting to small-town life. Even the way James and Karie Ford had instantly welcomed her into their lives with the offer of a place to sleep and a hot meal. Everything about this town had worked under her skin, become part of her. Despite her determination to keep her distance from the people here, she'd come to know and appreciate every single one of them. "Maybe that's why I should leave."

She hadn't meant for the words to slip, but she

couldn't take them back. A vise squeezed around her heart as deep brown eyes locked on her.

"I feel like we've already had this conversation when you snuck out my parents' bathroom window." Weston stood a bit taller, every ounce the hardworking police chief she'd come to admire. Committed, reliable, loyal—everything she hadn't realized she'd miss when she left her career, her friends and her life behind in Denver. "We agreed we have a higher chance of solving this case together."

Chloe fixated on the framed photo she'd discovered during her cursory search of her cabin, the same cabin Weston and his wife had occupied up until her death nearly four years ago. He'd already lost the most important person in his life. She couldn't be the one to cause him more pain. "Every minute I'm here is another chance someone I care about gets hurt, and I won't be able to live with myself if that person is you. I appreciate everything you've done for me, but I can't risk your life like that. Not when there's something I can do to protect you and this town."

"Whether or not my life is at risk during this investigation isn't up to you." Weston gently framed her jaw with the palm of his hand, forcing her to look up at him. A shot of warmth penetrated through the layer of ice that'd cut her off from feeling anything but fear these past few months. "I made the choice to put my life on the line when I became this town's police chief, Chloe. I knew the risk and so does my family, and I was willing to do this job anyway. And having you here... You're an integral part of this case. I need you here."

She'd become a cardiothoracic surgeon to save lives, to be the best option for patients who needed the finest care. She'd gone out of her way to ensure she'd never be put back in the same position she'd been in during her attack. Helpless, incapable, useless, but right then she'd never felt stronger. Weston needed her. Whether he'd meant personally or professionally, she didn't care. A shift rocked through her, and Chloe raised onto her toes.

She pressed her mouth to his.

His lips gave under the pressure a split second before he took control of the kiss, and the numbness drained from her veins. Her pulse ticked hard at the base of her throat as she parted her lips. He fit against her from her shoulders to her knees, and she swore right then her blood started boiling. A groan escaped up her throat as Weston fisted one hand in her coat collar. Her ears rang, every cell in her body on fire. For him.

He dragged his mouth from hers on a strong gasp. Regret contorted his features into a gut-wrenching mask. "We can't... We can't do this. I'm sorry if I gave you the impression I was interested in more than a professional relationship, but I'm not in a position to commit to anything but my job, Dr. Pascale."

Dr. Pascale.

Her fingers ached to hold on to him, even as he released his grip on her. Chloe cleared her throat as rejection burned through her. She stumbled back, all too aware of the thickening tension between them and the sting of tears forming in her eyes. "Right. No. I understand. I must've... You're right. I misunderstood. I'm sorry, too." She turned toward the door. He'd said he needed her, and something inside had jumped at the opportunity, but she could see now the circumstances that'd brought them together outweighed the kernel of hope in her chest. She should've seen it before now, should've known. Weston Ford could never be hers. Not when a killer had targeted her, and not when he'd gone out of his way to set the photo of him and his wife at his workspace. Eager to put as much distance between them as possible, she wrenched the door open, and a frigid blast of wind slammed into her face. "Do you think you could get ahold of Roberta Ellis's autopsy report? I wanted to run through my notes from Whitney Avgerpoulos's autopsy and compare them with hers. See if they have something in common."

Heavy footsteps closed in from behind. "Chloe, wait—"

A gunshot exploded through the darkening evening.

She automatically hit the floor, hands over her head, but this time there were no screams. No shattering glass. Craning her head up, she searched the limited view of the property framed by the cabin's front door. Her heart threatened to beat out of her chest as she waited for the pain, but it never came. "Weston?"

"I'm fine." Strong hands secured her against his chest as he pulled her out of the doorway and behind the small kitchen cabinet. The police chief shot to his feet and collected his sidearm from the counter. Balanced on both knees, he threaded his arms through the shoulder holster and grabbed for his coat from one of the kitchen chairs. Weston got to a low crouch to peer out the window over the kitchen sink. "That shot came from somewhere close by."

"How can you be sure?" Chloe asked.

"I've been in these woods enough growing up to know where every member of my family was while we hunted game." Hardness entered his expression.

"It could be one of them." She peered around the corner of the cabinet, meeting only darkness on the other side of the door frame.

"Not this late at night. Family rules. We only hunt in daylight, and we always tell each other when we're headed out." He bent on one knee, leveraging his other leg at a ninety-degree angle. Weston dropped the magazine from his weapon, seemed to count the rounds inside and shoved it back into place. He pulled back on the slide, and the soft click of a round loading into the chamber reached her ears. In less than three breaths, he'd transformed from the guilt-laden man she'd kissed into the police chief determined to protect his town. His gaze cut to hers. "Someone else is out here."

THE STORM HAD ARRIVED.

"Stay here. No matter what happens or what you hear, do not leave this cabin. Understand?" Weston stretched his dominant hand back and pried open the cabinet under the sink. He tore the weapon he'd taped to the underside free. Handing it off to her, he slid his finger alongside her inner wrist. Air caught in his lungs from the small point of contact, but it was nothing compared to the electrifying kiss they'd shared a few minutes ago. He couldn't think about that right now. Whispering Pines had been breached, and he'd do whatever it took to protect his family—to protect her—from the threat. He pulled a flashlight from under the same cabinet. "Safety is here. There are fifteen rounds in the magazine. Don't open this door for anyone until I come back."

Chloe nodded, those brilliant eyes wide. "Be careful. Please."

"You, too." Two simple words, but there was an unspoken weight behind them. In less than a day, she'd triggered his protective instincts and claimed a piece of him. How was that possible? He left the cover of the cabin. Flakes fell in a thin veil as the clouds rolled softly above. Wind kicked up through the trees and mimicked the chaotic storm churning through him. The exposed skin along the backs of his hands and neck burned as he stepped out into the open. The small porch protested under his weight. Snow crunched beneath his boots as he maneuvered into the clearing between the main cabin and the satellite structures around the property.

Muffled footsteps filled his ears from his right, and he raised his weapon, taking aim. Two figures jogged down the main cabin steps. The rack of a shotgun echoed through the night. Instant recognition hardened the muscles down his spine. "Whoever you are, I suggest getting the hell off our property before you have to spend the rest of your short life pulling buckshot from your gut," a familiar voice said.

"Mom, it's me." Weston lowered his sidearm, crossing the clearing. He pressed his back into the main cabin wall, and the outline of both of his parents, each armed, filled in. Their night robes dragged through the flurry of snow settling, their pajama pants tucked into their boots. "You both heard the shot."

"Wasn't us. We made the family rules. We have to stand by them. Lead by example and all that crap." His dad scanned the property with the barrel of the same shotgun he'd taught Weston to shoot with when he'd only been waist-high, leading the way.

"Thank goodness you're okay." His mother leveraged the shotgun in the crook of her arm and brought him in for a one-armed hug. "Where's Chloe?"

"In my cabin." He pulled back and studied the landscape. "She's armed. I told her to shoot anyone who came through the door, so steer clear."

"Sounded like a semi-auto pistol. Coming from near Easton's cabin." His dad motioned toward the far cabin. "But it couldn't have been your brother."

Easton hadn't picked up a firearm since he'd returned home. They all knew that. Unless his brother had felt threatened.

Panic flooded adrenaline through his veins. A killer had targeted Chloe. If the bastard had come for her... Weston caught sight of the footprints leading away from his brother's cabin. "Go back inside. Lock the doors."

"Like hell we will. Someone comes for one of us, they come for all of us. We'll stay near Chloe." His mother pushed him toward the far cabin. "You find the idiot who dared take on this family."

Weston dashed across the clearing, his boots slipping on the lightweight snow. He tightened his grip around his weapon as he traced the footprints back to their origin. Easton's front door stood slightly ajar. His brother was one of the most security-oriented men he'd ever met. He'd never leave his door unlocked, let alone open. Even out here where the only people he had to worry about were the ones who wouldn't let him disappear into depression and grief. He did a quick check inside. Empty. Outside, Weston rounded to the back, following the tracks there. The footprints disappeared into the tree line, but he'd grown up in these woods. There wasn't a single acre he hadn't memorized over the years.

He ran straight into the darkness.

Ice burned down his throat the harder he pushed himself. Easton was a trained Special Forces Green Beret, but the man who'd murdered Roberta Ellis and Whitney Avgerpoulos—the man who'd tried to kill Chloe—wasn't the kind of killer who'd cease fire upon agreed terms. Weston wasn't going to leave his brother to fight alone. He hit the power button for the flashlight. Pine needles scratched at his neck and face. The snow was falling heavier now. The footprints would be buried under a fresh layer of flakes in a matter of minutes. His breath crystalized in front of his mouth. "Damn it, Easton. Where the hell are you?"

The footprints ended. Impossible. He scanned the area around him, searching for an indication of where his brother had gone, but it was as though Easton had vanished. No sign of a struggle. No evidence his brother had simply turned around and gone back the way he'd come.

A branch snapped off to his left.

Weston dropped the flashlight, spun toward the

sound and hiked his pistol shoulder-level. One second. Two. The trees seemed to close in around him. The hairs on the back of his neck stood on end. Wetting his chapped lips, he whistled a short burst of varying notes, the signal he and Easton had used as kids when they'd gotten separated during hunts.

No answer.

Movement registered from behind, and Weston took aim. He hadn't imagined the sound of the gunshot. He hadn't imagined the footprints. Someone was out here, and his brother had noticed. Had Easton broken his own rules to warn him about what was coming? "You're trespassing on private land. Identify yourself."

The trees rustled with another round of movement. Weston held his ground, his weight evenly distributed between both feet, just as his father had taught him. The flashlight reflected back off something within the trees, and just as he fit his finger over the trigger, a ram cleared the tree line. Bleating filled the clearing.

Tension drained from his arms, and he lowered his weapon. "Damn it."

Someone slammed into him from behind.

His gun slipped from his grip and disappeared into the snow and brush a few feet away. Weston hit the ground. Flakes worked under the collar of his jacket as he wrenched one elbow back. He made contact with the assailant's skull. A groan of pain cut through the silence, but his attacker held on. Pain exploded across the side of his head with a right hook to his temple, and white streaks filled his vision.

Weston flipped onto his back and braced against

gloved hands wrapping around his neck. A dark ski mask hid his attacker's features, but the weight and shape pinning him to the ground was distinctly male. He widened his arms and dragged the bastard closer. "You picked the wrong family to mess with."

"Who said I'm here for your family?" The man above him countered the leverage Weston had around his wrists, crushing his own hands against Weston's chest. The son of a bitch hauled one fist back and rocketed it into Weston's face. Once. Twice. A third time.

Lightning overwhelmed his senses as his head rammed back into the ground. Darkness closed in around the edges of his vision. *Chloe.* The suspect shoved to his feet, and the pressure against his chest released. "You can't have her."

"You should've stayed out of it, Chief Ford." The man's outline blended in with the trees a split second before the sky tilted on its axis. "Now I'm going to have to hurt you and your brother to make sure you don't interrupt my plans."

His heels dragged into the snow and dirt. Weston clawed at the hand gripped around the back of his coat but couldn't reach. Dizziness arced through him. He tried to reach for the knife he'd secured under his pant leg, but his attacker released his hold before he had the chance. "Where is… Easton? What did you do with him?"

"Don't worry, Chief. You and your brother will have all the time in the world together. Chloe's going to pay for what she's done, and there's nothing you can do to stop me. I'd do you the favor of sedating you, but I only brought enough propofol for one." The man in the mask crouched over him, patting him down for weapons. He pulled the blade from the ankle holster under his pant leg and twisted it back and forth, back and forth. The killer straightened and set one foot against Weston's stomach. "I learned a lot from her escape a few months ago. My main takeaway? Dig the hole first."

A single push. That was all it took, and Weston was falling. Rock, snow and dirt scratched at his face and hands before the ground disappeared out from underneath him. He landed on something soft. His head cleared enough to recognize the familiar scent of bleach just before the lid secured him inside. "No!"

Pitch darkness engulfed him as the reverberation of chains echoed into the box. He pressed both hands against the lid, but the physics of being in such a confined space and the ache in his head stole his strength. His attacker had locked him in a meat freezer. The hard thump of rock and gravel hitting the exterior of the container punctured through the ringing in his ears. The suspect was burying him alive. Weston struck the lid again and pressed his knees into the door as hard as he could. It was no use. It wouldn't budge. "Damn it."

A moan filled the small space. "Language."

"Easton?" He tried to maneuver around to face his brother, but the space was too tight for the both of them to move comfortably. He was positioned directly on top of Easton, their backs pressed against one another.

"Bastard got the drop on me. I think I got a shot off, but my memory is a bit fuzzy after that. You know, from the concussion." Easton shifted beneath him, and his voice became clearer. "I know we're brothers and all, and we used to sleep in the same tent, but could you get your elbow out of my ribs?"

"In case you haven't noticed, we've been locked in a freezer and buried. Would you prefer one of my other body parts instead?" Chloe had been able to calculate how long Whitney Avgerpoulos had between the time the killer had put her in the freezer and the moment she'd taken her last breath. But with two adult men, that time didn't apply. With him and Easton out of commission, the woman he'd given his word to protect was in danger. "We have to work fast. We're about to run out of air."

Chapter Seven

A tremor worked through her despite the warmth from the fireplace.

The snow was falling heavier now and building on the edges of the windowsill. The gun slipped from the sweat building between her palm and the grip as she studied every shift in the trees. Nothing but the wind. Weston had left nearly twenty minutes ago. Where was he? Was he okay?

A knot of concern urged her to check on James and Karie, but leaving the cabin went against everything Weston had instructed. The second she stepped out the front door, she'd be exposed. It was her fault a killer had come to their town. Her fault the man who'd attacked her had killed again. She had a responsibility to make things right, but deeper, the loneliness of the past few months had ebbed the moment the Fords had brought her into their tight-knit fold. She couldn't leave them to pay for her mistakes, and she wouldn't leave Weston to fight her battles alone.

Setting the gun on the kitchen table beside the photo of the police chief and his wife, Chloe tucked her hair into her coat collar and zipped up. She could still taste him on her lips, smell him on her skin. Smoked birch and man mixed with a hint of peppermint. Soothing and exhilarating at the same time. She'd come to Battle Mountain to start over, to never have to face the helplessness she'd felt during her attack. The last thing she'd expected was him. And while Weston had made it perfectly clear he wasn't ready to give up the past, she'd reveled in the feel of someone else fighting to hold her together. That alone was worth the risk. "You can do this."

She collected the gun he'd lent her and clicked off the safety. The weapon was heavy in her hand. Nothing like her surgical tools yet just as deadly. Twisting the old brass knob, she wrenched open the wooden door and stepped out into the open. Winds whipped at her hair as snow melted against her face and neck. She hid in her coat's faux-fur hood, but nothing could cut through the freezing temperatures. Her ears burned with the wind chill as she narrowed her eyes against the onslaught of the storm. Her boots sank into the layer of snow as she headed straight for the main house. A low whistle filled her ears as another gust ripped through the trees. High peaks demanded attention around the property as though a thick layer of black velvet had been draped over them. She couldn't see anything out here, couldn't hear. One hand grasping to keep her hood in place, she picked up the pace toward the dim lights of the main cabin.

Her boots thumped against old wood as she climbed the

now-familiar steps leading to the front door. She'd barely lifted her hand to knock before the door swung inward.

"Chloe, what are you doing out here? Weston told us you're supposed to stay in his cabin until he gets back." Karie Ford, armed with one of the largest shotguns Chloe had ever seen, motioned her inside. "Come on, honey. No use in letting you freeze to death. I've got hot chocolate on the stove."

She ducked inside, brushing snow from her coat, and stomped her feet against a smaller version of the handwoven rug she'd noticed in the living room. Chloe pushed her hood back onto her shoulders. "I'm sorry. I just wanted to make sure you and James were okay. It's been almost thirty minutes since Weston left, and the storm is getting worse. You haven't heard from him, have you?"

"No." An internal concern slipped into Karie's brown gaze as the Ford matriarch set her weapon beside the door. "Temperatures are dropping, and he wasn't wearing more than his sheepskin coat, but my boys know these woods better than the backs of their hands. I'm sure they're fine."

"Boys?" Panic squeezed around Chloe's heart. "You mean Easton is out there, too?"

"The shot came from near Easton's cabin. I taught my boys how to track. The snow will complicate things, but they're good hunters. Whoever's out there doesn't stand a chance." James Ford rounded the corner with two steaming white mugs in hand and offered one to her and one to his wife. "Here, drink up. You look like you're about to fall over."

Both of the Ford sons had gone out into the woods in the dead of night in the middle of a snowstorm. Chloe stumbled back toward the door, the gun heavier than a minute ago. "I have to go. I have to find them before it's too late."

"Chloe, Weston would want you to stay here. You're safe with us." Karie handed off her mug back to her husband and countered Chloe's retreat. That sugar-sweet voice that'd greeted her when Weston had introduced her to these people solidified as hard as overcooked caramel. "You don't know the land or how to survive in these conditions. The second you walk out that door, you'll be putting yourself in danger, and my son did not risk his life to protect you for you to do something stupid."

"The man who tried to bury me alive, who killed Whitney Avgerpoulos and one of my colleagues, followed me to Battle Mountain. He won't stop until he gets what he wants." She squared her shoulders, more herself than ever before. "You and your family are the only ones standing between him and me. Whitney had nothing to do with any of this, and he killed her anyway. Do you think he'll spare your sons' lives just because they're not his original target, or do you think he'll eliminate anyone who gets in his way?"

One second. Two. Karie Ford notched her chin higher, but the hardness drained from her expression. "Honey, Easton is former Special Forces, and Weston has been police chief of this town going on three years. They've trained with weapons. What do you think you can do to stop whoever is after you that they can't?"

"I don't know, but I'm not going to be the reason you lose your sons tonight. I'm going after them, and there's nothing you can do to stop me." Chloe handed off the mug of hot chocolate and escaped out the front door, immediately tensing at the wall of cold seeping past layers and straight into bone.

"You're not going alone, kid." James Ford closed the front door behind him and secured a thick winter hat over his gray hair. With a rifle slung across his back, he slid gloves onto each hand and tossed a similar set of gloves and a matching hat to her. "Here, put these on. You're going to need 'em."

Hesitation crushed her from the inside, but she wouldn't deny she had no idea where she was going or how to track Weston's and Easton's movements. James had said it himself. He'd trained his boys. Who better to help her find them than the expert? Chloe leveraged the gun between her thighs as she donned the winter gear, but James was already on the move and walking around the back of the cabin. "You said Weston headed behind Easton's cabin. Where are you going?"

"Storm's getting worse. We need to move fast before the snow covers their tracks." He stopped in front of a garage and hefted the heavy door above his head. Inside, he stepped between two identical four-wheelers most likely used to tend the land. Throwing one leg over the machine, he twisted the key in the ignition, and the ATV growled to life. James hiked his thumb over his shoulder and reached back for a helmet. "Climb on."

She approached from the opposite side and maneuvered into position behind him. The machine vibrated beneath her as she clipped the straps of the helmet securely around her chin. Chloe clicked the safety on the weapon Weston had lent her and slid it into her pocket. She'd never ridden an ATV or a motorcycle before, and the fear of sliding off the back stuck in her throat. The chemical burn of gasoline and exhaust filled her lungs. "I don't know what I'm supposed to do."

James craned his chin over his shoulder, his voice barely breaking through the growl of the engine and the padding around her ears. "Put your arms around me, and hang on."

The all-terrain vehicle jolted forward, and Chloe held on for dear life. The garage disappeared behind them as they rocketed through the snow, the change of gears loud in her ears. Her heart rate shot into her throat as they raced across the property directly toward Easton's cabin. Snow liquefied against the helmet's visor, cutting off her view, but James seemed to know exactly which direction his sons had gone. Pine branches laden with at least two inches of snow blurred in her vision the faster Weston's father pushed the four-wheeler, but in an instant, momentum threw her forward as he downshifted.

They slowed to a stop, and James pointed to their right. Darkness fled at the spread of the machine's headlights to where she could almost make out dips in the snow alongside them. "Those are Weston's prints. Size ten. These other ones are Easton's. Size eleven. They headed this way."

James knew his sons' shoe sizes. Of course, he did. The ATV launched forward to the compression of the gas before she could respond, her hot breath building in the helmet. The curves of the rifle strapped to James's back bit into her arms, but she didn't dare release her grip or move in any way for fear of disturbing the delicate balance of the machine beneath her.

Pine trees thinned ahead before opening into a wide spread of clearing, and James slowed once again. A loud click notched her heart rate into her throat. The engine died as the Ford patriarch dismounted easily and rounded to the front of the ATV. He crouched, sliding gloved fingers through the snow before studying the landscape around them.

"What is it?" Chloe asked.

"Easton's tracks end, but Weston's…" He pointed off to his left. "There's another set of footprints I don't recognize, heading south. There's a small ravine where an old creek used to cut through our property. It dried up a long time ago, but that's where these tracks lead. Along with a set of drag marks."

Drag marks? Every muscle down her spine tensed. The third set of tracks headed toward the creek. Not Weston's or Easton's. "You think—"

The growl of another engine cut through the soft ringing in her ears.

James pushed to his feet, twisting around a split second before a second set of headlights illuminated the clearing from a break in the trees.

Chloe shielded her eyes against the sudden brightness but couldn't make out the driver.

A soft clink of chains reached her ears as the truck rocketed toward them.

"Chloe, get out of here!" James stepped between

her and the oncoming pickup and shoved her off the four-wheeler.

She hit the ground just as the scream of metal and glass exploded around her. "No!"

THE AIR HAD already thinned.

Weston gasped through the pressure building in his chest, but it was only a matter of time before their bodies exchanged what was left of the oxygen for carbon dioxide. No light. No way out. He pressed his elbow into Easton's chest to reach his cell phone, but his brother's groan told him to back off. "We have to get out of here. Can you reach my phone in my back pocket?"

"I can't reach anything with you on top of me, genius." The words growled from between Easton's teeth as his brother shifted beneath him. "Great plan, luring a killer straight to our property, by the way. You're doing a bang-up job, Chief."

"I asked for your help. You slammed the door in my face." Irritation burned through him, and Weston threw his elbow back into his brother's chest without guilt. Instead, his elbow hit the side wall of the freezer and shot nerve-numbing agony through his forearm and into his fingers. "Fine. I'll do it myself, just like I've done everything else since you came home and started feeling sorry for yourself."

He'd taken an oath to protect the people of Battle Mountain, promised to protect Chloe. Being buried in a freezer wasn't going to stop him and neither was Easton's self-pity. He craned his hand back behind him, joints screaming for relief as he skimmed the top of his jeans pocket with his middle finger. There was no way he could reach it. Not without more room to maneuver or Easton's help, and the wretch obviously wasn't in the mood to help anyone. Let alone himself. Weston slumped back onto his brother. They weren't going anywhere.

"Is that what you think I'm doing?" Easton asked. "Feeling sorry for myself?"

"Honestly, I don't know what you're doing." Weston set both palms straight ahead of him, but he couldn't get the leverage he needed to increase the pressure on the freezer door. Not as long as Easton took up more than half the space. He slid his palms down the length of the container. "All I know is you were my brother when you left on orders. Now you're a stranger. You hide in your cabin, you alienate the people who care about you and you shut us out when we try to help, but damn it, Easton, enough. I need your help to get out of here so I can stop a killer from getting to Chloe. It's time to think about someone else for a change."

The sound of their shallow breathing filled the space. Seconds distorted into minutes. He wasn't sure how long the silence stretched yet felt the weight of time slipping.

Exhaustion urged him to close his eyes, but drifting off, pretending they weren't going to die, would be too easy. Sweat beaded in his hairline, and a deep-rooted fear took control. Losing Cynthia had changed him. In an instant, he'd had everything he'd wanted out of life. A wife, a promising future at another mine up north. And it'd all slipped through his fingers the moment she was diagnosed. He watched her suffer, was there when the life drained from her gaze, and then he was alone. His parents had done what they could to be there for him, but it hadn't been the same, trusting himself completely to another person, of having that person trust him completely. He'd loved his wife, and it hadn't been enough.

How the hell was he supposed to protect Chloe when he couldn't even protect himself? Weston pressed one hand into the side of the freezer to feel for the size of the space.

Damn it. Harshness bled from his voice. "I'm sorry, Easton. I didn't mean... I have no room to talk. I lost Cynthia. I can only imagine how hard it must've been to watch your entire unit die right in front of you and not be able to do a damn thing about it." Weston let his body sink into the confines of the container, and the past rushed to meet the present. "When she died, I was a mess. I couldn't eat, couldn't sleep. I didn't want to talk to anyone or leave my cabin, either. Most of the time, I didn't even know what day it was or how long she'd been gone. Some days were better than others, but honestly, the only thing that helped me move on was becoming police chief of this town. It gave me a reason to get up in the morning, a purpose. That's all I want for you. You battled to save thousands of strangers in the Middle East, and now I'm asking you to help me save one more. Please, don't give up. I can't do this without you."

The tick of his brother's swallow reached his ears.

"Seven months, one week and two days." Easton's voice broke through the darkness. "That's when our convoy was hit by an IED. I lost everyone, and I don't go a single day without remembering their names or what they looked like when I pulled them from the wreckage. I was the only one who survived. A piece of shrapnel penetrated my helmet, but I remember every second of that day, Weston. You managed to pick yourself up and find something you believe in, but I'm not you. You're stronger. You always have been. Over there, I knew the things I was doing made a difference. Here, I'm nothing."

"You're my brother," Weston said, whispering so as not to use up too much air. "That's not nothing. All I ever wanted to be growing up was you. You went into the military and suddenly became this hero Mom and Dad were so proud of. All I ever managed was to stay alive down there in the mine. You…you were everything to me. You still are, and I don't want to lose you again."

His heart rate ticked off the seconds, the minutes.

"Forget the phone. You're not going to get coverage with this storm. Move to your left," Easton said.

Muscled arms reached past him as Weston followed orders, and his body sank into the space between the freezer wall and his brother's side. On level ground, he had room to straighten his arms out in front of him, and he set his hands against the door. "The bastard padlocked us in and buried us under at least a few inches of dirt."

"It's worth a shot. On my count." Easton shifted beside him, their arms brushing against one another. "One, two…three!"

Every muscle he owned protested under the pressure,

and pain scorched down his side and into the back of his neck. The door lifted slightly, and a wall of dirt cascaded down into the freezer. It peppered across his face and penetrated the seam of his mouth. Weston shook his head to dislodge it, and a wave of dizziness slithered through him. Time was running out. His arms gave out, and the door thumped back into place. They were burning through the last of the oxygen. "It moved…but the padlock…is still in place."

"We have to keep…trying. Use…legs," Easton said. "No time…for caution."

They could do this. They had to do this. There were no other options. Weston braced his feet against the lower half of the freezer door. "One, two, three."

He used every last ounce of strength he had left. Another wave of dirt fell into the container, half burying him, but he couldn't stop. Not yet. A groan filled the small space before a loud snap. The weight of the door disappeared, and frigid air dove into his lungs. A humorless laugh of relief escaped up his throat, but there was only a minimal amount of space to escape. Gasping for breath, he caught sight of storm clouds above. Bites of snow blew into the freezer and melted against his face. "We did it."

Easton pressed his back into the freezer door, giving Weston a chance to get to his knees. He swept his arm through the ten-inch opening and dislodged some of the dirt wall that'd held them prisoner. "The chains and padlock are still in place. We must've just broken the door handle, but it's enough. We can climb through here. You first."

Weston stretched one hand through the opening and hauled his body through. Turning back, he held the freezer door open as wide as he could as his brother followed behind. He hadn't heard a vehicle engine. The son of a bitch who'd attacked them could still be near. He helped Easton to his feet and released his hold on the door. "He couldn't have gotten far."

"You see that?" Easton asked.

Two beams of light penetrated through the trees to the north. A vehicle? A chemical burn replaced fresh air in his throat, familiar and nauseating. "Smells like one of the four-wheelers, but those lights are too tall to be from one of ours."

"Stay low, move fast. Use me as a shield if you have to." Easton used the trees as cover, Weston on his heels. They'd hunted together for years, shared an awareness of the other as though they were twins.

"You know I'm the older brother, right? I taught you how to hunt. I should be the one telling you to stay low and move fast." Weston pulled up short as they reached the trees and took cover behind one of the larger pines. The snow had lightened, and outlines materialized about twenty feet ahead. "That's a truck."

"And a four-wheeler. One of ours from the look of it." The weight of Easton's attention settled along one side of his face. His voice dipped an octave. "It's been totaled."

Weston scanned the area. No sign of movement or an ambush, but he hadn't seen his attacker until it'd been too late. His instincts prickled, and he stepped free from cover. Something wasn't right. He'd instructed Chloe and his parents to stay inside the cabin. What was one of their ATVs doing out here? His gut knotted as he approached the wreckage, and a familiar outline took shape draped over the front of the machine. Recognition flared. "Dad!"

His heart shot into his throat. He sprinted for his father. His boots slid across the layer of ice under pristine powder, and he went down. Scrambling to his feet, he ignored the bite of frost on his hands as he clamped onto one of the twisted handholds. James Ford lay motionless over the four-wheeler, pinned between the pickup and the ATV. His hands shook as he hesitated moving the older man, and Easton stepped into his peripheral vision. "It's going to be okay. We'll get you out of here." He reached for his phone in his back pocket but came up empty. They were at least a mile from the house. By the time the storm passed, it could be too late.

"Go." The single word punctured through the grief threatening to tear him apart. Blood trickled from his father's mouth, and there was nothing Weston could do to stop it. "Find…her."

"We're not going anywhere. We're going to get you out of here, okay? Hang on, Dad." A vise constricted around his heart and squeezed the air from his chest as though he were right there at Cynthia's bedside all over again. Weston stumbled back. Sorrow lodged in his throat, tears burning against his face. There was so much blood. "Just hang on. Okay? We're going to get you help."

"He took… Chloe. Go." James Ford relaxed against the mangled parts of his four-wheeler. A single exhale escaped past his lips, and then he was gone.

Chapter Eight

A shiver rippled through her.

Wind whistled low from between the slats of the abandoned structure, freezing her jeans solid against her legs. Dropping temperatures kept her from losing consciousness for the time being, but it was only a matter of time before her organs started shutting down to conserve energy. As long as she kept shivering, she had time. She twisted at the bungee cord tightly secured around her wrists. The last images of James Ford flashed across her mind, playing in slow motion. Another torrent of guilt and sadness thickened the sob in her throat. He'd put himself between her and the oncoming truck. He'd saved her life but ended up paying the price. This. This was what she'd been trying to avoid when Weston had brought her to Whispering Pines Ranch. The loss. The pain. The fear. A fresh cut twisted through her heart at the imagery of Weston learning of his father's death. He would blame her. He would hate her. He'd never forgive her.

Chloe dug her heels into the old planks of wood to get her bearings through one of the small windows above her head, but her body protested even the small movements. The man who'd dragged her through the woods—away from the crash—obviously knew this property better than she did. She struggled to get her eyeline above the bottom of the window at her back, but there was only darkness. Her captor had dropped her on the floor and left, but her instincts warned her he hadn't gone far. Was he waiting for her to try to escape? Finishing off Weston and his brother?

The small structure she'd memorized over the past few minutes creaked and groaned under the violence of the storm. No more than five feet by five feet, dark, isolated. A single wooden chair sat in one corner. An old hunting shed? A hunting shed with a crawl space? Another groan of wood shrieked over the constant drone of wind. She listened for crunching snow, footsteps—anything that would give her an idea of where her abductor had gone. There was only the storm. The muscles in her abdomen burned as she brought her heels in closer to her body. Her fingers ached as she skimmed the bungie cord cutting off circulation to her ankles and hands. "Come on."

Chloe tried to work her fingers under the bonds again. Her eyes sagged closed, the corners of the shed blurring at the edges of her vision. She had to stay awake, had to keep trying. Weston and Easton had gone into the woods to find her. Were they still out there? Were they safe? Her fingers curled into her palms against her brain's commands. Exhaustion increased the heaviness in her muscles. She could do this. She had to do this. The pulse behind her ears lightened, her exhales crystalizing in front of her mouth. The temperature had dropped well below freezing. Even with her winter coat and the hat James had lent her, she couldn't last much longer in these conditions. Not without a heat source.

There were five stages to hypothermia. From the quick inventory of her body, she surmised she'd already entered stage one. Shivering, temperature around thirty-three degrees. Stage two would complicate things. The tips of her fingernails had turned blue. From the cold or from lack of blood, she couldn't be sure right then. Didn't matter. "Just keep shivering."

The single door to the shed slammed against the outside wall, and a broad outline filled the door frame. A lantern highlighted dark pants, a heavy jacket, hiking boots. Her automated reflexes froze instead of firing, and she forced her hands away from her ankle binds. Recognition connected memories of her attack three months ago with the man closing the door behind him. Same shape, same build, same black ski mask. "You."

"Me." He secured the door, then turned to face her, removing his gloves in the process. "I've been looking for you, Dr. Miles. Thought I'd caught up with you a couple months ago in Vail, but just as I underestimated you in Denver, you'd already moved on. Here, to Battle Mountain."

The hard thump between her ears, combined with the effects of hypothermia, distorted her abductor's voice. Gravity pulled her upper body to the right, but she caught herself before collapsing to the floor. One of the planks near her feet wobbled under the pressure of keeping herself upright. "Why are you doing this? Why did you have to kill Whitney and James?"

"You dragged that old man into this the moment you accepted his help, Chloe. Just as you dragged the police chief and his brother into this. I'm not sure how else to make it clear to you. Nothing is going to stop me from making sure you pay for what you've done." The killer's footsteps reverberated through the uneven floor as he crossed the small space and dragged the chair into the center of the floor. Directly in front of her. He set an old oil lantern between them. "As for Whitney, well, she was simply in the wrong place at the wrong time. You see, I've spent the past three months hunting you down. I contacted your friends, your family, your co-workers. I even filed a missing person's report on your behalf, but the police had nothing."

He leaned forward, setting his elbows against his knees, and she caught sight of the streak of dirt along the outer edges of his gloves. "Then it occurred to me you'd actually left Denver. So I started branching out to smaller towns where no one would think to look for you. It turns out you make one hell of an impression on the people you talk to, just as you'd made an impression on me. It was only a matter of time before I caught up with you, but when I learned where you were staying and tried to break in to leave you a little gift, Whitney did what any concerned citizen would do. She confronted me. Unfortunately for her, it was her last good deed. I couldn't have her ruining my surprise. Turns out, she was better than the gift I'd chosen for you anyway."

"She had nothing to do with this. She had an entire

future ahead of her." Tears burned in her eyes as pieces of the puzzle settled into place, but three words stood out among the many. The police chief. She'd stopped shivering. Numbness climbed up her arms, past her ankles, but Chloe wasn't going to let him get away with this. No matter what happened, she'd make sure Whitney Avgerpoulos's parents learned of their daughter's bravery. "Why are you doing this? Why kill Roberta Ellis? Why try to kill me?"

A low laugh filled the shed as her abductor shoved to his feet. He closed the distance between them and crouched. His joints popped as he reached for the ski mask and pulled it from his head. Strikingly blond hair turned golden under the warmth of the lantern. Sharp features hazed as he turned an iced expression on her, but she could never forget his face. Thin lips rolled between the killer's teeth as he tossed the mask to the other side of the shed. He'd aged significantly in the past few months since she'd seen him. Where he'd greeted her on more than a dozen occasions with a quick smile and a softness, a hollowness had taken hold, and her heart plummeted in her chest. "Isn't it obvious, Dr. Miles? You killed my wife."

"Jonathan." His name left her mouth through her locked jaw, and she was forced to set her head back against the shed wall. "You're...doing this because of her. You blame me for...what happened."

"Shouldn't I? You promised me my wife's surgery was routine, that the chances of her surviving were over ninety percent." Jonathan Byrd reached behind him, pulling something solid and distinct from his back waistband. A gun. He pointed the barrel at her. Not just any gun. The one Weston had given her before he'd left the cabin. "Turns out she did survive the surgery. What killed her was the clamp you left in her chest."

Chloe struggled to shake her head. Her tongue caught between her lips, rough and dry. How had he found out about the mistake her team had made? She hadn't had the chance to tell the board, and the other physicians wouldn't have willingly put their careers at risk.

"I sat at her bedside every day. I watched her slowly suffocate right in front of me. She was in so much pain not even the morphine could help her at the end. I held her hand until she died, and a piece of me died right along with her." Jonathan straightened, standing over her with the gun gripped in one hand. "I'm going to find the rest of the doctors who were there that day. I'm going to end the lives of each and every single one of them, but today, you're going to know what it feels like to lose someone you care about slowly and painfully."

What? A board shifted under her foot, and Chloe clawed at the bungee cord around her ankles pitifully. It was no use. Her body was already starting to shut down, one organ at a time. She couldn't reach the binds. Not without Jonathan catching her. "I don't...understand."

"I've been watching you, Chloe. I've seen the way you look at him. I see the way you make him smile. You're falling for him." The killer inserted the blade between her ankles and cut through the bungie cord. The strands fell free, and he wrapped his free hand around her arm and hauled her to her feet. "I'd origi-nally brought the freezer out here for you and the police chief, but circumstances have changed. For his brother. Someone will find their bodies in a few days. After I call in an anonymous tip, of course. There won't be anything you can do about it, but I'll do you a favor. I'll bury you right next to them, and you can take your last breaths together."

Weston. A sob built in her chest but stuck under her sternum as he led her toward the shed door. No. She wrenched out of his hold with everything she had left and knocked the lantern over as she hit the floor. Hot oil spilled across the old wood and caught fire. Chloe stretched both hands out and tried to stand, but her body wouldn't obey her brain's commands. A gust of wind aggravated the fire, and she realized her abductor had vanished. Flames branched from the source and raced up the walls as she clawed toward the door. Instant heat burned the exposed skin of her face and neck as she struggled to shield her eyes against the fire closing in, but it was too late.

There was no escape.

THE SMELL OF burning wood filled his nostrils.

Weston trudged through shin-high powder as he followed the disturbances south across the property. Bare skin burned from exposure, but it wouldn't slow him down. The scent of gasoline still clung to his jacket from the wreckage he'd left behind, the chemical burn thick in his throat. Snow worked into his boots and numbed his fingers. He had to keep going. He needed her to be alive.

He'd left Easton at the crash site. The storm made

it impossible to get through to the station, but Easton would take care of their father. A swell of grief charged up his throat as the last few moments of James Ford's life played over and over again. His father had been a great man. Strong, loyal, selfless. There wasn't a single moment growing up Weston hadn't been able to count on him, even when the old man had been on military orders.

Tears stung his eyes. Damn it. He couldn't think about that right now. The next step, the next tree. That was all that mattered. The scent of smoke slithered through the pines ahead, and he picked up the pace. The bastard who'd taken Chloe had already killed three people. There was no telling how long she had before she joined that number. "I'm coming, Doc. Just hang on."

As hard as he'd tried to deny the connection building between him and the coroner, he couldn't ignore the panic exploding through his system now. He'd taken an oath to protect her and failed, but it was more than that.

He'd underestimated her determination to defend him and his family, this town even, against her past. He'd underestimated her influence on his thoughts, on his actions and his entire belief system. Her undeniable sense of right and wrong, of making up for the past, had broken through the wall of ice that'd kept him from letting anyone in since his wife's death. He'd never met anyone more committed to the well-being of others, more passionate to set things right than her. She'd made a mistake, resulting in a patient's death, but her sincerity had never been more evident than in the fact she'd convinced his father to join her in the race to find him and Easton.

But, hell, if he were being honest with himself, asking Chloe to see this case through until the end wasn't just about finding Whitney Avgerpoulos's killer. It might've begun that way, but really, he'd started to care about her, and there wasn't anything he wouldn't do to ensure she walked away from this investigation alive.

A waning orange glow pulsed through the trees ahead, and the hairs on the back of his neck stood on end. He slowed as his mind ran through the possibilities, each ending in only one conclusion. Fire. "Chloe."

Weston pushed through a wall of pines cutting him off from a small clearing on the other side. He was familiar with the area, even in the dark, but despite his position as Battle Mountain's police chief, he hadn't been prepared for this fight. Needles and branches sliced across his face and neck. His boots sank into undisturbed snow, slowing him down. Muscles burned with exertion down the front of his thighs. He swung his arms wide to keep momentum, his throat frozen with icy temperatures.

A lick of flame sprinted toward the sky, and he burst into the small clearing where one of their old hunting sheds had caught fire. Instant heat warned him not to get closer, but his instincts said she was here. "Chloe!"

The structure's roof groaned as bits and pieces flaked off and fell around the perimeter of the fire. The shed was going to collapse any second, and every cell in his body said Chloe was inside. Red, orange and yellow embers shot into the air. Nearby young trees smoldered as the flames drew near. Smoke thickened between him and the shed and stung his eyes.

A scream cut through the crackle of flame and cauterized his nerve endings.

"No." Weston sprinted toward what was left of the door, covering his face with both arms. The flames lashed out, and agony shot down his hands and across his face. Weston stumbled back. He couldn't get close enough. Not without some kind of protection. Ripping his coat from his shoulders, he draped it over his head and hands as best he could. Sweat dripped underneath his collar and pooled at the base of his spine. Shifting his weight onto his front leg, he bounced on his back foot and summoned the courage to try again.

Pain splintered across his left shoulder and thrust Weston forward.

He landed palms down into a smoldering pile of wood. His fight-or-flight system twisted him away as fast as his body allowed. He rolled onto his back as a wall of muscle brought down a large branch from above. He threw his forearms out and blocked the blow. An ache ripped through his arms. The attacker pulled back for another strike, and Weston rocketed both feet into the bastard's chest. His coat fell away and exposed more skin to the elements.

He scrambled to his feet. Heat struggled to overcome the stiffness in his bones. He set one foot into the shed. A dark feminine outline—unmoving—was all he recognized before strong hands tore him back. Fire and trees blurred in his vision as he hit the ground a second time. Snow stung down his back and across both arms.

"You just don't quit, do you, Chief?" His attacker closed the distance between them and fisted one hand into Weston's T-shirt. He pulled his free hand back and struck. One hit. Two. "Doesn't matter. I got what I wanted. You're too late. Chloe is going to pay for every single second my wife suffered, and there's nothing you can do about it."

"Over my dead body." Weston dodged the next strike and used the man's own momentum to launch him face-first into the snow. He slammed his elbow into the attacker's back, and a groan drowned out the sound of the crackling flames. He struck again and got to his feet. Hauling his boot into the son of a bitch's rib cage, Weston froze as the killer caught his foot and twisted. His knee planted into the ground and knocked him off balance as lightning arced through his ligaments. He fell forward, palms splayed out in front of him.

"That can be arranged." The killer fisted a handful of hair and forced Weston back onto his knees. The fire lit up sharp angles of the suspect's face and highlighted the curl of a thin mouth. Pain contorted his opponent's expression as his hand trembled against Weston's skull. Jonathan Byrd. The husband of the patient Chloe and her team had lost in the week following her surgery. "I know why you're doing this. I know the pull she has on you and everyone she meets. You think she's innocent, that she deserves your protection, but you're wrong, Chief Ford. She doesn't deserve your loyalty. She'll only use it against you."

The past few weeks flashed through his brain as he recounted his first meeting with Chloe, the way her smile had lit him up from the inside, how she'd gone out of her way to help elderly Mrs. Banes get her groceries to the car. How she'd empathized when he'd told her about Cynthia's diagnosis and death and somehow given him hope for the future in the same breath. No. There wasn't a single part of him that doubted her engrained goodness and honesty.

"I know exactly who she is." Debilitating throbbing gripped his body as Weston forced himself to his feet. The world threatened to rip out from under him, but he powered through. "I know what you're going through. I know how much it hurts to lose the one person you thought you'd be spending the rest of your life with, but you're wrong about Chloe. And there's no way in hell I'm going to let you take her."

He tackled the killer around the middle, and they hit the ground as one. Air crushed from his lungs as they rolled through the snow, each fighting for dominance.

Weston's head snapped back against something harder than ice, and the edges of his vision darkened in waves. A rock? Disorientation cleared enough for him to dodge the next strike aimed at his face, and he wrapped frozen fingers around the rock behind him. Arcing the heavy weapon as fast as he could, he slammed it against the killer's head, and the weight against his chest vanished.

Weston forced himself to sit up and shoved to his feet. He stumbled as dizziness took hold, but he couldn't stop. Couldn't give up. Blocking the heat from his face with both hands, he stepped through the shed's opening. A section of roof crashed to the floor beside Chloe, and he lunged. He gripped both of her ankles and pulled as hard as he could. Her outstretched hands barely cleared the doorway as the structure failed. He landed on his backside a few yards from the shed, and he scrambled to turn her over onto her back. He fought to catch his breath. "I've got you, Doc. It's going to be okay. You're going to make it. Hang on."

He pressed two fingers to the base of her neck. Her pulse was thready but there, and the battle-ready tension that'd pushed him this far drained. He split his attention from the dark smudges across the underside of her jaw and scanned the area where he and the killer had fought. Weston straightened, keeping one hand pressed to Chloe's neck.

Jonathan Byrd was gone.

For how long, he didn't know. Didn't care. All that mattered was getting Chloe help. He threaded his hands beneath her knees and along her lower back and hefted her against his chest. Every muscle he owned protested the additional weight as he climbed to his feet. He could do this. He had to do this.

Her head sagged against his arm as he retraced his steps through the trees and back toward the wreckage where he'd left Easton and his father. She cracked her eyes open, the distant glow of the fire reflecting back at him. "Bet you wish you'd let me leave now."

Chapter Nine

Her lungs burned.

Smoke inhalation, mild hypothermia, choking grief for someone she'd hardly known. Chloe closed her eyes against the onslaught of noise coming from the monitors tracking her vitals and the afternoon sunlight streaming through the window. Emergency personnel had rushed her to the small medical center located at the southern end of town once they'd been able to get to the main cabin and keep the fire from spreading. The neutral colors eased the headache at the base of her skull, the scratchy sheets long past their prime. What she wouldn't give to be able to go home, to pretend what'd happened out in those woods hadn't been her fault.

Flashes of fear, of pain, exploded through her as she memorized the gauze across her hands concealing the blisters underneath. Jonathan Byrd was systematically and methodically tracking down each surgical team member involved in his wife's death and seeking his own sense of revenge. Roberta Ellis had already paid the price, and he'd come for Chloe twice. It was only a matter of time before the grieving husband set his sights on the others. She'd severed contact with anyone from that life when she'd left Denver, but she wouldn't let anyone else die for a mistake she'd failed to notice during that surgery. No matter who was really at fault. She had to warn them.

Hospital staff had taken her clothes and bagged them as evidence and left a pair of dark blue scrubs as a temporary replacement. Shoving back the blankets, she set her bare feet against the floor and removed the sticky nodes from her skin. The tug of her IV catheter reminded her dehydration had been a large proponent of why she'd gone into hypothermia so quickly, but she couldn't afford to wait around for Jonathan Byrd to strike again. Not when he'd already destroyed so many lives.

She peeled the adhesive sticker from her skin, the sting intensifying at the entry of her IV, and discarded it on the bed. A couple drops of blood back-loaded into the line as she pulled the needle from her vein. She stripped the blood pressure cuff from her arm, the Velcro louder than she expected, and stood. Cold worked up through her heels and into bone as she shuffled to the end of the hospital bed. The monitors had gone quiet without anything to report. Dressing quickly, she tossed the thin gown over the blood pressure cuff and slid her legs into the scrub pants. She secured the drawstring and locked her jaw against the ache in her right side from being thrown from James Ford's four-wheeler. She nearly collapsed as she replayed those terrifying seconds over and over. She recalled the acceptance in his eyes as she stared up at him, the gut-wrenching sorrow that'd crushed her as effectively as the pickup slamming into the ATV. Only she'd been the one to walk away.

Chloe forced herself to thread both arms into the scrub top. She shoved her feet into the thin hospital socks with rubber grips on the bottom and realized the nurses had taken her boots along with her clothing.

Three knocks on the door electrified her nerves, and she sat back against the bed.

The mattress creaked under her as Weston filled the doorway, every ounce the police chief she'd needed out there. He'd changed, most likely because he'd surrendered his clothing as evidence as well, but even without the addition of his sheepskin coat, he was still the most rugged, handsome man she'd ever met. He removed his stained hat, circled as far from her as possible and took a seat in the chair a few feet from the bed. Exhaustion had set up in the finer lines of his face and darkened the circles under his eyes. He moved slowly, as though every step triggered another round of pain, and the invisible laceration cutting through her heart carved deeper. He'd been injured out there. Because of her. "Look who's awake. How are you feeling?"

"Like I owe you my life. I'm not sure I would've made it out of that shed if it weren't for you." Blisters stung beneath the gauze, but the low dose of morphine still clinging to her sympathetic nervous system muffled the pain. The last moment of consciousness, of staring up into his face as he hauled her away from the flames, had engrained itself into her mind, and she pressed her hands into the mattress to counter the emotion that came with it. "Thank you."

"Just doing my job, Doc. Besides, I'm sure you would've done the same for me." Weston settled back into the chair, his expression solid and hurt. "I'm glad you're okay."

She nodded, unable to meet his gaze. Tears burned in her eyes, and she lowered her attention to a single thread unravelling from the heavy blanket on the bed. Her heart squeezed from the obvious pain in his eyes. She swallowed through the thickness in her throat, but there were certain pains that couldn't be healed with anything more than time. "I'm sorry about your father. He... When he saw the pickup coming toward us, he pushed me off the four-wheeler so I wouldn't be caught in the collision. James saved my life, and I'll never forget that."

"He was always one to put others' safety before his own." Silence settled between them. A minute. Two. The heaviness he'd obviously been fighting charged to the surface. "I still remember one winter we were headed back to the ranch from picking up supplies in town. The road home was covered in at least a half inch of ice, but he'd driven that stretch so many times it was just another day for him." The police chief scrubbed a hand down his face. "An oncoming sedan slid into our lane, but instead of swerving to avoid them like most people would and going down the gulch, he slowed down, threw the truck in Reverse and aimed right for this family we could hear screaming from inside the car. My brother and I were never more scared in our lives, but James Ford simply let their car hit ours so he could help them stop. Worked, too. Everyone walked away that day."

The urge to reach out to him, to smooth the lines between his eyebrows, curled her blistered fingers into her palms. Another crack in her guard spread wider at the obvious respect he'd kept for his father, and a hit of grief crushed the air from her lungs. She knew what it was like to lose a parent—accident or not—and her heart squeezed. "Sounds like he was a great man."

"He was. My whole life I thought he was more interested in helping everyone but his own family, but now that I look back, I can see he was preparing us to do the same. To be there for the people who couldn't help themselves." Weston shifted in his seat. "Easton is working with Mom on the arrangements. They're going to try to have the funeral within the next few days."

"You should be with them. They need you." But even as she said the words—believed them with her whole heart—the hollowness in her chest throbbed with need. The need not to be alone, to have him close. The need for him to forgive her for bringing this violence and danger into his and his family's lives. These past couple days, while terrifying and filled with unimaginable loss, had shut out the loneliness she'd experienced since leaving Denver behind, and she didn't want him to go.

"I need to be here. As long as Jonathan Byrd is out there, you and the people you worked with aren't safe, and I wouldn't be any kind of police chief if I walked away from the investigation now. I've already filled in Denver PD. They're trying to get a location on the other three surgical team members who were in that surgical suite the day of Miriam Byrd's operation. There's a chance Jonathan has been so focused on you, he's temporarily given them a pass." Weston set his elbows on his knees, hands pressed together in front of him. "Chloe, look at me. Please."

The weight of his attention pressurized the air in her lungs until she gave in to her craving to look up. The combination of weariness and concern in his voice hiked her blood pressure higher, but she couldn't ignore the resulting warmth he triggered behind her rib cage.

"I need you to know I don't blame you for what happened. You are not responsible for my dad's death. Understand?" he said.

Her bottom lip shook under the swell of emotion the longer she met his gaze. "You and Easton were buried in a freezer. Your dad was killed. Everything that's happened...it's because of me. If I hadn't come to Battle Mountain—"

"He would've found you somewhere else. Maybe even killed more people to get to you." Weston rose to his feet, then maneuvered onto the edge of the bed beside her. The mattress dipped beneath his weight and pulled the left side of her body against him. Right where she needed to be. He swept callused fingers across her forehead, brushing a strand of her knotted and singed hair behind her ear, and her heart jerked in her chest. "None of this is your fault. Okay? I told you. My dad put others' safety before his own long before he met you. He knew exactly what he was doing out there. He knew a killer wanted to get to you, and he did what he had to to keep that from happening." Weston gathered her hair in one hand and swept it across her shoulders. "As for me and Easton, we got out, and being buried alive only forced us to work together to survive. You have nothing to apologize for, Doc. You're not responsible for someone else's choices, and I don't want you spending the rest of your life carrying that burden."

The hesitation she'd held on to, to keep herself from getting too close, cracked. Chloe swiped the back of her bandaged hand down her face to catch the tears escaping. "How can you just dismiss the fact none of this would've happened if I hadn't come to your town? How can you forgive me like that? You don't even know me."

"I know enough." He slid his hand down her back and planted it behind her. "We might not have known each other long and you're intense at times, maybe even a little secretive. But you're also the most intelligent, insightful and realistic woman I've ever met in my life, and I'm grateful I got the chance to work with you. I meant what I said when you were trying to sneak out of my parents' bathroom window. I can't do this without you, and I wouldn't trust anyone else to be my partner."

He leaned in close, his exhale brushing along the underside of her jaw. Anticipation coiled deep in her belly as he locked that mesmerizing gaze on her. Right before he kissed her.

HE'D NEVER KISSED another woman after his wife's death, until Chloe, and Weston couldn't keep his distance any longer. Fire scorched along his hands and up his neck as he threaded his fingers through her slightly singed hair. The flames had gotten too close. If he'd pulled her from that shed even thirty seconds later, it would've been too late, and the tightness in his chest only intensified.

So pale against the dark blue of her borrowed scrubs, Chloe looked as though one wrong word, one tiny ding in her armor, might shatter her into a million pieces, and his entire being turned inside out.

He kissed her, falling from about a thousand feet and landing with a velvet glide of tongues that threatened to unravel every ounce of his control. Their combined exhales filled his ears, nearly drowning the pound of his pulse at the base of his skull. Electricity tornadoed into a frenzy he hadn't felt in years, but with Chloe, the low buzzing of desire had always been there and suffocated the grief clawing through him.

He'd almost lost her out there, wasn't sure what he would've done if Jonathan Byrd had finished the job he'd started three months ago, but it wouldn't have made his father proud. His family had always had his back, but this was different. She was different. She was everything he wasn't and everything he hadn't realized he'd been missing all this time. A companion, a partner, someone who'd never turn her back on him or leave.

Weston pulled back slightly, his fingers grazing her jawline. But Chloe would leave. The IV line, the blood pressure cuff, the monitor nodes and her gown—all of it had been discarded on the bed as though she hadn't planned to stick around. It made sense. Once this case was closed, she'd go back to her life in Denver. She'd slip through his fingers just as easily as Cynthia had, and he'd be alone all over again. Hell, he'd barely recovered from losing his wife. It'd taken months and hundreds of threats from his parents to pull himself out of the suffocating blackness of grief the first time. What was he doing trying to put himself back in the same position?

He wasn't ever going to leave Battle Mountain, and Chloe… She had her own life. Her own friends, a career she cared about. She'd already lost it all once. He couldn't take that from her again, but the thought of letting her go completely didn't sit well, either. He ducked his chin toward his chest and forced himself to detach as he stood. "We can't go back to the ranch. I put out an all-points bulletin to the surrounding towns up to a fifty-mile radius for Jonathan Byrd and asked residents to call in with anything suspicious, but I don't want him to be able to track you."

Overwhelming pressure took up residence under his rib cage.

"Right. No, I understand. It's… It's fine." Chloe peeled her bandaged hand from his arm and intertwined her fingers in her lap, obviously sensing the sudden distance between them. She got to her feet. "Jonathan Byrd told me he was hunting down everyone involved in his wife Miriam's death. I need to know my colleagues are safe."

"That's where you were headed when I came in the room, before I told you I had Denver PD looking for them." A rock settled in his gut, and the tight thread of anxiety that'd pushed him to find her in those woods broke.

Confusion contorted her beautiful expression. "Weston—"

His heart thundered in his chest as he collected his hat from the chair. He skimmed his fingers across the brim. "I called in a favor to get you another place. Somewhere Jonathan Bryd won't be able to connect to me or my family. You'll have everything you need until I can bring him in."

"Wait. You want to work the case alone?" she asked.

"Isn't that what you want?" He motioned to the collection of medical supplies on the bed. "Isn't that why you've been trying to run since the moment you recognized the killer's MO in the mine, and why you were getting ready to leave the hospital?"

Chloe relaxed both hands to her sides and met his gaze head-on. Her voice deadpanned, calm and guarded as it'd been the first few times they'd met. "Actually, if you'd let me finish, I could've told you I was leaving the hospital to look for you, to make sure you were okay and to figure out a way to contact my team without tipping Jonathan Byrd off."

Well, damn. He hadn't expected that. Relief replaced the pain and settled his nerves. "So then you're not planning on escaping through the bathroom window again?"

"I already checked. I won't fit through it. I'm moving on to plan B." She closed the distance between them, her full lips stretching into a heartbreaking smile he'd remember for the rest of his life. Chloe angled her hands between his arms and rib cage and secured him in a hug. Setting her head against his chest, she held on to him.

Weston pressed his mouth into the crown of her head, inhaling the residual odor of smoke and pine, and his gut clenched. "Which is?"

"I'm going to let you take me to this new safe house so I can get a proper shower, find a comfortable change of clothes since you instructed the staff to take mine as evidence, a good night's sleep and let you feed me." Her laugh reverberated through him and revitalized an easiness he hadn't let himself feel since taking the position as Battle Mountain's police chief. "I'm thinking something with pasta and cheese. Carbs and fats are the gateway of comfort food and are guaranteed to put me to sleep the fastest."

"Anything else?" He grudgingly released her and the blanket of warmth her body heat produced and offered his hand to her. "A movie perhaps or some silk pillowcases?"

Chloe slid her palm into his, and a bolt of peace filled the cracks in his wounded armor, even with the bandages over her hand. "I'll take what I can get. I might even share." Her smile disappeared as she stared up at him, and his heart kicked in his chest at the abrupt change. "Do you really think this is the best plan? Leaving your family when they need you most?"

He wasn't sure what to say to that. His family had been there for him when Cynthia had passed away. Without them, he wouldn't be where he was today, but now he was leaving them to deal with their grief alone. His mom was strong, and Easton would be there for her until Weston brought his father's killer to justice. "They understand. Come on, let's get you checked out. The longer we stay here, the higher chance Jonathan Byrd has to catch up to you."

He escorted her into the hallway, and within a few

minutes she was released by the nurses at the floor's front desk. The safe house wasn't far. Maybe a twenty-minute drive, but enough distance that they might have the advantage the next time Jonathan Byrd came for her. Because he would come for her. Weston bet his entire year's salary on it. The man's hatred for the physicians responsible for his wife's death had destroyed any semblance of the husband Chloe had described. Now, there was only desperation and revenge.

They descended the stairs and exited the hospital from the east side of the building instead of the main doors. Less chance of an ambush. He threw his jacket over her shoulders and directed her toward a small black sedan on the other side of the lot. Macie had come through. He couldn't take any chances of relying on his own vehicle or anyone related to him. Not anymore.

Opening the passenger door, he helped Chloe into her seat and secured her inside. His exhales crystallized in front of his mouth with dropping temperatures as he rounded to the driver's side. Recovering the keys from the visor, he started the engine.

"Whose car is this?" Chloe took in the worn, stained upholstery, the slight hint of perfume permanently part of the vehicle and the two duffel bags in the back seat.

"Macie's." He pulled out of the hospital parking lot but didn't turn back toward the heart of town. They had to stay off the main road. It was the only way to ensure they weren't being followed. "I called her from the nurses' station, after the attending cleared me to leave, instead of using my own phone. I told her what'd happened and that we needed a vehicle that couldn't be connected back to us. Hope you don't mind, but I had her bring you a few changes of clothes, too."

She reached for the large hot-pink circular key chain knocking against his knee and smiled. A spike of desire coiled through him at the memory of those full lips under his, the softness, her taste. Honey with a hint of bite. "That explains the *coffee, chocolate and men, some things are better rich* key chain."

"Macie's very much an individualist when it comes to style. I'd take that as a warning before opening that bag she packed for you." He'd told her the truth when he said the safe house couldn't connect back to him. The small cabin he'd only been to once before sat at the base of Crystal Peak, northeast of town. The vehicle bounced too easily along the single dirt paved road as they wound around Lake San Cristobal. The lake had frozen over months ago, just now thawing in the middle. Colorado's second largest natural lake spanned two miles and brought in visitors from all over the state. Well-stocked with trout, it was often visited by moose hanging around the swampy shoreline and almost everyone within town during the summer. Although it'd been years since Weston had been on the water.

A single beam of sunlight pierced through the front windshield and highlighted the golden undertones of Chloe's hair as she leaned back in her seat. No matter how many times he tried to keep his attention on the road, she had a certain pull he couldn't ignore. He'd felt it the moment he met her all those months ago. She was sunshine wrapped in a hurricane on the darkest of days, and he wasn't sure he'd ever recover—that he wanted to recover—once this investigation ended. He directed the sedan onto a smaller road heading west. Several inches of snow clung to the pines, slipping from branches as they drove up the long driveway. The trees thinned about halfway up and encircled a single structure ahead, exactly as he remembered it. He swung the car around in front of the three-story cabin and peered out the passenger side window, his chest brushing against her arm. "Let's see Jonathan Byrd find you here."

Chapter Ten

"This isn't a safe house." Chloe slammed the car door a little too firmly as she stared up at the barely standing structure punctured with two trees up through the middle. He had to be joking. "This is a treehouse."

The house featured a grand outdoor spiral staircase leading to the front door and first level, which had most likely been custom crafted around a giant Douglas fir. Above an outdoor seating area seemingly constructed with two living trees, another level stared out over the roughly five-acre lot packed with several feet of snow. A beautiful brick chimney finished the artistically designed craftsman with a shed a few yards from the base of the staircase. She'd never seen anything like it. She locked her gaze on him. "What is this place?"

With what looked like barely more than five hundred square feet of living space with two outside deck areas made from living trees, it was a cozy abode, one in which Chloe couldn't imagine staying for long without running smack into Weston multiple times. He'd kissed her at the hospital, triggering a wave of confidence and strength, a confirmation of being his equal so gut-wrenching it'd stolen her fear in an instant. Then there'd been distance, regret, as he'd backed away, and every nerve ending that'd woken in awareness of him had gone numb. She couldn't even blame him. Losing his father in the past twenty-four hours, losing his wife to cancer nearly four years ago. She couldn't imagine the battle warring inside him to rise above the grief, to move on, but she had her own skirmish tearing through her. One she hadn't expected to face when she'd come to Battle Mountain.

"I told you. Macie has a very unique outlook on life." Weston wrenched open the back door of the sedan and hauled both duffel bags from the back seat. Shouldering one, he clutched the other in his free hand. "It's not that small once you get inside. I promise."

She'd fled Denver to survive, to never have to face the helplessness being a victim had engrained in her. The only reason she'd gotten this far was by keeping her head down, moving from one town to the next and not letting herself get attached. It hurt less that way, but instead she'd found him. Weston had worked through her guard and survival instincts and reminded her how strong she could be, that she beat a killer. Twice. Now the idea of leaving Battle Mountain, of leaving him and going back to the life she'd left behind... That hurt almost as much as the stab wound in her side had. Chloe followed the divots Weston left in the snow as he trod toward the base of the outdoor staircase.

His boots thunked against the cherry-stained wood as they climbed to the first level. The entire structure had been placed on stilts, and a sudden wash of vertigo had her holding the railing tighter than necessary. Snow melted under her fingers, and she froze. The air was suddenly thinner up here, or was that her brain playing tricks on her?

"Doc? You okay?" His voice sounded too far away. Wobbly. "All the color just ran from your face."

"I don't seem to be able to move anymore." She closed her eyes against the dizziness drilling down into her bones. Her knees threatened to give out straight from under her, and in her next breath she feared she might tip over the railing. Strong hands encircled her arms, and she opened her eyes.

"Don't worry. I've got you. You've been through a lot in the past couple of days. Just hold on to me." Warm brown eyes filled her vision. He scooped her body against his and leveraged one hand against the railing. Dragging her up the last few steps, Weston refused to release her until the front door swung inward and he'd stepped over the threshold. "Almost there."

Warmth tendriled down the V-shaped collar of the scrubs she still wore and spread across her skin. The world tilted on its axis as he laid her across a red padded bench. The edges of a raw wood table swam into her vision as she set her head back. Exposed beams crisscrossed fifteen to twenty feet overhead, and as long as she focused on one of them, the dizziness ebbed. She pressed one hand against her forehead, and the blisters under the gauze screamed in warning. A modern sphere-shaped chandelier swayed, and the worst of the wooziness faded. "I'm okay. I think it's just been a while since I've eaten. My blood sugar must be low."

"It's been a while, but luckily I can take care of that. You rest. I'll get something together for us." Hands leveraged on either side of her, Weston straightened, his gaze drifting to the exposed skin above her scrub pants. His mouth parted, eyes wide, and it was then she knew. The scar. "That's a pretty nasty wound. Doesn't look very old, either."

Chloe pulled her scrub top back into place and forced herself to sit upright. The edges of her vision wobbled slightly, but not nearly as bad as it had on the stairs. The coat he'd lent her weighed heavy on her shoulders, and she slid the thick sheepskin free. Embarrassment flooded her face with heat, but the simple fact was she hadn't left Denver without a physical souvenir in addition to the mental scars she suffered whenever she closed her eyes.

"It happened the first time he attacked you, didn't it?" Weston lowered himself onto an identical bench perpendicular to hers in the small seating area. "Couldn't have been a clean stabbing. The edges are too rough for a blade."

"It was a rock." A shiver chased down her spine. The memories of that day threatened to escape the box she'd locked them inside these past few months, but she couldn't hide from them forever. "I fell while I was trying to escape. The surgeon did the best he could, but there was no way I was going to walk away without a permanent scar."

Weston hauled himself off the bench and maneuvered beside her, and her heart jumped a little higher in her chest. "Does it hurt?"

"Sometimes, but to be fair, I really haven't given it a chance to heal. As soon as the detectives informed me they weren't able to find any evidence of the attack, I checked myself out of the hospital and drove for as long and as fast as I could. It's feeling better, though. I don't wince as much when I'm cleaning the exam room at the funeral home." All those miles. All that time wasted on fearing for her life when she could've been planning a better future. Who knew she'd end up here? With him. "For what it's worth, I've felt safer here in Battle Mountain than anywhere else. Up until a few days ago, I was actually starting to accept this was where I'd end up. I have a good job, a place to live and everyone in town has been so welcoming and kind. People actually remember my name. I have a couple acquaintances outside of work and a police chief who will go to extreme lengths to protect the people under his jurisdiction. What's not to like?"

"And now?" A thread of hope infused his voice and urged her to meet his gaze.

"Now I'm not sure what's going to happen." Her throat thickened as the fear for this town that'd accepted her without hesitation twisted tighter. She'd had a plan when she'd fled Denver. Stay on the move, stay alive, but it wasn't just the town or the sense of stability that came with it that had her reconsidering the two rules that'd brought her this far. It was the thought of never finding out if this connection between her and Weston—this pull—could lead to more, to a future.

She'd had boyfriends before medical school, not really anytime during and very few after she'd graduated, but she wasn't inexperienced. There'd been late nights of passion and flirty text messages that'd rocketed her blood pressure into dangerous territory, but none of them had compared to what she'd felt when kissing him. Her lips warmed in memory. She could still taste him, the slight hint of smoked birch and peppermint, and her scalp tightened.

That moment had started a chain reaction that'd triggered a heavy dose of desire and ended with a crushing wave of self-discovery. Her lungs emptied. Because she was in love with him. Two kisses and a hell of a lot of loyalty she didn't deserve, and she'd fallen in love with him. Chloe gripped the edge of the bench and old wood protested. "Jonathan Byrd blames me and my team for his wife's death. He won't stop until every single one of us is dead, and anyone associated with me is at risk, especially you. I can't justify you putting your life in danger for mine, but I'm grateful for everything you and your family have done for me."

Weston interlaced his hand into hers and knocked their knuckles against her outer thigh. "It's going to be okay, Doc. I've got the town on alert. Denver PD is working to put the rest of your team in protective custody, and Easton and my mom can take care of themselves. I'm not going anywhere. Understand? Your safety is my priority. Nothing else matters right now."

"Thank you." She squeezed his hand, and the tension in her rib cage released. "Now, if I remember correctly, there was talk of something to eat."

"Hope you like pancakes. They're the only food I know how to make." Bringing her hand to his mouth, he kissed the over-sensitized skin along the back of her wrist before getting to his feet. His head charged straight into the chandelier above, and he jerked out of the way with one hand secured against his skull. "I did not see that there."

Her laugh escaped easily, and for the first time in days, a weightlessness drifted through her whole body. Because of him. "That's what you get for putting me up in a tree house."

THE FIRE CRACKLED and spit embers into the clear midnight sky from the fire pit on the second deck.

No matter how many times he'd tried, Weston couldn't sleep. Not with Chloe mere inches away. He'd found a couple sleeping bags and heavy blankets tucked in the tree house's loft for the single queen-size bed, but space had become limited as soon as he'd rolled them out. He took a sip of the rich hot chocolate he'd discovered in the cupboards on the main level and let the liquid scald his mouth to counter the below-freezing temperatures. He'd let her sleep as long as possible before throwing her back into reality. The woman had survived a killer not once but twice, and there was only so much the human mind could shoulder before the cracks started to show.

His new phone pinged with an incoming message, and Weston tugged it from his coat. He and Easton had ditched their phones at the hospital. Lucky for him, his brother had serious trust issues and was able to provide him with a burner phone that couldn't be traced back to either of them or Chloe. He read the message. No one had tried to come for Whitney Avgerpoulos's remains. The woman's family was waiting patiently for her body to be released, but it seemed Jonathan Byrd was finished with her. What Weston wouldn't give for that to be the case for Chloe.

The heavy glass door slid back on its track, and the hairs on the back of his neck stood on end. He didn't have to turn around to know how close she'd gotten. Every cell in his body had become attuned to every cell in hers in a matter of days. He sat higher in the camp chair. Hints of the perfume Macie insisted on wearing 24/7 battled with the scent of burning wood and fire. "I didn't mean to wake you up."

"You didn't. It's just colder up there without another body to warm me." Chloe maneuvered to the second chair around the fire, one of the blankets he'd found around her shoulders and a Macie-original flannel shirt and thick knitted beanie with a faux fur pom-pom completing the outfit. Tipping her head back, she stared straight up into the clear starry night as the fire cast a warm glow over her skin. "I can't remember the last time it was so…peaceful."

"Hell of a difference from Denver, I imagine." He set his mug down beside him and reached for the box of hot chocolate and dumped it into his empty cup. Careful not to burn himself, he grabbed the teakettle perched over the flames, refilled the cup and handed it to her.

"Can't say it was all bad. It's where I grew up, where my parents are buried and where I built my career. I still had friends and some family there before I left. We weren't close. Not like your family, but they were mine." She curved long fingers around the ceramic before bringing the mug up to her mouth. Closing her eyes, she inhaled the steaming liquid before taking a sip, and the danger, the investigation, the loss—it all vanished in the wash of this single moment. "Mmm. That's good."

"Secret family recipe." He held up the box and couldn't help but laugh at the ridiculousness. He tossed the rectangular cardboard box into the third camp chair and leaned back in his seat. There'd been plenty of nights just like this with his family growing up. At least once a year, usually around Christmas, they walked down to huddle around the firepit his father had built on their property. His mom would give him, Easton and his father their own hot cocoa packet, then take turns filling up each of their cups. Then she'd hand out the peppermint candy canes to stir the mix in and spice up the taste. His father would complain about burning his mouth every time, but Weston hadn't minded. It was one of the costs of his favorite night of the year. He couldn't remember the last time they'd been together like that. He'd lost Cynthia when Easton had been deployed. They'd just…let life get in the way. Now there'd be an empty seat around the fire. Weston cleared his throat as a distraction. "Easton and I were with him when he died. My dad. He'd gotten pinned between the pickup and the four-wheeler, but he hung on long enough to make sure we knew you'd been taken. Stubborn old man."

Chloe hesitated, the mug halfway to her mouth. She set it into her lap. "I wish I would've gotten to know him better. I tried going into the woods to search for you and Easton on my own, but he wouldn't let me. Told me I wasn't prepared for what I would find out there. He was right."

"He usually was. About a lot of things, whether I wanted to admit it or not. He's the one who came to me about becoming police chief after Cynthia died. I fought him at first but, as usual, I ended up taking his advice. Turned out to be one of the best decisions I've made." He could still recall the unending argument he and his dad had gotten in that day about controlling his own life, but his father had never given up on him. "Charlie Frasier was looking to retire after forty years of protecting Battle Mountain, but he didn't have anyone to replace him."

"Why not?" she asked.

"The mining companies all pulled out after they ran out of money. The economy took a turn, and people lost their jobs. Part of that mining income went to pay for the police department. When it dried up, the few deputies Frasier had on staff couldn't afford to live here anymore. Ended up taking jobs with other departments around the state." Weston stared into the flames, the warmth of the fire constant and assuring. "A few years later, Frasier had a heart attack in the middle of the station. Doctor told him his police chief days had officially come to an end. I stepped in. Seems like a lifetime ago."

"Do you regret it?" Chloe brought her legs into her chest and set her cheek against one knee, studying him from his peripheral vision. Her mug steamed from where she'd set it on the chair's arm.

"No. People rely on me to be there for them when

they need it. Turns out, my father was preparing me for this my whole life. Starting with that car that slid off the road." He reached for the mug and took another gulp of hot chocolate, but he wouldn't be able to bury the loss boiling inside forever. The slightly watered-down flavor spread across his tongue. "It might be just me and Macie in that station, but the way I see it, we can still make a difference in a town this small."

"You've definitely made a difference for me." Chloe lowered her feet back to the deck and rose to stand, the blanket still wrapped around her shoulders. One step. Two. She towered over him a split second before sliding onto his lap. Warmth penetrated the icy shell that'd developed over the past hour he'd been sitting out here, and the need to keep her close took control. "If you hadn't tackled me to the ground when that bullet ripped through the funeral home or pulled me from that burning shed, I wouldn't be here now."

The bullet. He'd almost forgotten about the gunshot the day they'd discovered Whitney Avgerpoulos's body. Weston wrapped both arms around her waist. "Jonathan Byrd didn't attack me with a gun out there in those woods, and I didn't recover one in his pickup."

"He took the one you gave me for protection." She snaked her hands around the back of his neck and threaded her fingers through his hair. "I meant to tell you earlier, but—"

"I'm not worried about my gun, Chloe. His MO is abducting and burying the people he blames for his wife's death, not to mention the people who get in his way, in mine and Whitney Avgerpoulos's case. Why take a shot at you at the funeral home if he planned to put you in that freezer?" There was something they were missing. Weston made a mental note to message his brother to collect the bullet from the funeral home. It'd take time, but there was a chance ballistics could match it from the federal database if the weapon had been used in another crime. "It doesn't fit his pattern."

"But there was a gunshot, remember? That's why you went into the woods in the first place. And he didn't put me in the freezer. He buried you and Easton and left me to burn in that shed," she said. "Jonathan Byrd isn't a serial killer. He's a man who's lost the woman he loves, and he's desperate to make that pain go away in whatever way possible. I'm not sure his mind is clear enough to follow a pattern."

She had a point. This wasn't the work of a seasoned killer. There might not be any MO to follow as far as this case was concerned, which would make Weston's job only harder. No pattern meant less predictability. "Easton came back from his last tour determined never to raise a weapon at another human being again, but he still kept one in his cabin for self-defense. According to his statement, he'd noticed movement outside his window, but knew it wasn't me or our parents."

"The family rules?" she asked.

"As long as we are on Ford land, we follow them without hesitation. For all our sakes. Easton armed himself and went to check it out. His gun discharged when Jonathan Byrd ambushed him from behind, and I found my weapon right where I'd dropped it during our altercation. No other weapons were recovered at the scene." His vision unfocused the stronger his instincts grew. Weston locked his gaze on hers. "I don't think you getting caught in that shed was his plan. At least, not entirely. There was no way he would've been able to predict Easton would get involved, but the freezer was already in place. Why take the time to bury a container that will fit two people if you only plan on killing one?"

"When I was tied up in the shed he told me the freezer was meant for me...and you," she said.

"Makes sense. He knew I was protecting you. I was the one person standing in his way to get to you. What better way to kill two birds with one stone than to bury them alive together?" The memory of slowly suffocating next to his brother charged forward. "I don't believe Jonathan Byrd shot at us two days ago."

Chloe leaned back slightly, her grip tighter than before. "Then who?"

"That's what I want to know." Weston interlaced his fingers on her opposite hip, careful of the wound she'd revealed earlier. The outline, the jaggedness to the skin, flashed across his mind every time he closed his eyes, and he wanted nothing more than to return the damage to the bastard who'd caused it in the first place. He hiked his knees higher, forcing her weight to shift against him. She settled against his chest, and he tipped his chin down to get a good long look at the coroner who'd risked her life to save his. "But not tonight. Tonight it's just us. No bullets. No freezers. No bodies. Just us and this fire."

She leveled her mouth with his, scanning his face

from forehead to chin as though looking for permission to close the distance between them. "For how long?"

"As long as we need." He wanted her, and for the first time in years, he was ready. To move on, to heal. Ready for her.

Chapter Eleven

She shuddered awake.

Chloe cracked her eyes against the snow-white winter wonderland frozen all around her. Curling into the double-wide sleeping bag Weston had dragged out onto the deck once they'd finished their hot chocolate, she tried to hide from the frigid temperatures, only to realize the fire had been fed. Flames popped and crackled in uneven intervals as she clutched the edge of the sleeping bag and the heavy blanket. Goose bumps prickled down her spine as she sat up, the clothes she'd borrowed from Macie more than enough to fight back the cold.

Weston had slipped from the heap of blankets without her notice.

She skimmed her fingers across his side of the red flannel-lined sleeping bag. Still warm. He couldn't have gotten up more than a few minutes ago, but he'd given her the time to stretch and revel in a forgotten kind of muscle soreness she hadn't experienced in nearly a year. A smile pulled at one corner of her mouth as the memories of last night played in fractured sequences across her mind. The kisses against her skin, the feel of his hands memorizing every inch of her, the pleasure that'd swept her out of reality and stolen the nightmares of the past few days. He'd stripped the last of the armor she'd carried for far too long away in a matter of hours and barreled through her deepest fear: being harmed again.

No matter how many times she'd tried to convince herself otherwise, Weston got to her. Committed. Reliable. Willing to defend her until the end. He was nothing she'd expected when she'd come to Battle Mountain and everything she wanted in her life, and despite the timing and their situation, she'd already started falling in love with him.

The large glass door separating the tree house from the great outdoors slid back on its track, and every sense she owned homed in on him.

"Good morning. Hope you're hungry." His boots reverberated through the wood underneath her. Rich brown hair tussled to one side as he maneuvered through the door with two plates in his hands.

Chloe straightened. She took in his thick coat and strong thighs beneath his sweatpants. "Starving."

He stretched one plate of steaming food toward her. "We can go inside if you prefer."

She accepted the plate and breathed in the combination of pancakes, butter, maple syrup and sausage links. "I'm still pretty warm after last night, thanks to you." Chloe balanced the plate on top of the sleeping bag and dove straight in. She couldn't remember the last time someone other than his mother had made her a home-cooked meal. Most of her meals had been in the clinic cafeteria, considering she'd worked twelve-to-eighteen-hour days, and the food she'd kept at home stayed fresh in the freezer. The sweetness of the maple syrup coated her tongue. Who knew being hunted by a man who'd lost his hold on reality could come with so many benefits? "This is really good."

Weston took his seat in the camp chair they'd shared the night before. "I feel like I should warn you. Macie only eats breakfast food, so her pantry and fridge are stocked with pretty much everything you'd possibly want in the morning. And that's it."

"She lives here full-time?" Chloe recalled the single time she'd met the friendly redheaded dispatcher at Caffeine and Carbs, and now that she thought about it, she could definitely picture the woman living life on her own terms. "It's very generous of her to let us stay here and rummage through her kitchen. You might want to tell her she's going to need to wash these sleeping bags, though."

His laugh encircled her in a hug of warmth and lightness and stirred hints of the heat he'd stoked low in her belly. He took a bite of his own food, a string of syrup catching in his beard. "I think I'll wash them myself and leave her out of it. If she even gets a hint I've been with someone, I'll never hear the end of it. The woman has been trying to set me up for years."

"I didn't realize you hadn't been with anyone after your wife passed." The small amount of hope this could be something more exploded through her. Chloe set her fork on the plate, the ding of stainless steel against ceramic too loud in her ears.

His smile left his expression. "When Cynthia died,

I cut myself off from my friends, my family, her family. I got stuck in this cycle of grief I couldn't seem to pull myself out of until I took this job, but even then I wasn't ready to let myself get attached to anyone. Until I met you."

"You think I'm worth getting attached to?" She hadn't meant for the question to slip past her control, but there it was. Her heart, her future, on the line and exposed for the world to see.

"Is that a problem?" he asked.

"No." She shook her head. Butterflies stirred in her stomach. "Not at all. I'm kind of attached to you, too."

Weston used the side of his fork to cut another section of pancake but didn't take a bite. Veins threatened to escape the callused skin along the backs of his hands as he stared down at the contents on his plate. "So what do you think you'll do after we've caught Jonathan Byrd and this investigation is over?"

"I don't know." She stretched her feet toward the bottom of the sleeping bag, aware he held all the cards here. Physically, mentally, emotionally. "I ran from my life in Denver to survive. I trusted the detectives there to find the man who tried to kill me, even after all these months, but I knew they'd given up due to lack of evidence. I certainly didn't think I'd be here trying to catch him. I guess I've never really thought about what would happen or where I would go afterward."

He didn't move, didn't even seem to breathe, and the tension between them tightened. He was waiting for an answer, waiting for her to choose him. She could see it in his eyes, in the set of his mouth.

Chloe set down her plate on the slightly frosted deck, her fork skimming across the ceramic. "Battle Mountain has been my home for the past two months. There's something about this town that made me want to get to know the people here and stop running. I have a good job and an apartment I can turn into my own. Where else can I actually get a barista to write my name correctly on my cup?"

That earned her a smile, and her heart shot into her throat. "You make a good point."

She hugged her knees into her chest to counter the bite of early spring mornings and the instant reaction he seemed to pull from her with one look. "Honestly, I think I would like it here as long as I had someone to enjoy it with." His expression softened under her admission, and her pulse beat faster. "To be clear, I mean you."

"I was hoping you'd say that." Weston shoved to his feet. He tossed his plate into his vacated chair, and she looked up just in time as he closed in on her. He threaded his arms underneath her knees and low back, gathering the sleeping bag and blanket, and swept her off the deck. Tendons in his neck flexed under her weight, but he barely missed a step as he maneuvered her through the sliding glass door.

A wall of warmth encased her as he used his heel to slide the door closed behind them. She wrapped her arms around his neck but still struggled to keep her balance as he hauled her up to the second level without any sign of exertion. "What are you—"

The tree house blurred in her vision as he tossed her onto the single queen-size bed, and a squeak of surprise escaped past her lips. She clutched the sleeping bag tighter around her.

The mattress dipped under the weight of his knee as he crawled to meet her in the middle, his weight seemingly the only thing keeping her anchored in the moment. Threading one hand through the hair at the back of her neck, Weston brought her mouth to meet his, and the world, the investigation, the grief for an entire life she'd lost disappeared. There was only him. "I didn't think I'd ever find someone I trust as much as I trust myself. Then I met you. You're the most persistent, straight-talking, challenging woman I've ever met, Doc. You're everything I've been missing all these years. I've taken an oath to protect this town and everyone in it, but I'm not sure I'd survive if something ever happened to you."

"Good thing you don't have to worry about that. Because I'm not going anywhere." She pressed her mouth to his, framing both hands along his jaw, and brought him up to settle his weight onto her. Her chest ached at the thought of how much he'd already lost, but she could be here for him now. As long as Jonathan Byrd couldn't hurt them that would never change. "But I need you to promise me something first, Weston."

A furrow developed between his brows, and he leveraged his weight into his hands on either side of her shoulders. "What is it?"

"I'm not her." Chloe smoothed her thumb over the thick sheepskin lining of his coat at his collar. "I'm not your wife, and I don't ever want you to believe I could fill that space you still have for her in your heart. She was such a big part of your life, and I don't want you to stop loving her. She deserves better than that, and so do I. Promise me, that whatever this is between us, it doesn't have anything to do with her. Promise me you'll keep her memory alive but see me as...me."

A corner of his mouth quirked into a smile. "Hell, woman, I think I just fell a little bit in love with you."

"Promise me." The words left her mouth as nothing more than a whisper but held the weight of their entire future. She curled her bandaged hand into his coat. "Please."

Weston kissed her, sweeping his tongue past the seam of her lips, before setting his forehead against hers. "I promise."

THE GRATING PING of a cell phone shoved him back into consciousness.

Water ticked against tile from the only bathroom with a shower. A wall of humidity bellowed into the bedroom from the cracked door a few feet from the bed, and Weston scrubbed a hand down his face. He reached for the small clock radio on the raw wood nightstand built into the wall and knocked into the lamp instead. Shooting one hand out, he caught the damn thing before it hit the floor. "I'm awake."

The burner phone pinged again.

Ten in the morning. Damn, he'd passed out after showing Chloe exactly how much she'd meant to him over these past few days. He'd never slept so well in his life despite the grief simmering below the surface, and the pull of drugging sleep urged him to collapse back into bed, to forget anything that existed outside this ridiculous safe house. The sleeping bag and blanket they'd taken refuge under last night on the deck had slid to the floor, and he hauled himself upright before tossing both back onto the bed. He stood, knees popping at the effort, and shuffled down the winding staircase to the main level. The phone vibrated on the butcher-block countertop in the wraparound kitchen, and he slammed a hand down over it. Easton had moved on to calling him. Hitting the green button to connect, he brought the phone to his ear. "Yeah, what is it?"

"You've got another body on your hands." His brother's voice deadpanned. "You need to get back into town. Now."

"What do you mean another body?" The words replayed over in his head, but it took longer than it should have to make sense. Weston turned and raised his gaze to the second level, the constant white noise of the shower steady. "Jonathan Byrd is hunting Chloe and the rest of her surgical team. I can't leave her alone here, and I'm sure as hell not bringing her back into town to make her an easier target than she already is."

"That won't be a problem," Easton said. "Not anymore."

"What are you talking about?" he asked.

"I just found Jonathan Byrd's remains. I'm not a detective but he was murdered, from the look of it." Soft footsteps echoed through the line, then the sound of a passing car. Easton was on the move, most likely down Main Street. "I went back to Jacob Family Funeral Home to recover the bullet like you'd asked. Don't worry. I was careful. I pulled the discarded slug from the wall and bagged it without getting my prints on the evidence, but as I was leaving, I noticed the dead bolt to the exam room Chloe works out of had fresh scratches on the lock face. Someone had picked the lock. Horribly, I might add. The victim you found, Whitney Avgerpoulos, you told me you'd asked Frank Jacob to secure the remains after the shooting, so I thought maybe your suspect had come looking for her. Turns out, your suspect was there instead."

"Jonathan Byrd is dead." Weston gripped the edge of the counter. Son of a bitch. "How?"

"There's a bullet wound between his eyes. Entry wound looks to be the same caliber as the bullet I'm holding right now. Can't be sure until your coroner examines the body, but he was definitely tortured first," Easton said. "Whoever killed him wanted something."

"Chloe." Movement registered from above. His grip slipped from around his phone as Chloe stared down at him from the second floor. He caught the device just before it fell past his waist and brought it back to his ear. Not really paying attention to anything his brother said on the other end of the line. "I need to call you back."

He ended the call.

Wrapped in a clean white robe, hair dripping around her shoulders, she descended the stairs, every inch the woman who'd penetrated his strongest defenses and broken him down to nothing. She hit the bottom of the stairs, one hand still gripping the railing as though preparing for the worst. "Something's happened."

"That was Easton. I sent him back to the funeral

home to recover the bullet from the shooting so we could run ballistics." They'd known exactly who'd targeted her all those months ago, what kind of monster had driven her to flee Denver and go on the run for her life. Only now a new monster had stepped from the shadows, one they didn't know anything about.

"Okay." She folded her arms across her chest. "Did he find it?"

"Yes, but he found something else while he was there." He set the phone back on the counter and braced himself. "Jonathan Byrd's body. Someone tortured and killed him, presumably to get information from him."

"Information? What…kind of information?" The small muscles along her throat constricted with a hard swallow.

"As of right now, I think we need to assume it has to do with you." His stomach knotted tighter. They'd had him. The Creed and Silverton police departments had cut off Jonathan Byrd's escape by setting up roadblocks along both roads leading in and out of Battle Mountain, but now the game had changed. There was a new player, and they'd been forced back to square one. "Jonathan Byrd wasn't able to kill you. There's a chance he had a partner we didn't know about who's out to finish the job."

The color drained from her face, that full bottom lip he'd memorized with a dozen kisses merely an hour ago pulling away from the top. She shifted her weight back, and Weston closed the distance between them in case she collapsed. "This doesn't make sense. He was the one who attacked me in Denver. He was the one who buried you and Easton and killed your father. He left me in that shed to die. Now you're saying he was murdered by someone else."

He wound his arms around her waist and held her tighter than ever before. "Until we're able to determine when and how he officially died, you need to stay here—"

"No." She shook her head, all that dark brown hair sticking to her robe. "I can't do this. I can't spend the rest of my life looking over my shoulder. That's not a life, Weston. That's fear, and I've been letting it control me for too long." Chloe dug her fingernails into his arms. "I can't hide from this anymore. You asked me to stay and help you solve this case. That's what I'm doing."

He nodded, knowing exactly what she'd say next.

"I need to examine the body." Chloe maneuvered out of his arms as acceptance smoothed her expression. Tugging the robe tighter around her frame, she pushed wet hair out of her face. "I know that means leaving the safe house. I know that means putting my life at risk, but I trust you'll do whatever it takes to make sure I walk away from this alive."

Weston pulled her into his arms, and she melted into him. Running one hand down the thick waterfall of her hair, he clung to her as the last moments of Cynthia's life filled his head. The hollowness that'd carved into his chest that day ebbed, and for the first time in years, he was able to take a full breath. "I can't lose you."

"You won't." Pulling back, she squeezed his arms in reassurance. "But as much as I enjoyed last night under the stars, I'm not walking outside naked. I'm going to get dressed in every layer Macie owns."

His laugh escaped up his throat easily, and Weston forced his hands to release her. He waited until she'd ascended the stairs and the sound of the bathroom door closing behind her reached his ears. Collecting the burner phone from the counter, he called his brother. The line rang once. Twice. He didn't wait for a greeting as the call connected. "Where are you?"

"Across the street from the funeral home. I'm watching to see if anyone comes back to visit their handiwork." Easton spoke over the rush of cars along Main. "The guy could've easily bypassed the front door since the glass hasn't been replaced from your shooting yet. He had everything he needed to extract the information he wanted in that exam room. Looks like the bastard put it all to use, too. I reached out to a couple of contacts in Denver. He was a handyman. No military or law enforcement training. It wouldn't have taken long to get him to give up whatever they wanted from him, but I'm not going to lie. It's a mess in there."

"You're saying it's possible whoever killed Jonathan Byrd kept torturing him, even after he gave them the information they wanted." Hell. There was only one reason to inflict that much pain on another human being: rage. The pressure of three murders crushed the air from his lungs, almost as though he and Easton had been buried all over again. He'd put his family in danger long enough, but he didn't have the manpower or the resources to solve this case alone. Weston leveraged one hand against the live tree shooting up through the roof in the center of the living space. Rough bark scratched at his palms. "Listen, I was wrong before, Easton. These past few months I thought you'd given up, that you wished you'd been in that explosion rather than the men and women in your unit. I hated seeing you waste away in that cabin day after day when Mom, Dad and I were right there willing to do anything to help. We were best friends before you shipped out on orders, and I didn't understand why you couldn't just try to move on and be my brother again. I understand now. You're punishing yourself."

Weston tightened his grip on the phone. "I can't tell you you're not the one responsible for what happened to your unit. I can't promise you you'll heal. I wish I had the answers and that I could help you. I wish I could take away that guilt, but that's something you need to confront yourself. Just as I had to when Cynthia died. I know what I'm supposed to do now, and I need your help. I've already asked a lot of you, and we've had our differences over the years, but I can't do this without you, brother. I need you on my side now. I need you to help me protect this town and the people in it."

Silence bled through the line. His heart threatened to beat out of his chest, and Weston set his forehead against the tree, waiting. Memories of him and Easton growing up had been overrun by the anger, hurt and disappointment of the past six months, but right then none of it mattered. They were brothers. They'd get through this. Just as their father had taught them.

Easton's voice penetrated through the slight ringing in his ears. "Tell me what you need me to do, Chief."

Chapter Twelve

The Jacob Family Funeral Home looked almost exactly the same, yet everything had changed. In a matter of days, her new life had been ripped out of her control and turned into something she didn't recognize.

Chloe stepped through the empty glass door frame. Weston's brother had sent the bullet to the forensic lab in Denver, but it would be days, if not weeks, before any kind of ballistic results came back, and only if the gun had been used in a previous crime. Whomever Weston had asked to repair the door had swept away the glass, but the weight of standing here, of knowing exactly who was on the other side of the examination room door, cut through her as sharply as though she hadn't worn boots.

Bright scratches stood stark against the brushed nickel of the dead bolt lock face securing her room. Jonathan Byrd's killer had brought his victim here, tortured him for some kind of information and killed him when he was finished. Her hand hesitated over the doorknob, her heart in her throat. He'd wanted to send her a message.

"You okay?" Weston's voice soothed the rough edges

of her nerves. "I can call another coroner in from Silverton or Ouray."

"No." She shook her head. She could do this. She had
to do this. She pushed inside. A wall of odor slammed
into her. Upon death, the cells in the human body broke
down and released gasses, coppery and fruity at the
same time, and her stomach lurched. Dried red and
crusted brown spatter arced across the walls, counter
and cabinets, but the source of the blood was what consumed her attention. Jonathan Byrd had been strapped
against her stainless-steel exam table with what looked
like two stained yellow furniture straps, one across his
chest, the other across the thighs. His hands had also
been secured, a third strap encircling each wrist before
diving beneath the table and tightened to full capacity.

Awareness of Weston warmed the skin down her
back as he moved inside the small room with her. It'd
been only a few days ago he'd stood right here and
handed her coffee. Their fingers had brushed against
one another, and she'd gotten that burst of attraction
she'd cut herself off from so long ago. Now here they
were, standing over the remains of another victim, him
on one side of the room, her beside the table. What she
wouldn't give to go back to that moment of blatant de-
nial that Whitney Avgerpoulos's death had just been a
coincidence. She knew the truth now.

Chloe mentally inventoried the surgical instruments
Jonathan Byrd's killer had used during the torture and
the kit they'd come from at the end of the counter. Her
medicolegal kit. Every single one of these tools were
hers, and the realization pooled dread at the base of her

spine. Willingly or not, she'd played a part in this man's death. Pulling a fresh set of latex gloves into place, she watched where she stepped and unpocketed her phone. Just as she'd done at the scene where Whitney had been buried, she took photos.

"Does anything stand out to you? Anything that might tell us who we're dealing with?" Weston's voice dipped an octave.

"There's an outline of a phone in the victim's pocket. The killer primarily used the scalpel over there on that cart, judging by the width of these wounds and the amount of blood on the instrument. These are my tools. They're all from that kit. I left it here after Whitney Avgerpoulos's autopsy. I usually keep it in the trunk of my car." She surveyed the lacerations across the killer's—the victim's—thoracic, abdominal and pelvic cavities. Dozens, all of varying depths and lengths, which suggested more of a swiping motion rather than a premeditated incision. Whoever'd done this had wanted Jonathan Byrd to suffer as much as possible. "Considering the bullet between his eyes, I'm leaning toward gunshot wound to the head. Manner of death is homicide."

"When?" Weston asked.

A burning exhale escaped as she raised her gaze to the victim's face. Agony had contorted his features in his last moments, and her heart shuddered in her chest. Jonathan Bryd had killed her colleague, attacked Chloe in Denver, had tried to bury her and ripped the life she'd worked so hard for away in a single instant. He'd buried Weston and his brother alive, killed a man willing to sacrifice himself to ensure she made it out alive and stole the life of an innocent young woman—all to ease the rage over his wife's death. She'd feared for her life while comprehending the source of his hatred. In a way, she'd understood him. But this… This wasn't pain. This wasn't grief or revenge. This was animalistic, and nothing she'd ever seen before.

Weston's hand spread across her shoulder blade. "Chloe?"

"I won't be able to give you an exact time frame without an autopsy, but right now I'm confident he was killed approximately eight to twelve hours ago." While she and Weston were whispering promises of the future and losing themselves to ecstasy. Chloe took the last of the photos and handed her phone off to Weston. Some items in her kit hadn't been disturbed, but to use or move anything inside it now might compromise the investigation. A rough stab wound claimed her attention, and she spread the skin on either side wider to get a better view. "This wound is more jagged than all the others. Rougher. Most likely the strike that incapacitated him. The scalpel was driven deep enough to hit the kidney, but that kind of force would most likely dislodge the killer's grip. His hand would've slid down the blade, maybe even cut himself in the process. I'll need cotton swabs and evidence bags to collect samples, some tweezers, and booties so I don't contaminate the scene."

"I'll check with Mr. Jacob and see what I can recover from the phone's call history." Weston unpocketed the phone from the victim's front pocket and flipped the old device open. He left the room and headed down the corridor, presumably toward Mr. Jacob's office, and all four walls seemed to close in around her.

Four bodies. So much pain. Her fingers curled into the center of her bandaged palms, and she stared down at the blisters peeking out from the stretched edges of gauze and under the latex gloves. Jonathan Byrd had wanted her and her colleagues to suffer for the death of his wife, but she couldn't do that to the people of this town, to Weston. She couldn't keep risking their lives for her mistake. Chloe slid one foot toward the door. The streaks of blood arcing over the walls and cabinets seemed to pulse right in front of her. Whoever'd done this had known exactly where to strike the victim. They were familiar with human anatomy and comfortable with a scalpel and used that knowledge to torture and kill her attacker for information. Who would they target next to tie up loose ends? Mr. Jacob? Easton or Karie? Her throat swelled with a pent-up sob. Weston?

No. Her heart threatened to beat straight out of her chest as she took another step. Every nerve ending in her body caught fire as images of Weston replaced the face of the victim on the table. The blood pooling beneath the body didn't belong to the man who'd attacked her out in those woods, who'd killed James Ford and Whitney Avgerpoulos and Roberta Ellis. All she could see was Weston. Nausea churned in her gut as her spine met the door frame, and she jerked to a stop. He'd promised to protect her, to solve this case together, but the rules to the sick game Jonathan Byrd started had changed. There was a new piece of the puzzle to solve, and she feared neither of them would survive to see the finished picture. She couldn't stay here. Not as long as her proximity to Weston, to his family, this town was the one element putting them in danger.

She had to move. Chloe peeled her gloves from her hands with a snap and discarded them in the trash can by the door. She escaped the exam room and forced one foot in front of the other, picking up her pace with every step. The hairs on the back of her neck prickled as cool air guided her toward the front door. Tears burned in her eyes, but she wouldn't let them fall. Not yet. Weston had left the keys trapped in the driver's side visor of Macie's sedan. She could make it.

"I think I've got everything you need, Doc." His voice stabbed straight through her, but Chloe refused to slow down. A hint of panic infused his tone, and something struck the floor at the end of the hallway. "Chloe?"

She raced through the broken front door without bothering with the metal handle and pumped her legs as hard as she could. Her lungs seized as heavy footsteps pounded loud behind her. She didn't stop to see how close he'd gotten. Ripping open the driver's side door of the sedan, she collapsed into the vehicle, collected the keys from the visor and inserted the key into the ignition. Movement registered from the sidewalk a split second before she thought to lock the doors.

Weston slammed both hands onto the hood of the vehicle, those mesmerizing brown eyes locked on her, and her entire body flinched. "Don't do this, Chloe."

"I'm sorry. For everything." She shifted the car into Reverse and slammed on the accelerator. The vehicle lurched out from beneath the police chief's weight, and she swung into the middle of Main Street. Residents stared as she slammed the car into Drive. The tires screamed in protest but caught the pavement and shot her forward.

Weston's outline ran straight for her door out of her peripheral vision. He tried the handle but wasn't able to keep up as she sped from the scene. Within seconds, he centered himself in the rearview mirror, both hands interlaced behind his head, and her heart shattered.

The tears flowed down her cheeks the more distance she put between them, but she wouldn't stop. Couldn't. Thick green trees dissolved to open fields and rolling hills. She wasn't sure where she was going, how far she'd get on half a tank of gas or how she'd pay for her next meal. It didn't matter. She'd started over once before. She could do it again.

A single vehicle stretched across the road ahead, red and blue lights working to overcome the sun's morning rays, and her chest squeezed. The roadblocks. Weston had called in other departments from nearby towns to box Jonathan Bryd in. Chloe swallowed around the panic clawing up her throat. Had Weston radioed them to stop her?

She forced Macie's old sedan to slow to a crawl as she approached the single officer climbing from his patrol vehicle. Within a few seconds, he tapped his baton against the driver's side window and signaled for her to roll it down. She did, every cell in her body praying he'd let her through.

"Good morning, ma'am. We're looking for a wanted suspect in a homicide investigation. Mind if I see your license and search your vehicle?" the officer asked, wrinkles putting his age somewhere close to sixty if she had to guess.

Chloe unpocketed her fake license with her assumed name from her jacket pocket and handed it to him, hands trembling. "I don't mind. The car's not mine. I'm borrowing it from a friend. Macie Barclay? You might know her. She's the dispatcher here in Battle Mountain."

"Sure, I know Macie." He read the details of her license and holstered his baton. "Everything all right, ma'am? You look as though you've been crying."

A car horn from behind jolted her nervous system into overdrive, and she clenched the steering wheel harder. The officer waved as she checked the rearview mirror, half expecting Weston's truck. Instead, a darker truck, dark blue or black, revved its engine. Without much traffic out of town, they were the only two vehicles on the road.

"I'm fine. Thank you." She swiped at her face. "Long day is all. I'd really like to get going if you don't mind."

A second man materialized behind the officer, pulled the firearm from his belt and slammed the butt of the gun against the officer's head. The old man crumpled, and in her next breath, the attacker aimed the gun at her. "Hello, Dr. Miles. I'm so glad I was finally able to catch up with you."

DAMN IT ALL to hell. Chloe was gone.

The watery outline of Macie's sedan dipped below the horizon. He could radio the officer set up at the roadblock. He could stop her. But what would be the point? She'd made her decision, and she was an expert at running. Weston threw his hat against the pavement. What the hell had he expected? A car drove past, reminding him he was still standing in the middle of Main Street with another body on his hands. She'd left him. Despite her promise she wasn't going anywhere, she'd left him. And he wanted to know why. "Son of a bitch."

He'd already lost his wife, lost his father. Now Chloe. The hollowness in his gut exploded, destroying the security and support that'd built up over the past few days with her at his side. She'd made it clear from the beginning. She'd wanted to run the moment they'd pulled Whitney Avgerpoulos from that mine, and the burn of abandonment and betrayal shot his blood pressure into dangerous territory. Worse, she was out there, on the run, alone, while another killer had obviously gone out of his way to tie up loose ends.

Weston bent down to collect his hat and headed back inside Jacob Family Funeral Home to contain the scene. The only person able to tell them who'd strapped Jonathan Byrd to an exam table and tortured him until he'd bled to death had fled. He'd have to call in another coroner or a nearby medical examiner to complete the autopsy. He needed that evidence to find the bastard who'd killed their killer. The odor of death and decomposition drove into his lungs. Holding his breath, he pulled the phone from his jacket and froze. Chloe's phone, the one she'd used to take photos of the scene. She'd handed it off to him before sending him to get supplies to collect the evidence. She'd known, even then, he would've used it to track her whereabouts. So she'd gotten rid of it.

He dug for the burner phone in his coat and hit the only contact number stored in the memory. The line connected. No small talk. They were running out of time. "Tell me you were able to find something I can use."

"Both Gregory and Delphine Avgerpoulos were at the restaurant until late last night. I have statements from one of the busboys and the dishwasher corroborating they didn't leave until 2:00 a.m. this morning," Easton said. "Neither of them are your killer, and Mom slapped me when I asked her if she'd tortured anyone lately. None of them even knew what'd happened until I told them."

Relief fought to cool the rage that'd taken control. Of all the people who'd had a motive to want Jonathan Byrd dead, he'd had to consider Whitney's parents and his own mother. "Good. You got that bullet sent to Unified Forensics?"

"Just left the post office. I'm headed your way. Almost there," Easton said.

Weston scanned the hallway, targeting the medical supplies he'd dropped chasing after Chloe. "Meet me in the exam room. We've got work to do."

He hung up and picked up the swabs, bags, tweezers and booties. The phone he'd taken from the victim's pocket had logged only one call. To the Battle Mountain police station. Jonathan Byrd had placed the anonymous call informing dispatch of Whitney Avgerpoulos's body in Contention Mine. He'd still pull prints and run them against the database, but now he had proof the man on that table had a hand in a young woman's death. Unpacking the booties, he slipped one over each boot. Footsteps echoed down the hallway before Easton appeared at his side. He handed off another set of booties and waited for his brother to finish before handing him a set of swabs and bags.

Easton stared down at the supplies, then seemed to comprehend exactly what Weston intended for them to do. "When I said I'd help you with this case, I didn't mean getting my hands bloody. Where's your coroner?"

"She's not mine." The words left his mouth harsher than he'd intended. No matter what his current feelings for the woman who'd worked her way into his life, he had a job to do, and he couldn't wait for another town to send someone. "I watched Dr. Miles swab for evidence from Whitney Avgerpoulos's body in the mine. We've already got pictures. Now we need to collect anything that might tell us who did this."

Dr. Miles. Her formal title bit like acid on his tongue.

"Her name's not Chloe Pascale." Easton's easy acceptance of that truth punctured as loud as the snap of latex gloves over his hands. "Didn't seem the type to lie about that kind of thing, but given the fact she obviously came here to hide from the pincushion on the table, can't say I blame her."

"There were a lot of things she convinced us were true." Weston swabbed around the wound in Jonathan Byrd's knee and bagged the evidence. He handed it off to his brother and continued examining the remains. Silence descended between them as they worked. He didn't want to get into what'd happened between him and Chloe, and Easton wasn't the type to pry. Made things easier for now. He mapped out the pattern of wounds, but the wound she'd pointed out before, rougher than the others, stood out among the rest. "All of these across the abdomen are superficial. Like they were for show." He pointed to the smallest of the collection. "Chloe was focused on this particular wound before she left. She said the killer had used so much force, it was possible he'd cut his hand. I'm no coroner, but as far as I know, nobody can survive a direct strike to the kidney like that for long, can they?"

"You're right. It's slightly wider than the others." Easton leaned over the body. "Most likely made with the same weapon, but the killer twisted the scalpel after piercing the kidney. Your victim here never would've recovered. Whoever got to this guy knew exactly how to make sure he'd never escape until he was finished."

Special Forces? Weston scanned the remains for something—anything—that would fill the empty segments of this case forming in his mind. What were the chances Battle Mountain had become a hunting ground for not one but two killers within the span of a week? A theory patched together as he recalled the reason Chloe had been targeted in the first place. She was going to report the surgical team's mistake to the board of the clinic. She was going to take responsibility for Miriam Byrd's death. "Or maybe someone familiar with human anatomy?"

"I can see the wheels spinning in your head," Easton said.

"How did Jonathan Byrd know where to find Chloe after all these months? He's a handyman with a preference for '50s-era refrigerators. Doesn't seem like the kind of job where you'd have a lot of connections or the kind of resources he'd need to figure out she'd changed her name. That kind of work wouldn't have given him access to the propofol he used to sedate his victims unless he took contracts with hospitals, which I couldn't see in any of his previous work orders." Weston swabbed the area around the final wound and bagged the evidence. "He had help."

Easton straightened. "Someone gave him the coroner's location here in Battle Mountain, then set him loose, knowing he was going to kill her. Only when Whitney Avgerpoulos finds him trying to break into your doc's apartment, he has to take care of her. He blows the element of surprise, and now his target knows he's in town."

"Jonathan Byrd filed a malpractice suit the day before Chloe was attacked. She hadn't told the board what she and her team had done yet. So how did he find out, and why would he file the suit if he planned on killing her? So he can claim his innocence just in case he's accused of murder? I think someone got to him." It was the only scenario that made sense. "Chloe swore Jonathan Byrd wasn't the kind of man prone to violence, but as you and I both know, grief can change a person. Especially if that anger and resentment is fed rather than faced. Manipulating someone else's grief to act is a good way to keep your own hands clean if you don't want to be connected to a murder."

"Only problem is Jonathan Byrd failed. Chloe escaped. Twice," Easton said.

"And the puppet master has come to finish the job. I think I know who tortured and killed Jonathan Byrd, but it's going to take some time to prove it." Time he didn't have. His phone's ring pierced through the haze clouding anything outside this room. Weston ripped one glove from his hand and unpocketed the burner. "It's Macie." He swiped his thumb across the screen. "Yeah."

"Get out to the east roadblock. Now," Macie said.

Ice worked down his spine. He glanced up at Easton. "What happened?"

"Silverton PD just reported an officer down. It looks as though he'd stopped someone and was in the process of checking their identification when he was hit from behind." Macie's voice quaked. "Whoever it was took the officer's weapon."

Damn it. Battle Mountain and nearly every resident in its borders believed in the second amendment and made no qualms about showing it. Who the hell would attack a single officer just for his weapon? "Macie, I'm in the middle of collecting evidence off a fresh body. Silverton PD is going to have to take point—"

"There's more," Macie said. "He was still holding a driver's identification when Silverton PD found him, and they pulled the registration in the glove compartment of the vehicle she was driving."

She? Tension pulled the muscles tight across his back. "Spit it out."

"It's Chloe, Chief." Regret simmered beneath the dispatcher's words. "The car they found abandoned at the checkpoint is mine, but Chloe's gone."

Weston ended the call and stripped the latex gloves

from his hands, depositing them in the garbage can near the door. "Secure this room. No one comes in or out aside from you."

"Something's happened." Easton's voice remained even despite the obvious change in Weston's tone. "I can help."

"Keep collecting the evidence. There has to be something here that will tie us to the killer." Weston unholstered his sidearm from his hip, released the magazine, counted the bullets and slammed it into place. He pulled back on the slide and loaded a round into the chamber, then reholstered his weapon. As much as he trusted Easton to have his back after what they'd been through together, this was something he had to do on his own. Only Chloe had taken the vehicle they'd come into town in together, and his truck was still parked up at the ranch. "Keys."

No questions. No hesitation. Easton pulled his keys from his jeans and tossed them right at him. He caught them, and in his next breath, headed for the front door. Cold dissipated as determination—stronger than anything he'd felt before—burned beneath his skin. "I'm coming for you, Doc."

Chapter Thirteen

"You should've kept up your end of the deal, Chloe," a familiar voice said. "After all, you're not the only one who has everything to lose."

Muted sunlight warmed her face through the clouds above as she pulled her head away from one shoulder. An ache snaked through the tendons in her neck. She'd been unconscious. The last few moments of memory washed across her mind in waves. The roadblock. The officer who'd been checking her ID. The shadow behind him. Her heart rate ticked up a notch. He'd pulled her from the car, then pressed something into her rib cage and everything...had gone black. A taser?

Chloe set her head back against something solid, and the thud vibrated loud in her ears. Her shoulder sockets ached under pressure. She pulled at her wrists to bring them around to the front, but plastic dug into her skin. Zip ties. She rolled her head against whatever was behind her, back and forth, but it didn't lighten the shadows across the man's face any more. A slight breeze pushed her hair into her eyes. "Where... Where am I?"

"Somewhere that police chief of yours will never

find you." Her abductor stood from his crouched position a few feet in front of her, and the shadows cleared. Recognition flared as he settled dark eyes on her, and she pressed her heels into the ground to put as much distance between them as possible.

"You?" The blood drained from her face. "You did this?"

"I had some help, as you know. What better way to make sure you couldn't go to the board than to convince the patient's husband he needed to take matters into his own hands?" Michael Kerr, the resident surgeon who'd assisted her during Miriam Byrd's surgery, blocked the sun from her eyes. Stubble shaded a square jaw, which struggled to hide a layer of fat. Long, thick eyebrows, matching the light brown hair receding up his forehead, spiked in different directions, and accented a deranged set to his mouth. Crooked smile lines ended at the base of a wide nose broken at least once over the course of a forty-five-year life. He fanned his grip over the handgun at his side. Not the officer's weapon he used to knock the man unconscious. A .38 revolver she bet would match ballistics to the bullet shot at her and Weston when they'd been standing inside the Jacob Family Funeral Home and the entry wound set between Jonathan Byrd's eyes. Blood dried underneath his nose from where she'd struck him back at the roadblock. "We had a deal, Chloe. You broke that deal."

She shook her head. "I never went to the board about what happened."

"But you were going to, right?" He settled in front of her, his knees popping under his weight. Crusted dirt kicked up around him, a bright smudge of dust against his shined shoes. "You told Roberta Ellis you didn't feel right about keeping the patient's husband in the dark about what'd happened, that you couldn't lie to him. That you felt guilty for that woman's death. So what did you do? You went against the family's wishes, and you performed your own autopsy to find out what went wrong."

"Of course, I felt guilty," she said. "She died because of us. Because we left a clamp inside her chest. She was trying to tell us, but she could barely even speak she was in so much pain. We deserve to answer for what we've done." Her instincts kicked her in the gut, and she pulled her knees into her chest. The zip ties bit into her skin and wouldn't give way. Jonathan Byrd learning her location, his access to propofol… It all made sense. "It was you. The clamp. It was yours, wasn't it? You didn't want the truth coming out. You told Jonathan Byrd what really happened to his wife. He filed the lawsuit against me, but you played on his grief. You turned him into a killer, even with the possibility he'd come after you. Why?"

A thin smile contorted the laugh lines carved into his features but didn't reach his eyes. "You are so much more intelligent than I gave you credit for, Chloe, you know that? I mean, how many times did Jonathan Byrd try to kill you? Twice? I underestimated you." He stood again, rounding behind the solid surface keeping her upright. Old hinges protested as he lifted the lid, but she couldn't force her neck to twist around in order for her to keep him in her vision. "Before coming to

Colorado, I was the top cardiothoracic surgeon at the Mayo Clinic. I had it made. For seven long years, I saved hundreds of patients. I literally held their lives in my hands. I got to decide how long they had left on earth, whether they would see their children again, their grandchildren. That feeling of…playing God, it's very addictive, you know."

Chloe pulled against the zip ties. She narrowed her gaze as the clouds rolled above and exposed a sliver of sunlight. Her fingers brushed against cool metal, and her heart stalled in her throat. Craning her chin over one shoulder, she took in the pale blue color of the container at her back. No. He…he wouldn't. Her mouth dried on a sharp inhale, and she struggled against the binds again. The zip tie around her ankles would break under pressure, but she wasn't strong enough to break the plastic around her wrists. Not without injuring herself in the process. The lid compromised his view of her. It was now or never.

She brought her knees into her chest, the heels of her boots right against her pelvic bone. She splayed her knees out to either side as hard and as fast as she could. The zip tie around her ankle snapped, and she quickly pressed her knees together in case Michael had heard. She had to keep him talking, distracted. Using one foot, she pushed the broken tie to the outside of her hip. She forced her right shoulder to stretch as much as possible, and her fingers clawed into frozen dirt to get a hold of the tie. It slipped out of reach. Damn it. She tried again. "You made a mistake?"

"Too many." The distinct scent of bleach burned in

her lungs. Footsteps echoed from behind as Michael rounded into her peripheral vision, a soaked rag in hand, and she forced herself to relax, but odor permeated her senses. Wind lifted his hair as he stared down at her. His eyes glazed slightly, as though remembering some distant memory, and Chloe tried for the broken zip tie again. "I am a senator's son. If the truth had gotten out, the media would've been all over it. I'd become the black sheep of my family, the embarrassment. I couldn't let that happen. Not with millions of dollars of inheritance at stake. The heart and vascular center was my last option."

"You left your history with the Mayo Clinic off your résumé. You lied about saving lives in third world countries so we wouldn't look too closely." Dread pooled at the base of her spine. She'd hired a narcissist with a God complex, worked beside him, trusted him. Chloe curled the broken zip tie into her palm, then made quick work of angling it under the bind around her wrist. She gripped both ends in her hands and pressed her thumb into the center of the tie, working it back and forth against the other. She'd gauged his height to be around six-foot-two, maybe six-foot-three, but he had more than eighty pounds on her. It wouldn't be hard for him to subdue her if she ran. "And when you left that clamp in Miriam Byrd's chest, you altered her chart to make sure no one else discovered what you did. All for money?"

Those dark eyes centered on her, and a stiffness infused the tendons between his shoulders and neck. Faster than she thought possible, Michael shot one hand out and wrenched her to her feet. "You of all people should understand I did what I had to do, Dr. Miles, and I'll keep doing it as long as I have the chance to save the people who would die if it weren't for me."

"How many people other than Miriam Byrd died because of you? Two? Three? Including the officer at the roadblock? You don't give a damn about our patients. This is all about your ego." Heat climbed into her face at the thought of this monster holding another life in his hands, hers included. The weakened zip ties around her wrists broke under pressure, and Chloe swayed forward to keep Michael off balance. "And there's no way in hell I'm letting you get away with it."

She wound one foot behind his and shoved him as hard as she could. Michael hit the dirt, and she ran. The mountain sloped down, directing her back toward town. Branches scratched against her face, just as they had in the woods near her home in Denver, only this time the fear didn't get to control her. Because she wasn't alone.

Weston Ford hadn't just been her partner during the course of this investigation. He'd become so much more. A friend, a trusted ally, a lover. In a matter of days, he'd stripped away her isolated existence and showed her what really mattered. Family. James Ford had given his life for her, Easton Ford had dedicated himself to solving this case for her and Karie Ford had stood as a testament of true loyalty for her. She'd come into Battle Mountain alone, afraid and detached, but she wasn't that person anymore. Because of them.

Chloe wound through a minefield of loose rocks and knee-high grass, not daring to turn around. Her breath sawed in and out of her chest. Adrenaline drained, and her body slowed despite her internal fight to keep going. She'd been running on fumes for days. She wasn't going to make it. Taking cover behind a large pine, she tried to disappear into its branches. A woodpecker carved a new hole into the bark overhead, masking all other sounds of the woods. No movement. No sign Michael had followed her. Keeping her gaze locked in the direction she'd come from, she stepped backward down the slope.

And met a wall of muscle.

She twisted around, her fist connecting with one side of his jaw, but it wasn't enough. Massive arms encircled her rib cage and squeezed the air from her lungs.

"I've come too far to let you ruin this for me now," Michael said.

The edges of her vision darkened. She kicked out to throw him off balance and shot her hands back to claw at his face as he hauled her back up the incline. The light blue refrigerator came into view, and every cell in her body screamed in protest. Chloe fought harder, burning precious oxygen as Michael forced her into the too small space.

"I really wish you'd held up your end of the deal." He sealed her inside.

THE FRONT PASSENGER door stood ajar.

Weston struggled to stay on his feet as he approached the small four-door sedan Chloe had used to escape town less than an hour ago. It had become a crime scene. His boots echoed off the pavement. EMTs had already assessed the Silverton PD officer assigned to the roadblock.

According to his statement, he'd stopped Chloe Pascale to search her vehicle when a second vehicle had pulled up behind her. She looked as though she were under duress, crying, which had given the officer reason to search the car. The second driver had honked, as though in a hurry, and before the officer had any indication of what was happening, he was knocked unconscious from behind.

Now she was gone.

The weight of the Silverton and Creed PD officers' unspoken questions weighed heavy as he handled the driver's side door with gloves. Chloe wouldn't have left the vehicle voluntarily, which meant her abductor had to have taken her by force. The window had been rolled down, presumably for her to hand her license and registration to the Silverton officer when she'd been stopped. "I want prints taken from the door handle and the frame, and everything in this car bagged as evidence."

The officers moved on his orders.

He searched for something—anything—to tell him what'd happened in those few terrorizing seconds leading up to Chloe's abduction, but there was no telling how long the debris on the floorboards had been there. This wasn't her vehicle. They'd borrowed it from Macie, and without his dispatcher here to tell him exactly when each and every crumb had appeared in the vehicle, they were dead in the water.

He sat in the driver's seat and closed the door behind him. Twisting the keys in the ignition, he scanned the dashboard and steering column. The car instantly pinged with a warning light. One of the doors hadn't properly closed. He checked the driver's side again. Secure. Which meant... A sliver of sunlight outlined the seam of the passenger door. Her abductor wouldn't have gotten behind the wheel, but he would've had to reach inside if Chloe tried to escape out the other side.

Weston stretched the length of the car and reached for the opposite handle. "If she was over here, you would've grabbed her feet. Maybe she kicked you to get away." The scene played out in his head as though it were happening right in front of him, and a howling rage consumed him from head to toe. Damn it. Chloe had known there was another killer out here, that the bastard had tortured and killed Jonathan Byrd for information. Why the hell had she run?

He pulled his flashlight from his belt and hit the power button. Shadows fled the crevasses between the two front seats and the middle shifting column. With Jonathan Byrd decomposing on the exam table at the Jacob Family Funeral Home, he was back to his original suspect list. Someone who'd tried to stop Chloe from reporting the real reason Miriam Byrd had died after routine surgery four months ago to the board at the clinic.

The flashlight beam revealed a drop of liquid, and Weston moved in to get a better look. Blood. Impossible to tell whether or not it belonged to their suspect or Chloe, but from the location, his instincts said they had a direct link between her abduction and the bastard who'd skewered Jonathan Byrd. Chloe had fought back. "We've got blood. Hand me a bag and a swab."

"Here you go, Chief," one of the officers said.

Weston collected the evidence and sealed it into an

evidence bag. He moved to pull out of the car, brushing against Macie's oversize key chain, and froze. An ache radiated down his arm as he set most of his weight into his free hand and wrist and reached for a shiny rectangular pin facedown against the floorboards. He pinched the pushpin between his index finger and thumb and turned it over. An American flag. It must've popped loose during the struggle, but Chloe hadn't been wearing it when she'd left the funeral home, which meant…

"Son of a bitch."

He'd been right to suspect the bastard from the beginning. Weston extricated himself from the car. Handing off the pin to one of Creed's officers, he stripped the gloves from his hands and shoved them in his pockets. "Listen up!" All eyes shifted to him. "Our missing woman is Battle Mountain's coroner, Chloe Pascale. Your captains should've forwarded all of you her driver's license photo. Only her real name is Chloe Miles, a cardiothoracic surgeon out of Denver. I have reason to believe one of her fellow surgeons, Dr. Michael Kerr, is responsible for what happened here today. He's already suspected of torturing and killing one man in the past twelve hours and injuring one of our officers." Weston faced the two officers to his right dressed in dark blue uniforms. "Silverton PD, I want you to go through DMV records and narrow down the make and model of Dr. Kerr's vehicle. After that, check in with all of the car rental agencies out of Denver to see if he decided to road trip with a vehicle that couldn't be linked to him. Canvass the town, talk to anyone you have to. We need to find that car."

He turned toward the three officers dressed in black. "Creed PD, you're with me. This killer is intelligent and desperate to cover his tracks. There's a chance he'll try to use an MO we picked up at the start of this case to place blame on a dead man by burying Chloe alive. We're looking for a '50s-style refrigerator. He'll stay within the boundaries our original killer set to strengthen our case. That leaves Contention Mine and the woods around it where Chloe and I discovered the first victim. Let's move."

He wasn't sure about any of it, but his instincts said Michael Kerr would do whatever it took to keep his involvement in this case as murky as possible. Weston jogged around the hood of his brother's truck and turned back toward town. Adrenaline spiked his heart rate higher, and he drummed his fingers against the steering wheel as he and the two Creed patrol cruisers behind him tore back toward town.

She was alive. He had to believe that. He had to believe she would do everything to survive, to come back to him. Because he loved her, damn it. He hadn't been willing to see it before, but it was impossible to ignore now. He'd convinced himself he'd never find a partner to support him, to love him, after Cynthia had died. He'd accepted the fact, at some point, whomever he committed himself to would leave as she had, as his father had, as Easton had, hell, even as Chloe had, and he'd be left behind. Alone. Empty. But as he floored the accelerator to the opposite end of town and up the mountain, there was a certain clarity that drove straight into his chest.

Cynthia had let go to ease their combined suffering.

James Ford had sacrificed his life to save a practical stranger.

Easton had sacrificed his mental health for the greater good.

And Chloe... She'd sacrificed herself to protect him.

The people he'd come to rely on the most—who'd shaken his sense of security—had all put the lives of those they cared about before their own. Chloe had taken in the violence, the cruelty, of Jonathan Byrd's murder, and had chosen to draw the threat away from him, his family and away from the town he called home. And he loved her for it. Loved her protectiveness, her persistence and her strength, and he wasn't going to stop looking for her.

Main Street blurred in his peripheral vision as he led the way across town. Weston gripped the steering wheel harder as the truck's shocks absorbed the first climb up the dirt road leading to the mine where he'd discovered Whitney Avgerpoulos's body. This was where the investigation had started. Seemed only fitting this was where it would end. "Hang on, Doc. I'm coming."

The patrol cruisers cut their lights and sirens, dirt kicking up behind each one of them as the convoy ascended the mountain. Branches and leaves scraped against the side of Easton's truck, but Weston couldn't worry about the damage right then. The hood bounced as he forced the vehicle higher, then dipped just as the ground leveled out.

The tail of a dark pickup truck lodged into a grove of pines demanded attention. Weston skidded to a stop and slammed the truck into Park. In the same breath, he hit the dirt and unholstered his sidearm. Both officers left the safety of their patrol vehicles and followed his hand signals to approach the passenger side of the truck while he approached the driver's side. His wobbly reflection glared back at him from the tinted windows as he kept low and moved fast. Unhitching the door, he swung it open.

Empty.

"Check the registration and run these plates." Weston maneuvered toward the bed of the truck and scanned the patterns in the frozen dirt. Two depressed lines, about a foot apart, had been carved into the ground. Smooth and consistent. No tire tracks, but he was willing to bet Michael Kerr had borrowed the dolly Jonathan Byrd had used to get his victim's '50s-style coffins in place. He followed the tracks that disappeared opposite the small clearing in front of the mine, and his gut kicked hard.

He wasn't as familiar with these woods as he was with the land in and around his family's property, but the same rules applied. Determine the target, memorize a map of the area, know the dangers of going in on foot. Weston traced the dolly's tracks through the underbrush and scanned ahead. The clouds shifted overhead and shadows crawled up the mountain. Light brown rock stared back at him as he mentally matched the landscape to the map in his head. Michael Kerr wouldn't have been able to carry his victim and push the refrigerator up this incline at the same time. This was premeditated. He'd come into town for one thing: Chloe.

His chest tightened. Weston checked his weapon to

ensure he'd loaded a round into the chamber. He called over his shoulder to the two Creed officers running the truck's VIN number. "One of you with me. We're going hunting."

Chapter Fourteen

It was so dark.

Chloe ran her bandaged hands over the inside frame of the refrigerator, her breath coming in small bursts. Her fingers grazed over the rubber seal along one side, but no matter how many times she'd tried, the lid wouldn't budge. Michael had already buried her. The more she panicked, the faster she'd burn through what little air she had left.

She wasn't sure how long she'd been locked inside. Time had no meaning in the darkness. A soft moan escaped up her throat, and she closed her eyes. Weston and Easton had escaped the freezer Jonathan Byrd buried them in. She could get herself free. She just had to calm down. She had to think. Her soft exhale filled her ears, but her heart rate only notched higher. "Come on."

Slow, shallow breaths. Of course, the Ford brothers had had each other. They were stronger. They'd worked together. She kept in shape to stay on the run. Running, Olympic lifting, yoga. If she could squat over one hundred pounds, she could wedge her feet against the lid and get the damn thing open. She just had to try.

Chloe brought her knees into her chest, setting her boots against the lid. Her knees dug into her rib cage, and she automatically held her breath to pressurize the air in her lungs as though she were getting ready to lift. Only this time, she was fighting for her life. Not a personal record. She hadn't heard a chain or a padlock put into place when Michael sealed her inside. She focused the majority of her strength in her heels and pushed against the lid with everything she had.

The door lifted slightly, but a waterfall of dirt cascaded down into the refrigerator. She covered her face against the onslaught and turned away from the avalanche more likely to suffocate her than give her a way to escape. The lid settled back into place. A sob thickened in her throat as she streaked her hands down her face. It was no use. She could raise the lid, but she'd only manage to kill herself in the process. She couldn't open it completely and climb through the several tons of dirt crushing down on her. She was going to die here.

Weston.

His name materialized at the front of her mind, and a calm settled over her. The wishful part of her brain tried to convince her he'd found Macie's vehicle at the roadblock outside town, that the officer who Michael Kerr had knocked unconscious had come around and called in her abduction. It wanted to convince her he was doing everything in his power to find her, despite the fact she'd run. But the logical part of her brain, the one she'd relied on these past few months to stay alive, said no one was coming to save her. She believed in heroes, but she had to save herself.

Dirt caked the inside of her mouth as she searched her pockets. Michael hadn't emptied her coat before wrestling her into the refrigerator, and he hadn't noticed she'd emptied his when he'd captured her in the trees. She unpocketed the phone she'd taken from him. No service. The screen automatically lit up, and relief coursed through her as the slightest hint of light chased back the blackness. It wasn't much. It wasn't anything, really, but the agitation knotting in her stomach released.

Until the low battery warning flashed across the screen.

Her single lifeline of comfort was running out. Tears blurred in her vision as the phone went into automatic battery saving mode. The screen dimmed, but there was still enough light for her to get a measure of the refrigerator. "It's okay. You can do this."

Setting the phone up against the left wall, Chloe shifted to her right and turned onto her side. There wasn't a whole lot of room to maneuver. She had the strength to lift the lid, but without something to protect her face, the massive amount of dirt on top of her would suffocate her before she had a chance to escape. As much as she wanted to believe Weston had learned about what'd occurred at the roadblock, she couldn't rely on him this time. He wasn't the type of man or police chief to ignore one of his residents in danger—no matter the emotional repercussions—but hope wasn't a plan.

She tugged her coat cuff over her hand to wiggle free from one sleeve. Her elbow slammed into the opposite wall and triggered nerve pain straight down to her fingers. A groan escaped past her mouth, but she caught herself to hold on to as much air for as long as possible. Moving slower than she wanted to go, she slipped free of her left sleeve and settled onto her back. Time for the other side. Her heart thumped hard behind her rib cage, starved for oxygen. Her hand slipped free of the other sleeve. Cold from the plastic interior burrowed under her shirt. She couldn't stop the shiver from the abrupt change in temperature.

Spring had barely fallen across Battle Mountain, but out here, deep within the earth, the ground was still frozen, barren and lonely. Tremors worked through her hands as she raised her hips and pulled her coat out from beneath her weight. She didn't want to be alone anymore, didn't want to die. Despite the paralyzing fear of realizing not one but two killers had targeted her, she felt more cared for, loved even, than she ever had in Denver, surrounded by friends and what little remained of her family. The people here had taken her in, but Weston Ford had given her something she'd never imagined she'd feel again: a future. She wasn't ready to give that up. Not as long as she still had air in her lungs.

She'd have to move fast. Dirt and pebbles scratched at her skin as she leveraged her feet against the lid again. The second she opened the door, another round of dirt and rock would fill the empty space and bury her. Threading her arms through opposite sleeves, she ducked her head beneath the hood of her coat to protect her face and eyes.

She had one shot. Her last chance. One breath. Two.

She filled her lungs as fast as possible and shoved everything she had into the heels of her feet. Soreness echoed down her right side from being thrown from the four-wheeler, but the lid lifted. Another wave of dirt rolled into the space and displaced the precious oxygen she coveted. Dirt covered her almost instantly, and she struggled to keep the lid open while trying to sit up at the same time. The ticking of rock hitting the plastic filled her ears. She stretched out one hand, locking her elbow against the weight of the door, and felt for the cracked seal with the other. She tunneled through the wall of dirt slowly burying her alive and gripped the edge of the door. Yes!

Pressure built in her chest the longer she held her breath, but she couldn't afford to exhale. Not yet. Sweat beaded in her hairline as she lowered one leg, then the other. The door closed on her opposite hand, but the pain was nothing compared to the alternative of suffocation. Her heels hit dirt that had collected in the appliance. She dug her chest, face and thighs out from under the weight of loose soil and twisted onto her knees. The bones in her fingers trapped between the heavy door and the seal shattered under the weight, but she couldn't cry out. Couldn't scream. Her nervous system's automatic survival messages would force her to breathe if she lost consciousness. She had to stay awake. She had to keep going.

Rocks bit into her knees through her jeans as she set her shoulders against the door, but she couldn't leverage her feet under her with so much of the refrigerator's space eaten up by earth. Time was running out.

Despite the fact she couldn't see anything, granules of light prickled at the edges of her vision. She was going to pass out. Her heartbeat pulsed at the base of her skull. No. Not yet. Her head swam. Sliding her free hand down her left leg, she forced her boot through the dirt beneath her and tossed several inches to the bottom of the fridge. She could do this. She had to do this. She did the same for her left foot and had enough balance to thrust her shoulders against the weighted door.

A scream burst from her chest at the effort. Her lungs spasmed for air, but all she managed was a fraction of what she needed. The hood of her coat suctioned into her mouth. She was out of time. She couldn't hold the door open and climb through the opening at the same time. Her legs shook from the exertion, but she didn't have a choice. With the fingers of her right hand certainly broken, she clawed at the dirt still cascading into the refrigerator with the other. She couldn't breathe, couldn't think.

There was no way out.

Panic gripped like a tight vise around her heart. She was pulling in less and less air, her struggled inhales the only sound cutting through the silence. No. No, no, no, no. This wasn't how it was supposed to be. A wave of agony arced through her feet and up her legs. Her pulse shot into dangerous territory. Her heart was trying to get as much oxygen to the rest of her body as fast as possible, killing her while trying to save her.

She set her legs hip distance as best she could and raised the door another few inches. Pain radiated through her entire body as she gauged how many feet of soil she'd have to wade through to reach the surface. Her fingers tingled, her jaw ached from carrying the weight of the world on her shoulders. Literally. Tears burned down her face. The door lifted wider, but not wide enough for her to squeeze through. More dirt fell inside and surrounded her shins, and her strength ran out.

Her knees buckled, and the door collapsed closed. "No!"

WESTON AND THE Creed PD officer at his heels kept their distance from the set of tire tracks carved through the dirt. The killer had dragged Chloe and whatever he'd hauled on the dolly away from the mine for a reason. Chances were he'd come back this way when he was finished. Only Weston wasn't going to wait.

Sweat built in his palms as he crept along the man-made trail. The son of a bitch couldn't have gone far with such a heavy load, but he wouldn't want her found quickly, either. Branches swayed ahead, and Weston slowed, signaling the officer at his back to stop. Gusts of wind whistled through the passes above, but his instincts warned him he and his backup weren't alone anymore.

A gunshot exploded.

The rock to the right of his head caught the bullet and spit a veil of dust into his face. Weston twisted back to keep the obstruction between him and the shooter, but another bullet ripped through the trees and pegged the Creed officer. His backup went down, a groan following the echo bouncing off the peaks. Weston fisted the man's jacket and dragged him behind a boulder twenty feet back the way they'd come. Damn it. It was an ambush.

Chloe's abductor had been waiting for them.

Which meant he'd finished with his latest victim.

"Hang tight. Help is on the way." Crouching behind the boulder, Weston ripped his radio from his belt and pinched the push-to-talk button. "Dispatch, this is Ford. I'm taking fire near the entrance to Contention Mine. One shooter. Officer down. I repeat, officer down. Requesting Silverton and Creed backup as soon as possible."

Static filled the airwaves as Weston struggled to catch his breath. No movement. No sign the shooter had moved to get a better angle. The officer he'd left behind with Michael Kerr's truck would've heard the shots, but he couldn't leave the man at his feet to bleed out alone.

"Say again… Chief. Say—" Macie's voice dissolved.

Survival instinct bled into frustration. They were positioned between two peaks. The signal couldn't penetrate through the rock. Weston crouched beside the officer and pressed his palm into the bullet wound in the man's shoulder. Blood trickled up through his fingers and down the officer's uniform. Nichols, according to the nameplate pinned to the left side of his chest. "I'm going to get you out of here."

"You need to keep pressure on that wound," an unfamiliar voice said. "Otherwise, there's a chance your friend there will bleed out."

Weston ripped his bloodied hand from his fellow officer and raised his weapon, taking aim. Dr. Michael Kerr, the resident surgeon who'd assisted Chloe during the life-ending surgery of Miriam Byrd, stepped into view, a revolver pointed straight back at him. "Battle Mountain PD, put the weapon down. Now!"

A low laugh punctured through the groan coming from the officer at his feet as Michael Kerr took another step forward. A high widow's peak disappeared under a layer of hair whipped across the man's forehead, a few days' worth of beard growth shadowing an otherwise smooth face. "You're not going to shoot me, Chief Ford. Because I'm the only one who knows where she is." Kerr shook his head and took another step forward. "No. What you're going to do is let me walk back to my truck, drive down this mountain and out of this pathetic town, forget I was ever here, and no one else has to get hurt."

"You son of a bitch. You wanted her dead all along. You encouraged Jonathan Byrd to find her after you told him the truth about what happened to his wife, didn't you? But you couldn't risk him coming after you. You would've had to have done it anonymously. What'd you do? Get a copy of Chloe's findings when she did the autopsy and send it to him?" His shoulders ached from holding his weapon steady, but he wouldn't let this bastard get away with what he'd done. "You knew she was going to go to the clinic's board and tell them everything, and you couldn't risk being named in the malpractice suit. You used your mother's connections to find her, told Jonathan Byrd where she was hiding. Can't imagine what the senator might lose if her son was implicated in the wrongful death of a patient." Weston noted the slight crease in Kerr's mouth. He'd struck a chord. "You blamed Chloe for the mistake during that surgery. You used Jonathan Byrd like a weapon, and then you pointed him at Roberta Ellis and Chloe. All to save yourself, but something went wrong."

Kerr didn't answer, didn't even seem to breathe as his gaze flickered to the officer he'd shot at Weston's feet. The killer fanned his grip over the revolver in his hand.

"You lost control of your pet project. Jonathan Byrd was angry enough to kill anyone involved in his wife's death, but you couldn't afford his actions to link back to you or for him to catch you by surprise." Seconds ticked off in his head, each stacking against the one before it. "You had to put him down like the rabid dog you'd turned him into."

"That's a great story, Chief, but that's all it is. A story you'll never be able to prove, and the longer you try, the faster Dr. Miles suffocates." Michael Kerr's gun lowered a fraction. The man was a surgeon. While he saved and destroyed lives with a steady hand, he'd most likely never trained with weapons as long as Weston had. His arm was getting tired.

"You sure about that?" Weston nodded toward the small piece of gauze and tape wrapped between Kerr's thumb and index finger on his right hand behind the gun's grip. "Because the way Chloe saw it, whoever tortured Jonathan Byrd stabbed him with so much force, his hand slipped down the handle of the scalpel. The interim coroner is collecting samples from the remains right now. What are the chances the victim's DNA isn't the only blood the lab finds or that we won't be able to tie the clamp Chloe removed from Miriam Byrd's remains back to you?"

Shock smoothed Kerr's expression.

"That's right, Kerr. She outsmarted you, but you still have one bargaining chip here." Every muscle down his spine hardened with battle-ready tension, and Weston was the one to take a step forward this time. "Tell me where she is, and the district attorney might take your cooperation into consideration when filing charges for three counts of conspiracy to commit murder and first-degree murder."

"You remember the part where I said I'm walking out of here, Chief? Nobody is taking this from me. Not even you. Now you can get out of my way, or you can die as slowly and painfully as she is right now." Michael Kerr pulled the trigger.

The gun jammed, but faster than Weston thought possible the killer threw the weapon straight at him. Steel struck the side of his head, and he wrenched back, losing his aim. Pain splintered across his temple. Kerr lunged. Jumping off a rock between them, his attacker got the upper hand and swung a hard right hook. Lightning struck behind his eyes, and his weapon discharged a split second before Kerr knocked it from his hand. A solid kick to the sternum thrust him into the rock at his back. Strong hands wrapped around his throat and pushed him down. His knees threatened to collapse out from under him as Weston spotted his weapon a few feet away.

The wounded officer had lost consciousness. Chloe had been buried alive. Backup had no idea where he was.

Pure survival twisted Kerr's face into something unrecognizable, and a thread of spittle hung from dry, cracked lips. "Did you know seventy percent of strangulation victims are found with a broken hyoid bone? You see, it all depends on your age, the shape of the hyoid and whether or not the hyoid synchondrosis have fused. I wonder how much pressure it'll take to break yours."

His heart thudded loud behind his ears as he tried to breathe through the grip around his throat. Weston dug his hands into the man's forearms. The clock ticking at the back of his mind intensified. Chloe. She was out here, alone, afraid, dying. He wasn't going to lose her. Not again.

Weston released his hold on Kerr. He didn't know anything about human anatomy, but he'd gotten into plenty of fights with Easton to strike where it hurt. He rocketed his knee into Kerr's left kidney. The pressure around his throat released, and he gasped for air. His vision wavered, but he didn't let it stop him from fisting what was left of Kerr's hair. He slammed his knee into the bastard's face, and the good doctor collapsed. Unconscious. "Wonder which bones of yours are broken now."

He struggled to catch his breath. He wiped the blood from his temple with the back of his hand and collected his weapon. Flipping Michael Kerr onto his face, Weston handcuffed him to the downed officer, whose pulse was still strong, just as his partner exploded through the trees, weapon raised. "I've got an officer down and one suspect in custody. Call it in!"

Weston didn't wait for confirmation as he retargeted the dolly tracks he'd followed into the woods and headed up the mountain. His body hurt, his throat raw. He protected his face against the branches clawing at his face, desperation drowning the burn in his lungs. The tracks wound through a thick grove of trees, and he burst through them, out of breath.

The tracks ended.

In their place, a disturbed area of loose soil. Just as he'd noted before finding Whitney Avgerpoulos's remains. Weston collapsed to his knees and started digging. "Chloe!"

Dirt packed under his fingernails and numbed his hands. Blood dripped into the soil underneath him. Every cell in his body caught fire as he uncovered the smooth metal of a refrigerator too small for even her to survive inside. Weston repositioned himself to the longest side of the container, his boot striking a shovel discarded in the weeds. He made quick work of digging around the perimeter of the refrigerator and tossed the shovel. His hands blistered from the combination of dried wood and the sheen of sweat on his palms, but he didn't stop. Kneeling into the moat he'd created along one side, he hauled the door above his head.

A single pale hand reached toward the surface, her fingers swelling at odd angles. Broken. Unmoving. He worked faster, harder, unburying her inch by agonizing inch from the dirt that'd filled the refrigerator. "Hang on, baby. Hang on!"

He freed her left arm and scrambled to uncover her head and shoulders. Her coat crumpled as his hands tangled in long brown hair, and his heart stopped. She'd covered her face with the hood of her jacket to keep the dirt from choking her. She'd tried to escape. Weston pushed his hands beneath the loose soil and positioned his arms beneath hers, pulling her from her makeshift coffin.

"Come on, Doc. Don't you dare die on me. Don't let him win." Lowering the hood from her face, he smoothed her hair back. Streaks of dirt marred her complexion. He set his ear against her perfect mouth. No breathing sounds. Laying her flat, Weston interlaced his hands and centered the base of his palms beneath her sternum and compressed. "One, two, three, four." He set his mouth against hers and breathed every ounce of desperation, hope and love into her lungs, then got back to chest compressions. "Wake up, Chloe. You and I aren't finished. We'll never be finished."

Chloe's back arched off the ground as she gasped for air.

Chapter Fifteen

Coming back to life hurt more than she expected.

It was nothing compared to the ache of slowly suffocating to death, but she'd take any kind of pain she could get at this point. It was better than feeling nothing at all.

Chloe huddled into the space blanket provided by the EMT who'd stayed behind for her as she recounted to one of the Silverton PD officers what'd happened after her abduction at the roadblock. Pines swayed against the constant hum and whistle of wind, and a shiver chased down her spine. The truck bed of Easton's pickup bounced as the tech wrapping her broken fingers in splints maneuvered around for supplies. Sunlight glared off the light brown rocks of the peaks demanding attention outside Contention Mine. Four days ago, she'd responded to a call from the Battle Mountain PD dispatcher, which had set this nightmare in motion. Here she was, outside that same mine, alive in the end. These trees, these mountains—they'd stood the test of that time, but everything had changed. Exhaustion stole the last of her energy, and she settled against the cold steel of the truck bed.

Dirt crusted her hairline and fell in uneven batches with every movement. The idea to keep her coat over her face as she'd fought to escape the refrigerator had kept the soil out of her mouth, nose and lungs, but it had worked beneath her clothing and stuck to everything else in the worst way possible. The short hours she and Weston had spent in the tree house she'd vowed to hate seemed like a lifetime ago. What she wouldn't give for a hot shower and the comforting scent of the honey soap she'd used there, for the thick robe and the warm man against her.

Her hands shook despite the blanket draped over her. She'd treated enough patients during her ER rotation as a med student to watch for signs of shock, but it would still be another thirty minutes, at least, before the EMT would clear her. The officer who'd been shot had been rushed to a full-service hospital in Grand Junction in the town's only ambulance. She'd have to wait, but the fact she was still breathing said she'd walk away from the scene on her own two feet. The EMT explained there would be chest pain over the next few days as her body adjusted to the lack of oxygen over a sustained period of time, but her vitals were steady. She would live.

The scene buzzed with controlled chaos as three different police departments collected evidence and put the last pieces of the investigation on paper. It was over. Jonathan Byrd's remains had been collected by the coroner out of Creed, and the samples Easton Ford and the interim coroner had taken from the body were already on their way to the lab in Denver for testing. Considering the amount of force it'd taken for the killer to drive a scalpel into Jonathan Byrd's bone, the lab would most assuredly find DNA that forensically identified who had wielded the scalpel that'd killed her attacker. But there was no doubt in her mind—Dr. Michael Kerr's blood would match.

Anxiety coiled in her stomach as two officers, one being the unforgettable man who'd pulled her from her own grave, escorted her former colleague to a waiting police cruiser. The officer Michael Kerr had knocked unconscious at the roadblock had quickly identified the vehicle of his attacker as a dark blue pickup, matching the rental the disgraced surgeon had used to abduct her and transport the refrigerator he'd buried her inside. Preliminary ballistics had already compared the bullet recovered from Jonathan Byrd's head wound and the last bullets found in Kerr's gun. They were a visual match.

A man she'd worked beside for years would be charged with first-degree murder, attempted murder and three counts of conspiracy to commit murder. While he hadn't killed Roberta Ellis or Whitney Avgerpoulos, he'd enlisted a grieving husband to do the work for him. He'd spend the rest of his life behind bars and lose any claim to his family's fortune. From what little Chloe had overheard from the Silverton officers a few feet away, Senator Kerr herself had already held a press conference to deny her knowledge of her son's actions and remove him from the family trust.

The heart and vascular clinic would hear the news soon. The truth would come out. Chloe and the rest of her surgical team who'd been in the operating room that day would be suspended until the investigation was complete. With Jonathan Byrd dead, his malpractice suit filed against her would be dismissed, but the board would be forced to investigate all of her other surgeries. The press alone would hurt the clinic and the patients who'd relied on their physicians to get them through the scariest times of their lives.

She was going to lose everything. Her medical career was over.

But with the thought came an undeniable peace. She'd planned to tell the board what'd happened to Miriam Byrd before her attack in Denver. She was going to take responsibility for Michael Kerr's mistake and step down as the head of her department. Only now, the man she thought would be replacing her would spend the rest of his life in prison.

She curled one hand into the reflective space blanket. Michael turned that dark gaze to her, and her heart rate kicked behind her ribs. She forced her blistered hand to relax as Weston blocked her killer's line of sight, and the uneasiness from having to face her attacker eased. Because of him. The police chief who'd never given up on her, even when he'd had the chance.

Weston settled both hands on his waist, his back to her, as the other officer pushed Michael Kerr into his seat. The patrol car's siren chirped once as it pulled out of the small clearing and headed down the mountain back toward town. She wasn't sure what would happen to the surgeon now. Once she handed over the clamp she'd removed from Miriam Byrd's remains and all the forensic evidence had been verified, the state would presumably have Michael transferred to a larger holding facility, possibly back in Denver, while the district attorney filed official charges.

Battle Mountain's police chief turned to face her, and the fear, the investigation, the mine—it all fell away as though it'd never existed. There was only Weston. Her partner. Her friend. Her everything. He closed the distance between them, and Chloe pulled away from the truck bed frame to sit straighter. "Fancy meeting you here, Doc." That crooked smile she hadn't known existed a few days ago punctured through the fear and isolation that usually controlled her, and she couldn't help but smile in return. "For the record, crime scenes are not my favorite place to bring dates."

"Is that what this is?" Her chest ached as a laugh escaped, and she set her hand over her sternum to hold herself together. In vain. She'd done nothing but try to keep herself from shattering into a million pieces since learning Roberta Ellis had been buried alive, but her control had worn thin. She was supposed to feel relieved—happy, even—they'd solved the case, but all that was left was…emptiness.

Concern wiped Weston's amusement from his expression, and he stepped into her. Placing one hand between her shoulder blades, he set the other over her hand on her chest. "Deep breaths, Doc. I've got you. Whatever you need, I'm here."

"Thank you." Chloe settled her forehead against his shoulder and matched her breathing to his. The softness of his flannel shirt warmed under her temple, and suddenly there was nothing she could do to stop the flood of terror and guilt she'd tried to bury at the back of her mind. A sob wracked through her. Tears streaked down her face, but Weston only held her tighter.

She was so tired. Tired of being someone she wasn't, of lying, of running, of merely surviving. She just wanted to go home. She wanted somewhere she could call home. Somewhere she could be herself, where the hardest part of her day would be figuring out what to make for dinner, and she didn't want to do it alone. She wanted a partner, someone she could trust, talk with, laugh. She wanted Weston. She wanted to be loved by him.

She brushed her unbroken fingers against Weston's collar and buried her nose against his neck. Committed, dependent, loyal. There wasn't an ounce of her that hadn't fallen in love with him over the course of this investigation, but her brain had locked on to the fact he wasn't ready to move on from his wife. Swiping at the dirt caking under her eyes, she forced herself to take a shaky breath and put some distance between them. "I'm sorry. I'm sure you don't want to stand here and get cried on."

"Don't ever apologize for feeling what you have to feel. The past few days have been harder on you than anyone else. Well, maybe not the people who were killed, but you get my point." Callused hands framed her jaw, and Weston urged her to look up at him despite what the two of them must look like to the officers still working the scene. He traced the top of her cheekbone with the pad of his thumb. "Besides, I never liked this shirt anyway."

He was trying to set her at ease, and it was working. Damn him. Her mouth tugged at one corner as the pressure of breaking his gaze won out over the moment. Chloe winced as she tried to bend her broken fingers around the edge of the space blanket. "I'm sure you have a lot of work to do here. You don't have to stay with me. I can wait for the ambulance to come back from Grand Junction or have the EMT drive me to the clinic."

"Chloe," he said, his voice dipping into dangerous territory. Her name on his lips urged her to bring her gaze to his. "Stop wasting your energy on trying to get rid of me. It's not going to work. I almost lost you out here. Again. I'm not going anywhere. Just tell me what you need from me."

A weightlessness slid through her at the sincerity in his voice, in his expression, in the way he held her as though he couldn't stand not to touch her, and the anxiety building in her stomach dissipated. A fresh round of hot tears welled in her eyes. "I need a shower, and a hot meal, and a nap, and for you to be there when I wake up."

Strong arms secured her against his chest, and Weston set his chin on the crown of her head. "Let's get you home."

WHITNEY AVGERPOULOS WAS finally able to go home.

Home. That single world had a different meaning now.

Wasn't just where his phone connected to Wi-Fi automatically. It'd become so much more than that over the past few days. It'd become a person. Chloe. No matter where they went from here, he'd never look at the Whispering Pines the same again. Still, they needed somewhere to recover from the events of this investigation, and he doubted Chloe would be comfortable in his one-bedroom, one-bathroom apartment long. Especially given his limited cooking skills and men's hygiene products.

Denver PD was sending two detectives to Battle Mountain to review the recent investigation and officially close Dr. Roberta Ellis's case. The forensics lab wouldn't have the results from the tox screens or DNA evidence from each victim for another few days, but from what the district attorney had said, Michael Kerr and his public defender were already looking at making a deal. The senator's press conference had done its job in making it clear she hadn't known anything about her son's activities, that she and her staff had severed contact with the good doctor and that Kerr had forfeited his future inheritance.

The Silverton officer who'd been knocked unconscious during Chloe's abduction had officially put in his retirement papers, claiming he'd seen enough excitement in an otherwise uneventful career. While the officer who'd taken a bullet during the shoot-out had already tried to discharge himself early to get back on shift. Both had been invaluable to the investigation. Without them, he could've lost Chloe forever.

Weston pulled up the long drive, the shocks of his pickup doing their best to absorb the change in elevation. Didn't seem to bother the sleeping beauty in the passenger seat, whose ordeal had ended a mere twenty-four hours ago. He doubted a nuclear bomb could wake her now. He shoved the truck into Park as a single figure descended the main house's porch stairs. His heart protested at the absence of the family patriarch who'd always been at Karie Ford's side to greet him.

His mother folded her arms across her chest as he shouldered out of the truck, her usually quick smile waning. Her flannel shirt bellowed wide as she stretched her arms out. She brought him in for a too-tight hug before scanning him from head to toe as a mother often did. "Easton told me about what happened out at the mine." Her watery brown gaze shifted to the passenger in his truck as she pulled away. Long fingers with soft loose skin interlaced with his, and she patted the back of his hand. "That one of her fellow surgeons tried to bury her alive to save his own skin. Thank goodness you were there. How is she?"

"She's tired, overwhelmed by everything, but she's strong. She just needs a few days to recover. The DA says their case is solid. I've turned everything over to Denver PD, including the refrigerators from all three crime scenes and Jonathan Byrd's remains and the pickup truck he used to…" Weston swallowed to counter the thickness in his throat. "Chloe told them where they could find the clamp she hid from Michael Kerr, too. They were the ones to first catch the case. Makes sense they'd wrap it up."

What then? He couldn't stop the thought from worming its way into the front of his mind. With Jonathan Byrd dead and Michael Kerr headed for a life sentence behind bars, Chloe was safe. Free to go wherever she wanted. Whether that meant going back to her old life or including him in her decision, he had no idea, but nearly losing her like that had ripped open a part of him he believed lost after Cynthia passed. He didn't want to be alone anymore, but it was more than that. He needed Chloe in his life. This town needed her. Her confidence and temper, her softness and strength. Every cell in his body craved every cell in hers. Because he loved her. Weston turned to his mother. "How are you holding up?"

Karie shifted her weight, a familiar move when she wasn't comfortable with attention. "Oh, you know, your father took care of most everything around here. We built this place to raise our kids, but the income from tourists is what pays the bills, groceries and our…my health insurance." His mother slid her hand out of his, pulling her shoulders back. "Hard to imagine keeping it going without him. I don't really see any other option than to sell. Neither you nor your brother are in a position to help me run things around here." Her voice wavered. A strand of white hair blew in front of her face. "Easton's taken care of all the funeral arrangements for tomorrow, but sometimes I catch myself telling your father to come eat lunch or trying to show him a story in the paper. It's not real yet."

Karie Ford had stood as a strong example of fortitude and kindness all his life, but right then all Weston saw was a reflection of the same grief he'd suffered after losing Cynthia in his mother's eyes.

"I'm sorry, Mom." He encircled her in his arms. His

heart lodged in his throat at the thought of her having to sell off the property he'd called home his entire life.

"Oh, honey, I don't blame you. For any of this. Your father made his choice. He knew what he was getting into going out there. He dedicated his life to helping those less fortunate or that couldn't help themselves. It's only fitting that's how he left. On his terms." She put a foot of distance between them, cleared her throat and swiped at her face. "Now you two get cleaned up and settled. I'll make sure you have something to eat when you're both ready."

"Thank you," he said.

His mother reached out, brushing the pad of her thumb across his cheek. "You remind me so much of him, Weston. Putting everyone else's needs and safety before your own. Just remember to put yourself first every once in a while." Karie's gaze slid to the passenger in his truck. "You deserve to be happy."

He nodded as she turned back toward the main cabin and ascended the stairs. Weston stared after her, seeing the cracks beginning to form as his mother tried to hold herself together. Losing a spouse changed a person, and finding that kind of support and love again was rare. Unless you were lucky enough for it to move into town unannounced and respond to a dead body. He rounded to the passenger side of the truck and opened the door softly. Setting his hand beneath Chloe's elbows, he took her weight against his chest and swung her legs up. "Come on, Doc. You're raining dirt."

"Where are we?" The question barely left her lips as more than a whisper.

"Home." He carried her across the property toward the satellite cabin he'd taken up during the investigation. As comfortable as he was in the one he and Cynthia had shared during her treatments, it was time to start something new, fresh. He'd never forget his wife. Hell, how could he forget someone who'd been such a large part of his past? His mother had been right. He deserved to move on, deserved to live, to be happy. The door swung inward, and Weston maneuvered her through the opening. "No offense, but you've smelled better."

Her laugh spiked his blood pressure higher as he set her in one of the chairs around the small kitchen table. "The people I work with don't care what I smell like."

"You mean because they're dead." He couldn't help but smile as he slipped her boots from her feet and tossed them out the front door to contain the amount of dirt inside. Weston set his hands at the backs of her arms and pulled her upright into his chest. Right where she belonged. Pale green eyes gazed up at him as he smoothed her crusted hair away from her face, and her smile waned. He had to know where they stood, where they went from here. In that moment, his future stood on the edge of a blade. Tip it too far one direction and he'd lose everything. "Chloe, I know the case is closed and you have an entire life and career and friends back in Denver, but I—"

"I'm not going back to Denver." She reclaimed some of her own strength, although she seemed to still need help balancing. Her mouth curled at one corner as she set her hand over his heart. "I knew exactly what I was giving up when I ran three months ago. I knew I'd never be able to go back with my reputation intact or that I'd be able to pretend I hadn't been involved in the preventable death of a patient, even if it wasn't my fault. I convinced myself once this investigation was closed, I could still have that life, that I'd be happy."

His gut clenched as he prepared for the final blow.

"But I've built a better life here." She rolled her bottom lip between her teeth. "It sounds silly, but I like that Reagan remembers my name when I order coffee. I like that people smile at me when I walk down the street and bring me dinners for no apparent reason other than they made too much. I like my job and the people I work with at the funeral home, which sounds weird, but it's true. I feel more at home here than I've felt anywhere else. Battle Mountain isn't just the town I used to escape my past. It's my future, and I hope, with time, I can earn back the trust they've shown me these past few months." She fisted his shirt in her unbroken hand. "And I want you to be part of that future, Chief Ford. Late-night emergencies, family dinners, helping you and your mom maintain this place—I want it all. I want you. Forever."

"I love you, too." Warmth exploded through his chest as he crushed his mouth to hers. Weston threaded one hand through the rat's nest of her hair but quickly pulled back. "Does that future include a shower?"

"For the record, you didn't smell great either after you'd been buried in that freezer with your brother, but I pushed past it." She pressed her hand into his chest, forcing him across the cabin backward until he hit the closed bathroom door. Chloe notched her chin higher and leveled her mouth with his.

"You're right." He reached behind him and twisted the bathroom doorknob open. They fell in a tangle of limbs and surprised protests as Weston latched onto her hips. "I'll just hold my breath."

She swatted his arm as she whispered against his mouth. "Careful, Chief. Out of all the people in this town, I'm the one who knows where the bodies are buried."

Epilogue

Easton Ford folded his hands, one over the other, as he stood beside the coffin.

A bite of cold infused an already grim day as he, his brother and a few of his father's friends waited for the signal to carry the casket from the church down the short path to the cemetery.

His mother secured her hand in Chloe Miles's from the front row of pews, her skin too pale and streaked with tears. It seemed as though the entire town had come to pay their respects, a testament to how many lives James Ford had touched in his too-short sixty-three years. His father had been a great man, one who'd taught his sons loyalty, responsibility and, more importantly, duty to a man's town and family before himself.

Those same principles had gotten the old man killed.

Easton served his country believing his father had been right, and he'd lost everyone in his unit because of it. He held his head high as the pastor ended the service. He wrapped his grip around the handle and hefted the weight of his father's remains above his shoulder with the other men in the procession. This wasn't the first funeral he'd attended since coming home, and it wouldn't be the last, but as Battle Mountain's first reserve officer, he'd make damn sure he wouldn't be caught unprepared again.

* * * * *

AN OPERATIVE'S
LAST STAND

JUNO RUSHDAN

This is for Team JIKA. You made this series possible.

Prologue

Eighteen months ago

Hunter Wright strolled down the seventh-floor hallway of the Waterfront Hotel alongside Kelly Russell, aka the ice queen. She was his team handler and supervisor, for all intents and purposes. For five years, they'd worked closely, executing some of the CIA's toughest covert assignments to eliminate high-value targets abroad, with him leading his Topaz unit in the field and her managing their intel as well as logistics from Langley.

This was the first time they'd ever been one-on-one. Alone. Outside the Washington, DC, metropolitan area.

A possibility he'd imagined many times, though, if it were up to him, they wouldn't be freezing their keisters off in Boston. This TDY—temporary duty—attending an international industrial technology conference had been a last-minute thing. They had been sent undercover to spy on attendees after the two operatives who had been scheduled to be there got food poisoning from a buffet restaurant, a total fluke.

Kelly had been the first to volunteer. Naturally, there was no way on God's green earth Hunter was going to miss the weeklong opportunity to work as partners with her while indulging in long dinners and playing tourist.

Now their time had come to an end. This was the last night of the conference. Tomorrow morning they had to catch a nine o'clock flight out of Logan International.

She stopped at the door to her room and slipped her heels off with a sigh, as though she'd been looking forward to that moment all day. His room was right across the hall, but he lingered beside her, taking her in. Even with her hair tucked in a twist, the conservative pantsuit that did nothing to flatter her lithe body and the barest touch of makeup that let her freckles shine, none of it downplayed her stunning beauty.

After a sixteen-hour day, which had started with them both in the gym at 5:00 a.m., she looked worn-out and a little tipsy from one too many drinks at the bar. Not that Kelly was at a disadvantage. She could hold her liquor, stayed sharp and aware, never letting her guard down.

He knew he should just keep his mouth shut—to speak his mind would be playing with fire. Still, he leaned on the door frame and said, "Hey, think you might be interested in a last nightcap, in my room—*or yours*—instead of the bar?"

She looked up at him and smiled, her eyes a deep cobalt blue, dark fire-red hair, her skin pale and creamy, those angular features, her full pink mouth, the effortless sensuality. It all hit him like a gut punch. God, she was breathtaking.

"A drink? No." Amusement rang in her voice, and something inside him sank.

"All right," he said nonchalantly. He forced a smile, swallowing his disappointment, and stepped across the hall. Of course. Some things weren't meant to be. This was for the best anyway. Everything came at a price. To be with Kelly Russell might cost him his soul. "I'll let you get some sleep. It's been a long week, and we've got an early flight."

"Hunter," she said, and he glanced back at her. "Who said anything about sleeping? I *am* interested in the euphemism behind your offer of a nightcap." Another smile, this time flirty, sexy. Full of promise. "And to answer the second part to your question, my room."

Every muscle in his body tightened with need, making it difficult for him to think of anything else, least of all playing it cool.

"We need to establish the rules of engagement first," she said.

All business. Always in control. Even now. For some inexplicable reason, it only added to her allure.

He strolled back across the hall. "I'm listening."

"This has to be a one-night-only situation. It can never happen again."

He reached out and tucked a fiery strand that had escaped her twist behind her ear. Her skin was warm and soft, with a perfect porcelain texture. "My mother always told me, never say never."

"I'm serious, Hunter." She slipped her key card in the slot, unlocked the door and opened it. "One night to assuage our mutual curiosity."

Curiosity. Chemistry. Semantics. "If we enjoy ourselves, why only one night?"

Standing on the threshold, she held the door open with it at her back. "We need to keep things professional in the office. Neither of us can afford to let whatever happens tonight cloud our judgment or impact any hard decisions we might have to make in the future."

If it ever came down to her choosing between him and national security, she didn't want emotion causing her to hesitate or think twice about that choice. She was destined for greatness. One day, she would be the director of the CIA, and she didn't want anything or anyone getting in the way of her climb up the ladder. He understood—it was the same for him. Nothing would ever cloud his judgment professionally, either. Not even one night with the incomparable Kelly Russell.

"Is that it?" He slipped into the doorway in front of her. They stood so close in the narrow space that their bodies almost touched. He was so physically aware of her that he felt as though he were standing in the middle of a magnetic field, electric current flowing between them, with the air snapping and sparks flying.

"One more thing." She took a step closer, and her chest brushed his suit. "What happens TDY, stays TDY. We'll never discuss it."

He didn't need to talk about it to replay it in his head. "Agreed."

Grabbing his tie, she pulled him into her room and tossed her shoes.

Desire coiled and tightened in his gut. He'd never been attracted to weak, helpless women who needed protecting. There was nothing weak about Kelly.

She was as fierce and deadly as a switchblade.

The door slammed closed behind them. There was a sweet, faintly spicy scent in the air that overrode the generic flatness prevalent in hotel rooms. His blood stirred—from the proximity to her, from anticipation, from the sheer reaction to the feminine smell, universal in some ways, exclusive to her in others.

"I do have a condition of my own," he said.

As she undid his tie with a gleam in her eyes, he slipped his hands into her hair, something he'd longed to do, and plucked out the pins, throwing them one by one to the floor.

She raised a perfectly groomed eyebrow. "Which is?"

"It's more about clarifying parameters rather than a condition per se." He found the last pin in her hair, and the sophisticated twist tumbled down her back. The long, silky strands flowed in loose waves around her shoulders. "The *night* doesn't end until the sun is up."

Her mouth quirked in a sinfully sexy grin. "I can live with those terms."

He fisted a hand in her hair and pulled her luscious body against his, aching to taste every inch of her.

There were a hundred reasons, all of them good, why he shouldn't have Kelly in his arms, why he shouldn't want this one night with her more than he wanted his next breath, but in that instant, none of them mattered…even though the price for this night might be higher than he could possibly imagine.

THE NEXT MORNING, in the light of day, Kelly pressed her forehead to the cool bathroom door, shriveling on the inside from regrets. Great, big, screaming regrets.

Not because the night with Hunter hadn't been off-the-charts amazing. On the contrary. It had been unbelievable. Better than any fantasy.

But what had she been thinking? To be so weak as to give in to a physical urge.

A conflict of interest of this magnitude could jeopardize her career and everything she'd worked so hard to achieve.

Although she had told him they'd never speak of this—and she wouldn't with him—at the first opportunity, she was reporting this *incident* to Human Resources. She could not afford to have this come out during a counterintelligence polygraph.

That was how operatives were compromised. Blackmailed.

What would happen if the unfortunate day ever came when they were on opposing sides instead of the same team?

Sometimes the unthinkable happened, interpersonal dynamics thrown into a tailspin due to politics, ambition, greed. One thing trumped all others to her—national security.

Cracking the bathroom door open, Kelly put her stealth skills to good use. She slipped into the main room, fully dressed, with her packed carry-on and shoes in her hand.

Sunlight peeked through the curtains, falling on Hunter's naked body in her bed, with only his lower half covered. She watched him sleeping for a moment and memorized the sight of him like this. Smooth skin marred by scars. Every ridge and valley of ripped muscle in his chest and abdomen. Those strong arms that had held her close.

She had wanted Hunter with a blind, ferocious need, a craving she couldn't suppress no matter how hard she'd tried. And for hours she'd fed that particular hunger until they'd both been sated and too exhausted to move.

A pang cut through her, but she vowed, *never again*.

This was lust, nothing more. Certainly not some other four-letter word.

With a deep breath, she steeled herself.

He stirred, his head rolling to the side, blond hair mussed, his hand touching the empty space beside him. His bright blue eyes opened, his gaze finding the clock before locking on hers. A delicious smile spread across his devastatingly handsome face, and her chest tightened.

"Why are you dressed?" His voice was husky, with a gravelly rasp that caressed her senses, making her thighs tingle. "We've got three hours before our flight. Come here, Red."

That was the first time he'd called her the nickname, and it had her belly turning to mush.

With a lazy grin on his face, he reached out for her.

She wanted nothing more than to take his hand and

climb back into bed with him. To stay there all day, for another night at least. To forget the outside world existed.

But there was far too much at stake.

"The sun is up, Hunter. The night is over. It's time to go home." Her tone was stone-cold, her gaze unflinching, her expression serious. His smile fell. "I plan to report this indiscretion to HR." She owed it to him to give him a heads-up. "I highly recommend you do likewise. Since this is a onetime thing, I don't think I'll be pulled as your team handler."

Planting a forearm on the bed, he lifted up with a be-wildered look, but she pressed on, forcing herself to stare into those crystal-blue eyes and ignore the wild flutter in her chest. "A rideshare will be here in fifteen minutes to take us to the airport." She'd ordered one in the bathroom along with changing her flight to one an hour earlier to spare them the awkwardness of sitting together. Maybe it was a coward's move, but she'd told herself it was a smart one. "If you're not in the lobby by the time it arrives, I'm leaving without you."

Turning from him without giving him a chance to re-spond, she wheeled her carry-on to the door and stepped into the hall. With the click of the lock behind her, some-thing splintered in her chest, a chilling emptiness settling behind her breastbone. The sensation didn't slow her as she hurried for the elevator, afraid she might be tempted to go back into that room, crawl into bed and climb on top of him.

She was almost running down the hall…escaping. From him.

Chapter One

Present day

Never in a million years had Hunter Wright expected to find himself in this position—disavowed, falsely accused of treason, on the run. And now, taking up arms against the CIA, an organization he'd served for more than half his life, had sacrificed and bled for.

All because of the machinations of one woman.

It was the ultimate betrayal.

He wanted to be immune to the raw emotions bubbling inside him, but he wasn't. If only he knew why she had set them up. Getting an answer was a priority, but not the highest at the moment. Notwithstanding an explanation, Hunter was determined to clear his name along with the rest of his Topaz unit.

First, they had to survive the night.

Clenching his jaw so hard that his teeth ground together, he settled into a prone position in the hunting stand nestled between two palm trees with the sniper rifle in his hands. The spot was protected from thermal imaging with a multilayer combination of Mylar foil, which was impervious to infrared radiation and reflected heat, synthetic microfiber spray-painted to match the environment, and he'd covered it with a final layer of nylon camo netting that would take on the ambient temperature. He'd made the perch to blend seamlessly into the landscape.

Two others from his rogue team, Gage Graham and Dean Delgado, were concealed in a similar manner, each with a different vantage point. Ready to bring shock and awe to those coming. Mercenaries—scumbags, not loyal operatives, who had no reservations about committing atrocities—hired to do the CIA's dirty work.

Her dirty work.

But Topaz was prepared, primed for war and wouldn't go down without a fight.

Zenobia "Zee" Hanley, the fourth member, was on the mainland. She and her fiancé were conducting surveillance with their daughter in tow. Gage's and Dean's significant others, both civilians, were no doubt fretting as they stayed at a safe distance from where the action was about to take place.

This was the beginning of the end. Waiting for the enemy to come and lay waste to the island that Topaz—*his family*—had forged into a home wasn't the hardest part for Hunter. What got to him, deep down under his skin, was thinking about the cause of this gross injustice…*her*.

The thought made his gut burn.

"Incoming," Gage said in his ear over comms. "Five hundred yards out."

They'd be here soon. Using inflatable boats with a quiet engine. His guess was electric power propulsion. The strike team would stop more than two hundred yards away, before they could be heard. Then they'd swim the rest of the way.

"How many?" Hunter asked.

"Three boats. Twenty-four men."

Swearing to himself, Hunter gritted his teeth. In his gut, he always knew it would be more than a baker's dozen. *Still.*

"Twenty-six," Dean corrected. "You missed two. They're hard to see this far out, cloaked in the shadows."

"Twenty-four, twenty-six, it's twenty too many," Gage said.

Dean grunted in agreement. "You have to hand it to her, Kell—"

"Do not speak her name," Hunter warned.

"The ice queen," Dean corrected, using the nickname for the woman who was always poised, in control and cold-blooded to the core, "made sure to send plenty of re-inforcements."

That she had. "She's excellent at tying up loose ends." Determined, too.

He'd stopped thinking her name a week ago. After he'd learned *she* had been promoted in the wake of Topaz's in-famy. Fast-tracked from team handler to deputy director of operations, no less. There was only one way in the world that could've been possible.

She'd set them up and sold them out.

"I'm sorry." Dean's voice was thick with remorse. "It's my fault they found us."

It was *and* it wasn't. The ice queen had spearheaded an operation targeting Dean, who had been in hiding in Wyoming. Rather than kill him, they tracked him and his girlfriend here to this island off the coast of Venezuela, unbeknownst to either. The two of them had led the CIA straight to them, where every other member of Topaz had found short-lived sanctuary.

"No time for a pity party. We've got work to do," Hunter said, needing his team to focus on the monumental task at hand. Not dwelling on mistakes that they couldn't undo. They had to fight as one with singular resolve. There wasn't room for anything else. "I need you both razor-sharp. Once those men have boots on the beach, we have to be ready to push hard and fast. Got it?"

"Roger," Dean and Gage said in unison.

The night was calm and quiet as expected at 3:00 a.m.— the perfect time to launch an assault. A chilly breeze swept over Hunter. To a small degree it was soothing, though he doubted anything would cool his rage other than making her pay for every dirty rotten deed that had caused his team to be branded traitors and marked for death.

KELLY RUSSELL, THE CIA deputy director of operations, stood at the head of the conference table in the vault of the Caracas station. Consular services of the US Embassy in Venezuela had been suspended for quite some time, and diplomatic personnel had been withdrawn years ago. In light of the significance of this covert operation and her need to have boots on the ground as close to the action to get it done right, she was given special dispensation to monitor it from here. She had arrived with the SAC—Special Activities Center—chief, Andrew Clark, and a small contingent of marines to open this section of the embassy and provide security.

Her boss, CIA director Wayne Price, had warned her about going to Venezuela. *Obsession by its nature precludes equilibrium*, he'd said to her. She was known for her steadiness, her ruthlessly cool approach to everything. Except in this.

She wouldn't have stability in her career, her life, even in her thoughts, not until this was finished and Team Topaz was eliminated.

Kelly stared at the high-definition screen that dominated the far wall, watching the live footage from the Predator drone hovering above the target location.

Operation Cujo was in full swing. A fitting name considering Topaz had once been her most envied team, idolized and lauded. She'd even made the disastrous mistake of caring about them. More for one in particular than the rest. Then they turned on the CIA, betrayed her trust and made a mockery of everything she stood for and believed in when the Topaz unit accepted millions to assassinate a top official in Afghanistan which led to the destabilization of the country.

Now, like the pack of rabid dogs they had become, they were about to be put down permanently.

"Coffee?" Andrew asked, shoving a hot brewed cup in her face. The man had the aggressive, animalistic tenacity of the weasel he resembled. Alert, dark beady eyes, sharp features and dishwater-brown hair. Always so eager. So bold.

His wool suit was rumpled, the same one he'd worn on the long, private flight, suitable for the mid-March temperature of the Northeast. Unlike hers, which was fresh and lightweight, and more appropriate for the change in climate. The journey seemed to age him, making him look fifty instead of forty. He'd skipped shaving, so he had scruffy stubble that looked coarse enough to sand wood. At least he'd run a comb through his wiry tuft of hair.

She waved him off. "No. Thanks."

After downing two espressos in her hotel room at zero dark thirty and with her adrenaline pumping full throttle, the last thing she needed was more caffeine. Besides, she'd never accept one from Andrew. It might be poisoned.

"You seem…" Andrew said, studying her. "On edge."

Of course she was. This was the most important op of both their lives.

A year ago, while Andrew had been in charge of all covert operations as the SAC chief, she'd been Topaz's handler when the agency's most revered operatives went rogue. Leaving her to take the heat, to clean up the mess and to stitch back together the tatters of her career thread by thread. The suspicion that had hung over both their heads, the interrogations they'd been subjected to—a living nightmare for months.

But she had clawed her way out of that black hole, only to rise even higher, like a phoenix from the ashes.

Everything hung in the balance with Operation Cujo.

The question churning in her head now was: Why wasn't Andrew on edge? Instead of being the picture of reserved poise.

She drew in a deep breath, struggling to find the calm center that had served her so well most of her life.

"We need this to succeed," she said matter-of-factly, hiding the desperation pooling in her belly. "We can't afford to let one of them slip through our fingers. Again."

Topaz had made fools of them all since they went on the run. Constantly evading capture, managing to slip out of every trap they'd set. The only member of Topaz they'd never been able to get a bead on until now was Hunter Wright.

Her gut clenched at the thought of him, but it was that fist-tight squeeze around her heart, despite the anger simmering in her veins, that she despised.

She cursed that man's name and rued the day she'd slept with him.

The CIA's failure, her failure, regarding Topaz was getting ridiculous at this point. Another embarrassment was simply something she would not abide.

Those despicable traitors needed to die before sunrise.

"I never thought I'd ever have to say this to you, much less think it, but," Andrew said, leaning over and lowering his voice so that the two marines in the room couldn't overhear, "pull yourself together."

Kelly snapped her gaze to him, bristling at the proprietary tone he had used. How dare he speak to her like that?

Once he'd been her supervisor, but now he was her subordinate.

"You work for me," she said, her voice soft, but her tone full of grit. "You would do best not to forget that."

The smug look fell from his face as Andrew blanched. Catching himself, he washed emotion from his expression. "I only meant you have a reputation to uphold. You're the ice queen, after all."

She gave him a sidelong glance.

"Come on, you know what they all whisper about you. The fear you instill is part of your mystique. But if you're afraid, then it means the rest of us should be quaking in our boots," he said.

She let herself take the slightest comfort in the compliment. "I'm not afraid." She was terrified. But there was no way she'd ever let anyone see her sweat.

"Topaz has no idea we're coming, thanks to your plan to manipulate Dean Delgado," Andrew said. "We have the element of surprise, the tactical advantage, and I put together the best group of mercs. Zulu team will stop at nothing to get the job done. This op is in the bag."

It was true that Zulu was the best of the best. Most were former Special Forces commandos, but it would only be in the bag once they had four confirmed kills on Hunter, Gage, Zee and Dean. Then she would be able to sleep well at night, knowing her greatest shame and the biggest threat to national security had been neutralized.

"I hope you're right," she said. For both their sakes.

She twisted the large, bulky ring on her right hand. It had been her father's United States Military Academy class ring she'd had adjusted to fit her. Heavy men's casting and embossed with the West Point seal where the stone

should have been set. Her father had made it all the way
to chairman of the Joint Chiefs of Staff, principal military
adviser to the president and the secretary of defense, before a heart attack claimed his life. She couldn't help but
wonder if he could see her now, what he might think of
her and the mistakes she'd made.

Her godmother, Judith Farren, the first female director
of the NSA, had already chided her numerous times for
getting too close to Topaz. To Hunter.

The phone rang, and Andrew shot her a glance.

Well aware who was on the other end of the line, she
gave Andrew a curt nod. "Put him through on speaker."

Andrew answered the phone as she instructed.

"Director Price, Andrew and I are both here. Do you
have a visual?"

"I do," he said from his office at the Langley campus.
"This is the closest we've come to eliminating Topaz in
almost a year."

Eleven months, two weeks, five days. Not that she was
counting.

"I dare say this op might be our best and last chance
to finally put an end to this." The tension in Price's voice
resonated clearly over the secure line. "Operation Cujo had
better go off without a hitch or heads are going to roll."

It wasn't going to be Kelly's. She was many things, but
above all, she was a survivor. They should be calling her
the phoenix instead of the ice queen. She would rise again
and again from the ashes, no matter how many times she
got burned.

Andrew cleared his throat. "Yes, sir. Rest assured we
have the situation under control. This ends now."

Don't make promises you can't keep.

Then again, the more promises he made, the easier it

would be to ensure Andrew's head was the one on the chopping block in the event this went sideways.

The one thing she'd learned a long time ago was to never underestimate the enemy, and Hunter Wright was the last foe the CIA wanted to have. He was a former Delta Force operator. The CIA liked to recruit them, but Hunter was special. His contacts ran deep, his resourcefulness was never-ending and his ability to see three moves ahead made him a formidable adversary. Hunter saw angles and possibility where others saw chaos, danger and a problem not worth tackling.

She glanced at the screen.

The strike team had left the boats and was in the water swimming to the island. Almost thirty battle-hardened warriors against eight—seven, really, since one was an adolescent. They had orders to make every effort to ensure no harm came to her.

No matter what, Kelly didn't want to see the young girl end up as collateral damage. She was ruthless, but she'd never intentionally hurt a child or use one as leverage. There were some lines that should never be crossed.

Authorizing Operation Cujo had been a tough call. A painful one.

Topaz had brought this on themselves, and that innocent child, the second they decided to put their self-interests before their country and commit treason.

The strike team had the numbers and the overwhelming firepower, but Hunter would not "go gentle into that good night," as Dylan Thomas once wrote.

He would rage, taking down as many as he could, until his last breath.

HUNTER SIGHTED THROUGH his scope, past the assortment of palms and other vegetation, but his vantage point didn't give him a clear visual of the sea. His line of sight covered the shoreline and up to the house. Ripples tickled the shore, all was calm, but there was no peace. "Give me an update."

"The boats have stopped," Gage said, blowing out a heavy breath. "After checking their gear, they slipped into the water."

"How far out are they?" Hunter asked.

"About three hundred yards. One guy stayed behind."

That man would keep the boats from drifting. "We have three minutes before they come ashore. Have either of you spotted the Predator?"

For a strike mission of this size to eliminate four critical targets and their known collaborators, there would be a drone deployed so the higher-ups could watch the scene unfold on the ground in real time from the safety and distance and comfort of a situation room.

"I have," Dean said. "Eyes in the sky is within visual range. I can see it pretty clearly thanks to the full moon."

It was the sight of a Predator conducting reconnaissance within the past forty-eight hours that had tipped them off that the CIA was about to make their move. A strike team of this magnitude would never be sent in without first verifying the targets' identities and confirming they were on-site.

The Predator was blind to Hunter and his men. The house was currently empty, though it wouldn't appear as such. Eight heat signatures would be detected inside.

A calm stole over him as he closed his eyes and searched his gear by touch, making sure he could put his hands on any part of it without looking, knowing the other two men would do the same thing.

"Is everything ready?" Hunter asked, opening his eyes.

"Yes," they responded at the same time.

Each man had an objective. The three of them had to be coordinated, calculated, precise in their actions.

"Set your timers," Hunter ordered. "Radio silence from here on out until I give the signal."

The radio went quiet as his men complied. This was the calm before the storm. Within minutes they would be in the thick of the action. There was no room for failure. Anything short of success would not only cost them their lives, but also jeopardize the others on the mainland, who were counting on them.

Movement in the water close to shore had him tightening his grip on the long-range rifle. He was capable of taking down targets a mile out, but tonight he needed to bide his time and draw them into the trap they'd set.

After Hunter had found the GPS tracker the CIA had planted when Dean arrived, he knew it would come to this. An incursion on the island. The only way to save his team and clear their names was to face the onslaught head-on. No more running. No more hiding. No more evasive action.

Now they were playing offense.

Twenty-five men emerged from the water, dressed in tactical dry suits, carrying assault weapons, wearing night-vision goggles. Red laser-sight beams painted the night. All those men were prepared to shed blood and ensure no one on his team survived.

Hunter caressed the trigger of his weapon, tamping down his dangerous emotions. He ached to take them out one by one, but with the first shot fired, Hunter's team would lose the upper hand. Without surprise on their side, things would get far more dangerous. They needed to keep the advantage at all costs if they were going to win this battle.

Chapter Two

Conducting a successful operation required the ability to juggle several balls at once, never dropping a single one, while staying focused on the objective. It took training and talent and the gift of knowing when to listen to one's gut.

"Connect the Predator mission commander to the call," Kelly said to Andrew.

"Hold the line, Director, while I patch them in," Andrew said to Price before dialing.

The two-person Predator crew that consisted of a pilot and a sensor operator, a company-grade officer and senior airman respectively, were sitting in a Conex box out in the desert at Nellis Air Force Base. One or both were probably wired from energy drinks.

"This is First Lieutenant Matthews," a female voice said.

"Kelly Russell, here, as well as the director."

"Yes. We're in position."

When Predator missions were conducted in daylight, following a car or target, they always flew too high to be spotted or heard. At night, though, a false sense of confidence had a tendency to set in.

"What's your altitude, Lieutenant?" Kelly asked.

"We are at a half-nautical-mile standoff at eight thousand feet."

"You're a little close, aren't you?" Two nautical miles at twelve thousand feet would've given Kelly a warm and fuzzy. She didn't expect Hunter to be awake at this hour, but there was no sense in taking unnecessary chances.

This wasn't good.

"We were briefed there was no danger of the target catching sight of us, much less hearing our engines, ma'am," Lieutenant Matthews said.

Kelly stiffened, her pulse spiking. "Briefed by whom?"

"SAC Chief Clark, ma'am."

Andrew pressed his lips together, avoiding eye contact with her for an interminable moment. "It's three o'clock in the morning," he finally said, trying to muster a dismissive tone. "Topaz has lowered their guard thinking they've gotten away with it. They don't have anyone on watch. They're all asleep in their comfy beds."

"We hope," she said, knowing that there were no guarantees.

Andrew's scoffing laughter slithered under her skin. "The Predator's altitude is fine and won't have any impact on the mission."

Every factor, every tiny detail could have an impact on the outcome of an operation. This was only further proof to substantiate why his head should roll and not hers.

Taking a deep breath, she refused to let Andrew distract her. She wasn't going to be sidetracked by someone else's incompetence. So, she let it go. For now.

Andrew watched her a moment before taking a seat at the conference table and facing the monitor.

She turned her full attention to the op in progress on the screen. There was a picture in picture. The larger one was the real-time Predator footage, and the smaller picture that was set off in the upper right corner showed the feed from Zulu Prime's body camera.

Zulu team ascended from the water, weapons at the ready, and swept up the beach, approaching the house.

"Here we go," Kelly said, her gaze glued to the monitor.

Silence filled the room.

Thus far, the sneak attack was going smoothly, as planned, and that's what worried her. The men moved unimpeded. No concealed claymore mines were tripped and detonated. No hidden dangers emerged.

Yet the sinking feeling that something bad was going to happen churned inside her.

"Switch to thermal imaging," Kelly said to the Predator commander.

On the screen, the display changed. Twenty-five men became glowing images as they moved in a single line up the beach.

There were heat signatures in the house. Eight. The same number that had been detected earlier.

Still, warning prickled her skin. She scanned the surrounding area, not only for the telltale orange-red glow of people hiding in wait to launch an ambush, but also for any black holes—a clear indicator that someone was deliberately masking their heat signature.

Though someone shrewd, a seasoned operative like Hunter, would know how to effortlessly disappear without a trace.

Maybe she was being paranoid, looking for a trap where there was none.

She had played out this operation evening after evening in her head, envisioning the outcome, and she needed this victory so badly she could taste it on the tip of her tongue.

"Satisfied with the thermal imaging, Kelly?" the director asked.

Not by a long shot, but what could she say? *I've got a bad feeling this op is going to backfire in our faces.*

To get the director and Andrew to listen, she needed something concrete, not simple conjecture of what she guessed was going on. They already thought she was losing her cool. She couldn't have them thinking she was losing her nerve as well. "Yes, sir."

"Switch it back," the director said, "so I can see what's happening."

The Predator crew toggled back to the first sensor.

Some of the tactical strike team mounted the porch steps swiftly yet methodically while the others maneuvered around to the back of the house. Four climbed up onto the roof of the porch, prepared to go in from the top floor.

The men halted a moment.

"Zulu Thirteen, are you in position?" the voice of Zulu Prime, the team leader, filled the situation room.

They could listen in on the strike team's comms, and their end was muted to them. Kelly would only speak to them if absolutely necessary. It was better to let those mercs focus and do their job.

"In position," another deep, low voice said. "Sweeping our entry point."

Kelly's fingers tingled from unease. Drawing in a calming breath, she rubbed her father's ring for good luck.

THE STRIKE TEAM had swept up the beach headed to the big white house. Hunter's home. The place where they'd held family dinners, gathered to talk and to play games. Where they had hatched this plan and discussed the intricacies and potential complications and strategized various scenarios at length.

This was the one constant that would not vary. Any tactical team sent would go for the main house, the location of the signal, and begin eliminating targets there before expanding their search.

Finger on the trigger, Hunter breathed deep, steady, slow.
Hold.
Hold.

His men would do likewise. The smallest slipup, any premature act, and everything would be ruined. Their one chance at this would be lost. No matter how tempted they might be to leap into action. Their discipline and training would ensure they waited until the enemy was in the kill zone.

Dean had come up with this snare, and Zee's fiancé, a former Navy SEAL, had helped him put the components in place.

The covert operators crept up to the house and surrounded the perimeter. One outside light that Hunter had deliberately left on blinked out into darkness. That meant the power had been cut.

Ten men moved, silent as ghosts, up the steps and onto the porch. The point man raised his fist, giving the signal for them to stop. Then he pressed fingers to his ear. To his Bluetooth comms device. Probably listening and waiting for the others to get into place at the back door of the house. Four men climbed the roof of the porch.

The men huddled at the front entrance pulled out a device and slipped it under the door. A camera. They were checking for trip wires and booby traps.

Smart, but Hunter had anticipated that, and it wouldn't be enough to help those mercenaries.

A minute later, the point man waved two fingers forward, giving the directive to breach.

This was it. Hunter sighted through his scope. "On my mark," he whispered into his comms. "We're going to rain hell down from on high."

THE SITUATION ROOM was quiet enough to hear a pin drop. Tense and watchful, Kelly waited. She clutched the back of the chair she stood behind and dug her manicured nails into the cushy leather. The *ticktock* from a clock on the wall that still worked reverberated through her.

Andrew propped his forearms on the table, clasping his hands almost as if in prayer, and leaned in toward the screen.

Zulu team had cut the power, but surely Hunter had an alarm system with a backup battery. The alarm would go off, screaming like banshees, the second the team breached the house, waking everyone inside. Zulu would have to move fast. That was why they had men positioned on the upper floor.

About a hundred things could go wrong, and there was only one way this would go right. Everything had to work exactly as planned.

"All clear," Zulu Prime said.

"All clear," Thirteen responded.

Zulu Prime gave the signal. The front door was busted in.

An alarm went off, the screeching sound over their comms rubbing her already raw nerves like sandpaper. The team rushed inside, and the Predator lost visual of them.

Quickly, she typed in commands on the keyboard to swap the picture-in-picture screens, giving the team leader's body cam footage the larger display.

Choppy orders from Zulu and curt responses bounced back and forth across the line. The heavy thud of boots pounding across a floor filled her ears as they searched the house. Doors opened and closed as they called out *clear*, notifying the others a room was empty.

"Damn, that isn't good," someone said. "This is Zulu Five. There's no one upstairs."

"What?" Zulu Prime asked, slowing down as he spoke. "We have confirmed heat signatures up there."

"They put SmartDummies in the beds."

Thermal manikins. Human models designed for scientific testing that could be programmed to reach twenty to thirty degrees Fahrenheit over ambient room temperature. They were hard to come by unless you had the right connection.

But if the eight individuals they had surveilled while doing recon weren't in the house, then where were they?

Zulu Prime eased forward into the next room. There was something stacked up on the center of a table with a blinking light.

"What is that?" Andrew asked, peering at the monitor.

Zulu Prime drew closer to the object. "Oh, no." His tone sent chills up Kelly's spine. "Get out! Get out! Retreat!" He whirled around and ran for the hall.

The airwaves cracked like a living thing. A series of loud pops resonated followed by a hissing sound.

"Halothane," someone said.

The men in front of Zulu Prime dropped like puppets with their strings cut. A split second after, Prime fell, too.

Then in the smaller picture window, an explosion ripped through the air behind the house.

What was that? A generator?

She checked the feeds from the other body cameras. The majority of the team was down. Knocked out in one fell swoop.

Hunter must've had canisters of halothane hidden throughout the whole house. The clear, colorless gas had a sweet chloroform-like odor. The amount needed to flood the place would leave those men nauseous and vomiting with chills and severe headaches once they woke up.

Shock seized her every muscle as the undeniable reality hit her. Zulu had walked into a trap set by Hunter. He'd known. Somehow that man had known they were coming, and rather than flee with his tail tucked between his legs, he'd stood his ground and fought.

Andrew hung his head, holding it in his hands.

Kelly put the Predator footage back on the main screen.

The Zulu stragglers who hadn't been incapacitated were racing down the beach, desperate to reach the water. Muzzle flashes erupted on the screen right before three individuals emerged out of nowhere. Lighting up the beach with live rounds and tracer fire were Hunter and two others. Her guess, it was Gage and Dean.

Crafty devils. They were using classic guerrilla warfare tactics to level the battlefield. A show of force to make her think twice. But she would not be so easily deterred.

Even as part of her recognized their elite skills and unwilling pride swelled in her heart, the other part of her loathed them for being the bane of her existence.

To think her father had held Hunter in such high esteem, thought he might make a suitable partner for her if he ever left the CIA and became a contractor. An equal in every way. Provided she dared to open herself to a relationship.

If her dad could see the traitor Hunter had become, one who was besting her, he'd roll over in his grave.

Aghast, she watched the remaining men from Zulu fall one after the other and eventually stop moving.

Suddenly, the beach went dark. Except for the blazing inferno behind the house.

"This can't be happening," Andrew whispered, on the brink of panic. "This *can't* be happening."

But it was happening. To her.

No battle plan survives contact with the enemy. The axiom her father had ingrained in her slid through her head.

"When a plan falls apart and mistaken suppositions

come back to bite you, be prepared to sink your teeth into something—or someone," her father had told her.

Shaking her head, Kelly snapped out of her shocked stupor. She whipped out a secure cell phone, a burner, and hit the only number programmed on speed dial. "It's me," she said when it was answered.

"Do I have a green light?" the baritone voice on the other end asked with a hint of twisted amusement. The *thwomp, thwomp, thwomp* of rotator noise played in the background.

"You are cleared hot to go. Topaz doesn't leave that island alive."

She heard the smile in his voice as he said, "Yes, ma'am. It'll be my pleasure."

Kelly disconnected, and nausea bubbled in her stomach. Had she just unleashed a bigger devil than the one she was trying to catch?

Andrew turned to her as if waking from a trance. "Wh-who was that? Who were you talking to?"

"Beta team." Her contingency plan. "I had them keep out of Zulu's sight." And far from Andrew's purview. "They're two minutes from having boots on the island." They were coming in by helicopter and would rappel in.

Beta wasn't led by the best of the best. Their team leader was the worst of the worst, as in bad to the bone. He was an unscrupulous man who had no honor, cared nothing about collateral damage and would go through his own grandmother to get the target if the payday were big enough.

But desperate measures and all.

"Maybe this can be salvaged, after all," the director said. "Good thinking, Kelly."

She wanted to thank him, but that would've been premature. Her Beta team had to get to that island ASAP and finish the mission objective first. In the event the tide didn't turn in her favor, she needed to be prepared.

Kelly beckoned to one of the marines, and once he was close enough, she leaned in. "Prepare to lock up in case we need to make a hasty exit. Then have the vehicles ready and waiting," she said in a hushed tone.

"Yes, ma'am." The marine left the room.

Andrew stood, his mouth agape, his face mottled red, his eyes narrowed, seething. "You…you had a backup team and didn't tell me? How could you keep this from me? I should have been informed."

"I don't answer to you." She cut her gaze to him. "You work for me, not the other way around. Remember?"

Chapter Three

They did it. Their plan had worked, and they'd gotten rid of the private army that had been sent to terminate them.

This was a temporary victory, since the war had yet to be won. Hunter wasn't deluding himself about their situation, but he would gladly take the win.

As they took the slightest moment to catch their breath, he didn't allow himself to relax. He stayed tense, ready for anything. They still had to make the trek to the other side of the island to reach their egress point and get away without the Predator tracking them.

"Hey," Gage said, looking around, "do you hear that?"

"No, what is it?"

Gage tilted his head back and searched the sky.

"There!" Dean pointed. "We have incoming."

Hunter followed the direction Dean had indicated.

A black helicopter was inbound. A tactical stealth model.

The hairs on his arms and the nape of his neck lifted as he experienced a disconcerting sense of déjà vu. In the moonlight and with the open doors, it was easy to make out a secondary strike team with men strapped in as well as riding the external benches, locked and loaded, coming in hot and heavy.

"A damn backup team?" Hunter's rough estimate was

ten men in the helicopter. There might be more in that bird. He wouldn't know for certain until they dropped in. But he wasn't sticking around long enough to find out.

The ice queen was gunning for them. That was for sure. She'd had a secondary strike unit waiting in the distance just in case the first failed. If there had been any question in his mind that she was responsible for setting them up, it was now gone.

Without a shadow of a doubt, she wanted Hunter and his people dead.

His fury was a hot fire, and this only stoked the flames to burn hotter.

Hunter tore his gaze from the helicopter. "Those men will be overhead and rappelling down within two minutes."

"I take it we're not sticking around to greet those guys," Dean said.

"Definitely not." Hunter wasn't one to get rattled. Panicking never solved a problem. Every step they needed to take was solid in his mind. "Go to your hidey-holes and grab your thermal imaging shielding. They can't track what they can't see." He glanced at his watch. "You have sixty seconds. Meet me at the rendezvous point. Hustle, hustle!"

They dispersed, taking off in different directions. Hunter bolted through sand and grass to the tree stand. He climbed the trunk faster than a monkey. Inside the platform, he tore off the DIY shielding from the top and around the sides of the stand. He tossed it over the edge, down thirty-five feet, hoping it didn't break apart on the branches of the trees below, and then he leaped off the platform with his rifle in hand.

Jumping was easy. Anyone could jump. Landing without breaking multiple bones was the trick. He plummeted through fronds, branches whipping at his face and arms.

It was all he could do to keep one arm in front, preventing the branches from hitting him in the eye.

The ground rushed up at him. He landed on the balls of his feet and into a tuck and roll unscathed. Luckily, his shielding remained intact.

The Predator wouldn't be able to track them with thermal, but it had other sensors that would still detect their movement. The smoke from the explosion would help cover their trail, but they would not be invisible.

The faster they moved, the higher the odds of them surviving this second-wave attack.

The *thwomp, thwomp* from the rotor blades drawing closer pounded in his ears, driving his pulse harder. A crew of former Special Forces turned guns for hire was about to descend on them, and he'd already played his trump card.

Taking out the enemy was no longer the priority. They needed to get off this island. Now.

The helicopter was directly over the beach. Four ropes dropped and dangled from the bird.

Scooping up the thermal shielding and wrapping it around himself, he hustled toward the rendezvous point before incoming gunfire was bearing down on him and tearing up the foliage around his head.

Hunter was highly trained and had a laundry list of skills, but dodging a bullet wasn't one of them. He sprinted through the thick undergrowth. Fifty yards north and thirty yards west. That's where they were meeting.

As he raced through the small patch of jungle, his pulse throbbed in his head, his heart hammering steady as a metronome despite the danger. Mentally, he kept count of how far he'd traveled and instinctively knew when to turn. He shoved branches out of his way, leaping over a shrub, and pressed on to the other beach.

Bursting through the dense vegetation, Hunter caught

sight of Dean, who was waiting and geared up, ready to go. But where was Gage?

Time was of the essence. If they got embroiled in a shoot-out with those commandos, it wouldn't bode well for them. The only way off the island in that event might be in a body bag.

But there was no way he was leaving any of his people. One team, one fight. No man would be left behind on his watch.

Four men attached to the ropes dangling from the helicopter and rappelled down, disappearing on the other side of the trees near the house. Four more prepared to follow.

Come on. Where are you?

"Get going," Hunter said to Dean. "I'll stay behind and wait for him."

Dean shook his head. "We stick together. If that team catches up and things get hairy, you'll need me in a fight."

This was what Hunter loved about his unit. Any of them would sacrifice for the sake of the team, and no one put their own needs first. They'd been together for nearly a decade and operated better than a well-oiled machine.

An extra man with a gun could make a world of difference if it came down to that, but Hunter was going to do everything in his power to ensure it didn't. "Get in the water. Now. That's an order."

Gage sprinted from the tree line, armed and cloaked in his thermal imaging shield.

Good man. Saved Hunter from going back to look for him.

Gage ran up to them breathless. "They're not far behind." He panted. "They'll be on us any minute."

Hunter and Gage dug out the equipment they needed from their packs. They put on fins and slipped diving masks over their faces, the same as Dean had already done.

The thudding of footfalls in the woods headed their way grew louder in tandem with the whoosh of branches.

Staying in motion, not allowing distraction, they shoved their arms through the straps of their oxygen tanks and put the regulators in their mouths.

Each of them grabbed a DPV—diver propulsion vehicle—and ran for the water.

Gunfire kicked up behind them, smacking into bark and spitting into the sand.

Fire bit into his arm, and he felt the hot trickle of blood but paid it no mind. It was a flesh wound, and he'd have to worry about it later.

Once they were deep enough, they dived into the dark water just as a barrage of bullets followed them under. Slugs speared through the current around them.

Holding the small yet powerful DPVs by the handles, they switched them on and zipped off. Gage and Dean both held steadfast, and if either was injured, Hunter saw no sign of it.

The underwater scooters towed them through the sea, allowing them to ride in the slipstream, away to a safe distance. Normally it only had a top speed of nine miles per hour, but their former SEAL, John Lowry, had brought his skills to bear and upgraded the motors to go three times that speed.

The Predator drone wouldn't be able to detect them in the water at their current depth.

Using his GPS, he charted their course and held the line. They were twenty-five miles from the mainland, but they had someone waiting to pick them up in a boat seven miles out at a prearranged location.

A red light in the water came into sight. It hung from the boat that was there to pick them up.

They slowed their speed, and once they were close

enough, they cut the engines. Hunter surfaced first and climbed onto the waiting motorboat. He dropped to a knee under the Bimini top, which consisted of a metal frame supporting canvas that was open on the sides, covering a portion of the boat.

Hope Fischer, Gage's girlfriend, and Kate Sawyer, the love of Dean's life, hurried to his side, taking his oxygen tank and other equipment once he'd removed it and setting everything to the side.

"Are you all right?" Hope asked. "Is everyone okay?"

"I believe so."

Kate gave him a quick once-over. She was a veterinarian and for the duration of this mission also their emergency medic. A role she wasn't thrilled about, since she'd reminded them a hundred times about the difference between animals and people, but she was willing to pitch in and help in any way she could.

"Your arm," Kate said, examining his wound.

Hunter put a hand on her shoulder. "It's not serious. It can wait."

Dean climbed up next, followed by Gage. Neither appeared injured.

Relief flooded Kate's face as she went to Dean's side and took his tank.

Hope threw her arms around Gage's neck before he could take the regulator out of his mouth. She pressed herself to him, getting the front of her clothing soaked. "Thank God you're okay."

Drawing back and giving him a chance to catch a breath, she helped him get the tank off and slipped the diving mask from his face. She ran her hands over him, inspecting him, to be sure he hadn't gotten hurt.

"I'm good." Gage put a palm to her cheek, calming her. "We're all fine."

"We were so worried," Hope said. "From here it looked like World War III had broken out on the island. My head started spinning, and horrible scenarios raced through my mind. What if something happened to you? What if I didn't get a chance to see you again? To tell you how much I love you. To tell you that I want to spend the rest of my life with you. Oh, Gage." Tears streamed down her face as she trembled. "I'm pregnant."

"What?" Gage gaped at her.

Everyone else already knew or had guessed. Everyone except Gage.

Hope had been a ball of nerves about telling him. They'd only been a couple for a few months, thrown together by life-or-death circumstances. Their love was new and blossoming under the harshest of conditions. It only added to her anxiety that Gage never spoke about fatherhood as something he wanted.

Their situation was complicated.

It was high time she'd told him, but Hunter hadn't expected it to be like this.

"There were so many times I tried to tell you," Hope said, "but the timing never seemed right, and I thought that if I waited there would be this perfect moment. Only it didn't come, and then I realized I could lose you in all this."

"Honey." Gage wrapped her in a tight embrace. Shock was tattooed on his face.

Dean ran a hand over Kate's hair with love gleaming in his eyes. He gave her a quick kiss and then exchanged a look with Hunter. They both understood Hope was in a fragile place emotionally. One wrong word from Gage could turn her into a ticking bomb when they needed everyone to be solid and focused.

"Are you mad?" Hope pulled back and stared at Gage. "I was so used to receiving a text message and a phone call from my doctor's office when I was due to get my next contraceptive shot. But we came here, leaving our cell phones behind. I didn't think about it, and when I did, it was too late. Because I was late. Are you upset?"

"I'm not mad or upset, just…surprised. It takes two to make a baby, honey. I love you. You're everything to me. Both of you." He put a hand on her stomach, and she sobbed harder, but they were tears of joy.

Crisis averted. Hunter exhaled in relief.

With that settled, he moved to the front of the boat and got behind the wheel. He turned the key, firing up the engine, and moved the handle into the forward position, taking off.

Once they made it to the hotel, they would regroup with the others and go over Zee's intel. Then Hunter would do something no one in the CIA would expect.

He was going home to Virginia to snatch the ice queen from her ivory tower and confront her. Finally find out why she had betrayed them, upending all their lives.

Nothing on earth would stop him.

Or save *her*.

"MA'AM," THE BARITONE voice said over the speaker, "the targets have escaped. The Predator lost them in the water. They could be making their way to any number of port cities along the coast or heading to a different island. Do you want us to search the remainder of the islet to be sure no one else is here besides the other team?"

Hunter was too smart and cared too much about his people to leave any behind on the island. But she wasn't in a position to take chances. "Search the island." It wouldn't take them long. The patch of land was small, and Hunter's people had been the only inhabitants. "If you find anyone, keep them alive for questioning. Then meet me at my hotel. There's a helipad on the roof you can use."

She hadn't determined yet whether they would fly back Stateside with her or stay in Venezuela.

The first team would be able to make their own way home. They still had a man out on the water with their boats.

"Understood, ma'am." The Beta team leader disconnected.

This was an unmitigated disaster. Topaz had been within her grasp, and now they were in the wind and on the run once more. She drew in a slow, steady breath on a count of four and released it in the same four-count manner to keep from busting a blood vessel.

Hunter and his people would leave the country as soon as possible, but while they were still here, this wasn't over. CCTV was prevalent in this country. More so than in the United States. After a major Chinese telecommunications company helped the Venezuelan government construct an advanced citizen surveillance program, there were eyes and ears everywhere.

"Director, will you hold? I need to patch in an analyst," Kelly said.

"Go ahead."

She entered the code that would connect the analyst she had standing by in Langley to the call. "This is Deputy Director Russell."

"Yes, ma'am," Ebony Williams said. She was a veteran analyst who not only kept her composure under pressure but thrived in the high-ops environment.

"I need you to concentrate the full force of our facial recognition program here. I suspect all four targets may be within country. Tap into the Venezuelan big brother program," she said, referring to the robust surveillance infra-structure already established, "and find them."

"I'll do my best."

She needed more than her best. She needed a mira-cle. "Also, keep an eye out in case they use any of their known aliases." That would be highly unlikely. Consid-ering Hunter had time to procure thermal manikins, his team would surely have impeccable fake credentials. This was a shot in the dark, but one she needed to take. "Let me know the second you find anything."

"Of course."

She disconnected the analyst from the call.

"Kelly, Andrew," the director said, "I want you back on a plane to Virginia. As soon as possible."

Keeping up the pretense that she had this under con-trol and that her nerves weren't screaming, she mustered an even-keeled tone for the director and an unflappable expression for Andrew. "But, sir, they're still here within country. I'm certain of it. Our window to find them be-fore it's too late is small." And shrinking every minute.

"Your Beta team will find them. You can give them in-structions from anywhere in the world."

She straightened, rolling her shoulders back, and gave the hem of her suit jacket a little tug down. "Of course."

"Update me with your ETA from the airport," the di-rector said. "As soon as you land, I want to see you both in my office. I don't care what time it is. Am I clear?"

She fiddled with her father's ring. "Crystal, sir." At least it was a good thing she'd had the foresight to prepare to close the embassy, though, given more time she was cer-tain she could make headway in finding the Topaz unit.

The director hung up, leaving a dial tone since she had already cut the Predator crew from the call earlier.

The flight would give her plenty of time to formulate

her thoughts and put together an argument that would protect her. An even more pressing concern was finding Hunter and his cohorts. They were in some coastal city or town. Sooner or later, they would expose themselves, make the slightest mistake, and Beta team would have them.

She had to believe that.

"I know what you're thinking," Andrew said through clenched teeth, rising from his chair, fiery daggers shooting from his weasel-like eyes, his tone blistering.

"If you're a mind reader, I'm the tooth fairy." She gathered her things. "I suggest you put what talent you do have to better use than trying to infer what's going through my head, considering I could outthink you with a concussion."

"You're going to try to pin the blame for your fiasco on my head!"

"I plan to do no such thing." Going for Andrew's jugular would be too obvious. No, she would not be reduced to a game of pointing fingers and sniping at one another in the director's office.

To save her career, she needed to get Andrew to dig his own grave.

"If you go after me in front of the director, so help me, I'll get you and make you pay, you lying bit—"

"Language, Andrew," she said, cutting him off in a smooth voice deliberately modulated by her Ivy League education and years of breeding. "We're both professionals capable of proper decorum, even under the most trying of circumstances. Such vulgarity is beneath us. Besides, you wouldn't know how to *get me* if you had step-by-step instructions." She slung the strap of her purse on her shoulder and fixed him with an icy stare that made him recoil. "I never thought I'd ever have to say this to you, much less think it, but pull yourself together."

A trickle of sweat slithered down her back as she

grabbed her things and spun on her heel. She hated confrontation. It always made her anxious, jittery to the point her hands often shook, and that was the reason she tended to clench them or fold them in her lap. That didn't mean she hadn't learned how to spar verbally. She could hold her own with the best of them.

Kelly strode out the door, headed for the stairs. The only reason she dared turn her back on Andrew without fearing he'd literally stab her in it was the marine standing as a silent sentinel in the room with a loaded sidearm holstered on his hip. She'd brought the military contingent to protect her from all hostile forces—including Andrew.

Chapter Four

In the hotel suite in Caracas, Hunter's entire team gathered around him, as well as John, Zee's fiancé, Hope and Kate. The only one missing from their little tribe was Olivia. The eleven-year-old was asleep in one of the connecting bedrooms.

Zee, their hacker extraordinaire, had messed with the city surveillance system along a specified route as well as the hotel security cameras to ensure they wouldn't be detected once out of the water and making their way to the hotel room.

After Hunter finished giving everyone an unfiltered sitrep—situation report—Hope and Kate, the two civilians unaccustomed to this precarious lifestyle, turned to their partners and clung to them. The embraces were poignant and full of gratitude, highlighting just how close they'd come to death. Zee and John, a former SEAL with more than seventeen years under his belt, exchanged a look that was no less sentimental, brimming with such affection that it made something inside Hunter ache.

They all had someone they loved. Someone who suited them, someone to bolster them through this dark time.

Hunter envied them and was happy for them at the same time. Most of all, it fortified his determination to clear their names so that they could have the futures they deserved.

No such thing as happily-ever-after for a man like him, and that was okay, so long as his team, his family, got theirs.

For one night back in Boston, he'd thought he might have found what every other member of his team had—a partner worth fighting for. The makings of a love you would do anything to protect. But he couldn't have been more wrong.

He had been nothing but a one-night stand to satisfy the ice queen's curiosity.

"What's our next move?" Hope asked with an arm around Gage's waist, leaning against him while he had an arm slung over her shoulder, clearly wanting to keep her close as well.

Hunter stretched his bandaged arm, gritting his teeth through the ache. "I'm not exactly sure." He needed an update from Zee first. To analyze all the available information before making a decision. "But it's looking as if we're going Stateside."

"Won't it be more dangerous there?" Kate asked. Dean stood behind her with her head tucked under his chin and his arms wrapped around her in a loving cocoon.

"Yes, it will be." He couldn't sugarcoat the reality of it. "But there's no way around it. The proof we need to clear our names will be back home. Zee, you'll need to initiate the diversion protocol."

With a nod, she went to her laptop, which was already powered up. She hit a few keys and pressed Enter. "It's done."

Zee was a computer genius. Her program would have the CIA looking for them in all the wrong places, giving them an opportunity to get back to Virginia without being apprehended.

He'd start with the ice queen and work his way to the evidence that would prove they had never specifically targeted that Afghan official. Topaz had been set up to believe the official had been working with a terrorist and financing him. At a supposed meeting between the official and the terrorist, Khayr Faraj, Topaz had been instructed to eliminate Faraj. But instead of taking out the next Osama bin Laden, the explosion had killed the Afghan official, who was the head of military intelligence, and a tribal leader.

All based on intelligence from their team handler. The ice queen. As if that hadn't been bad enough, their egress plan out of the country had been leaked. They had barely made it out of Afghanistan alive.

They later found out that Faraj had never even been there, and the Afghan official hadn't been corrupt. He and the tribal leader had been innocent men.

None of it made sense, and it was time he got answers.

Before he could make a concrete decision about their next move, he needed solid intel he could rely on, and there was no one he trusted more to provide it than Zee.

"What have you learned?" Hunter asked her.

"Kelly Russell is here. In Caracas."

His heart stuttered, and the room spun a moment. That was a bombshell he hadn't been prepared for. Why had she left the safety of Langley? Did she want to see his dead body with her own two eyes, up close and personal?

"Where?" he finally managed to ask.

Pressing her lips tight together, Zee lowered her head. Dark spiral curls curtained her light brown face. "I think it's best you don't know."

"What!" Kelly was here, in the same city, with boots on the ground, and Zee didn't want to spill the location? What was she thinking?

They'd never get answers without going through Kelly first.

He stormed up to Zee, but John stepped in front of him

with a palm raised. John was a big guy, bigger than Hunter. A Special Forces operator who was prepared to kill to keep Zee safe. Not that she was in any danger in this room.

"We know this is important," John said, using a careful tone, "but…"

"But what?" Hunter snapped.

Zee raised her head and met his gaze. "You're too emotional where Kelly is concerned."

Hunter rocked back on his heels. "She set us up—of course I'm emotional. We all are."

"I think it's more than that for you," Zee said. "I think it's been a lot more since you two went TDY to Boston together."

A chill skittered across his skin. How could she possibly know?

Hunter had been so careful. Played it subzero cool when they had gotten back after the way Kelly had thrown up an Arctic wall between them.

Looking around the room at the others, he noticed Gage and Dean exchanging baffled looks.

Well, at least they hadn't known until now.

"Wait a minute." Dean let go of Kate and stepped up to him. "You slept with her? You slept with the ice queen?"

Gage moved away from Hope and joined Dean. "The woman who set us up?"

In his defense, he had slept with her before she'd set them up. "Once," Hunter admitted reluctantly, struggling not to turn away from them in shame. He had to face this.

"In Boston," Zee said, closing the circle around him.

Gage looked at Zee. "How did you know?"

Yeah, how did she?

"When you two got back, you were both…weird. Staring at the other when you shouldn't have been, keeping your distance more than normal. There was tension in the room when you two were together. Sexual tension. And you got snippy, Hunter."

Snippy was never an adjective that should be used to describe him. "No, I was myself."

"You weren't," Zee insisted. "I was going to pull you aside and ask you about it, but then I realized that these two," she said, gesturing to Gage and Dean, "hadn't noticed. So, I figured, maybe I should let sleeping dogs lie."

"Was it only once?" Gage asked with his eyes narrowed.

It had been many times but only during the one night that he'd never wanted to end. Like a fool. "Yes," Hunter said.

Zee shook her head with a reproachful look on her face. "Kelly played you."

"I wasn't played." Hunter bristled, putting his fists on his hips. "I initiated it."

Rolling her eyes, Zee crossed her arms. "She let you initiate it. Probably on the last night of the TDY, right?" When Hunter didn't respond, she said, "I bet she lingered outside her hotel room door after you two had a few drinks down at the bar."

That was true.

"But while you had those drinks, she made physical contact of some kind to let you know subconsciously she'd be receptive to the idea," Zee said. "A hand on your shoulder, perhaps a graze of her fingers across your cheek, leaning into you while she shared something confidential, personal."

Kelly had leaned in, putting her hand on his forearm, which had later brushed his thigh and eventually rested on his knee as she'd talked about her father. Shared with him stories about her dad, a man he'd known and respected. Told Hunter how she wore his ring in remembrance of him.

He'd thought they had connected, bonded, that those intimate gestures had been a natural by-product.

"She was the one who suggested you both go upstairs to your rooms because it was late. Didn't she?"

Thinking back on it, Kelly had made the suggestion. She'd yawned and asked for the check.

"I take it your rooms were conveniently close together," Zee continued as if reading from a seduction playbook. "Either side by side or directly across the hall from each other."

A sickening sensation churned in his gut.

"I bet Kelly could've simply said good-night and gone into her room and that would've been the end of the evening, but she didn't," Zee said. "She lingered in the hall, giving you an opportunity to make a pass at her."

The shoes. Kelly had taken the time to slip off her high heels, and although he'd thought he had been the one stalling, it had been her all along.

Maybe Kelly's motives had been more insidious back then. Perhaps she had slept with him as part of a grander plan to manipulate, use and discard him like trash.

How had he not seen it?

He was a veteran operative, knew what to expect from the enemy.

Kelly had been his blind spot. A supposed ally he'd been attracted to. Not just physically. Yes, she was gorgeous, but she was also brilliant and fierce.

Deadly as a switchblade. He always should've known that she'd cut him some day, and she was now going after his jugular.

"You had sex in her room, didn't you?" Zee said, driving her point home. "On her terms."

Kelly had lured him in and played him. She'd even had a new box of condoms in the nightstand. He had been so excited, so thrilled to be with her that he'd chalked it up to her wanting him, too.

"Damn it!" Hunter said, hating himself for the outburst.

"See?" Zee gestured at him. "You're too emotional where she's concerned."

"Where is she?" Hunter demanded.

"This would be a mistake," Zee said. "Going after her like this. You need to be calm. In control."

"Where. Is. She."

Still, Zee hesitated.

"If I have to go outside and get myself locked up in a Venezuelan jail to get her in front of me because you won't follow an order, then so be it." He knew how to pick handcuffs, and he didn't need to break out of a jail cell to wrap his hands around Kelly's throat and squeeze the truth from her lips.

"Okay, I'll tell you. But for the record, I think this is a colossal mistake."

"Duly noted. Where?"

"If you're going to go, you can't go alone, agreed?" Zee asked.

If? Nothing short of a nuclear bomb detonating would stop him from going. Zee was looking out for him, trying to protect him from himself, but her concern only served to annoy him. He was a big boy and had experience channeling his rage when necessary so that it worked for him rather against.

"Fine," he conceded with a wave of his hand. Although he was *their* team leader, he'd go with a chaperone.

Before giving him the information, Zee added, "Andrew Clark is also here."

Hunter stifled a groan over the insipid man's presence. Clark could certainly complicate things.

"One more thing, and it's *important*." Zee caught his gaze and hesitated.

More important than the fact Kelly Russell was in Caracas? That got his attention. "What is it?"

"The secondary team that Kelly brought in. I tracked them from the airport. There was no way to get a message to you and warn you they were coming." They'd had tight communication protocols to ensure they hadn't inadvertently tipped their hand about the ambush. "But I know who's leading them."

Hunter knew it wasn't going to be good. They had enough to deal with and didn't need any further complications, but if it was as important as Zee claimed, then Hunter needed to know. "Who is it?"

"Mickey Quinlan."

Hunter's stomach roiled as Dean, who wasn't big on religion, made the sign of the cross over himself.

"Oh, man," Gage groaned. "That dude is a lunatic. Why would Kelly hire him?"

Because she was desperate. It was the only reason.

Quinlan wasn't sane. No sane person enjoyed killing as much as he did, but Quinlan could be bought. For the right price. Topaz couldn't afford to use their personal resources on Quinlan, but supposedly there was two million dollars sitting in offshore accounts that they'd never seen or touched.

Maybe Zee could pilfer those funds and put them to good use.

"Where is she?" Hunter asked. Kelly Russell had ruined his life and the lives of the people who meant the most to him. Those standing in this room, shoulder to shoulder with him.

That sin was unforgivable.

Getting to her here, in a country that had a strained relationship and no formal diplomatic ties with the United States, was better than trying to do it on American soil.

"She has a marine detail escorting her," Zee said, stalling.

Speed bumps. Those marines would slow him down, but they wouldn't stop him from getting to her. Nothing would. "I'll handle them. Please don't make me ask you again."

Zee rattled off the name of the hotel and the room number. "I'll go with you."

"No way." John shook his head as his features tightened in a fearsome expression. "You said yourself he's not thinking straight when it comes to that woman."

Zee turned to her fiancé and clasped his shoulders. "That's why Hunter needs me. Gage and Dean won't know where to draw the line with him. They won't see if he's about to go over the edge. It has to be me. Either I go or Hunter doesn't go."

Hunter gave a dark chuckle that carried zero humor in the sound. He was going.

One way or another.

Chapter Five

Hurrying around her hotel room, Kelly finished packing her carry-on. She hadn't brought much with her and had only taken out what was necessary to freshen up before they went to the embassy.

Her cell phone rang. The burner. She could tell by the ringtone.

She took it from her purse and answered. "Yes." Hoping for good news was too much after the events of the past few hours—still, she did pray for the tiniest lead.

"There was no one else on the island," Quinlan said, which didn't come as a surprise to her. "We're here, in the lobby. Drawing quite the audience."

They were hard to ignore. No doubt the staff and other hotel guests in the lobby were staring at them. "Hang tight. I'll be down momentarily."

She wanted to give him his instructions face-to-face, and there was the fact she was still working out what those orders would be.

"We'll be waiting."

She did one last sweep of the room to be sure she hadn't left anything behind, and then she stepped into the hall, where she had two marines standing by just in case Andrew had decided to stop by her room to finish their little chitchat. Nothing like two buff, armed men to make a guy acting on bad judgment think twice.

Not that she needed them to handle Andrew. Her father had ensured she was able to take care of herself by having her trained in Krav Maga and jiujitsu since she was six years old.

Andrew would've needed the marines to get *her* off *him*, but she wasn't foolish enough to lay a finger on him without witnesses to justify any force she might use. He'd have bruises or worse and then it would be his word against hers, along with his injury report. An HR nightmare.

As she made her way to the elevator, her secure work cell rang. She glanced at the screen. It was a Langley number. The generic 703-482-0000 always came up on incoming calls from headquarters. Without the extension she had no way of knowing exactly who was on the other end.

"This is Russell."

"Yes, ma'am," Ebony Williams said, her voice soft yet firm. "I have a lead."

Thank goodness. "What is it?"

"Aliases for all the members of Topaz pinged. They're fleeing Venezuela. By different modes of transportation. One by train, one by bus, one by boat and one by air. All different destinations as well."

Kelly stopped midstride, processing what she'd heard. "You got hits on known aliases for *all four* members of their unit? In the span of an hour?"

"Yes, ma'am."

How odd, and not a good-luck kind of odd.

One member slipping up using a known alias was possible. She'd buy that and check it out, but all four was more than suspect. There was zero chance that the entire team would take such a gamble, and Hunter wouldn't be caught

in such a stupid mistake. Not when they had time to prepare that ambush and escape without a trace.

This was deliberate, calculated. Topaz was trying to
throw them off.

"I'm sending the information to your tactical team on
the ground, Beta, as we speak," Ebony said.

It was protocol for the analysts to follow up on such
leads, and Kelly appreciated initiative, but not in this case.

She hit the call button for the elevator. "No, don't do
that." It would send her strike team on a wild-goose chase,
which she suspected was the point. "The odds of this lead
panning out are slim to none."

Hunter wanted them chasing after their tails instead
of after him.

"I concur with that assessment, ma'am, and wouldn't
have contacted the tactical team, but SAC Chief Clark
asked me to."

"Come again?" Surely Kelly had misheard the woman.
"When did you speak to Clark?"

"A few minutes ago, ma'am. After you and I spoke, the
SAC chief called me and asked me to report all updates to
him first. In fact, he said there was no need to apprise you
of this because you were swamped and he'd handle it, but
I thought it best for me to call you regardless."

Anger flooded through her. "When did Clark give you
the instructions to notify him first?"

Ebony gave the precise time.

Kelly had been in a vehicle separate from Andrew on
the way back to the hotel when that dirtbag tried to cut her
out of the loop on her operation.

"I've documented everything, ma'am," she said, and Kelly
was reminded why she had chosen this particular analyst.

Not someone beholden to Clark, who would forget to
annotate the little things.

"Thank you. As I've said, do not pursue this. It isn't a lead. It's a diversion," Kelly said. "And good work. Keep it up. But from here on out, you call me regarding this matter and only me. I'll deal with Clark."

"Yes, ma'am."

Kelly put her phone away and collected herself, checking her reflection in the steel doors. She smoothed back her chignon, making sure her hair was in place.

The elevator chimed, and the doors opened.

Andrew was inside the car, holding the handle of his suitcase. He flashed a tense grin, looking as cagey and untrustworthy as ever.

Kelly adopted a composed smile—calm, pleasant, tempered and aloof—not hinting at the fury boiling in her veins. Releasing the handle of her hard-shell carry-on, she turned to the marines. "Would you catch the next one and, if you wouldn't mind, please bring my bag down with you."

"Of course, ma'am." One of them took her bag.

Kelly stepped inside the elevator next to Andrew. They had a long, colorful history together, and she was familiar with the man's capabilities as well as his weaknesses. She was going to exploit that to teach him a lesson.

The doors closed and the car went into motion, headed down.

"The secondary strike team is here, waiting in the lobby for me to give them their instructions," she said without mentioning she'd spoken to the analyst.

Andrew was in the dark. Precisely where she wanted him to stay.

"I'm sure they'll get a lead that'll help them track down the team. Surely Topaz is trying to get out of the country. Beta team should check the manifests of the trains, buses, boats, airlines. Leave no stone unturned."

"That is one idea. But I think I'll send them in a different direction." What that direction was, she had yet to figure out.

"It's standard protocol, and it makes the most sense for Topaz to run. You would be wise to listen to my advice. I should be the one leading the Beta team as is. A recommendation I'll make to the director."

So, that was his angle.

"Your advice holds about as much value as a can of poppycock." She let her smile widen, meeting his eyes in the reflection of the shiny doors, wanting to rile him up because he would let his anger override common sense. And he deserved it after pulling that little stunt with the analyst. All the while she paced herself, timing this tête-à-tête to perfection.

The elevator stopped.

"You're a little man with little ideas, Andrew."

The chime sounded.

"If you were wise, you'd stay in your lane before you get mowed down," she continued.

The doors opened.

"I'd hate to see you reduced to roadkill." Kelly stepped forward.

Andrew snatched her arm, jerking her to a stop as he called her the foulest thing one could say to a woman, loud enough to draw attention. But he didn't stop there. "The higher you climb, the harder you'll fall." He tightened his grip, squeezing to intentionally hurt her. "You don't know half as much as you think you do. You'd better watch your mouth and the way you speak to me, or I'll make you regret it."

Kelly caught the gaze of the other marines in the lobby, who were already in motion to assist to her, as well as those on Beta team, to be sure she had witnesses who'd seen that Andrew had put his hand on her in an aggressive manner first.

Then she pivoted, raising the arm that he had snatched up in front of her. She locked her other hand under his wrist, bending and rotating it along with his entire arm. A light kick to the side of his leg at the knee, not hard enough to break a bone, had him crumpling to the floor of the elevator. His wrist and shoulder were wrenched at a painful angle, and his face was twisted in agony.

"If you ever put your hand on me again, I will break it. Do you understand?"

"Y-yeah, yeah, let me go, Kelly." The fear in his eyes told her that her message had been received.

She dropped his wrist and gave her suit jacket a tug at the hem. He clutched his arm to his chest like a wounded animal.

Andrew hated her because she'd been promoted over him to deputy director. It didn't help that she was four years younger, even though she had more experience. The crux of his problem was her sex. She hadn't realized it until her godmother had pointed it out to her. Andrew was never condescending to male colleagues, never called them vulgar names no matter how incensed he became. And in all the years she'd worked with him, she'd never seen him grab another man's arm.

At least he'd think twice before touching her again.

When she turned back around, several marines were in front of the elevator with their hands on the hilts of their weapons. "Are you okay, ma'am?" one asked her.

"I'm fine. But he might need assistance." She hiked a thumb back at Andrew, who was still hissing in pain behind her, and strode off the elevator to Beta team.

Quinlan laughed as she approached him. The sound

was dark and chilling. "Remind me never to get on your bad side."

The joke registered. She was no match for this man in any universe. He was six-two and pure muscle, but so was Hunter Wright, and she was fairly certain the outcome in a melee with Hunter wouldn't be a given. She'd learned how to fight an opponent who was bigger and stronger. The physical factor wasn't what would give Quinlan the winning edge.

The difference wasn't about skill or cunning. They were both highly trained.

It didn't even boil down to the fact that Quinlan was a brutal sociopath who lacked a conscience. Sure, he enjoyed his profession of killing and the only person he ultimately served was himself, but there was a darkness in him that frightened her.

Andrew had been right about one thing. If she was afraid, then everyone else should be quaking in their boots.

"I can take care of him for you." Quinlan gestured with his chin at Andrew, who was being helped out of the elevator. "Put him in a ditch where he'll never be found, and in the event that he is, he'll never be identified. I assure you."

As tempting as the idea was and as vexing as Andrew could be, that wasn't her style. He was still a colleague, even if she didn't respect him and he often got in her way. She didn't hire mercenaries to resolve a difficult working relationship.

The Topaz unit was a special case. She'd love nothing more than to bring them to justice and see the lot of them rot in a supermax prison. But they'd committed treason by killing Afghanistan's head of military intelligence, someone who had been crucial to prevent the Taliban from taking over, and had accepted payment to do so while acting under the guise of the CIA. Putting them on trial, airing dirty laundry along with government secrets and publicly tying the United States to that politically charged crime simply wouldn't happen. Could not happen under any circumstances.

Although she'd never admit it to anyone, this whole mess broke her heart.

Once such fine operatives. How had it come to this?

How had Hunter strayed so far off course?

At her lack of an immediate response, Quinlan added, "I'd even cut you a discount. I never did like him."

"Thanks, but no, thanks. I can handle Andrew Clark."

"Yes, you can." Another grin from him that made her skin crawl.

She glanced around at the prying eyes. "Walk with me. Let's talk in the Suburban."

They left the air-conditioned lobby, briefly transiting through the heat.

"We're not to be disturbed by anyone, not even Clark," she said to the marine standing next to the vehicle before she climbed in and slid across the seat, making room for Quinlan.

He shut the door. "We received partial information from headquarters. Something about a train and a boat. Known aliases used. Do you want us to pursue it?"

"No. It would be a waste of your time."

Quinlan scrubbed a hand over his bald head. "Then what do you want us to do? They're not going to stick around in this country, that's for certain. An island was one thing. But here on the mainland where the surveillance is on steroids, they wouldn't last long," he said, and she had to agree. "Do you think they might try to go Stateside? Head back to Virginia?"

"Go home?"

She would've dismissed the idea as preposterous eleven

months ago. But since Gage and Dean had both been found in towns where they'd grown up, anything was a possibility. Zee had been hiding in a location that contradicted her profile, which had been smart, but still, she'd popped up on their radar as well.

What reason would they have to go back to Virginia?

That would be a huge risk for Topaz to take, and she couldn't see the potential reward.

"Go to the Cayman Islands," she said. "I'll send you the details about their offshore accounts. To our knowledge, some money has been withdrawn, but there's still quite a bit left just sitting there."

If they'd been so brazen as to set foot in the bank before, they'd do it again.

She'd seen video footage of Hunter waltzing into the bank, and the same day, a quarter of a million dollars had been withdrawn from his offshore account.

Almost as if he'd been thumbing his nose at her and the CIA, acting as though he were invincible. It only solidified her determination to catch Hunter and put an end to this travesty, which was a blight on the CIA's record.

"I'd also like you to leave a couple of men behind in Caracas," Kelly said. "To keep their fingers on the pulse of things and to make certain no one from Topaz is able to hide here."

"I'm one step ahead of you. I've reached out to a contact I have in the SEBIN," he said, referring to the internal security force of the repressive intelligence directorate of the country. "He'll keep an eye out. If Topaz pops up, he has men loyal to him who will eradicate the problem."

Quinlan was an outside-the-box thinker.

"Thank you." She gave a slight nod.

"No need to thank me. I'll send you the bill for this add-on."

Of course. Having an inside man in the Venezuelan intelligence service wouldn't be cheap, and Quinlan never acted out of the kindness of his heart.

"Your team should fly with us. We can drop you off." Getting the Beta team into Venezuela and geared up had been a logistical headache. Flying them private would be the most efficient way from here on out.

"Fine. It'll be faster to take the helo to the airport rather than drive, especially with all the attention we're garnering. Clark should ride with us. An open door, faulty seat buckle, a sharp turn—it's possible he takes a tumble and has a convenient accident."

The prospect horrified her.

Kelly plastered on a soft grin while gritting her teeth. "As much as I appreciate your resourcefulness and desire to go above and beyond, he's off-limits."

The corner of his mouth hitched up. "I bet when you return to Langley, you'll look back on this moment and wonder if you should've made a different choice." He chuckled. "No worries. You know my number in case you change your mind."

Andrew was a thorn in her side, right between the ribs. He would make things difficult in the days ahead. The man was an aggravation. Not a criminal or the enemy of the state.

What Quinlan proposed was revolting.

She would never regret doing the right thing.

They hopped out of the SUV to go back inside and take the elevator to the helipad on the roof. As she walked around the vehicle, a shiver skated over her, like a warm finger dipped in honey sliding down her spine.

She was being watched. Considering the circumstances and the gaggle of armed men around her, that wasn't unexpected.

What surprised her to the core was she had the sense

that *he* was watching her. Kelly had only ever gotten that warm sensation when Hunter's gaze had been on her.

Remembering it, him, their time together in the office, in the hotel room, in bed together, sent a bittersweet ache seeping through her.

Whenever they had shared the same airspace, a bright, scorching heat flared to life.

What she felt now was more subtle, distant.

Was he really so reckless as to spy on her in Caracas? Or was she on edge with her senses misfiring?

Turning, she scanned the surrounding area.

PEERING THROUGH HIS SNIPERSCOPE, Hunter adjusted the sight, clarifying the image. He'd been desperate for more than a glimpse of her. Desperate to make her pay.

Now here she was in the flesh. In his crosshairs.

Kelly spun in a slow circle, her forehead creased in concentration as she looked around, giving him a 360-degree view of her, and his gut clenched.

Clad in a tailored ivory suit and wearing bone-colored high heels that showed off her long, lithe legs, she was a vision to behold. Flaming red hair pulled up in an impeccable twist. Thinner than the last time he'd seen her, but her svelte figure was no less captivating. Her complexion was the same color as her suit. Softer. Luminous in the early-morning light.

Stopping, she angled her head in his direction, and he would've sworn that she looked right at him, through him.

His heart locked in his chest.

The odds she'd spotted him on the covered top floor of the nearby parking garage were nil. The sun was to his back, and there wasn't anything to cause a glare on his scope. Of that he was one hundred percent positive. With Zee on his right side and John, who had insisted on tagging along as a backup babysitter, at his left, they'd double-checked to be certain nothing gave away their position.

All Hunter needed to do was squeeze the trigger. Squeeze it and he could end her with one bullet.

His gaze was still trained on her, his finger caressing the trigger, his heart threatening to burst from his chest.

How had she gone from making love to him all night, wrapping herself around him, sharing her cold, dark past, fueling his belief that they'd shared a connection, to feeling nothing for him—besides the desire to see him dead?

"Our hands are tied here," Zee said, dragging him from his torturous thoughts. "She's with Quinlan and his men."

"A few marines would have been tricky, but doable. This?" John grunted. "No way. I'm sorry, Hunter. Going after her here and now is a no-go."

Zee put a firm hand on his shoulder. "She's untouchable."

No one was untouchable. He could reach out with a bullet and touch her right now.

But then he'd never get answers. Never know why.

Without Kelly, he didn't have a chance at tracking down irrefutable evidence that she had set them up. In order to have a future and prevent more teams from coming after them, they had to clear their names.

He had no choice but to let her live. It was the only reason he didn't open fire.

Or so he told himself.

He needed the truth and the proof to substantiate it. He was resolved to be as cold and merciless as necessary in finding it.

Hunter's scope was still locked on her as he watched her.

Quinlan must have said something to Kelly, because she glanced at him as though her attention had been broken. Her lips moved. She gave one last look around before walking into the building with her armed entourage.

Hunter lowered the rifle.

Zee and John were right. For now, there was nothing he could do, even with their help.

But Kelly Russell wouldn't have bodyguards with her 24/7.

Sooner or later, there would be an opportunity to get his hands on her and make her talk. When that happened, he'd be ready to seize it.

"What do you want to do?" Zee asked.

The battle for the day had been won, but those men who had stormed the island were merely foot soldiers. The real war was with Kelly and, by extension, the CIA. It could only be fought in Northern Virginia.

They had to leave Venezuela.

Hunter drew in a heavy breath. "It's time for us to go home."

Chapter Six

Giving her father's ring one final twist on her finger, Kelly crossed her legs at the ankle, seated before the director. She folded her hands in her lap, her back ramrod straight, her expression reserved despite the exhaustion and worry pressing down on her.

Andrew was in the chair beside her, being his usual eager, predictable self. "Did she tell you that she contracted that psycho Mickey Quinlan to head up her Beta team?" Agitation was stamped on his face, his voice hoarse with anger and fatigue. "The man is unhinged. There is an unspoken rule that we aren't to work with him. That alone should tell you she's not exercising sound judgment. She's shooting from the hip in desperation."

Director Price's gaze swung to her. "I'm inclined to agree with Andrew. In light of Quinlan's history, I'm having a hard time understanding this decision, Kelly. He leaves a bloody mess wherever he goes."

"My choice is somewhat unorthodox, I admit." As Price stared at her with his gray eyes, waiting patiently for her to say more, she sat taller and drew a breath. "But it was one I had to make. I didn't have the opportunity to choose the primary strike team or to sign off on them. Look how that turned out."

Andrew shifted uncomfortably in his seat. "The only

reason they weren't successful is because her—" he jabbed a finger in her direction "—former team got one up on us."

"Topaz did." Kelly gave a curt nod. "Because the reconnaissance executed by the Predator crew was compromised. They were given incompetent instructions from a higher-up." Not once had she spoken Andrew's name, or glanced at him, and she definitely hadn't pointed a finger like a five-year-old having a tantrum. "They should've been flying at twelve thousand feet with a standoff of two nautical miles. Those are the instructions I would've given them, but my authority was infringed upon. Topaz must have spotted the drone before the strike team's arrival. That's how they knew we were coming."

From her therapy sessions with her father as a teenager, she'd learned to use *I* statements and to stick with the facts. It was a communication strategy that was less accusatory and allowed for the actual issue to be clearly defined and addressed.

"The Predator mission commander should have known better." Andrew stabbed the arm of his chair as he spoke. "They do this all the time, tracking terrorists. This was no different."

"Until someone made it different by telling them they could disregard normal mission parameters because it didn't matter. Sir, really, is this the drone crew's fault?"

Price clenched his jaw as his gaze slid to Andrew.

"It's her fault," Andrew snapped. "Come on, we both know that. Everyone in this building knows it. I get that she's your favorite pet and you're grooming her to take over someday, but I think this proves she's not up for the task of executing Operation Cujo, much less running this place."

"I'm flabbergasted by this hostility toward me." Sighing with a disappointed shake of her head, she held the director's gaze. "This is the twenty-first century. I'd like to believe this organization won't tolerate the presence of violent misogynists who are incapable of controlling themselves."

"Violent!" Andrew jumped to his feet. "Do you know what this bitch did to me in the hotel elevator? She nearly broke my wrist. Go on, tell him about that."

Language, Andrew.

She didn't have to say a word. The director was well-informed.

Before they'd taken off from Simón Bolívar International, she'd had every single marine who had witnessed what had transpired in the elevator send an email to their immediate supervisor documenting it, and one went so far as to call. Marines worked round the clock. Surely their lieutenant colonel had reached out to the director posthaste.

"You need to calm down," the director said to him.

"Name-calling, the vulgarity." Kelly dropped her gaze to her father's ring. "I find it offensive. This kind of behavior only serves to create a hostile work environment."

"Sit down." The director gestured at Andrew. "And do yourself a favor by shutting up."

Andrew balked, but he lowered himself, silently, into the chair.

"Kelly is spearheading Operation Cujo," the director said, "but she asked to do it alone. You came crying to me, Andrew, wanting to dip your fingers in the pie and get a slice of the success. Well, you mucked things up. The waters are so blurry now, I don't know if she would've accomplished it without your interference. What I do know is that you have been more of a hindrance to her than a help. You are to take a back seat on this going forward and stay out of her way."

"But I should be leading Beta team. I'm the one—"

The director raised his palm. "And I don't ever want you

to use such inappropriate language with a colleague. Right now, I'm not sure who is more unhinged, you or Quinlan."

"Sir," Andrew said on an exhale, making the one syllable sound as if it was deflating.

"Take a couple of days off. Go home. Cool down. Spend some time with your wife. Focus on other things in your life that are important."

His wife had left him six months ago, and Andrew was trying to keep it quiet. He didn't have anyone to go home to.

Then again, neither did Kelly, and the twinge from that emptiness was with her every time she entered her house.

"Work would really be the best thing for me," Andrew said. "I just need a little sleep and I'll be right as rain."

"It wasn't a suggestion." There was an awkward pause as Price stared at him with pity. "That was an order. Go home, why don't you? You never take leave and you've spent years working hours you've never claimed. I don't want you back in this building for seventy-two hours unless you're summoned. Understood?"

Slowly, reluctantly, Andrew nodded and stood. "I want it on the record that I think she shouldn't remain in charge of Operation Cujo. She's unfit."

"Okay. Sure." Price gave him a sympathetic nod. "I will document your personal feelings."

"Not personal feelings. My professional assessment."

"If you push this, then I'll have to document other things. Such as the aggressive behavior you just displayed in my office and your foul language directed at a coworker. Your superior, no less. I'm trying to help you out here. Go home. Get some rest. Enjoy the time with that beautiful wife of yours, and tell Leslie I said hi."

Without a word, Andrew skulked out of the office. Beaten. Tail between his legs.

Kelly actually felt bad for him, even though she shouldn't. He'd behaved horribly, but she understood some of what he might be feeling in this moment beyond the defeat.

She was a workaholic, too. Without this job, this place, what did she have?

The same thing Andrew had. Absolutely nothing.

They sacrificed everything for this job, and not once did she ever question if the heavy toll was worth it.

This was for the greater good of this country, for national security, to make the world a better, safer place. Someone had to do it. Her father had raised her to do this and ensured she had the perfect skill set to be successful.

"Can you handle this?" Price asked her.

"Yes," she said unequivocally, though doubt rattled through her.

She had no choice but to handle it. Everything was on the line. She could not afford to make another mistake. The gamble was that Topaz would mess up before she did. No one was perfect. No matter how much talent they had, everyone got tripped up. To complicate the odds for her, Topaz wasn't working alone. They had assistance from a former Navy SEAL and two civilians. The SEAL worried her. He'd proven to be a formidable force when the CIA had sent a team after Zee.

While Kelly only had herself to rely on.

"I believe in you," Price said. "Don't prove me wrong. You won't survive the scrutiny a second time around if this op goes south."

He didn't mean her career. She'd barely survived eleven months ago. Guilt by association until proven innocent was the way it worked in the hallowed halls of Langley. The one thing that'd saved her had been admitting to her onetime indiscretion with Hunter immediately after it had happened. If their night together had come out in a polygraph in the aftermath of Topaz's treasonous act, she would've been done for.

With a nod, she acknowledged him and stood, smoothing down her skirt.

Then he added, "We can't risk any exposure on this. If Quinlan wreaks havoc, crosses the line, it will fall solely on you."

She wouldn't have it any other way. Theirs was not a risk-free business, and she had rolled the dice on Quinlan. "I'll take full responsibility for his actions. I chose him."

"That you did. Be careful."

"I always am."

IN FAIRFAX, VIRGINIA, Hunter and the others were getting settled in the closest thing to an unofficial safe house. Zee had arranged their lodgings. The woman was not only a genius but also a magician. With a few clicks on her laptop, she'd found a nearly vacant, no-frills budget motel with limited CCTV coverage that was willing to take cash for a short-term stay without asking too many questions. The best part was the location. She'd rented a block of rooms to ensure their privacy, and they had quick, easy access to both I-66 and I-495. In the span of a short drive, they could be in McLean, where Langley was located.

The rental of a private Cessna to take the team from Venezuela to a landing strip just outside Fairfax County had eaten up a significant chunk of the cash they had left. The motel rooms had been cheap in comparison, but their hard currency was dwindling. They weren't strapped by any means. Zee had started investing in Bitcoin a few years back and had done remarkably well. The cryptocurrency was in an account the CIA wasn't aware of, because they'd gone into hiding before her next financial disclosure had been due, but they had a problem. Most people didn't take digital currency as payment. The pilot had wanted cash. The hotel wanted cash or a credit card. Sorry, no Bitcoin accepted.

Digital currency ATMs weren't so easy to find abroad. On American soil was a different story. She could tap one thirty minutes away. But Zee was an ethical hacker. She hadn't tried to hide her identity when she'd created the account. As soon as she made a withdrawal, the CIA would pick it up. Then there was the issue of anyone getting close to an ATM due to security cameras.

They had to be cognizant of all CCTV.

Every move they made had to be careful, calculated.

The slightest misstep would put them in a bind at best. At worst, it could cost them their lives.

With the eight of them crammed into one room to talk, tension was dense as fog. Everyone felt it in varying degrees, especially the civilians in their forged family. Kate, a veterinarian turned into their resident doctor, was used to a slower pace and the security of a small town. Danger was nothing new to Hope, a photojournalist who had often found herself in precarious situations for a job. But neither was accustomed to this grueling high-ops tempo with threats around every corner.

Olivia might be a child, but Zee had trained and prepared her to handle this type of pressure.

Hunter wanted to keep the three of them as far removed as possible. He didn't want them being used as leverage or put in harm's way.

If he could accomplish this on his lonesome and clear their names without jeopardizing any of his people, he would.

"Is everyone clear on the next step?" Hunter asked.

Heads nodded around the room.

"I'll need Zee to come along to handle the alarm system," he said, "and one more person." The backup would be essential in this case.

John stepped forward. "I'll go."

"No, you have to stay here." Zee put a hand on his broad chest. "I thought about it on the flight. I need one of us to always be with Olivia from here on out. In the event things take a turn for the worse—"

"We can't think like that," John said.

A sad smile tugged at Zee's mouth. "But we have to."

Olivia climbed off one of the double beds where she was sitting and went up to John and her mother. "I'll be okay with everyone else. Isn't it better for you, Mom, if John goes?"

John would put Zee above everything, even at the expense of their last-ditch mission to clear their names. He wasn't Hunter's first or second pick to go.

"It's better for you, sweetheart, if one of us stays," Zee said to her daughter. "That way, no matter what, you'll be taken care of."

The subject was hard to tiptoe around, the prospect of things not working out in their favor. The possibility of this ending with a funeral instead of a celebration. Hunter admired their efforts to try as well as the courageous way Olivia was facing this.

Not many men would embrace the challenge of having an instant family. John had accepted Olivia as his own, and Zee knew that he would love and protect that little girl for the rest of his life.

"Okay. I'll stay." John wrapped one arm around Zee, the other around Olivia and kissed each of them on the head.

Looking at the three of them, huddled together, was enough to make a cynic like Hunter believe in destiny and true love and hope they got their happily-ever-after. They deserved it. As did the other two couples in the room.

Before Gage could offer to go, Dean did. "I'll be the third."

Gage, never one to shirk duty, was about to protest, but Hope took his hand and caught his gaze.

"The three of us will handle it," Hunter said to reassure Gage. "You should stay."

Gage and Hope hadn't had a chance to talk privately since the baby bombshell. Taking some time to decompress, to process the news that they were expecting, was important. They had to seize any moment for normalcy when feasible.

Nodding, Gage interlaced his fingers with Hope's.

"If we're not back in four hours or if you haven't heard from us…" Hunter stopped short of saying *you should assume we are dead* in front of Olivia. The insinuation was clear.

They would be on their own and would have to run. Limited cash would make it tough until they could access Zee's crypto savings, but Hunter was leaving them with everything they had left.

"Just make sure it doesn't come to that," John said, hiding his concern behind a hardened warrior's stare.

"I'll do my best," Hunter said, hoping that his best would be good enough.

ALMOST TWO DAYS with no sleep, and Kelly had hit a mental wall. She hadn't been able to rest on the flights to or from Venezuela, and after talking with Director Price, she'd gathered her team of analysts.

Quinlan had discovered all the accounts in the Cayman Islands had been emptied through wire transfers and closed. With nothing else to go on, he was headed back

Stateside. Kelly had pushed her analysts for the past several hours to figure out where the members of Topaz would go. Would they stay together? Would they separate to make it harder to find them?

They were stitching together everything they knew about them from their profiles and history, in conjunction with their current behavior and the information they'd dug up on their collaborators: Hope Fischer, John Lowry and Kate Sawyer.

From there they would extrapolate, because other than getting false positives on the use of their known aliases, they had nothing else to go on. Not a single hit on facial recognition.

Either they were hiding off the grid somewhere or Zee was keeping them from being detected using her ace hacker skills. Or it was a combination of both.

Pinching the bridge of her nose as she squeezed her eyes shut, Kelly realized she had to pack it in for a few hours. Go home. Take a shower. Get some rest and food. Then come back and tackle this with a fresh perspective.

"I'm heading home," she said to the analysts who had done a shift change before dinner. "If you find anything, notify me and only me immediately."

"Yes, ma'am."

She grabbed her overcoat and purse and left the private operations room where Cujo was being conducted. Others steered clear of her in the halls, and no one initiated conversation in the elevator. Her reputation as the ice queen was well-known. People feared her. Most days that didn't bother her, but what she would've given to have an ally. A friend on her side.

Once this was resolved, she'd take a few days of leave. Maybe spend the vacation with her godmother. Judith had managed to juggle a husband for a decade when she was younger, and the marriage had given her a son, Zachary, who was five years older than Kelly. Somehow, he had turned out easygoing, content with a nine-to-five job as the head of public affairs at the NSA.

The vacation would probably come down to Kelly and Zach. Judith stayed busy, rarely had time for herself. Then she'd be stuck with Mr. Mellow, who never stressed about anything and didn't understand the pressures of a high-powered position. He was a nice guy. The big brother she never had. They were simply cut from a different cloth.

Perhaps Kelly would retreat to her godmother's house in West Virginia. Fresh air. Good wine. Great food. And she could enjoy it alone.

Always alone.

Ignoring the sting of emptiness, she passed security as she crossed the lobby and left the building. One perk of her position was a nearby parking spot. With color-coded lots befitting Disneyland, the benefit was nothing to scoff at. She hurried to her car and climbed inside, out of the cold.

On her way home, some of the tension dissipated, draining from her shoulders. But the knot in the pit of her stomach refused to loosen. Her hands tightened on the steering wheel. A storm of emotions swirled inside her. Anger, frustration, loneliness, uncertainty, regret.

If only she'd seen the warning signs that Topaz might turn traitor, maybe she could have prevented things from getting to this point.

Regardless, their fates were linked now.

Hitting the button to open her garage, she pulled up the driveway of her home in Vienna. The four-bedroom brick colonial where she grew up. Her father had bequeathed her the house in excellent condition with the mortgage paid off to ensure she wouldn't have to worry about money.

Even in death he looked out for her.

She turned off the ignition, closed the garage door, got out of the car and entered the house.

The alarm chirped. Kelly entered the four-digit PIN, turning it off, and dead bolted the door.

Rolling her shoulders and stretching her neck, she strode down the short, narrow hall. She dumped her purse and keys on the entry table and entered the kitchen.

A second before she spotted him, she sensed him. That warm finger sliding down her spine.

Hunter Wright stood in the moonlight on the opposite side of her kitchen island, waiting for her.

For a long moment, they both simply stood and stared. The air between them vibrated with an awareness that was nearly palpable.

Painful memories sliced through her brain in a rush. Late nights in the office, side by side. Flirting disguised as witty repartee. That TDY in Boston. The taste of his mouth. The smell of his skin. The feel of his body on her. Inside her.

She struggled to breathe, her lungs squeezing, her heart throbbing like an open wound.

Then a surge of adrenaline had her springing into action. She spun around, lunging for the entry table. Yanked open the drawer where she kept a loaded nine-millimeter Glock. Grabbed the handgun and whirled as she thumbed off the safety.

She aimed center mass. The way her father had taught her. Not at the limbs or the head, and she certainly didn't want to mess up that gorgeous face of his. The man had won the genetic lottery big-time and deserved an open casket.

Hitting a target was harder than it looked on TV or in movies. So she pointed the gun at his chest, where a bullet was likely to strike the aorta, the vena cava, a lung, the spine.

She drew closer, the click of her heels on the wood floor the only sound in the room.

Out of all the places in the world he could've gone, he was in her house. Before she pumped him full of lead, she'd find out why.

"Raise both hands, slowly, where I can see them." She stopped, close enough to strike her target, but with distance between them to prevent him from disarming her.

He moved his arms, bringing his hands into sight, both clenched into fists. Once he reached his torso, he froze, only a second. Then he opened his hands.

Bullets fell from his palms, raining down on the marble countertop. "I found the Glock and the Beretta while I was waiting."

Damn it. He'd unloaded both.

But maybe he'd forgotten the round she kept chambered.

Kelly squeezed the trigger. *Click!* She threw the gun at his head, cursing the fact she was in a stupid skirt. It would limit her range of motion in a fight. She could put more power behind a well-placed kick than a punch.

Nonetheless, she could still knee his groin, and there was nothing like a stiletto heel to a kneecap to make someone feel blinding agony.

Hunter stalked around the counter toward her, moving like a predator.

It was unnerving and sexy as hell at the same time.

She raised her fists and widened her stance. "Come on. I'll teach you not to break into my house."

The floorboards creaked and groaned under shifting weight. *Behind her.*

Kelly's whole body flashed cold as the realization occurred to her that Hunter hadn't come alone.

She pivoted to turn, but someone slipped an arm around her throat, locking her in a choke hold.

Stalking closer, Hunter smiled, so brazen, so cocksure, as though certain he had her.

Kelly kicked off the kitchen island in front of her, sending her and the second assailant stumbling back and crashing into a table. Slamming the spike of her stiletto onto his foot, she used every ounce of force she could muster.

A guttural curse left his mouth, and his arm slackened around her throat from the unexpected jab of pain. Kelly unlocked her knees and sank down, grabbing the man's forearm with both hands. Then she bent forward at the waist with a sudden jerk, sending him flying over her head and to the floor.

Dean Delgado.

Two against one. They should be ashamed of themselves.

She stomped her heeled foot in his midsection, bearing down with her full weight.

Howling in pain, Dean grabbed his stomach. After she dealt with Hunter, her next kick would be to Dean's throat.

Hunter was almost on her now, crossing the kitchen.

She leaped over Dean's writhing body and dropped to a knee just as Hunter swung for her and missed. She threw a fist to his groin. Once he doubled over from the sucker punch, she rammed the heel of her palm up into his face, driving him backward.

A shadow slipped into her peripheral vision. A third person.

Kelly whirled, scrambling to her feet—too late. She caught sight of Zee and then the electric-blue sparks of the Taser right before the crackling stun gun was thrust into her side. The sudden shock of voltage felt like being punched by a gorilla. Kelly's legs stopped working and she collapsed as the world went black.

Chapter Seven

At the motel, Hunter and Dean were still recovering from Kelly's attack.

Although Hunter only had a bloody nose, the memory of being struck between the legs and the agonizing pain that only a man understood was fresh in his mind.

Kate had determined that Dean had bruised ribs. It could have been worse. At least none were broken, and she hadn't punctured a lung. He was in his room resting now.

This was why Hunter had wanted a three-person team to subdue Kelly. The woman was not to be trifled with. If they hadn't taken the time to search her place for weapons, she would've shot them dead. Instead, she'd only beaten them up.

Humiliating as it was, that was the truth.

Hunter turned off the faucet of the tub, figuring there was enough tepid water in it. Stepping into the bedroom, he caught the handcuffs that Zee tossed his way. He shoved them into his back pocket.

Kelly lay on the king-size bed, unconscious from the light sedative they'd given her to keep her knocked out while they transported her to the motel. Zee had removed Kelly's suit, leaving her clad in her underwear and a slip. The mint-green satin chemise had lace trim around the neckline with the hem falling high above the knee. He was viscerally aware of her bare arms and legs, lean and toned.

The old tug toward her was still there. More of a hard yank, really, if he were being honest, and he hated it. Why couldn't he ignore his attraction to her?

There was a knock on the door before Gage entered the room, carrying two twenty-pound bags of ice and a plastic shopping bag.

They were ready for the next step.

Zee took Kelly's temperature with a forehead thermometer. "Every five minutes I'll check her to be sure her body temp doesn't drop too low."

Hunter gave a nod. Then he pushed up his sleeves to keep from getting his sweater wet and scooped Kelly up from the bed. Her head fell against his chest as he cradled her in his arms and walked into the bathroom. She was so warm and soft, he loathed feeling the slightest enjoyment from the contact, from her skin against his.

He took comfort in the fact that it would be short-lived. In the next minute, she'd be wide-awake, hissing and clawing like a wildcat, trying to kill him.

Gently, he eased her into the water, not wanting to hurt her—at least not physically, despite the whupping she'd given them. In her house, he'd swung at her with enough force to knock someone out, but he had doubted he'd would've been able to land a single blow.

Kelly was highly trained and fast, and he'd been right about her.

She stirred, groaning, her head rolling from side to side.

He took the handcuffs from his back pocket and slipped the chain around the safety grab bar bolted to the wall. Then he cuffed her wrists tightly to be sure she couldn't slip out of them. Her ankles were restrained with zip ties.

Nodding to Gage, Hunter gave him the go-ahead.

Gage brought the bags of ice into the bathroom. They each opened a bag and dumped the freezing contents into the tub.

With a sharp gasp, Kelly's eyes flew open. Her frantic gaze landed on them, and immediately she started jerking on the cuffs like it was possible for her to rip the metal bar from the wall.

"Might as well settle down, because you're not going anywhere." Not anytime soon.

"What's going on?" She jerked her arms again. "Where am I? What are you doing?" she demanded as though she were in charge of this situation.

"You're here to give us answers," Hunter said, calm and composed. It was going to take drastic measures. They were prepared to do what was necessary to get honest responses.

"If you wanted to chat, all you had to do was call. You've got my number. No need to ambush me in my own home. Three against one. Pathetic," Kelly said, her tongue sharp as ever, and damn if he didn't admire her spunk. "Cheaters. No honor. No shame. I should've expected nothing less. Couldn't even be man enough to fight me one-on-one."

Swallowing his frustration and anger, he clenched a hand. "This needs to be done face-to-face. So I can tell when you're lying." Reflecting on it in hindsight, everything that had come out of her mouth had probably been lies. He needed to see her eyes to tell when she was speaking the truth.

Kelly barked out a scathing laugh. "Is this just a pitiful excuse to get my clothes off again?"

"You seduced me," Hunter said, "not the other way around."

"Is that how you remember it? Guess our recollections differ."

Hunter turned to Gage and Zee, who both stood silent, observing, analyzing everything. "Out. Both of you."

"What about the interrogation?" Zee asked. "We should be here for it."

"Interrogation?" Kelly laughed again, shivering from the ice bath. "Is this supposed to be some kind of torture? It'll do wonders for my pores." Another chuckle rolled from her pink lips. "I've already been through real torture thanks to this traitorous little unit. Did you know they took me to a black site after you all went rogue?"

"Oh, please." Hunter sighed, kneeling beside the tub with an arm propped on his thigh. "Is that what you call a promotion these days, torture?"

"Everyone thought I had taken vacation days until the dust settled." Her face took on a feral sort of look, her eyes becoming catlike. "I was getting a tan under hot, bright lights I had sweltered under while they played loud heavy metal music to keep me awake. No swimming, I'm afraid, but they did waterboard me a few times. I only got a break from it during the polygraphs. Over and over. To be sure I wasn't a no-good traitor like the rest of you. So have at it. Give this your best shot, because once I get free, I'm going to kill *all* of you."

She would most certainly try, and they were prepared for that, too.

Hunter stared at her, studying her. "You must be the only person in history to leave a black site and get a promotion. To deputy director."

"Price has been grooming me. The promotion was given to me early as an apology for the torture once I proved my innocence."

Hunter considered what she had to say. It was a good story, definitely intriguing while invoking the right note of sympathy for her. Too bad it was a lie. Kelly was Scheherazade and knew how to spin a good tale. She'd run them around in circles all night if given the chance. They had a limited window to get answers.

The deputy director of the CIA couldn't go missing for days on end. They had hours before someone started looking for her.

Hunter held out his hand to Zee. "Give it to me."

Zee pulled a syringe from her pocket and placed it in his palm.

Hunter flicked off the cap and tapped the tube to get out the air bubbles.

Alarm flared in Kelly's eyes as she jerked back. "What is that?"

"Something I picked up in Venezuela. Better than sodium pentothal." It was an ultra-short-acting psychoactive drug used to obtain information from those who were unwilling to give it. The stuff caused consistent and predictable truth-telling. Combined with the ice bath to enhance the effects, no one could lie. Kelly was about to spill her guts. Hunter leaned forward with the hypodermic needle, and Kelly began thrashing in the tub. "I've got more of this, plenty of other needles, and I can have Gage and Zee hold you down. Fighting this is pointless."

Kelly clenched her jaw and stiffened, accepting there was no avoiding this.

Hunter injected her in the arm and depressed the plunger. "I'll handle this alone," he said to Zee and Gage.

"We're staying to hear the answers." Zee stood her ground, and he wondered if that was the real reason.

"I'm not going to kill her." Not yet anyway. First, he needed proof of their innocence.

"I agree with Zee," Gage said. "We stay. But we can hang back a bit in here to give you space to work."

That was as good as it was going to get. They were both

afraid to leave him alone with Kelly. Maybe he couldn't be trusted for more than one reason—half of him wanted to strangle her, and the other half wanted to kiss her.

"Fine," Hunter gritted out.

They moved into the bedroom, staying close to the open bathroom door, where they could hear without being seen.

Hunter turned back to Kelly. The drug was taking effect. Her pupils were dilated, and she looked woozy despite the cold making her teeth chatter.

"Where were we?" he asked.

Her cobalt blue eyes narrowed to slits. "Discussing how pathetic you are. If stripping me and getting me wet was what you were after—"

"In your dreams, sugar."

There was nothing sweet about Kelly. She was all fire and secrets. He preferred the heat of her passion over her wrath, but right now he was after those secrets.

"More like in your fantasies, I bet." She rested her head back against the wall.

"Don't flatter yourself."

"I don't have to. You already did. Remember? That one night. TDY. Boston." She licked her lips, and he recalled the feel of her mouth on him, their tongues tangled, the sweet heat that'd blazed through him, melting away all his defenses.

Hours of pleasure, lost in each other, but it had been more than that, at least for him. The sense of connection, that feeling of hope, had been everything. In the euphoria of their lovemaking, he had flattered her. The words had been genuine. Heartfelt.

Thinking back on it brought him nothing but misery.

"After I'd had too many drinks," she added, "and you seduced me."

The drugs must not have fully kicked in yet if she was

still running with the lie that he had been the one acting from a playbook.

"I vaguely remember the night," he said, sounding bored, but the memory of the way her body had moved beneath him, over him, dominating and surrendering, was burned in his mind when none of it had meant anything to her. He put the mental brakes on, refusing to go there any deeper. "But it sounds as if you recall everything in vivid detail."

"Oh, please," she scoffed. "Of course I do. Retaining information is part of the job."

"That's all I ever was to you. A job. A tool to be used. Like a hammer."

"You once had the precision of a scalpel. Until Afghanistan. When you took money and turned traitor. Betrayed your country. Betrayed me."

He grasped her chin between his thumb and forefinger, turning her face to his. She stared at him until, after a long moment, she took a shuddering breath.

"You've got that backward." His voice was low and hard. "You set us up with that op. You were the one who betrayed *us*."

She had picked their team for the mission in Afghanistan. She had verified the target, which, in the end, had been the wrong man. She was the one who had arranged their exit plan out of country. And all of it had gone to hell in a handbasket.

To make matters worse, when they'd finally made their way back to the United States and asked her to meet them so they could find out what in the world had gone wrong, a kill team turned up. They'd barely gotten away and had been forced to go on the run.

Kelly had ruined their reputations and destroyed their lives like it had been a game of climb the ladder to her. It brought him to a level of rage that he hadn't experienced in a long time.

"Is this sick joke part of the torture?" She pulled her chin out of his grasp. "I was horrified by what you did. Not just against this country. Against the agency. But…" She lowered her gaze and shook her head as if trying to clear it.

"But?" he prodded. "Don't hold back now. You never have before with your lies and manipulation."

"You betrayed me!" She stared up at him with glassy eyes. "Not the other way around. When you went rogue, Hunter, you broke my heart. I believed in you. Thought I could count on you. I trusted you more than anyone." Her bottom lip quivered as a whimper escaped her.

He couldn't tell if the wounded sound was from the cold or something else. Then she went on.

"Do you know how hard that was for me?" Her voice was tight, ragged with emotion. Deep, strong, real emotion that astounded him. "God, I thought I was f-fall…" Shaking her head again, she pressed her lips together.

"You thought you were what?"

"It doesn't matter! Not anymore. It stopped being important the day you betrayed me and left me behind. To be humiliated. To be interrogated. To be judged. For what you all did." She bared her teeth and growled, but tears leaked from the corners of her eyes. "I want to wrap my hands around your throat and choke the life out of you."

He'd been so angry for so long he hadn't allowed himself to feel much else.

Now, a sudden swell of pain surged through him, knocking Hunter back on his heels. His chest ached. His throat burned. He hadn't expected to feel *this*.

Even without the drug, he would've believed her. Never, not once in all the days he'd known her, had Kelly let her icy control slip enough to show such gut-wrenching vulnerability.

The sight of this strong, fearless woman in tears frightened him.

Zee came to the doorway. "It's a little past five minutes, but I didn't want to interrupt."

He waved her in.

Zee put the handheld device to Kelly's forehead and scanned her. Once it beeped, she glanced at the screen. "You're good to keep going, but not for much longer." She left the room.

Hunter swallowed hard, watching Kelly shiver and sob in the ice bath. "Were you really tortured?"

"For seven days." She looked up at him. Her gaze open, glassy, wounded. "While you were on a lurid, postcard-perfect beach off the coast of Venezuela—golden sand, aquamarine sea, enjoying your freedom and the money you took to kill an innocent man."

These past eleven months he'd sworn it had been Kelly. It was the only thing that made sense. But this left him with more questions than answers.

"If you didn't set us up to murder the Afghan official, then why didn't you show up after I contacted you for a meeting? Why did a kill team come for us instead?"

Confusion swamped her face. "What meeting? I don't know what you're talking about."

"I sent you a text from a burner phone. Used our code that no one else knew. You confirmed the meet. But you didn't come. You sent a hit squad."

"No." Kelly shook her head. "I never got any text. You never contacted me. I would've come. To hear your explanation before I slapped your face." She jerked her hands, the cuffs clinking against the bar. "How could you think

I would ever set you up? I was your handler! Your advocate! I defended you until I was forced to accept the truth."

This was no act to disguise her guilt. She really did believe they were traitors, that they had become hired guns. Turned on their country, on her, for money.

Zee came back into the bathroom and scanned Kelly's forehead. "We've got to get her out and warm her up." Drawing in a deep breath, Zee shook her head. "It wasn't Kelly. She didn't do this to us."

He agreed. Hearing someone else acknowledge it had a tingle of relief loosening the fist that was around his heart.

But if Kelly hadn't set them up, then who had?

"I need one more minute with her," Hunter said to Zee. "Sixty seconds. No longer."

He nodded. Thirty would suffice. "I'm going to take you out of the tub," he said to Kelly. "Give me your word that when I uncuff you, you won't get violent."

"I won't attack anyone." Her voice was throaty and trembling. "Not until this drug wears off."

That he believed, and it was good enough for him. The psychoactive drug affected the central nervous system. Even if she did try to attack them, she wouldn't be able to do much damage, but he didn't want the hassle of fighting with her.

He unlocked the cuffs and removed the restraint from one wrist. She grasped hold of the grab bar and lifted herself up. He reached for her to help her out of the tub, but she slapped his hand away.

Kelly managed to lurch out of the tub, shivering so hard she could barely stand.

Hunter caught her just as she started to fall, gripping her by her shoulders and holding her upright.

"Don't touch me." She jerked free of him and leaned against the counter.

Swearing under his breath, he forced himself not to go to her. She might appear weak and fragile, but it was temporary and didn't extend to her iron will.

Zee draped a towel around Kelly's shoulders and ran another one over her, drying her hair and legs.

Pushing off the counter, Kelly staggered and swayed. Her knees began to buckle, and all hesitation left him.

Hunter was by her side before she hit the floor and picked her up even though he knew she'd protest.

Instantly, she tensed and tried to twist out of his arms, but she lacked the strength to put up a real fight. There was no way she'd make it to the next room on her own.

"Hang on," he said, carrying her into the bedroom. Her pale skin was freezing cold, which had been the point, and her teeth were still chattering. He regretted putting her through that, especially after learning what the CIA had done to her at a black site, but it had been the only way to find out the truth. "I'll put you down in just a second. I don't want to touch you any more than you want to be touched." It was a good thing for him that he wasn't under the truth serum. Now that he knew she wasn't responsible for what had happened to his team, nothing felt better than having her in his arms.

On the bed was a new pair of sweats that Gage had picked up from the store while he'd been out getting the ice. Hunter sat Kelly down on the edge of the bed next to the fresh clothes. Then he grabbed the thermos on the dresser that was filled with hot broth. It would warm her from the inside out.

"I'll help get her changed," Zee said, taking the thermos from his hand.

"I don't need your help, either." Kelly sat with her head hung, trembling, her hands clenched and shaking on her legs.

Zee sucked in a long, hard breath and exhaled in the same drawn-out manner.

Kelly's obstinacy knew no bounds.

"Suit yourself," Zee said, "but I'll hang around to supervise. Make sure you don't get any dangerous ideas."

Hunter gestured to Gage, and the two of them left the motel room and stood outside in the fresh air.

"All this time we've been blaming Kelly when she's not responsible," Gage said.

The thought of what she had gone through at a black site had rage mixed with horror making his gut burn. He wanted to tear into whoever was responsible and rip them to shreds. They were still no closer to figuring out who that person was, and there were too many unanswered questions.

Deep down he sensed that somehow Kelly was the key to getting to the bottom of it.

"We need her help," Hunter said. "Someone on the inside to dig around."

A harsh breath left Gage's mouth, crystallizing in the air. "As if she'd help us now."

"I'll talk to her."

"Yeah, good luck with that. I'm pretty sure she hates us more now after that ice bath."

And the drugs. Kelly wouldn't let him forget that.

"She'll help." At Gage's skeptical expression, Hunter said, "She will." She had to, and Hunter believed that once he finally explained their side of the things, showed her what evidence they'd scraped together, that she would feel compelled.

He hoped like hell that was how it would work out. The bottom line, Kelly was a professional. She understood better than most at Langley the lengths an operative had to go to at times. If anyone would get the actions they'd taken tonight, his money was on her.

Zee opened the door, holding Kelly's wet things. "I'll get this stuff cleaned and dried."

"Thank you," Hunter said. "Do I have permission to speak to her alone?"

Zee gave him a rueful smile. "Sorry about that, but I needed to be sure."

"Of what?"

"That you wouldn't strangle her in a fit of rage. At least, not before we got answers, and now we've confirmed that she's innocent."

It was a great relief to know Kelly wasn't the enemy, but it did little to ease the tension knotted in his chest.

Hunter stepped inside the room. "Get some rest while you can."

"When are you going to sleep?" Gage asked.

"I'll sleep when I'm dead." Hunter closed the door, locked it and shoved a wedge-shaped rubber stopper under the door. An old habit from whenever he deployed.

With her back to him, Kelly was curled up on the bed in the fetal position under the covers.

He went to the dresser and pushed it in front of the door. That was to slow her down in the event she made a run for it once the drugs wore off and she got her strength back. They'd already unplugged the landline and hid the phone, and they'd made certain to leave both of her cell phones at her house.

There was no way for her to contact anyone. Not while she was in this room with him.

Hunter walked around to the other side of the bed and sank to the floor with his back pressed to the nightstand. The impact of hitting a brick wall rather than breaking through one hung in the air, settling on his shoulders.

Pulling his legs to his chest and resting his arms on his knees, he looked over at Kelly.

She was awake, so calm, clutching the covers to her chest. No doubt fuming on the inside.

Not that he blamed her.

"I'm sorry I put you through that." His voice was low and soft. "I had to be certain you told us the truth."

She was pale, hollow-eyed, and she didn't say a word.

The silence between them was dark and deep. He wanted to cross it. At the same time, he feared he never would. Finding a way to walk the line between the civility she deserved, now knowing she wasn't behind what happened to them, and the violence this path demanded seemed impossible.

Maybe this wasn't the right time to explain everything to her, present his argument of how they were innocent. It was better to wait until the drugs wore off. That way he could be certain her mind was clear to process everything.

But in this moment, with her unable to lie, there was one last thing he needed to know.

"In Boston," he said, hesitating a second, "if you didn't sleep with me to manipulate me, why did you seduce me on our last night?"

"You seduced me." Her voice was a whisper. "*And* I seduced you. I thought it had been mutual. That we'd wanted each other. You flirted. I flirted back. Gave you a chance to make a move. That's how I remember it."

Thinking that Kelly was the enemy had colored and framed so many things.

Everything.

His next question danced on his tongue, his pride making him reconsider whether to ask at all, but this was his one chance. He wanted, no, *needed* to know the truth. "Did you enjoy being with me, our one night together?"

She squeezed her eyes shut and tears leaked out, trickling down her cheeks. "Yes."

"Then why? Why were you so cold to me the next morning? Why did you leave the way that you did?"

"It doesn't matter. It was a year and a half ago."

"And here I sit. A fugitive, running for my life, and I'm still asking you. Whether it's been two years or twenty, it matters to me." He'd spent so many sleepless nights replaying that night, wondering, questioning. "Why?"

"Because I felt too much for you." She opened her eyes and shifted her sad gaze to his. "Not just the sex, which was amazing, but…" She trailed off and swallowed as though her throat hurt. "I was falling for you. Hard. I'd been into you for so long, and sleeping with you made it so much worse. It scared me." Tears starred her lashes. "I thought a clean break was for the best. That I was sparing us the pain of wanting something more, something we couldn't have. Not while we worked together."

He reached for her, slowly, and brushed her cheek with the back of his hand.

Just as he thought they were making a different kind of headway, she pulled back from his touch and rolled over, curling up on her side with her back to him.

After all this time, after the misconceptions, the lies, the fallacies on both sides, they were within arm's reach, but it might as well have been the Grand Canyon between them.

"I wish," he muttered. "I wish…" He wished so many things he didn't even know where to begin.

"Yeah," Kelly whispered, saving him from having to finish his statement. "Me, too."

If he had known back then, if she had taken ten minutes to tell him that had been the reason she'd acted as though she couldn't bear to be in the same room with him, he would've quit his job. Turned in his badge and gone to work as a contractor with his pick of security firms.

Then maybe none of this would've happened.

But she hadn't.

Kelly had chosen silence, the CIA and service before self over any chance of happiness with him.

The grim reality of the situation grabbed him by the throat, and he could barely breathe.

Now he needed Kelly to put him and his entire unit first. Ahead of the institution and principles that meant the most to her.

Otherwise, they'd never get exonerated, never be free. The eight of them couldn't run forever. They were operating on borrowed time.

Without her help, they'd never survive.

Chapter Eight

"Kelly." A deep, faraway voice tugged at her.

The sleep her body had craved for so long had her in its tight grip and wasn't letting go. She was warm, so tired. Needed to keep her eyes closed for just a little longer.

"Kelly." A rough shake accompanied the voice this time.

Sleep receded like an ebbing tide. She opened her eyes and Hunter came into focus.

He was crouched low next to the bed. Those piercing crystal-blue eyes were locked on her. His gorgeous face was so close she could touch him.

Then she remembered she wanted to smash that face to pieces. She jabbed out at him with a fist. Too slowly to do any damage. Unfortunately.

He'd rocked back out of reach with ease. "Before you start something I'll have to finish with a Taser, I suggest you have a cup of coffee. Then we can talk."

She pushed upright, setting her bare feet on the carpet. Her vision blurred, and dizziness swamped her. Once the room stopped spinning, she said, "Whatever you gave me sure does pack a doozy of a hangover."

"Coffee." Standing up, he hiked his chin at a cup with a plastic lid on the nightstand. "Black, two sugars. Hope that's the way you still take it."

"I've cut out sugar." And carbs. The stuff was toxic and

not doing wonders for her waistline. The older she got, the more closely she had to monitor what she consumed. Some women pulled off slim with little effort. She wasn't one of them.

"I'll remember that for next time," he said. "For now, a little sugar will make you feel better."

"Next time implies a future cordial exchange. There won't be one." She grabbed the coffee, flipped off the lid and took a sip. Letting out a low moan, she savored the next swallow of hot nirvana. Whether it was the effects of the drug or the fact that she'd given up sugar for the past six months, Kelly wasn't sure, but this was the best cup of coffee ever. "How do you see this playing out?"

"I was hoping for the easy way."

She chuckled. "Frankly, I think we're way beyond that, don't you?"

"Things could've been a lot harder in my perspective."

"Let me tase you, pump you full of an illegal psychoactive drug I picked up in a foreign country, dunk you in an ice bath and see how *easy* you think that is."

"Touché." He leaned against the far wall near the door, which was barricaded, and crossed his legs at the ankles. "For the record, I've apologized for that already."

He could take his apology and shove it where the sun didn't shine. "I don't know about easy, but this is pretty simple." She took another gulp of coffee. "Once I get my strength back, either I kill you or you kill me." Neither was a good choice, or one that she wanted. It was necessary.

Hunter and his team had to be eliminated. For the good of Langley. The country. So on and so forth.

His mouth quirked. "There is a third option."

She rolled her eyes. He wasn't naive and she wasn't gullible. There was no third option, but she'd play along. Stall. Sooner rather than later, someone at headquarters would wonder where she was, and then they'd send a team to find her.

"I'm listening," she said.

He pushed off the wall and edged forward. "Have you asked yourself why my team and I would risk our lives coming back here to Virginia just to speak with you when we could be halfway across the world?"

No. No, she hadn't. Her brain was still fuzzy, and last night she'd been preoccupied with other matters. Namely fighting and getting through a freezing-cold interrogation.

She glanced at the clock. Three thirty.

"I'll address the elephant in the room," he said. "I've got four, five hours tops to convince you of our innocence before the bloodhounds will be unleashed to find you."

If time was the elephant he was referring to, then there was a whole herd in the room. "Whether it's four hours or four hundred, you wouldn't be able to convince me. The best you could hope for at this point is to restrain me and run."

"We're done running." He took another step toward her, closing the gap between them. "Why would we come back here? What sense does that make unless we're innocent?"

His questions from last night replayed in her head. Each one had been about her possible guilt. Her setting them up. *Her* betrayal.

What game was he playing?

"Maybe you realized you can't win this," she said. "Not in the end. Sure, you made it off that island. Score one for the Topaz unit, but the CIA can't afford to lose this war. So, you're making a last-ditch effort to bring me over to your side. And if that's the case, it's quite desperate of you, not to mention futile."

"Someone set us up in Afghanistan to kill the wrong person. Our exit plan was blown, and we were attacked, but the team sent to take us out failed. Once we made our way back home, I texted you, arranged a meeting at the Tysons Corner Center. You confirmed, but instead of showing up, another kill team came in your stead."

That was the same story he'd spewed last night. But there had been no text from him. As far as she was aware, Hunter hadn't set foot in the United States again until now.

"You sent teams after Gage, Zee and Dean. They failed, too. Just like your two teams on the island."

Technically, Dean hadn't been a failure. In fact, he was the only success. The count was actually six to one in Topaz's favor.

"I'm not desperate," Hunter said. "Not yet. Trust me when I say you won't want it to come to that."

Desperate, out of options, cornered...that was precisely where she wanted them. "Really. Why not?"

"Because it means I have nothing else to lose, and then there won't be anything to stop me from burning Langley to the ground."

The idea of that was more chilling than the ice bath.

Bleary-eyed, she let her gaze travel over him, truly taking him in. Something she hadn't had a chance to do last night. His bearing was confident, bordering on cocky. Not in the least homicidal, which boded well for her. His golden-blond hair had grown out, but the shaggy look worked on him. Added to his rugged handsomeness. As did the tan. A collarless white pullover with sleeves pushed up to his forearms stretched across his muscular chest, and hip-hugging jeans encased his long legs. His physique was no less hardened by the months of frolicking on a Venezuelan beach. But his eyes were unreadable.

Why was he here? What could he possibly want from her?

"You've known me and my people a long time," he said,

his voice growing softer as he held her gaze. "What we stand for. What's important to us."

"I thought I did." In spectacular fashion, they had proven her wrong. "After you went rogue, I had to reexamine everything. Question everything. Everyone."

For months, she'd been paranoid about traitors lurking around every corner. It was no way to live. She was burning the candle at both ends. Unable to sleep. Unable to decompress. In a constant state of suspicion and anxiety at home and at work.

If she still had a therapist, they'd have a field day with her.

"You need to ask yourself why we're here," Hunter said again. "What do we have to gain?" He let the question hang in the air before continuing. "There's only one reason all of us would come back here, in spite of what happened at Tysons eleven months ago. We're innocent. We thought you were the one responsible. That it had to be you since you were the only person who had access to everything. Not only the mission details but also our exit plan. But we didn't come for blind revenge. We came for the evidence we need to clear our names."

They could have killed her last night. There was no question of that, and right now they were expending precious hours on her, talking, when they should be running for their lives.

None of it added up.

She held the cup in both her hands, churning everything over in her mind. "If a kill team had come for you like you said, I assume gunfire was exchanged." The CIA were masters at cleaning up a scene, but Tysons Corner Center was a mega shopping mall. The place was massive, the largest in the metropolitan DC area. Always packed with civilians. In the age of smartphones, something would've been captured on video and aired on the news.

Nothing had been reported.

"There was a shoot-out," he said.

Shaking her head at his lie, she lowered her gaze and sighed.

He folded his arms across his chest. His biceps naturally flexed under his shirt, drawing her attention where it shouldn't be. "It was a Thursday at 10:00 a.m. Zee drove. She let us out in parking garage C. The rest of us entered from the southeast entrance and went to the third floor of Bloomingdale's. The shoot-out took place in the furniture department near the mattresses. The fire alarm had been pulled. It was the only reason civilians weren't injured. I'm sure the team got their dead out and that Langley wiped the security footage of the store."

"Of course they would've, and any cameras they missed are useless now. It's been almost a year. Stores only keep security videos for thirty days. Ninety, max. It's standard, as well you know. Conveniently makes it difficult to verify your story, doesn't it?"

He would have to try much harder than this to convince her.

"Let me show you what we have." He gestured to the small desk on the other side of the room.

A laptop was on the table, open, powered up and waiting.

She glanced back at Hunter. It wasn't as though she was able to take him in a fight, not yet, and access to the computer would give her a chance to send a distress email.

"All right," she said. "Show me." She stood, padded to the desk and sat in front of the computer.

"In the spirit of full disclosure, Zee made sure the laptop is air-gapped."

In layman's terms, the computer wasn't connected to the internet. So much for her chance to send an email.

Hunter put a hand on the back of the chair and leaned over beside her, looking at the laptop's screen.

She could feel him, the warmth from his body. She could smell him. No cologne. No aftershave. The scent was all his, and her belly tightened against it.

"Zee stayed in the vehicle. To be our eyes, she plugged into the live security feeds, monitoring things." He moved the mouse past several documents on the screen and clicked on an MP4 file. "She recorded it."

The video began as a montage of several feeds rolling at once. Various angles and positions in a mall. It looked as though it could've been Tysons. Then she noticed several stores that were only located at that particular mall in the area.

Date and time stamps lined up with what he'd told her. Although it was easy enough to doctor those.

"Footage can be altered," she said, staring at the recorded feeds.

"Just watch."

Hunter, Gage and Dean entered the mall. Not together. Staggered seconds apart. They were wearing ball caps, and their heads were lowered, faces turned away from the cameras. Still, she pinpointed them. The self-possessed swagger and their muscular builds gave them away. Also, she knew what to look for.

They made their way to Bloomingdale's, using different routes, and took up positions on the third floor.

The screens changed, showing a second team enter. Six men. Three from the southeast. Three more from the west. Same swagger. Similar body frames. No doubt mercenaries contracted for this purpose.

"It was at this point Zee gave us the heads-up about the other team."

"You would've had ample time to leave without engagement." She looked up at him. "Why didn't you?"

He turned his head and met her gaze, bringing his mouth dangerously close to hers.

Unwanted heat flooded her face, bled lower through her body.

"Because I was waiting for you," he said. "At first, I thought you were being cautious by having a team there as protection. Then this happened."

She turned back to the screen, grateful to break the up-close-and-personal eye contact.

One man approached Hunter in the furniture department. The guy waved, flashed a tentative smile, drew closer saying something.

"He knew our code word," Hunter said.

"Thermopylae?" The battle where a small force of Greeks made their last stand, despite overwhelming odds, and faced a vast Persian army. They'd decided on the phrase because if it was ever used, then it meant things were dire. An operative was out in the cold and might have to disappear or make a last stand.

Never had they thought the day would come when it would be needed. They were both pragmatists, long-range planners who didn't expect the world to end but wanted to be prepared in the event it did.

"How would he know, Kelly? Unless you had been the one to send him," Hunter asked.

Unease trickled down her spine as she stared at the footage.

The man drew first, holding a gun with an attached sound suppressor. He had Hunter in his sights, would've killed him if not for Gage.

The rest of the kill team had taken a prime position. Topaz was surrounded. The elevator was to their backs.

Muzzle flashes erupted from a different angle. Somewhere behind the mercenaries.

"Who helped you?" Kelly asked.

"Zee. Once she spotted the team, she parked closer to the store and made a beeline to our position."

On the video, Hunter and his men made it inside the elevator. Someone tossed a smoke grenade. Had to have been Zee.

White emergency lights began flashing.

The fire alarm must've been pulled.

Kelly racked her brain for every reason she shouldn't believe the veracity of the video. All the ways it could've been staged, altered, manipulated for effect.

"You don't want to believe what you've just seen," Hunter said. "Right now, you're running through a list of excuses not to. You've clung to the lie you were fed for so long, it's hard to accept anything else. But think about it. Furniture had been smashed. There were bullet holes in mattresses. Even if none of the employees witnessed what happened and the security footage is gone, the damage would've been reported. There also has to be a record of the fire department responding to the alarm."

Details so in the weeds someone might have forgotten to clean those up. No one would generally look that deep.

She turned toward him, their legs brushing as she looked at him. The contact was unexpected, brief, but enough to send a tingle through her. "Let's say I check it out and there is a security report. It would only prove something violent happened there on the day you specified. Not that you're innocent of murder for hire."

"It would also prove that we went there to meet someone. A friend. Instead, a kill team was sent. If not by you, then who?" Hunter lowered in front of her and knelt, putting himself in a physically vulnerable position.

She was aware he knew this, and he did it anyway.

Near her right hand on the desk was a ballpoint pen. A makeshift weapon within reach. This was her chance. The tip was sharp enough to puncture his throat if she used the right amount of force and provided her reflexes had recovered.

She could end this, here and now.

Using her middle finger, she rolled it slowly, discreetly into her palm. It was solid, heavy. One jab, maybe two, was all that it would take, but something stayed her hand.

To hurt an enemy in self-defense, to send a team of bloodthirsty mercenaries to handle the elimination, yes, she was capable of that.

To kill Hunter when he was pleading his case, staring her in the eyes, close enough to kiss…

She let the pen go and pressed her palm to the desk.

"Your father trusted me," he said, making anger spike through Kelly.

Her father had admired him, thought him to be a shining example of what was the best at headquarters. She'd been foolish enough to think the same. "You don't get to talk about him."

"You once trusted me, too," he added, putting a hand on her knee, and an old wound opened inside her. "After our mission, did you ever look into why someone would want to have Ashref Saleh murdered?"

He made it sound so ordinary, so small. As though they had taken out a low-level diplomat, someone inconsequential.

Ashref had been the deputy director of intelligence for Afghanistan, second in rank and power only to the president. Topaz had been sent to kill Khayr Faraj, a terrorist. Langley had intel that indicated Ashref was financing Khayr. If Topaz had caught him in the act, handing over a payment, then and only then had they been given authorization to eliminate Ashref. That could've been justified, explained. Hailed by the US and Afghanistan as a joint success.

In place of a triumph, Topaz had created a political quagmire that threatened to destabilize an ally.

"Of course we looked into why you did it." She shoved his hand from her leg.

His mouth compressed into a thin, hard line. "What answer did you come up with?"

"Ashref had struck a deal with the tribal leaders and farmers to reduce the number of opium poppy fields in exchange for government subsidies. The Taliban and warlords weren't happy about it, but they didn't want to eliminate Saleh themselves. It might have started a civil war. Instead, they paid you to kill him and a tribal leader who had rallied the farmers to support him."

He frowned. "I would never sell my honor and integrity. None of us were paid. We heard about the supposed offshore accounts in our names, but none of us have touched one red cent of that blood money."

Hunter was good. Truly. He almost had her.

Talk about convincing. He spoke with such conviction, like he believed this story. Either he was a pathological liar, or he was suffering a break from reality.

She snatched the pen and pressed the tip to his throat, right at the carotid artery. "Before they shipped me off to a black site, I was hauled into Price's office, where Andrew played a video for me."

Rather than defend himself, he leaned into the tip of the pen, daring her to give it a good, hard shove. "Of what?"

"*You.* Waltzing into the bank in the Cayman Islands.

The very same day you withdrew two hundred and fifty thousand dollars. The video was also date and time stamped. You didn't even have the decency to hide your face from the camera."

Hunter recoiled as though he'd been physically hit. The man looked genuinely surprised. "I've never been to the Cayman Islands."

"I saw the video."

"It must have been fabricated. Real footage of me manipulated by whoever is behind this."

"But I'm supposed to believe without a shadow of doubt that the video you showed me of Tysons Corner is real? Not manipulated in any way to produce a desired effect."

His jaw hardened.

They were at an impasse when it came to the videos. One of them had been doctored.

She'd believed in him once, accepted anything he told her. Those days were long gone.

Never again would she allow herself to be a fool.

"David Bertrand didn't think we were traitors," Hunter said, trying a different course of persuasion. "He knew something was awry with the mission and started digging around. That's why he was fired, went into hiding."

"What?" David had been an analyst assigned to Topaz in a support role back at Langley. He had worked on their last mission and had been privy to the details of the op and how it had all taken a turn for the worse. "No, he wasn't fired. He quit."

"Why do you think that?"

"After I was released from the black site and returned to Langley, I noticed he was gone and asked about him. An analyst told me he'd quit."

"Zee spoke to him minutes before David and his fiancée were murdered by the team you sent after Zee."

Kelly stiffened. David Bertrand was dead?

Whether he had been killed accidentally or specifically targeted, why hadn't she been briefed?

She sat back, lowering the pen. "Where did this happen?"

"In Idaho Falls."

Kelly recalled mention of the location from the sitrep about Zee. The clever hacker had evaded the kill team with the help of John Lowry.

Not one word regarding Bertrand had been in the report.

"David told Zee that he found discrepancies in files related to our mission, such as what Khayr Faraj looks like." There were no pictures of Khayr, only sketches based on a compilation of oral descriptions. "We were under the impression he had a birthmark shaped like an apple on his right cheek. David found a conflicting one that specified it was on his left cheek, not the right, and resembled a tree. Subtle discrepancies that led us to believe the tribal leader was Khayr."

A subtle disparity could make a world of difference. Something small would be easy to overlook, especially in the case of this operation. The mission had been assigned at the last minute. Top priority. From the very beginning, it had been rushed and no one had thought anything of it. When a high-value target like Khayr popped up on the radar, everyone scrambled to get them. Time was always of the essence. It was the nature of those types of assignments.

"What are you saying? Someone deliberately changed the mission details?" she speculated, struggling to think coolly.

"That's precisely what I'm saying."

If Topaz had been set up, then that would have been the best way to do it. Feed them misinformation that had them taking out the wrong target, all the while leading them to believe they were following orders, just doing their job.

"When David dug around after the mission," Hunter said, "he couldn't find any substantive intelligence that supported the claim Ashref Saleh was funding terrorism or financially backing Khayr. It was a lie."

"The whole mission was predicated on it. If Ashref had no illicit dealings with Khayr, the two of them wouldn't have had a reason to meet."

"And they didn't. That's why Khayr wasn't there. He was never supposed to be, because he wasn't the intended target. Ashref Saleh was."

Kelly's stomach did a long, sickening roll. David had been fired after finding discrepancies; he'd gone into hiding and was murdered, and she had been none the wiser.

"Everything we've found on Ashref shows that he was clean." Hunter knelt forward and opened a folder on the laptop. "Zee activated a zero-day virus in Langley's system that allowed her to retrieve these documents."

Kelly set the pen on the desk and looked through the files in the folder. Page after page added credence to his argument. She had to wonder if it was real. Had they manufactured this? With Zee's virus, did the hacker import these documents onto the CIA server to leave behind as supposed evidence?

It was possible.

"On every assignment," he said, "we always chose how to execute it. Except on this one. We were instructed to use explosives."

"That's not true. I remember the mission parameters. You were given the normal leeway to handle it as you saw fit."

"Did you brief us on that?" he asked.

"No. There wasn't time."

Things had moved at warp speed when they'd learned about the planned meeting between Ashref and Khayr. Every member of Topaz was highly experienced. They didn't require her oversight. At the time, she'd been managing a second team that was green and needed guidance on their first few missions. Her attention had been divided, but with Hunter leading his unit, she hadn't thought twice about it.

"Can you say without a doubt what parameters were specified on the classified laptop we were given?" Hunter asked. "Did you load it? Did you verify it? Or did you trust the system?"

The sickness in her stomach sneaked into her throat and tasted foul.

Hunter went on and on, marshaling the facts to support his claim that Topaz had been used and set up to assassinate Ashref. The more details he picked apart, the more on edge it put her.

Her brain felt broken, like it couldn't process all the facts. Perhaps due to the lingering effects of the drugs. Or perhaps it was because the tsunami of information put her on the wrong side of this war.

"Stop." She lifted her palm, needing a breather. They'd been going at this for hours, on an empty stomach, no less. "Give me a minute."

Getting up, she stretched her legs, sucked in a deep breath.

She went to the bathroom, ran the water, corralled her thoughts.

Plenty of things about his story rang true. Some details she would be able to verify on her own: a security report at the mall about damage on the day of the ambush, the fire department responding to the incident, whether David had been killed in Idaho Falls, the discrepancies in the mission.

The money in the offshore accounts could be explained as part of the scheme to incriminate the Topaz unit. Two million dollars sounded like a big number at first. Not so much when divided four ways. If they had been guilty, had been hired to kill Ashref, why wouldn't they simply come back home after the mission?

They could've claimed they thought the tribal leader had been Khayr. Mistakes happened.

As strange as it sounded, guilty people wouldn't have run. Not for five hundred thousand apiece. Dirty law enforcement kept playing the game, biding their time, building up their financial stash, eliminating those who knew the truth.

The certainty of it struck her full force.

Someone else at Langley was behind this. Someone dirty who wanted Topaz out of the picture, because they were innocent. Forced to run after being attacked on their way out of Afghanistan and once again at Tysons Corner.

But the surveillance footage of Hunter strolling into the bank as casual as he pleased, smiling, no less, still bothered her.

It was the one piece of evidence that had cemented his guilt in her mind. After watching it, there was no way she was able to continue making excuses for them, and she had finally acknowledged them as traitors.

She looked in the mirror, past her haggard appearance, and stared into her eyes. "How stupid can you be?"

Whoever had done this knew that she'd believe the video. Knew she wouldn't question it. Knew it would sever the last threads of loyalty she had to Topaz.

Kelly splashed water on her face, patted her skin dry with a towel and left the bathroom.

Hunter stood, leaning against the desk with his arms crossed. The lethal glare of his eyes had her hesitating, told her something had changed. "If it wasn't you, *Red*, why were you promoted?"

A nervous thrill fluttered in her chest. Calling her the intimate nickname, after everything that had transpired, shouldn't affect her, but it did.

"I buy that you were interrogated at a black site." He stalked across the room. "But you didn't quit," he said, getting closer, lifting a hand and curling it around the side of her neck. "I'm having a tough time understanding why you were promoted if you weren't a part of this. Why would they reward you?"

"I told you. Price has been grooming me." She stepped back, trying to break his hold, but he wouldn't let go. In fact, he tightened his grip.

He dipped his head, bringing their faces as close as possible without their noses touching, and captured her gaze. Disquiet and desire quivered in her belly in equal measures, her skin heating at his touch.

She hated the fact that he still had such a powerful effect on her. Threads of the deep, lingering attraction tugged at her, making her yearn to be even closer to him.

"After being the handler for a team that goes rogue," he growled, "after being interrogated, tortured, they promoted you over Andrew Clark, to the position of deputy director of operations. You don't think that's odd?"

"I've been working for this position most of my life. You know that. The long hours, the endless sacrifices. Price told me this was always meant for me. I almost lost it, but I proved my innocence at the black site." Hunter didn't understand the agony she'd suffered through for an endless week. The nightmare of it had messed with her head for months—it still tormented her. "The promotion was an early reward because of what I had endured."

His jaw grew tight as he studied her. "From where I'm

standing, it looks like a bribe. Not a consolation prize."
He let her go. "But tell yourself whatever you need to if it
lets you sleep at night."

As he stepped back, she realized she was trembling
from top to toe. From the proximity to him, but more so
from his words. Each one she'd felt, and combined, they
had alarm bells clanging in her head.

A bribe implied corruption at the very top.

Dr. Evil did exist, and his name was Wayne Price.

She drew in a long, steady breath, suppressing the rising sense of dread. "Let's say I'm willing to swallow the
possibility that your team is indeed innocent. Then this
wasn't about the Taliban and government subsidies. Why
do you think Ashref was assassinated?"

This all boiled down to the *why*. Without that answer,
they'd never find proof.

Hunter shrugged. "We need you to find the answer to
that question."

Great.

"Hey, Red."

Her body strung tight, her thighs tingling, and she
cursed the visceral reaction.

"My people and I have a lot at stake, and we're betting
everything on you. Eight lives are in your hands. I've got
to ask. Can I trust you to help us?"

She wanted to say yes.

She wanted to trust him.

She wanted him back in her life. Not as an enemy. As a
friend. Hell, they'd been much more than that since Boston. She'd be a liar if she didn't admit that he was the only
man she'd longed to have on a deeper level.

But years of wariness, the lingering burn of them going
rogue, made it impossible for her to utter the word.

She wouldn't make him a promise that she wasn't certain she could keep. So, she told him the only honest thing she could. "You can trust me to find the truth. About all of it. Even my promotion."

"Thank you." He pulled her into a careful embrace, and she let him.

It seemed pointless to fight it. With his arms wrapped around her, he pressed his cheek to hers. His stubble brushed her face, and she was rubbed raw, not on her skin but deep inside.

The tenderness brought tears to her eyes, but she refused to cry and fall to pieces. Not when she had to steel herself to fight the real enemy.

No matter what it cost her, she wouldn't stop until she found the truth.

Chapter Nine

"You just let her go!" John said, getting in Hunter's face as though there had been a better choice.

"This wasn't something I did lightly. I weighed the decision carefully, factoring in the risks." Hunter kept his voice flat and moved around the room, looking at everyone else to prevent the conversation from escalating into a brawl. The only two not present were Kate and Olivia. With the likelihood of things getting heated, Zee didn't want her daughter in the room, and Kate had offered to keep her company. "Kelly agreed to wear a transmitter. We can see and hear everything she does."

His gut knotted at how badly this could backfire. He tried to defend himself mentally against John's rational arguments and common sense that agreed with the little voice in his head screaming this was a mistake.

"What good will that do us with the deputy director of the CIA?" John asked. "I take it she can't simply waltz into Langley wearing a device like that."

"No, she can't," Hunter admitted. "But there is a way around the sensors in the lobby. She'll have to remove it, temporarily, and hide the transmitter in the base of a specially lined travel mug that she has."

"When that happens," John said, "we'll be in the dark. The possibilities for Kelly Russell will become endless while we're exposed, with our possibilities shrinking by the minute."

It was true. Hunter wouldn't bother trying to deny it. This plan had holes, big gaping ones, but it was the best course of action. He hoped. "We all agreed that she's not the one who set us up," he pointed out.

"She didn't do it," Zee said, backing him up.

"If Hunter planted enough seeds of doubt about our guilt, then she'll help us," Dean chimed in.

"That's a mighty big *if*." John shook his head with frustration written all over his face. "We don't know what's going through her head. There's nothing stopping her from standing by and allowing her team to kill us, if for no other reason than to make her life easier."

Putting their heads on proverbial spikes would simplify Kelly's life and ensure her position as deputy director, but she was better than that. Hunter was certain of it. She loved the CIA, being a part of something greater than herself, being of service to her country. Letting this conspiracy continue would go against everything she stood for.

"Integrity will stop her," Hunter said. In the end, she would do the right thing.

"Do the rest of you agree with his assessment?" John looked around the room. "Are you willing to bet your lives on it?"

Before they were divided on a decision that couldn't be undone, Hunter turned to everyone. "I gave her a chance to take me out." He'd deliberately placed a ballpoint pen next to the laptop. Heavyweight. Textured rubber grip. Stainless steel, with a sharp tip. A solid crude weapon in a pinch. Then he'd lowered to a knee, giving her the perfect angle to strike and succeed, even if she hadn't fully recovered. Gage had been on the other side of the motel room door, ready with the Taser in the event things went south. "But she didn't. Instead, she listened and asked the right questions."

"Can you look me in the eye and tell me she's one hundred percent Team Topaz?" John asked.

"No, I can't." Hunter shook his head, and John gave a heavy sigh. "But she is on the side of the truth. She'll find out who is responsible. Of that, I have no doubt."

"Forgive me if I don't share in your confidence," John said. "We can't stay here. This location is compromised."

"I agree." Hunter looked at Zee. "Has everything already been arranged?"

"Yes," she said. "I've booked new rooms in a place similar to this but near Bailey's Crossroads."

That was much closer to Arlington, Alexandria and McLean than their current position. There would be an uptick in CCTV coverage around the new location. They'd have to take additional precautions.

"The rest of you will relocate," Hunter said. "I'll stay here and monitor the surveillance feed. That way when I meet with her again, I won't expose you all."

"John made valid points," Dean said. "When Kelly comes back here, she might not be alone. It'll be a tough spot for you to get out of on your own."

"I can hang back." Gage stepped out of the corner where he'd been monitoring the surveillance feed on Kelly, and Hope's eyes flared wide with alarm. "If she brings Quinlan and the others—"

"I'll handle it," Hunter said. "Alone."

"This isn't a smart move," Zee said. "Let one of us stay."

"It's not up for debate." He was grateful they were willing to have his back on this, even if it cost them. "Get moving. I'll check in regularly with updates."

This would work. It had to. He was betting on Kelly and that she would come through. In the event he was wrong, no one else should have to suffer for his error in judgment. They all had others who loved them, needed them to survive this.

If Kelly betrayed him, he would be the only one to pay the price.

KELLY HURRIED DOWN the hall at Langley, headed toward the operations room.

After Hunter had dropped her off at home, she'd grabbed her go bag, which was packed with essentials, and quickly changed her clothes while keeping on the pendant necklace with hidden camera and audio. The only time she'd taken it off was to get it through the lobby undetected.

Getting caught wearing the device would be considered treasonous, but she understood the necessity from Hunter's perspective. He was trusting her, once again, with the lives of his entire team. His level of faith in her only bolstered her growing fears that the Topaz unit had been unjustly persecuted.

The CIA had been their judge, jury and would-be executioner.

She was appalled by her part in it. By how she had allowed someone in these hallowed halls to play her for a fool.

Kelly pushed through the tinted door of the operations room and stopped cold.

"How nice of you to finally join us," Andrew said.

"What are you doing here?" she asked, swallowing the profanity she'd wanted to use.

"Your job, apparently, since you were missing in action." The corner of his mouth hitched up. "There's been a development. The analysts have been trying to reach you, to no avail."

"I was indisposed." Both of her cell phones were dead

when she got home. She'd charged them in the car and had been in such a rush she hadn't checked the messages. "That doesn't explain your presence in my ops room, much less the building."

Andrew was still staring at her with a hint of a smirk. "I stopped in to make sure I didn't leave anything outstanding and to check that ops were fully covered before I started my vacation. It's a good thing I was here."

"You just happened to stop in?" She regretted the question as soon as it left her lips. They both knew he hadn't. She wouldn't be surprised if he'd never left the building and had slept in his office. He was a cautionary case of what not to become. "Is Price aware you're here?"

"When I updated him, he was the one who said I was, and I quote, *invaluable.*" The smirk turned to a full-blown smug smile now. Patronizing. "He sees now how much I'm needed."

She swallowed the nasty retort building on her tongue, not wanting to sling mud with him in front of the analysts. The man was teeth-grindingly aggravating. "What's the urgent development?"

"We have reason to believe the entire Topaz unit is here. In Virginia."

A chill ran through Kelly, like someone had walked over her grave. "Based on what?" she asked, keeping her voice level and her face deadpan.

"Show her," Andrew said to Ebony.

The lead analyst hit a few keys, changing one of the displays on the wall of monitors at the front of the room. An image of Gage came up.

"How did we get this?" Kelly asked.

"Pure luck." Andrew clucked his tongue.

"We haven't had any hits on CCTV, not even from passive surveillance like security cameras on ATMs or traffic cams," Ebony said. "This photo of Gage Graham is actually in the background of the main photo. It's been zoomed in and enhanced. Two women were taking a selfie and caught Graham behind them in a parking lot. Our facial recognition program got a ping after they posted the pictures on Facebook and Snapchat. We pinpointed the location to a big-box store that's only twenty minutes away."

Hunter was monitoring the live feed from the necklace. He would take appropriate action to ensure his people stayed safe. At least that was one thing Kelly didn't have to worry about.

"If one of them is here in the local area," Andrew said, "I think it's safe to assume they all are, but I haven't been able to figure out why. I contacted your attack dog, Quinlan. Beta team is all over this." Andrew turned to her. "What's wrong with you? Why don't you look thrilled?"

"I am." Kelly tore her gaze from the monitors and looked at him. "This is great news."

"This is still your op." Andrew shoved his hands in his pockets. "Price made that clear. But I'll stick around and help you cover down on this. A lot of moving parts. Figured you'd need an extra hand, so we don't miss anything."

She could use this to her advantage. "That's fine."

Andrew narrowed his eyes. "Really? You're not going to give me any pushback on this after yesterday?"

"I'm a professional. Not a territorial animal incapable of rational thought and civility. Besides, I know this mission means as much to you as it does me."

"That it does. Topaz went rogue on both of us."

"Since you've already got things under control, why don't you run the op today?" Handing over the reins to Andrew would free her up to dig around in Topaz's last mission.

He hesitated a moment. "What's the catch?"

"Absolutely none. If this fails, I'll still take full responsibility."

Giving a slow nod, he didn't hide the suspicion from his face. "Okay."

Kelly turned to leave, but when she reached the door, she stopped. "Out of curiosity, whatever happened to David Bertrand?"

"David?" He walked up to her, drawing close enough for her to smell his cheap aftershave mingled with sweat. "He quit."

"Did he give his resignation to you?"

He edged even closer and lowered his voice. "I was at the black site with you when he decided to leave." His stale-coffee breath fanned her face, and her stomach turned. "One of the analysts updated me. Why?"

She took a step back. "He was so good at his job, it would be nice to have someone like him working on this, too. Never hurts to have too much brainpower. Be sure to brief me on any updates."

Eyeing her warily, he nodded. "I will."

Kelly shoved through the door and hurried down the maze of corridors to her office. At seeing Price's door closed, she let out a small breath of relief. She didn't want more questions about her whereabouts earlier this morning slowing her down.

"Good morning, Ms. Russell." Her executive assistant, Steve, smiled. "Can I get you coffee?"

Another wave of nausea rolled through her stomach. "No, thanks. I'm fine. Unless there's something urgent, I don't want to be disturbed for any reason before lunch."

"Understood," Steve said, flashing a pleasant smile. He was one of the most efficient assistants at Langley,

Juno Rushdan 125

and with the flip of an internal switch he could become the ultimate sentinel.

Closing the door to her office, she took off her overcoat and hung it up. She slipped into her chair behind her desk, shoved her ID into the smart card reader and booted up her computer. Looking around her office, she noticed, perhaps for the first time, what everyone else must see when they walked in. The space could belong to anyone. There was nothing personal to mark it as hers. No photos. No unique artwork. Not a shred of sentiment. The room was as cold and sterile as her life.

At home, she had a few pictures of her parents and godmother on the mantel above the fireplace. Still, none with friends, on vacation, celebrating a major life event. She even kept her trophies from martial arts tournaments boxed up in the garage.

Turning to the computer, she logged on, entering her lengthy password, and opened a bottle of water while she waited for system authentication. Finally, she was in. Another password to access the most restricted database. Red banners on all sides of the screen highlighted words denoting different compartments, additional levels of classification. She clicked past a series of screens acknowledging the sensitivity of the information. Accepting the consequences of disclosure—going to jail for a very long time.

This endeavor was a gamble. A big one. Provided she learned anything, she'd have to share it with Hunter, which would only drag her into this deeper.

There was a sinking feeling in her chest, but she'd made a vow, not only to Hunter, but also to herself. She needed the truth.

In the search engine, she entered two keywords: *Ashref Saleh*.

Links to a multitude of files popped up on the screen.

A combination of data ranging from the low side to the highest possible classification.

She scrolled past anything labeled *unclassified*, *confidential* or *secret*. Everyone in the building with access to a computer had clearance to read those files.

Instead, she focused on the top-secret documents that were labeled with an additional code word based on sensitivity. She tapped on a file, opening it.

She gave it more than a cursory glance, zipping over every word. Five pages of information she already knew, confirming Ashref's efforts to thwart the opium industry in Afghanistan with subsidies to farmers.

The next two were more of the same. Nothing on a connection to him and terrorism or Khayr Faraj. What if it didn't exist?

One link at the bottom of the screen had a code word for a highly classified electronic surveillance program. The intelligence community had several running at the moment, but this file could only be accessed by a handful of people at Langley. Not even David Bertrand would've been able to get to it.

She moved the cursor and clicked the link.

The document opened, and what she saw set her nerves on fire.

It was redacted.

Two pages. Ninety percent of the lines had been blacked out. At her current clearance level, she had access to everything the president was briefed on. Nothing was redacted. Until now.

This was it.

In her gut, she knew that whatever was in this document was the reason Ashref had been killed.

All she could make out was his name, that he had been

talking to someone about something, and it'd been deemed a "grave threat to US national security."

If Khayr Faraj had been mentioned, there was no way for her to tell for certain, but she doubted it. Keeping the terrorist's name visible would've supported the reason for Topaz's last op, and anyone who saw this would draw the natural conclusion.

This redaction was to cover up the truth.

She kicked herself mentally for never going through any of the files before, for not searching for hard evidence of her own.

Everything had happened in a whirlwind. The mission had gone awry, and the team had disappeared. Her biggest fear was that they had been killed. A flurry of reporting had come out about Ashref and the tribal leader. As they'd scrambled to piece together what had happened, news came in that the pilot who was supposed to transport Topaz out of Afghanistan was dead.

Still not a word from Hunter, or so she had thought.

Then the money in the offshore accounts had been discovered. Two days later, she was watching the video of Hunter going into the bank in the Cayman Islands. Before she had a chance to investigate, they'd hauled her off to that black site.

After the weeklong interrogation, the torture, she'd been so grateful, to be alive, not to be implicated with a team of suspected traitors, to have her reputation intact, to be rewarded with a promotion.

In the aftermath, she didn't want to think about any of it. She had wanted to forget and move on.

But all this time, she'd been stuck.

Voices outside her door pulled her from her thoughts. Steve and another man. Not Andrew.

Director Wayne Price.

Without a knock, the door swung open. Price strolled in with Steve on his heels.

"I'm sorry," Steve said to her, "I tried to explain you were busy."

"Leave us." Price shooed him out of the office and shut the door in his face.

Kelly closed the file and screen locked the computer. "To what do I owe the pleasure of you coming across to my side of the hall?" Something he had never done. She'd always been summoned.

Price walked to the large window that provided a view of the Potomac River in the distance. He clasped his hands behind his back and gazed outside. "Your predecessor, Matt, was brilliant, a workaholic, perceptive and stubborn as a mule. In many respects, you're very much like him. After three years of working seventy-hour weeks, he finally took a vacation with his family. To a ski resort in Vermont. His wife told him not to go down this one treacherous trail on the mountain. The Beast. There were signs posted about the dangers. Warnings that it was for the most advanced skiers only. But Matt insisted he had to do it. Wouldn't listen. He might've made it, too, but there was an avalanche. You know, they never did find his body."

Kelly's throat tightened as she stiffened in her chair. She considered saying something but thought better of it. The accident had happened not long after Topaz's mission.

She recalled someone had told her in passing how avalanches in Vermont were as uncommon as getting the measles.

But she hadn't paid it much attention. Everyone had chalked up the accident to bad luck. Shortly after, she'd been promoted.

Price turned around, fixing her with his gaze. "Matt had the potential to lead this agency one day. He would've achieved great things, too. If only he'd recognized the danger. Heeded the warnings."

Kelly fiddled with her father's ring, twisting it around her finger.

Price crossed the room slowly, as though he had all the time in the world, sat on the edge of her desk beside her chair and put a hand on her shoulder. "Some things are better left alone." He glanced at her computer screen and looked back at her. "A curiosity you don't dare indulge. Because like the Beast, it can get you killed." His pointed words sent a chill through her. "You have the potential to succeed me, to run the CIA one day, to achieve great things. I want that for you. Truly." He patted her shoulder, giving a soft smile that made her skin crawl. "We all need to know when to submit to greater forces and choose a different course of action in the interest of self-preservation."

He was threatening her. A veiled but nonetheless clear threat.

The sensitive files about Ashref were flagged. Once opened, Price must receive a notification about who accessed them. That was how he'd known David Bertrand had been digging around.

Kelly cleared her throat and shifted in her chair so that his hand fell from her shoulder. "Since Andrew is here, overseeing Operation Cujo, I think I'll take those couple of days off that you offered him."

Surprise flickered across his features. "That sounds marvelous." Eyes brightening, he nodded his head emphatically. "Yes, absolutely. Get out of the office. Take your mind off this horrible business with Topaz. Let us handle it. I would've suggested a little downtime, but you can be so stubborn."

"As a mule." She pulled on a forced smile. "But I understand your words of wisdom." Advice that her conscience wouldn't allow her to heed.

"I'm relieved to hear it." He stood and walked to the door. "I'll let Andrew know. We won't bother you unless it's to notify you that the situation has been resolved."

Resolved. What a placid way of saying that a team had been slaughtered.

She tightened her smile and turned to her computer. "I'm logging off as we speak."

There was little point in sticking around. One call to the IT department, and he would be able to monitor everything she accessed.

Kelly pulled her ID from the card reader and grabbed her coat.

Price opened the door, and they headed out together.

"I'm taking a couple of days off," she said to Steve.

His jaw dropped. "What? Why? Are you sick?"

The questions were partly out of concern for her, but mostly for himself. "No, I'm not contagious or anything. You can relax."

Steve sagged with relief. "Good to know. Enjoy your time."

Price walked her to the hall that ran between their office suites. "It's a prudent decision to take care of yourself. I would hate for anything to happen to you," he said. Then, as though it was an afterthought, he added, "From the stress of overworking. It can be a hazard to your health."

"I would hate that, too." She might not be able to find what she was looking for at Langley, but there was someplace else she could get answers.

She was nothing if not resourceful.

With a curt wave, she turned and hustled down the hall. A little maze of turns took her to the elevators. She'd wait to remove the necklace in the lobby bathroom before she got near the sensors. The need to get out of there as quickly as possible pushed in on her.

She hit the call button, strategizing her next stop. The ODNI—Office of the Director of National Intelligence— was a closer drive, but her presence there would raise all sorts of alarm bells, and Price would get a phone call ten minutes after she set foot inside the building.

The elevator dinged. The doors opened. She hopped inside the empty car and hit the button for the lobby. The doors started to close, but someone shoved an arm between them, engaging the safety sensor and forcing them to open.

Ebony got on and hit the button for the second floor. Once the elevator slipped into motion, she met Kelly's gaze in the reflection of the doors. "I heard what you said about David Bertrand."

The comment about wishing he were on the team. It had only been a cover to keep Andrew from getting suspicious. She hadn't meant to offend anyone. "You're a top-notch analyst. I wouldn't have anyone else leading the team."

"I know. My ego isn't fragile as eggshells."

Grinning, Kelly turned to her.

"Don't look at me. In case they're watching," Ebony said. The surveillance of the elevators didn't have audio, only video. "David didn't quit. He was fired. Security escorted him out the day they sacked him."

Her desk had been next to his, separated by a cubicle wall panel. Of course some of the other senior analysts must've witnessed what had happened.

"This past December," Ebony continued, "they killed him."

Kelly washed all expression from her face. "How do you know he's dead?"

"I was the support analyst assigned to the team that was sent after Zenobia. A kill order came in on David one night. It was in the same location where they had tracked Zenobia. According to protocol, I passed it along to the team leader."

"Where was this?"

"Idaho Falls."

Just as Hunter had told her. He'd been telling the truth about everything, and she'd doubted him, had sent two hit squads after him. Her actions filled her with shame. "Who initiated the kill order on David?"

"I don't know."

Damn.

But it must've been Price. He might have been able to get the order through without her knowledge, but every analyst's report on anything Topaz-related made it to her desk. She remembered this one, and there'd been no mention of David.

"Why didn't you include this information in your situation report?" Kelly asked.

"That's just it. I did." The elevator chimed. "Once it was completed, I sent the report to Clark for review." The doors opened. Ebony stepped off, and without looking back she said, "David deserves justice."

David Bertrand, the pilot in Afghanistan, Ashref Saleh, the tribal leader who had died alongside him and every member of Topaz deserved justice.

Kelly was going to do everything in her power to make that happen.

Chapter Ten

At the front desk of the National Security Agency head-quarters, Kelly signed in. Langley had an impressive campus sitting at 258 acres. The NSA dwarfed CIA headquarters in comparison. The behemoth agency occupied one and a half times as much land on Fort Meade in Maryland.

A guard passed her a visitor's badge, and she clipped it to the lapel of her suit jacket. Once he cleared her through the security checkpoint, she spotted Zach.

Tall and lean, he strode toward her wearing a suit with a slim cut and an impeccable fit. A light salmon-colored shirt flattered the olive tones of his skin. His thick black hair was brushed back, not a strand out of place.

"I hope you didn't come out on my account." Kelly gave him a quick one-armed embrace before he had a chance to wrap her into one of his bear hugs.

He'd always had a thing for her and had been the first boy to kiss her when they'd both been teenagers. Immediately afterward she knew she'd never see him as anything more than a brother.

"They always notify Public Affairs when a bigwig such as yourself," he said, waggling his eyebrows, "pops in unexpectedly." He walked her to the bank of elevators, hit the call button, and the doors opened. "What brings you by?"

They stepped inside together. Kelly hit the button for the top floor.

"I need to see Judith to get some information."

"Anything I can help you with?"

"I wish, but I need an analyst." Someone with complete access at the highest levels who could comb through a mountain of information quickly.

"Don't you have a legion of those at your command at Langley?"

"I do, but it's complicated."

The ride up was smooth, and he got off with her, sticking to her side.

"I'm going to hit the restroom first. It was great to see you."

"Oh, I'll wait for you."

Smothering a groan, she entered the ladies' room and ducked into a stall.

IN KEEPING WITH the agreement that she'd made with Hunter, she pulled the insulated thermos from her handbag—it was a large leather tote that held everything but the kitchen sink—and retrieved the surveillance necklace hidden in a compartment in the base.

Quickly, she put it on, hooking the clasp. She held up the pendant to her face. "As promised." It was the least she could do, even though it was like putting a Band-Aid on a gunshot wound.

She wished she'd had a phone number so she could speak with Hunter. To discuss everything. To apologize. To beg his forgiveness for falling into the designated role of adversary when he'd needed her. If she could go back in time, she'd make different choices. Starting with the morning after in the hotel room in Boston. To do it over again and confess how she'd felt about him.

If only she hadn't been such a coward, they might have figured out how to be in a relationship given their jobs and found a way to be together.

Although she didn't have his number, she was willing to bet that he had hers. But he hadn't called her on the long car ride from McLean, Virginia. Probably for operational security. It was safer to stay off the phones, especially one the CIA could hack and eavesdrop on.

Kelly stowed the travel mug in her bag and left the bathroom.

The security guard had already notified her godmother, Judith Farren, that she was on her way up. Kelly didn't want to keep her waiting. Judith always had a jam-packed schedule and was willing to give her two minutes. She couldn't afford to squander the opportunity.

In the hall, Zach stood patiently. He flashed a bright white smile worthy of a toothpaste commercial at her, and she couldn't help smiling back. Zach was like a breath of fresh air—in small doses.

"I really don't need an escort," she said.

"It's no trouble. Not where you're concerned."

He offered his arm, and she took it as they walked down the hall.

Judith's assistant greeted them and waved her into the office.

Her godmother was already on her feet behind her desk, gathering some folders and a notepad. With a smile, she held out a single arm in welcome. "How lovely of you to drop by, my dear." They gave each other air kisses, a custom they had in public since Judith was meticulous about her makeup. "I haven't seen you since Christmas. Far too long."

A pang of guilt sliced through Kelly. She only reached out to Judith when she needed something, and that wasn't often. Not because she didn't love her or enjoy her company—on the contrary. They were both compulsive workers, addicted to the grind. Or perhaps the emptiness in their lives made them cling tighter to their jobs.

"I've been meaning to get together to do lunch," Kelly said, glancing at Zach, who stood silent and observant like a fly on the wall.

"You picked a hectic day for a visit, but I trust you didn't drive to Maryland for a social call." Judith stayed in motion as always, only pausing in front of a mirror long enough to tuck a loose strand of hair in her chignon and check her teeth. Then she was headed for the door. "Walk with me. I have a meeting I can't skip. Sorry."

"No need to apologize. I'm the one who showed up unannounced."

"What can I do for you?"

There were others in the hall, also in a hurry. Although Judith had a presence that couldn't be ignored, no one seemed to be paying any attention to their conversation. Other than Zach, who traipsed alongside them.

Still, precaution never got anyone killed. "I need information that I can't get at home," she said, assured Judith would understand that she meant Langley.

"Problems with Father?" Judith asked.

"Let's just say I've been denied full access."

"You think you can find what you need in my house?"

"Yes." Without a doubt. It was related to a surveillance program. What the NSA didn't have control over, they had full knowledge of.

Judith stopped outside a conference room door. "Care to share with me?"

"I'd rather not." Kelly put a hand on her forearm. "I don't want to get you involved any more than I have to. Father is on the warpath."

Judith studied her with concern. "Are you safe?" The words, filled with alarm, snagged Zach's attention, bringing him to Kelly's side.

She looked between mother and son. "I can handle myself."

"It better stay that way. I had to bury Elliot," Judith said, referring to Kelly's real father. "I won't bury you, too. A parent should never have to go through that. I may not be your mother, but I love you like my own."

Kelly's mother had passed away when she was too young to remember her. Judith had stepped up, filling in the role as best she could. In so many ways, Kelly emulated Judith as the one female role model she admired. Everything she knew about how to dress, do her makeup, wear her hair in a professional environment, carry herself, she'd learned from Judith.

Zach put an arm around Kelly. "We both love you."

She wondered in what form his love came—familial or romantic. She could never shake the vibe that it was the latter.

"I'll be fine." Kelly stepped out from under his partial embrace. "It's nothing for either of you to worry about." In her experience, downplaying the severity of the matter was better than getting Judith worked up.

The conference door opened, and one of Judith's aides stuck his head out. "There you are. The general is ready to get started."

"I'll be there in a moment," Judith said easily, never one to get flustered. When the aide disappeared back inside the conference room, Judith turned to her. "You want to put one of my analysts in the crosshairs of whatever tiff you're having at home?"

"I'll do what I can to protect them. I only need them to do research. Nothing more."

Judith nodded. "Pick whoever you want. Tell them I give permission for them to clear their plate of everything else until they get you what you need. If you have any hiccups, let me know."

Kelly smiled. It was nice to have powerful people she could rely on. "Thank you."

"Do you need a list of analysts to consider? I can have my assistant give you some names."

"That won't be necessary." She had worked closely with the NSA for years and had made it her business to form a rapport with a few of the analysts, but there was one in particular she had a long history with. "I already have someone in mind."

"I'll take you over to Analysis," Zach offered.

"That won't be necessary. I'd rather go on my own." Kelly patted his forearm.

"Zach, I'm sure you have a full plate," his mother said, understanding Kelly didn't want him hovering. "If you don't, then we're paying you far too much."

"I was only trying to be helpful. I'll go back downstairs to my cubbyhole in Public Affairs."

Kelly kissed his cheek, relieved to be rid of him.

SEATED IN A small, private conference room next to Kelly, Freddie Herschel rubbed his forehead. His pale face was taut with worry, twisting his features. "Why couldn't you have told me all this outside? Now I need a cigarette."

Kelly crossed her legs and sat back in the ergonomic chair. "Smoking can kill you."

"Apparently, so can this fact-finding mission you want me to undertake. I can't believe they killed David Bertrand over this. Why did you come to me?"

Freddie was wearing a long-sleeved T-shirt with the Starfleet insignia designed out of smaller pictures of different starships and the slogan 100% TREKKIE written across the top, which suited him perfectly. He looked like a combination of geek and the friendly guy next door. The man you asked to house-sit or translate a message written in Vulcan.

"I trust you," she said. "Implicitly. You're one of the good ones." She was taking a huge chance by sharing details with him, but he needed to understand what was at stake and the risks of getting involved. The last thing she would do was drag someone into this completely blind.

"It doesn't pay to be a nice person. David was a good one, and look where that got him."

She agreed, but saying so wouldn't encourage him to help. "All I need you to do is find out which surveillance program is tied to Ashref Saleh. The redacted document I saw was dated thirteen months ago."

"Well, that's easy enough. We only use Arcane and Silent Shadow in Afghanistan."

The Arcane program was eavesdropping at its finest. Only on allies. Everything from phone conversations to internet activity on worldwide providers based in the US, such as Google, Facebook, Microsoft. Data gathered included emails, videos, photos, even file transfers.

Silent Shadow involved intercepting routers, servers and other network hardware being shipped to targeted organizations in foreign countries. Covert firmware was installed before they were delivered.

Both programs were vital to the continued success of CIA operations overseas. If Ashref found out about either, it would be a motive.

"I need to know which one and exactly what made Ashref Saleh a threat to Langley. Anything you dig up on him and the program, print it out and get it to me." Speculation wasn't going to cut it. She needed documentation clearly connecting the dots.

"Whoa. Hang on a minute." Freddie raised his palms. "You never said anything about wanting me to become the next Snowden."

"That's a gross exaggeration of what I'm asking."

"The guy printed out classified documents, stuffed them in his pants and smuggled them out of NSA headquarters so that he could go public with the information."

Okay, phrasing it that way did make it sound exactly like what she was asking him to do. Ninety-nine percent of the computers at the NSA didn't have a USB port, to prevent someone from downloading classified information on a flash drive. Printing the documents and sneaking them out was the only way. "This isn't to betray your country, and I don't plan to go public."

"Then how are you going to clear the Topaz unit?"

She hadn't gotten that far in the plan. Her priority was getting the rest of the pieces to the puzzle. "There are smarter, better courses of action than going to the press. I suspect the documentation I'm asking you to get will provide a clear motive. That, combined with other evidence that I have, will be enough for the director of national intelligence to exonerate the Topaz unit." The DNI guided the entire intelligence community. To ensure nothing got swept under the rug, she would insist that the secretary of defense be in the loop on everything.

"Where did you get this other evidence if you're locked out at Langley?"

The evidence was Hunter's, but she didn't want Freddie to know that she was in contact with him. Not yet. After she got her hands on the NSA documentation, she'd be willing to share more. "From a friend, but their hands are tied at this point. I need you."

Freddie lowered his gaze to his lap. "The DNI will have to conduct an independent investigation for verification before taking action. In the time that takes, I could be exposed. Someone could make me disappear."

"The independent investigation would only be a formality. To make things official. It would be done quickly and quietly due to the sensitive nature of the circumstances. You could take a well-timed leave of absence."

"I don't know." Freddie rubbed the bald spot at the top of his head. "Did Director Farren give authorization for me to smuggle out documents?"

"I don't want to make her complicit in this part." She didn't want to open her godmother up to the possibility of reprisals. Judith had worked too hard for too long to become the first female director of the NSA. Kelly wouldn't ruin such a remarkable achievement for her. Judith would have a far-reaching impact for years to come.

"Do you know how risky this is? What if I get stopped and searched on my way out of the building? What am I supposed to do if I get caught? This is my career, my life we're talking about."

"Not just yours. There are eight others with everything on the line. Ten if you include me." She was all in and had already crossed the point of no return. This was do or die.

"You're asking a lot from me," Freddie said. "I'm no hero. I'm not a risk taker. I don't even bluff when I play poker."

"Real heroes are ordinary citizens who decide to do what's right even though they're afraid." Despite her fearless facade, this conspiracy terrified her. But turning a blind eye wasn't an option. She waited to give Freddie a chance to think. The tension between them swelled, and when he didn't seem swayed, she said, "You could always log me in to a computer and walk away. Let me do it."

She owed Hunter more than she could ever repay. Regrets were worthless. Nothing short of full exposure of the truth and Topaz exonerated would suffice. And she was willing to do whatever was necessary to make it happen.

"As if," Freddie scoffed. "When this all comes out, it'll look ten times worse on me if I let someone else use a computer under my log-in."

Asking another analyst for assistance increased the likelihood of Price finding out about this gamble. Freddie was the only one she completely trusted not to spill his guts and to actually follow through. "If you don't help me, think about what will happen to the Topaz unit. Hunter, Gage, Zee, Dean. They have civilians with them." Freddie had met some of the operatives. Intel was a small world. Playing on the fact that he could put faces to names felt dirty but necessary. "Zee's daughter is caught up in this. She's only eleven."

Freddie tipped his head back and sighed. "Using the kiddie card is so unfair."

It was, and she was sorry for it. "Defending our nation. Securing our future." That was the NSA's motto. Words Freddie took to heart.

For a long moment, he said nothing, his gaze roaming around the room, then he nodded. "All right. No more twisting my arm behind my back. I'm your man."

"Thank you. How long do you think it'll take you?"

He shrugged. "It depends on how many systems I need to access. Maybe a few hours. You want me to be thorough, find absolutely every thread that could be a motive, right?"

"Yes, of course." Exactly what she needed. "Can you do it discreetly without accessing any files that are shared with Langley?"

"I don't know. I'll sure try."

"If you do access shared files, don't go home. I'll rent a room for you at a hotel in cash, untraceable."

Freddie grimaced like he was having second thoughts. "What'll happen to Coco?"

She wasn't aware he had a girlfriend, not that she knew a lot about his personal life. It was another reason she had chosen him. No immediate family to endanger, or so she had thought. "Who is she? Do you live together?"

"She's my cat."

Kelly suppressed a smile. "The hotel would just be a precaution in the event you open shared files. If it comes down that, I promise your cat will be cared for. Maybe even get you a room that will allow small pets." She wrote down her cell number for him. "Don't use any related keywords over the phone in case my line is being monitored. We'll meet in person once you have something. Give a place and time. Also, use a code word if you found pay dirt, something concrete."

"What about 'avocado'?"

Kelly frowned. The word was a solid choice, unrelated to the subject matter. It had simply taken her by surprise.

"I love avocados," he said. "I eat them every day."

"Okay. On the flip side, if its inconclusive, say something like—"

"Okra." Smiling, he pushed his glasses up the bridge of his nose. "I can't stand it."

"Are you sure you haven't done this before? You're a natural." She patted his hand. "Don't say anything else on the phone. Not even your name."

Freddie nodded again, clearly uncertain about the task ahead of him. "When I contact you, don't be late. If you're not there at the specified time, I'll leave and shred whatever I have. I'm not hanging around anywhere with classified documents. I mean it."

Based on the look in his eye, she could tell he was serious. "Fair enough, and this should go without saying, but don't trust anyone else on this."

"Got it. I won't." Freddie stood to leave.

"One more thing. Be careful."

HUNTER HIT A button on the laptop, stopping the recording from the surveillance necklace, and opened the motel door before Kelly had a chance to knock. His heart jumped at the sight of her. When she stepped across the threshold, she wasn't the deputy director of operations. She wasn't the enemy he had to recruit. Right then, she was the woman who had put the welfare and future of his team above herself and her own ambition.

"Sorry it took me so long to get back." She removed her coat. "I wanted to make sure I wasn't followed. I didn't want to risk leading anyone back here to the entire team."

It had taken her three hours since she'd left Fort Meade. She was thorough, he'd give her that.

He locked the door and watched her dump her bag in a chair and kick off her shoes while he glanced over the long, sexy muscles running the length of her slender body.

"I'm also sorry for doubting you," she said. "I do know you. Who you are at your core, and I should've trusted in that." Averting her gaze, she lowered her head, and he imagined how difficult this must be for her. "I'm so ashamed for my part in this. For the way I led the hunt on you all. Can you forgive me, for letting you down, for not being there when you and your team needed me most?"

"After everything you went through, your actions are understandable."

"You didn't answer my question."

He brushed the back of his hand across her cheek, along her jaw and tipped her chin up with a knuckle, meeting her tortured gaze. "I can forgive you anything." The words spilled from his mouth without him thinking, but he realized they were true.

For a second, those agonizing moments, forced to go into hiding, running for his life, trying to survive on the island, Kelly in the crosshairs of his sniper rifle, the interrogation he'd subjected her to, the anger… It all evaporated.

The past tangled with the present as heat speared through him.

All the affection he had for her had never gone away—suppressed, not erased—and now it surfaced along with the memories. Her warmth mingled with his, the feel of her skin, her hair brushing across his abdomen, her lips kissing his scars, as confident with her body as she was in her career, her sensual self-awareness that constantly enticed him, how he'd memorized the map of her freckles and the very scent of her.

Big things, little things, none he'd been able to forget.

He took her by the arm and drew her closer, bringing her body flush with his. He didn't question whether what he felt for the woman he was holding was nothing more than infatuation. Or a simple case of unrequited lust.

Without a doubt, it was more. Deeper.

Kelly was beneath his skin. In his head. In his heart.

He leaned in, lowering his face to hers slowly, giving her a chance to push him away, but she was the one who pressed closer and kissed him.

No tentative, exploratory kiss, either. It was a full, open-mouthed assault he welcomed.

Rising on the balls of her feet, her arms circling his neck, she held on to him as if he were a lifeline, her fingers running through his hair as she deepened the kiss. He tightened his arms around her waist, lifting her off her feet as he devoured her mouth like a starved man.

He didn't have to worry about barricading the door this time out of fear she'd try to get away. She hungered for him as much as he did for her, and that knowledge made Hunter feel heady and turned on all at once.

She tugged him to the bed and pushed him down. Still standing, she took off her blazer, tossing it, unbuttoned her silk blouse and slipped it off, revealing a sexy bra of pale blue lace and silk that barely restrained her full breasts.

He swallowed, astonished at how they'd come full circle, back in a hotel room. "You're stunning," he said, his voice husky. Her body, her brains, her bravery—it was all stunning. She took his breath away.

She smiled. "You're pretty incredible yourself." She unzipped her pants and slid out of them. Her panties, what little of them there were, matched her bra.

His mouth went dry.

She turned around, giving him a view of her perfect heart-shaped backside as she pulled the pins from her twist. Her red hair tumbled down her back before she faced him again.

Climbing on the bed, she straddled him, leaned over and kissed him. His hands went up to hold her face to his.

Her barely clothed body rubbed against his chest and groin, making him unbelievably hard. He held her close, so tight, afraid something might ruin the moment. He slipped his fingers through her hair, so soft, so silky.

He swallowed a moan of pleasure. His straining erection wasn't a reminder of how long it had been since he'd slept with a woman—eighteen months, no one since Boston—but how much he wanted to lie between Kelly's thighs again. Needing her more now than he had a year and a half ago, he kissed her jawline, her neck, took in the scent of her luscious skin. He breathed into her ear and nipped the lobe, feeling her shiver in his arms.

"Hunter," she murmured.

While he was still capable of thinking straight, he had to ask. "What are the rules this time?"

She stared down at him, her hair falling and brushing his cheek. "None." She pressed her mouth to his in a soft kiss. "No more rules, no more boundaries between us. The only thing I need from you is honesty."

"You'll always have that. And more…"

He wanted to give her so much. He loved her like he'd never loved anyone or anything in his whole life, but before he could finish, her lips crashed down onto his. Her kisses were hungry, urgent, almost desperate.

This was everything he'd craved. The peace of mind of having her fighting at his side rather than against him. The anticipation. The desire. The love he had for her that he was finally able to feel without the burn of anger, too. Most of all hope. That's what she gave him.

Hope they'd have a future, and that, for the little while that they were in each other's arms, nothing else mattered.

Chapter Eleven

This wasn't lust.

This was affection and fire and a kind of burning need that had her shaking at her core. It wasn't like the first time they'd been together, when it had been all about fun and pleasure with no thought of consequences. This was much deeper.

She realized now that she'd been so hurt by his supposed betrayal not simply because it had been a breach of sacred trust, but also because she loved him.

Only someone she cared for so deeply could break her heart.

Despite how hard she'd tried to deny it, ignore it, resist it, she'd been in love with Hunter Wright for years. The intelligent team leader who surpassed all the others. So intense that being near him made her tingle. An indomitable will that left her in awe.

He'd forgiven her for putting him and his people in harm's way *and* he wanted her. Still.

Any reason to be scared of this connection was obliterated by his mouth on hers, his calloused fingers skimming over her body. In the middle of this hell that threatened all their lives, and with him having every justification to hate her, he made her feel like she was the center of the universe.

She didn't deserve his warmth, not after what she'd done, but she'd take it.

Grabbing the hem of his shirt, she peeled it over his head and tossed it. She ran her hands up his solid chest and over his defined shoulders, holding his gaze.

"I want you, Red."

She reached down and stroked the bulge between his legs. "I want you, too."

He stilled, his body going rigid. "That's not what I mean." He moved her hand and lowered over her, resting on his forearms. "You're so strong and resilient. You've done this for so long on your own. I don't want you to be alone anymore. Not ever again. Everybody needs someone. I want you."

He wasn't staking claim to her in some possessive way. He was opening his heart and his life to her.

She didn't know what to say, what to think. Her father had taught her to be tough, self-sufficient, to rely on no one else unless she wanted to be disappointed. Every lesson Judith had reinforced until it was ingrained in her. *Tough love*, she'd called it.

The Topaz unit had been a huge part of her life before their last mission, the closest thing she had to family besides her godmother. But there was so much of herself that she kept protected behind a wall from everyone. Price. Judith. The entire team.

Only once had she let down her guard and allowed someone else in. Hunter. In Boston.

He stroked her hair, his attention fully focused on her. It dawned on her why he had risked coming to Northern Virginia, the most dangerous place on the planet for Topaz, to see her. He'd believed she would listen to his story, watch the video of what happened at the mall and chase after the truth. Even when she'd doubted, would've sworn it wasn't possible, he'd believed.

Hunter might know her better than she knew herself.

She wasn't sure what to do with that, but she wasn't going to retreat. No more running. "I don't know how..."

He lay on his side, bringing her with him, his thigh slipping between her legs, her chest pressed to his. Sliding her arm around his waist, she held him tight, not wanting to lose *this*.

Stroking her hair, kissing her forehead and temple, he brushed his stubble against her cheek, setting off every nerve ending inside her.

She shuddered, reveling in his touch, astounded by his tenderness and patience.

"Let me be the one you turn to, you lean on." His mouth glided across her cheek and jaw, stopping where her pulse pounded in a wild rhythm. "Let me be the one you share your fears with. Let me be the one who gets past the wall." Gathering her tightly against him, he placed a searing kiss on her lips, and she nearly came undone in his arms.

She'd told him no boundaries, but he sensed her restraint. The last safeguard she still had up. He was asking her to let it go, to let him in.

Goose bumps chased tingles over her skin. He understood her in ways no one else had. Or ever would.

Pressing herself closer, she kissed him back hard and long, soaking in the heat of his body, the pounding of his heart against her chest, as desperation and desire slid into every stroke of her tongue against his.

The world outside, all the fears, faded away until the only thing that remained was Hunter. With him, she could be herself, vulnerable, flawed. This was real. Raw. Something so beautiful she'd never imagined having it in her life.

She let out a soft moan. "Yes, I want you," she said, accepting his gift of devotion and protection. Of what she hoped was his love. She was tired of doing this alone, putting her life on hold for the sake of her career. It was so hard. So lonely. He was offering her a chance at a type of happiness she'd never known, a future with a different kind of security—if they survived this. She wanted that, with him, more than anything else. "I need you." The last part slipped out without her permission.

Her father always told her that to need anyone was a sign of weakness.

Maybe Hunter was her weakness, but he was also her strength. Someone who would always have her back. Support her. Believe in her when no one else would.

Since he'd been on the run, she'd been a hot mess. On edge. At a constant nine on the Richter scale of anxiety.

But not now. Here in his arms, she was safe.

"Not a day has gone by since Boston that I haven't thought about you. Wanted you. Many times, I'll admit, with mixed emotions," he said, and she didn't doubt that on occasion he'd wanted to strangle her. "But one thing is clear to me. I need you, too." The sincerity in his voice warmed her from the inside. "All your fire and ice and everything in between."

Smiling at him, she chased down the fear slithering up the back of her throat, determined to be undaunted. Whether or not they'd have the opportunity to explore a future together was unknown. Their mutual confession, their commitment to each other was enough.

"Tell me what you want, right now," he said. "To talk about everything that you've learned? To be held? To eat? You haven't had much today. I have food for you. Just a sandwich, but it's more than you've had all day."

No one had cared for her before. Put her needs above their own.

Hunter was like no other.

She wanted all that he offered. A conversation needed to be had, probably several of them, but she was going to take this reprieve from the danger and enjoy it. He'd earned it. He'd forced her to earn it as well. She was going to take and give and remember what it felt like to share all of herself with him.

Kelly reached for his belt and undid the buckle. "I want you to make love to me first."

He caressed her face, her breast, her back, her hip, every inch of her. Everywhere he touched had her shivering with anticipation; every breath across her skin squeezed a moan from her throat. He slid a hand into her panties, and his fingers stroked her where she throbbed and ached for him.

She spread her legs, giving herself over to him, freely, happily, with no walls between them, and she was lost.

THEY'D MADE LOVE again in the shower, cleaned up and hadn't bothered to dress. He sat on the bed with his back against the headboard, watching her devour a chicken salad sandwich.

The only thing she wore was the surveillance necklace. A feat of engineering that was stylish and waterproof.

He looked over her gorgeous body, appreciating every curve, every elegant line. Her milky skin showed love bites on her neck, shoulder and thigh. He hadn't meant to mark her, but they'd gotten carried away.

Their lovemaking had been hungry, but it hadn't been frantic. Once they'd found their sensitive spots, the things they each liked and enjoyed, the things that made them both lose control, hadn't changed, they'd slid into a rhythm. The urgency building until they'd slipped over the edge, and it was as if Boston had been yesterday.

Kelly looked up from the to-go container, and her smile pierced straight through him.

He was a goner, completely caught up in the one and only Kelly Russell. At times, the memory of their one night in Boston had sometimes seemed like a fantasy he'd rebuilt in his head. Making it hotter, sexier than it had really been.

But she was more beautiful and captivating than he remembered. Her skin softer. Her mouth hungrier, sweeter. She was thinner, not eating enough, but the visceral attraction that drew him to her hadn't been diminished in the least.

Shifting closer to him, she ran her hand up his leg, her lips pressing to his as her fingers teased the muscle and tendons of his thigh. Heat and searing need flooded him in an instant, and he was helpless to hide it.

Her grin widened. "Looks like somebody is ready for another round." She reached for the rigid proof of his arousal.

But he captured her wrist gently, stopping her. They were in a bubble of joy and desire. There was no other place he'd rather be. If he could, he'd stay in it with her forever.

Like all bubbles, it had to burst sooner or later, and they had so much to discuss.

"You have to stay away from Price until this is done," he said.

Her smile faltered and faded. "I know. I will." She pulled her hand free and wiped her mouth with a napkin. "But it's not him I'm worried about. Not directly."

It didn't take a mind reader to understand what she meant. "Quinlan."

She nodded. "Funny, Price was the one who warned me about using him. Provided Price doesn't find out that we're working together, it shouldn't be a problem."

Although as long as she was with him, she was in danger. Quinlan was out there right now trying to find Gage and the rest of them. Hunter had notified the team once he'd heard Andrew's good news about spotting Gage at the store. They were all on high alert, trying to remain invisible.

He tucked her hair behind her ear and brushed crumbs from the corner of her mouth. "I can't figure out Andrew's part in all this. Are you sure he was sent to the black site?"

"Yeah. We were together when they bagged us and transported us with hoods on. In the van and helicopter."

"How do you know he wasn't cut loose?" Maybe it had been a ruse for some reason.

"We talked along the way. Whispered, really. He was at the black site. We traveled back together, too. I'm not sure what they did to him, but he had bruises."

Hunter scrubbed a hand across his jaw. "The lie about David is what I'm hung up on. He knew he was killed from the report. Why hide it from you?"

"I've been tossing that one over, too. I don't have an answer for it."

A cell phone buzzed.

Kelly reached down over the side of the bed and picked up her pants. She yanked the phone out of her pocket and looked at the caller ID.

"Who is it?" he asked.

"Unknown number." She hit the green icon. "Hello?"

"Avocado." It was Freddie. He'd hit pay dirt, found the evidence they needed. "Get pen and paper." His voice was steady, perhaps even excited. Good signs no one had him under duress. There was background noise like he was in a car or on public transportation. He was definitely traveling.

She scrambled off the bed and went to the desk, picking up the ballpoint pen. "Go ahead."

He gave the address of a restaurant. "Twenty minutes." The line went dead.

She checked the time. "How long for us to get to Pentagon City from here?"

"About thirty-five minutes, depending on traffic."

She swore under her breath as she raced around the room, collecting her clothes. "We have to be there in twenty. Otherwise, Freddie will leave and shred everything he found."

Hunter jumped off the bed. "He didn't give us much time."

"I think that was his point." She already had her underwear on and was buttoning her blouse. "He probably wanted to keep the window small to reduce the chances that someone other than me showed up."

He shoved into his jeans. "We won't make it in twenty minutes."

"Didn't you hear what I said? We have to."

"I'm capable of a lot, but the miracle of freezing time isn't one of them." He pulled on his shirt and found his phone. The others were close enough to make it. "Who on my team would Freddie be the most amenable to talking to?"

"I don't understand how that's relevant."

He hadn't gotten a chance to tell her the others had relocated. "Who?"

Sighing, Kelly slipped on her shoes. "Probably Zee. He's met her and when I mentioned her daughter, it got to him."

Hunter dialed her number. As soon as she answered, he said, "I need a favor. It's something John won't like. I understand if you can't do it." She listened as he explained the details. "I need a yes or no."

"Yes," Zee said without hesitation.

"You have seventeen minutes. Try to get Freddie to wait. If you can't, then just get the documents."

"Got it." She hung up.

He pulled a ball cap on his head. "Zee will meet him." They grabbed their coats and hustled out the door. "She's good at winning people over."

"I'll drive," Kelly said. "The less your vehicle and plates are exposed, the better."

Good thinking. He climbed into the passenger's seat as she started the engine.

Kelly backed out of the spot, whipped the car around and hit the road. "Explain how Zee can make it to Pentagon City in time when we can't." The sharpness in her tone told him she was less than pleased with his omission.

He stifled a groan. "Bringing you to the motel compromised the location. I had to move the others. Even if they hadn't insisted, it was the smart call. I wasn't hiding it from you. We hadn't gotten around to it. There were more pressing matters to discuss."

She tightened her grip on the steering wheel, her knuckles whitening as she took the on-ramp for the interstate. "They still think I can't be trusted, after what you all put me through last night? They might not have confidence in me, but they should in that stupid drug you gave me. I'm sure you tested its efficacy beforehand."

"We did. On me." If anyone was going to be a guinea pig, it had to be him.

She shot him a concerned side-eye glance. "You must've been really desperate."

"For the truth? Yes." Besides confirming the drug worked, he needed to understand the side effects before giving it to anyone else. Including Kelly, even when he thought she had betrayed them. "John doesn't know you. He only wants to keep his family safe. You can't fault him for that. You have to admit it was possible for this to have played out a hundred different ways. Most not in our favor."

Kelly nodded. With her hair loose around her shoulders, she looked younger, innocent. Almost fragile, though she was anything but. In her head, she probably agreed with the things he'd told her, but in her heart...

"The others thought you'd help us." Hunter put a hand on her knee and squeezed. "I *knew* that you would. I didn't doubt you." Staying behind at the motel, with no backup, was proof.

"Thank you." She stared straight ahead at the road, going well over the speed limit as she changed lanes and cut around cars. "You're right. It was smart to move the others. You shouldn't tell me where they are."

What? "Kelly, you're risking your career and your life. You're entitled to know everything."

She shook her head. "No. I need to earn their trust. The way I earned yours. And we need to think worst-case scenario. The less I know, the better. Under duress, I can't give information that I don't have."

He glimpsed the sadness and hurt that tightened her features. "You would never."

"Oh, Hunter." She tapped a finger on the steering wheel. "There's one thing I learned at the black site. Everyone, no matter how tough or stubborn, eventually breaks." She whisked a tear from the corner of her eye, but she didn't let a single one fall.

He wanted to wrap her in his arms and hold her, love her, make her forget.

Then he wanted to kill Price. For orchestrating all this. For subjecting Kelly to such pain and humiliation. That's what they did at black sites. They broke your body, your mind, your will. Bit by bit until you cracked.

She took the Pentagon City exit.

His mind was racing nonstop about the meeting with Freddie and whether Zee had made it in time. About what Kelly had endured at a black site.

But why would Price send her there when he knew she was innocent?

For appearances, to make it look good since suspicion would naturally fall on the team handler?

Or had it been for another reason?

What if it had been to keep her mind occupied on the fear and horror of the torture instead of looking for the truth?

The thought sickened him to his core. The CIA had been an anchor he had placed his entire trust in. Kelly had done the same. If Price could go to such lengths, then there was no such thing as good. The world was just a mess of gray.

Wayne Price wasn't inherently evil, but nothing else explained what had happened to his team. To Kelly.

At least, he could answer one of his questions by calling Zee. He shoved his hand into his pocket and realized he had run out of the motel so hastily he'd left without his mobile. *Stupid, stupid mistake. One for an amateur.*

"What's wrong?" Kelly asked, driving toward the restaurant.

"I forgot my cell. I can't call Zee."

"Use mine," she said, then she tensed. "No, don't. If my phone is being monitored, I don't want her cell number linked. I can't become an even bigger liability."

Precisely why he hadn't called Kelly earlier, despite how much he'd wanted to talk to her.

Not only could Zee not contact him for anything, such as an update or verification for Freddie that Kelly had sent her, but he also couldn't make sure that Zee was safe.

Out the window, Hunter glimpsed four police officers

running down the sidewalk in the opposite direction, heading somewhere behind them. He turned in his seat, catching them race down the stairs of a nearby Metro station.

Hunter faced forward and glanced at the clock. They were running so late. It had taken them twenty-five minutes. The traffic had been lighter headed closer into the city as commuters were going home to the suburbs in the opposite direction, which had worked in their favor. Kelly had made great time, but not fast enough. If Zee hadn't convinced Freddie to hang around or give her the documents, they were back at square one.

"Park there." Hunter pointed to a spot. The restaurant was a block away.

"It's a tow-away zone."

"We won't be long. Two minutes. Ten at the most." She was riveting with her fiery-red hair loose around her face, but it also made her stand out. "Do you have anything you can use to cover your hair?"

"I think I have a scarf in my purse."

Kelly was the type of woman who was prepared for anything.

She pulled into the spot and cut the engine. Taking her handbag, she rummaged around inside and whipped out a large, expensive-looking silk scarf. She wrapped it over her head and tied it under her chin. She tucked the rest of her hair that hung loose in the back of her coat.

"Perfect." He lowered the bill of his cap down. They got out of the car and hurried down the street at a trot. Glancing at his watch, he saw it was five ten. He took Kelly's hand. "Come on." They broke into a run.

He could see the restaurant about three hundred feet away on Twenty-Third Street between South Fern and South Eads. Four people were standing around outside, chatting. None of them were Freddie or Zee.

If Freddie had left in the past couple of minutes, they should be able to see him. But there was no sign of him. Hunter had interacted with him face-to-face on a couple of occasions and would've been able to spot him in a crowd.

They waited for the light to change, allowing them to cross the street. After a couple of seconds, Kelly seemed too anxious to wait any longer. A break in traffic presented itself, and she tugged him across the road at a sprint. They passed a little side alley lined with dumpsters for the various stores and eateries and headed for the entrance at a quick pace. He could see inside through the plate glass window and strained for a glimpse of Zee or Freddie.

There.

Zee sat at a table in front of the window alone. Her long spiral curls were up in a bun, and she had on a wide-brimmed, floppy wool hat. As she looked around, he caught her eye. She threw her hands up in question, as if to say Freddie had never showed. She stood, gathering her things, a laptop and some other items from the table.

The squeal of tires snatched his attention. An SUV swung onto Twenty-Third Street at a high rate of speed, tires smoking. The vehicle slowed down, the right-side window lowering.

A man wearing a ski mask stuck his head out and lifted a submachine gun.

What the hell?

Hunter stopped walking, jerking Kelly to a stop alongside him as he processed what was happening, his body tensing to react.

The guy shoved the barrel of the automatic weapon out the window. The muzzle was aimed at the four people standing in front of the restaurant. The next thing he knew, gunfire ripped loose, spraying the front of the restaurant with hot rounds. All four individuals were hit instantly, spinning and falling to the ground.

Time slowed, everything stretching out at half speed. He strategized his options from one breath to the next, but there was no way out of this. They were in trouble.

Standing in front of the plate glass window of the restaurant, they had no immediate protection in sight. Nothing at all to stop the rounds that were about to tear into them, not even a sidewalk bistro table.

He considered hauling Kelly to the side alley behind them about forty feet away, but there was no time.

The man was still spraying bullets on full automatic, the slugs shattering the plate glass and stitching toward them like a sewing machine. The assailant's gun hand began to lose control from the vicious recoil of the weapon, giving Hunter a slim opening.

Rolling down the street at a crawl, the vehicle continued forward, only ten feet away now.

Hunter shoved Kelly down to the ground and did the only thing he could. He took the gunman head-on.

If Hunter miscalculated in the slightest, he was dead. He launched himself at the SUV. The man's eyes, framed in the balaclava, widened with shock as he spotted Hunter charging toward the gunfire. The assailant tried aiming the weapon directly at him, but Hunter beat him in the blink of an eye. Right as the bullets were about to riddle his body, he closed his hands on the hot barrel and jerked it upward.

With the man's finger locked on the trigger, the weapon cycled rounds, blasting bullets skyward, inches from Hunter's face. The guy struggled to regain control, and when the driver accelerated, the gunman almost succeeded. But the sudden change in speed allowed Hunter to wrench the submachine gun from his hands.

The vehicle hurtled down the street, the tires squealing again as it rounded a corner.

He watched as the SUV raced away, disappearing from sight, then he scanned for any other danger.

Kelly had made a beeline for the small alley that they had passed on the way to the restaurant, most likely seeking cover behind a dumpster. It was the perfect spot to seek shelter. But he found her locked in a ferocious brawl with another man wearing a balaclava who must've been waiting for a target to run there.

Hunter pulled the trigger, letting the remaining rounds in the magazine pepper the side of the building, chipping the bricks over their heads, without getting close enough to hit Kelly by accident.

The man turned tail and took off down the alley.

Hunter ran to Kelly. She was winded and the scarf had slipped down to her neck, but she didn't appear injured.

"Are you okay?" he asked, pressing a palm to her cool cheek, making sure.

She nodded. "I'm fine."

He thought about the wild spray of bullets. The plate glass window shattering. The bystanders who had been shot.

Zee.

Turning, Hunter bolted for the restaurant. Out of the four civilians who had been standing in front of the window, two were dead. A woman sat upright, holding her arm that had been shot. One man lay on his back, rolling left and right, clutching his chest. Blood stained his hands, dripping on the pavement.

Hunter's first instinct was to help him, but when he glanced inside the restaurant through the shot-out storefront, he didn't see Zee. Maybe she had been able to take cover and was staying low. He had a tough choice to make.

As much as his conscience demanded he help the man, he chose his family instead. Once he knew Zee was safe, then he could help the wounded man.

He yanked open the restaurant door and rushed inside, frantically looking around.

Zee was down on the floor, the laptop beside her, blood pooling in her abdomen.

No!

Chapter Twelve

Her mind spinning, Kelly scrambled into the restaurant behind Hunter.

Everything had happened so fast. One minute she'd been focused on meeting Freddie, terrified that they'd missed him, and the next, Hunter was shoving her down to the sidewalk.

And then gunfire had ripped through the air.

Hunter dropped the submachine gun and fell to his knees beside Zee. She'd been hit. A red stain was sprouting on her abdomen.

A strangled wail came from Hunter, the awful sound reverberating through Kelly. He scooped Zee into his arms. She was alive and conscious, sucking in gulping breaths.

"I'm here. I've got you." He placed her hands over the wound. "Apply pressure. As much as you can."

Zee did as he told her and winced from the pain.

"It's going to be okay," he said. "Stay with me."

Zee. God. Kelly couldn't believe she was severely injured, bleeding out in a restaurant. She felt like she was dreaming, trapped in a terrible nightmare and couldn't wake up.

Glancing around dazedly, Kelly saw other customers down on the floor who had been shot or were still cowering under tables where they'd taken cover.

Sirens approaching split the air. The sound was grow-ing louder with each passing second.

"We've got to go, now," Kelly said. "Come on."

Holding Zee, Hunter stood and rebalanced her weight in his arms.

"The laptop," Zee groaned. "We need it."

Kelly took off her scarf and wiped Hunter's fingerprints from the submachine gun, then she grabbed the laptop and hurried after them.

Hunter had taken off at a jog, headed back to the car. Kelly quickly caught up to them and dashed ahead. She raced into the street, holding up her palms to stop traffic and give Hunter a chance to cross with Zee.

Once they had made it to the other side, Kelly ran at a dead sprint. At the car, she opened the back door. Hunter got Zee into the car, carefully laying her down on the back seat.

"I'll drive," Hunter said, which made the most sense, since Kelly didn't know where they were going.

It wasn't as if they could take Zee to a hospital, but she needed urgent medical care.

Kelly threw the keys to him and climbed in the back, putting Zee's head on her lap. Needing to do something to help her, she reached for her go bag in the foot well. She unzipped it and rifled through the contents.

Hunter started the car and zipped into traffic, cutting off another vehicle. Several horns blared as he sped away down the street.

"Where are we going?" Kelly asked.

"To the motel, where the others are staying. Kate can help her."

Alarm streaked through her. "I can't go there." She couldn't endanger everyone else.

"We're out of options. I'm not going to pull over and

just let you out on the side of the road. We don't have time to spare to drop you somewhere safe."

She considered protesting, but it would do little good. If anything, it would only add to the stress of an already dire situation.

Kelly pulled her emergency medical kit from her go bag. Controlling Zee's bleeding was the most pressing concern. She found a packet of gauze that was pretreated with a hemostatic agent.

Before using it, she needed to see if there were multiple wounds and how bad they might be. Kelly folded back the sides of Zee's jacket. "I need to take a look."

Zee nodded and moved her hands.

Kelly lifted the hem of her sweater, peeling it up over the sticky spot where blood pooled, and gasped at what she saw.

"What is it? What's wrong?"

"She's wearing a bulletproof vest." Kelly lowered the zipper on the side of the vest, slowly, gently.

"Did the bullet hit her somewhere she wasn't covered?"

"No." Kelly tried to stop her hand from trembling. "It penetrated the vest."

"That would mean they used armor-piercing rounds."

At least the vest had slowed it down and hopefully minimized the impact. The internal damage wouldn't be nearly as bad as if she hadn't been wearing one.

Kelly pulled up the lower part of the vest to see the injury. Only one gunshot wound. She pressed the gauze with hemostatic agent on the wound and used her hand to add pressure.

"The AP rounds," Hunter said, "the man waiting in the alley. The one any trained operative would have used for cover. This wasn't random. It was planned, coordinated."

"In under twenty minutes?" She moved her hand from

the wound. The gauze was soaked through with blood. She peeled it off, put on a fresh piece and applied more pressure.

"It's the only explanation," Hunter said.

"But how?"

"Price has to be monitoring your phone. He must've identified the call as Freddie's and put two and two together. Quinlan and his men must've been close enough to respond."

Kelly had hoped their precautionary measures would have been enough. She bit her bottom lip, wanting to scream in frustration. The only reason she didn't chuck her cell phones out the window was the specialized app she'd had a tech guru download on them. It constantly bounced her position between cell towers within a hundred-mile radius of her true location so no one could trace her actual whereabouts.

She'd even had an ace hacker test the app. It was airtight, tamper-proof.

There must've been a lookout, waiting for her or Freddie to arrive.

"Did you see Freddie?" Kelly asked Zee.

"No." She groaned, her head lolling from side to side. "I was monitoring the CCTV cameras on the street from my laptop. I never saw him."

Where was he? "Maybe he got cold feet at the last minute and decided not to follow through." She hoped that was the case. The alternative was that something had happened to him.

Kelly cradled Zee's head while keeping pressure on the wound. Her tawny brown skin was ashen. Hunter needed to hurry before she went into shock.

The pretreated gauze was slowing the blood loss, but there was no way to tell what kind of internal damage she'd suffered. If an armor-piercing bullet had struck a major organ or artery.

"Hold on. We'll be there soon," Kelly said to her, even though she had no clue where the motel was located or how much longer it would take to reach it.

Zee was the glue that held Topaz together, a sister, a mother to the entire team. The one who made sure they all ate balanced meals in the field and didn't subsist off junk food. The one who gave them advice about their personal lives. She was the calming voice of reason when too much testosterone drove heads to grow hot and had mouths running even hotter.

They couldn't lose her. It would devastate all of them.

Kelly put a hand to her clammy cheek. "Hang in there, Zee." Light glinted off something, catching Kelly's gaze. A diamond ring on Zee's left hand.

Zee was engaged to John?

The realization only added to the pressure building in her chest.

"We're here." Hunter pulled into the parking lot of a motel and stopped in front of room 151. There was a black sedan in the spot beside them.

Kelly looked around for any passersby. No one was around. In this quadrant of the motel, there were only two other vehicles. Both must've belonged to Topaz.

Hunter opened the back door, and Kelly helped him get Zee out of the car. He picked her up, and she could tell he was taking great care not to add to her discomfort. "Knock on 150," he said, hustling around the car.

Kelly pounded on the door with a fist.

The door swung open, and she faced Dean. His eyes narrowed, his body tensing as he prepared to strike.

"Zee's hurt." The words rushed from Kelly's mouth.

Dean looked past her, spotting Hunter. "Kate!" He

called over his shoulder as he stepped back, letting them inside the room.

Hunter laid Zee down on the first of two queen beds closest to the door. "Tell Gage to keep a lookout," he said to Dean. "I don't think we were followed, but I can't be sure. We need to be prepared and go get John. Don't let Olivia come."

Dean gave a curt nod and took off like a shot out of the room.

Kate came out of the bathroom and froze, taking in the scene. Then she rushed over to examine Zee. "What happened?"

"Gunshot wound," Hunter said. "AP round through her vest."

"What's AP?" Kate snatched a medical bag from the desk and pulled on latex gloves.

"Armor-piercing. It tore through the vest."

Kate's eyes widened in alarm, but she didn't slow down. She pulled out a large plastic sheet. "Help me."

Kelly hurried over to assist. They spread the plastic sheet over the second bed. Kate tossed her a bundle of sterile surgical sheets.

"You're prepared," Kelly said, unable to filter the surprise from her voice.

"I needed to be ready in case anyone got seriously injured in Venezuela."

"Laptop," Zee said through a strained breath.

"Shh." Hunter knelt beside her, took off her hat and stroked her hair. "Don't try to talk. Conserve your strength."

"There's a program. Hit control-F7 to activate it." Zee took a deep breath and winced as tears leaked from the corner of her eyes. "You'll be able to monitor the CCTV in the surrounding area. Spot suspicious vehicles or activity. See them coming."

"You're something else, you know that?" Hunter said to her.

"That's why you chose me for Topaz."

"Yeah, it is. You were the best. Even at twenty years old. You still are. We can't lose you. So, you've got to hang in there."

Hunter had handpicked each member of his team. Kelly remembered how Zee had been the one holdout. The young woman had only been with the CIA for a year, after being coerced to join or go to jail. Suffice it to say, she had legitimate issues trusting the company. But Hunter had been relentless and had eventually persuaded her to put her trust in him.

Their team had been together for over a decade. Celebrating achievements together, sharing in the pain of their difficulties, helping one another through injuries, sticking side by side no matter the adversity.

Now, one of them was critically injured.

The door flew open and a man stormed in. John Lowry.

Kelly had only seen pictures of him from his impressive service record as a Navy SEAL. His enraged presence sucked all the oxygen from the room.

John's gaze fell to Zee and then swung to Hunter, who was standing up as if preparing himself. John stalked around the bed, snatched Hunter by his jacket, swung him around and shoved him back into a wall.

The thud resonated through the room.

Dean closed the door but didn't move. Nobody else moved. Kelly was stunned, uncertain what might happen next, but it was clear that whatever it was, Hunter had no intention of defending himself.

"You were supposed to protect her!" John said, slamming Hunter against the wall a second time. "I knew this would happen. That you couldn't keep her safe!"

"I'm sorry." Hunter kept his hands at his sides. "I'm so sorry. If I could trade places with her, I would."

"But you can't. Can you?" John's hand clenched and he cocked his fist back as Kelly launched across the room to stop him.

She grabbed hold of his arm, ready to do more if necessary. She recalled from his record that he'd suffered a leg injury. If necessary, she'd exploit it. "This is my fault! If you want to hit someone, hit me."

John glanced over at her as if coming out of a murderous trance. "What in the hell are you doing here?" he said, like he was noticing her for the first time. He glared at Hunter. "Are you kidding me?"

"Honey," Zee called weakly.

John turned, looking over his shoulder. Suddenly, his hands unclenched as he let Hunter go.

Zee held out her hand to him, and he hurried to her side, sitting on the bed. He took her bloody hand in his, and his entire demeanor immediately changed. Everything about him softened as he leaned in over her.

"Oh, baby." His kissed her forehead. "What happened to you?" His voice was as gentle as cotton, but it scored Kelly's heart.

There was no doubt in her mind how much this man loved Zee, that he would move heaven and earth for her.

"It's not Hunter's fault," Zee whispered.

"It never is. Always someone else's." John looked at Kate. "Can you help her?"

"I think so." Kate was setting out equipment in a neat line along the edge of the surgical sheet. "I'm going to do my best."

"We're done with this," John said to Zee. "We're finished."

"No." She tightened her fingers around his. "The team—" she swallowed and groaned in agony "—they need us. All h-hands on deck. Numbers matter."

Topaz did need all the quality help they could get, but John was also right. Zee was injured and they had a child to think of.

"We can't be done until our names are cleared," Zee said. "Please."

"We'll discuss it later. You need medical attention."

"I'm ready," Kate said. "I need to get the bullet out, check for internal damage and stop the bleeding. Bring her over here."

Hunter stepped forward to help.

"Stay away from her," John growled. He picked Zee up and set her down on the other bed.

"Dean, I'll need your assistance," Kate said as she put on a surgical gown. "John, you can stay if you can be still and quiet."

"I will," John said.

"Kelly, Hunter, I need you two to leave," Kate said.

Hunter grabbed Zee's laptop, and Kelly followed him out of the room.

"Are you okay?" she asked, putting a hand on his chest.

"No. I won't be all right until Zee is."

She understood the sense of responsibility he carried. The weight of their lives on his shoulders. "This *is* my fault. Not yours."

He shook his head. "You were the target, but this is Price's doing."

It should have occurred to her sooner. With so much happening so quickly, she'd barely had a chance to process everything. Price wouldn't have expected Hunter or Zee to be at the restaurant. That drive-by shooting had been meant for her.

Price wanted her dead, and since Hunter had been with her, now the man knew they were working together.

Gage seemingly materialized out of thin air and approached them. "How is she?"

"Kate's trying to help her now," Hunter said.

Gage tossed him a room key, and he caught it. "It's yours. On the corner of the second floor."

"Zee has a program set up where we can monitor the CCTV in the area. I'll activate it. Keep an eye on the footage. If you hear anything about Zee—"

"We'll let you know. How's John taking it?"

Hunter shook his head. "Not well."

"I'm surprised he didn't beat you within an inch of your life."

"I wasn't going to let that happen," Kelly said, not even if Hunter's guilt would've allowed it. They were in this together. All of them. The only way to survive was by working as a team, not beating each other up.

Gage gave her a two-finger salute. "I'll stay outside for a bit. I've got a nest on the roof with your sniper rifle."

"We'll take shifts," Hunter said. "One of us on the computer and the other on the roof. Every three hours we'll rotate."

Kelly shivered. "It's freezing out here. Wouldn't every hour be better?"

"Not from an operational standpoint," Gage said. "The fewer rotations, the less likely we are to give away the position. I've got blankets, hand warmers and a thermos of hot coffee. It'll be fine."

Hunter nodded in approval.

They were all hardened, dedicated. She'd never done fieldwork. It was best to leave it to the professionals.

Hunter took her hand and led her up the staircase to the room.

Inside, he set up the laptop on a desk and initiated the program. He sat in front of the computer with his gaze unwavering, clenching and unclenching his hands.

As she stared at his grim face that was etched with grief and worry, she couldn't deny this was reality. She detested feeling helpless and had no idea what to do. How to make this better for him. For any of them. Since they'd enlisted her to their side, they were no closer to proving that Price was behind everything.

She'd only managed to make things worse.

HUNTER WATCHED THE live video feed of six different CCTV cameras in the area while listening to the news. Kelly had put on the television once she'd stopped wearing a hole in the carpet by pacing around the room.

She made coffee and offered to take over monitoring the screens, but Hunter needed something to do.

Anything to keep his mind off how much he hated himself right now.

When he had recruited Zee all those years ago, he'd seen a beautiful, capable, strong, young hacker who was wicked smart. With the genius-level IQ to back it up. He'd also seen someone vulnerable. Someone who needed to be surrounded by people who would look out for her, take care of her. Of course, she'd wanted nothing to do with joining a team. Especially not his, where they were supposed to go into the field and eliminate high-value targets.

He'd been twenty-nine, ambitious, so self-assured that he'd lacked the foresight to consider their current predicament could ever be possible. Recruiting the best of the best for his team had been his only concern.

Then one day, she came to him with a problem. A deeply personal, painful problem. He didn't help her in a shady attempt to gain her trust. He had stepped in on her behalf because it had been the right thing to do. What she had endured at the hands of a low-life operative had made him livid. Raging mad.

But it had also been the thing that had convinced her to join Topaz.

For more than a decade, they had watched out for each other, supported one another through everything. Gage, Dean and Hunter had been like uncles to Olivia since the day she'd been born. Zee was their sister, the heart of their tribe.

They weren't a family through blood. They were a family forged by choice.

And it had been his shortsighted choice that had roped Zee into this. He could have left her alone after she'd rejected his offer the first time. She would be an analyst at Langley. Safe. Not hurt, but assured to watch her daughter grow up.

If Zee didn't pull through, he'd never forgive himself.

"Still the same hogwash," Kelly said, gesturing at the television.

During the past two and a half hours, the news coverage hadn't changed. The Arlington County Police Department was covering up the drive-by shooting, no doubt from the strict instructions of Director Price that had trickled down to their level. They were calling the incident that had killed five and wounded seven, not including Zee, *gang related*.

"What an unbelievable farce," she said, starting to pace again.

It wasn't easy being on the other side of a cover-up. He would know.

The television screen flashed a Breaking News banner and switched to a different reporter standing on a Metro station platform.

"I'm Juan Dowding reporting live from the Pentagon

City Metro station, where a man was killed earlier in a tragic accident. Police have finally identified the man as Frederick Herschel."

Hunter turned to Kelly. She grew still as stone. Her chest rose and fell in shallow rhythms as she stared at the television, wide-eyed and unblinking.

"He was a dedicated, hardworking analyst at the National Security Agency in Fort Meade. Earlier today an eyewitness saw Mr. Herschel slip from the platform and fall in front of an oncoming train."

"They killed him," she said. "They killed him because I dragged him into this."

Hunter got up and went to Kelly, bringing her into his arms. First Zee and now Freddie. "We needed the documentation." They still did, desperately. "Price forced us into this position. Not you. Don't forget that."

He didn't want her beating herself up over Freddie's murder. She was under enough pressure. They were all barely keeping their heads above water. Today's events had only compounded the strain.

"Freddie didn't deserve to die," she murmured. "Especially not like that."

No, he didn't. Not any more than his team deserved to be hunted or she had deserved to be tortured by her own government that she'd selflessly served since she was twenty-one.

They'd find a way to balance the scales and get justice for everyone Price had wronged.

"I've got to get Coco," Kelly said, her voice sharpening.

"Who is that?"

"Freddie's cat. She's all alone now. I promised to take care of her if anything happened."

A ferocious mix of grief, anger and dread swelled out of nowhere and hit him hard at the mention of the cat. It wasn't about the pet who'd lost an owner. Freddie was someone's son, possibly someone's brother or uncle. There were others in his life who'd miss him. Hunter also thought about Zee. About John and Olivia. About Zee's parents. She had a strained relationship with them, but Hunter had no doubt that they loved her, their only child, with all their hearts.

He swallowed past the thickening lump in his throat. "We'll get the cat once it's safe to go to his house."

"What are we going to do about Price?" She pressed her face into the crook of his neck.

Tightening his arms around her, he sucked in a deep breath. The truth was, he wasn't sure. He was sorry that Freddie was gone, sorry they'd gotten him involved, and he was furious with Price.

But all he could think about was Zee and whether or not Kate would be able to save her life.

There was a knock at the door.

"Don't worry. We'll figure it out and get through this together." Hunter kissed Kelly's forehead and went to open the door.

Hope stood with a somber look on her pale face, her eyes pink and glassy from crying. "It's Zee," she said in a shaky voice.

Hunter's heart clenched.

Chapter Thirteen

The cold air penetrated through her clothes straight down to bone without her coat, but they'd been in too much of a hurry to bother putting them on.

Kelly rushed alongside Hunter down the metal staircase to room 150. Hope trailed behind them, dotting her eyes with a tissue. Kelly's heart pounded with fear. Every frigid intake of breath seemed to seize her lungs.

Hunter hadn't given Hope a chance to spit out what she'd come to say. He tore out of the room and Kelly stayed at his side.

They had no idea what to expect. But she braced for the worst. Prepared herself to be strong for Hunter and the rest of the team.

Hunter pushed open the cracked door, and they stepped inside the warm room.

Zee was propped up in the bed. Her eyes were open but weary and glassy, like she was still under the effects of whatever drug Kate had used on her.

Relief poured through Kelly at seeing Zee alive. She said a silent prayer of thanks, even though she wasn't the praying kind. So many lives had already been lost. She was grateful Zee was with them.

John was sitting on the left side of the bed, and Olivia,

the girl who was the spitting image of Zee, sat on her mother's right side.

Kate had cleaned up any traces of the medical procedure. "I was able to stop the bleeding. She's lost a lot of blood," Kate said, "but not enough to need a transfusion. I got the bullet out in one piece. No fragments. And no major internal damage. It was a good thing she was wearing the vest and that the bullet didn't hit the aorta or puncture her stomach. She got very lucky. So did you two, from what Zee told us."

Hunter took a step toward Zee and then stopped, as though he reconsidered getting any closer to John.

Kelly put a hand on his shoulder. She understood how badly he must've wanted to hold Zee's hand, kiss her cheek, simply soak in the fact that she was alive and would be on the mend soon, but he also didn't want to intrude any further.

Behind them, Hope sniffled and blew her nose. "I was so worried about you pulling through. I'm happy to know you're going to be all right. I'm sorry I can't stop crying. Greeting card commercials have me in tears these days. My hormones are such a mess," she said, putting a hand to her stomach.

Was Hope pregnant?

Only a member of the Topaz unit would go on the run and find a way to fall in love, father a child and get engaged.

Kelly wiped the surprise from her face. "We're all relieved, Zee."

"You did good work, Kate," Hunter said. "Thank you."

Dean smiled at her and put an arm around her shoulder, bringing her in close against his side.

"No need to thank me," she said, resting her head on Dean's shoulder. "I'm only glad I was able to help."

"What I said earlier stands." John tore his gaze from Zee and looked at Hunter. "We're out."

"I understand," Hunter said. "I respect your decision."

Zee pulled John's hand to her chest, dragging his attention back to her. "I don't regret joining Topaz and following Hunter all around the world. It was the best decision I ever made. I can't even regret what happened in Afghanistan. If we hadn't been forced to go on the run and hide, I never would've met you. Other than Olivia, you're the best thing that's ever happened to me. It's because of all this that I found the love of my life."

John caressed her face with his other hand. "I love you, too, honey. You and Olivia have changed my life for the better. Saved me from self-doubt and pity. Brought me more joy than I ever thought possible. Filled up a dark place in my heart with so much light and love."

"It wouldn't have happened if I wasn't a part of this family," Zee said. "They need us, now more than ever. All hands on deck, sailor."

He lifted her hand to his mouth and kissed the back of it. "You're right. They need help, baby, but that can't be with us going forward."

Zee's eyes flared wide. She struggled to sit up in protest, her face lighting up with a fresh edge of gut-wrenching pain. John placed a steady hand on her shoulder, keeping her from moving farther. "Don't worry." His voice was soft and reassuring. "We're not abandoning them." John turned back to Hunter. "I called some friends. They'll have your back and take our place."

"You shared this situation with civilians?" Kelly asked. "Can they be trusted?"

John gave a slow, sad chuckle. "Coming from you, lady, that's pretty rich."

Taking her hand in his, Hunter captured her gaze and

shook his head while giving her fingers a slight squeeze. The gesture was curt, subtle, but she recognized the meaning. He wanted her to stay out of this.

"Hold on," John said. "Are you two together?" He went to stand, but Zee gave his arm a tug and he stayed seated. "Talk about sleeping with the enemy."

"Who did you call?" Hunter asked, redirecting the conversation as he let her hand go.

"SEALs. Not civilians." John's steely gaze slid to Kelly, and she forced herself not to flinch. "Four of them on leave. One is really good with computers. He's no Zee, not even on a good day, but he's the best I could get on short notice who was willing to help with few questions asked. They're driving up from Virginia Beach and will be here before sunrise. You may be losing two of us, but you're gaining four."

"SEALs," Dean said with a hint of excitement. "Good job, man."

Hunter nodded. "You didn't have to do that. I appreciate it."

"I didn't do it for you. I did it for Zee and the others." John patted Zee's hand and stood. He crossed the room, coming closer than Kelly would've preferred. "I like you, Hunter. Respect you. There have been no issues between us until things became about this woman." He gestured to Kelly while staring at Hunter. "I have a big problem with the choices you've made recently. I have an even bigger problem with her continued involvement."

"I like you, too," Hunter said, his voice even, firm. "I think you're great for Zee and Olivia. I appreciate your perspective. More than that, I respect your honesty. You've been of tremendous value to this team. But when it comes to Kelly, you no longer have a say, because you're out. For what it's worth, she isn't the enemy." He stepped away from her and John and went to Zee, lowering to his knee beside the bed. "I didn't keep you safe. I'm sorry." Zee opened her mouth, but he continued, "It is my fault. I'm in charge. I sent you there. I put you in harm's way. John is doing the right thing by pulling you guys out. You need to recover so you can be there for Olivia."

Zee glanced at her daughter, and the young girl smiled in return.

"I won't stop," Hunter said. "Not until our names are cleared. I swear it."

John glanced at Kelly, sending a look of poison through her.

She figured it was time for her to clear the air. The only person missing was Gage, but this felt like a now-or-never situation. "I owe all of you an apology. I've made serious mistakes and have done unconscionable things because I believed the lies that Price told me. He was very convincing. But I shouldn't have doubted any of you. I shouldn't have doubted my own judgment. I don't expect you to forgive me." She looked around the room, even at Hope, who was still teary-eyed. "But from now on I'll fight *for* you." She would fight to her last breath for them. "It's the very least that I can do."

IN THEIR ROOM on the second floor of the new motel, Hunter lay in the bed, with Kelly curled against him, and stared at the ceiling. The sun was rising. Soft morning light peeked through the curtains.

After seeing Zee would be all right, he'd relieved Gage from his post on the roof and taken over as lookout. If they had been followed, the strike team could've been waiting for the wee hours to attack when they thought everyone would be asleep. Although they had Zee's program active, monitoring the CCTV of the surrounding area, the cameras had blind spots. That's where a lookout on the roof ensured no one sneaked up on the team.

Three hours in the cold, in position in the nest, had numbed his feelings and clarified his thoughts. He finally saw a way forward.

Kelly stirred, running a hand up his chest. "Have you gotten any sleep?"

"I dozed a bit." Solid sleep had eluded him. The catnap would have to suffice.

"Do you think John's friends have gotten here?"

He hadn't heard any vehicles approach or car doors close, but they were special warfare operators who excelled at stealth. And killing.

"I'd be surprised if they haven't." He tightened his arm around her. "Do me a favor."

"Sure, anything. Name it."

"Stay out of their way," he said, and her body tensed against him. "I don't know what John has told them about you. Or me, regarding you."

"You need to mitigate any potential friction."

"Yeah." With Quinlan and his team in the mix, they needed the backup of those SEALs.

She leaned up on her forearm and stared down at him. "I shouldn't have said anything last night. I only wanted to smooth things over. As if that were possible."

He tucked her hair behind her ear and caressed her face. "You gave a good speech."

"Think so?"

"It came from the heart. Zee, Dean, Gage, they get it. I'm sure they appreciated what you had to say."

"I wonder if Hope was able to relay the message without crying."

They both chuckled, and she lay back down, putting her head on his chest. He smoothed her dark red hair away from her face and trailed his fingers in a slow stroke down her long, elegant throat and over the sexy sweep of her collarbone. Pressing his nose to her hair, he breathed in the scent of her. Cinnamon and vanilla. Spicy and sweet. She always smelled like that.

"I have an idea to get us out of this," he said.

"What?"

"I go to Price's house. Find out the motive firsthand."

Kelly shot upright in the bed and stared at him, horrified.

"Not alone." Should be easy enough to squeeze the truth out of Price, and taking the others along as an intimidation factor wouldn't hurt.

"You told me to stay away from him. I think you should follow your own advice and do the same."

"It's the only way. If you take what we currently have to the DNI, it'll seem like a reach. But if you also had a solid motive the DNI could verify through independent research, we might have a real chance."

Kelly shook her head. "We need that documentation. I can't go to the director of national intelligence half-cocked. I need concrete proof of a motive I can put on his desk. Not the word of the man we're implicating who was made to talk under duress. Can't you see how that would muddy the waters? Possibly even incline him to take Price's side in this?"

"How are we supposed to get it?"

"I'll do what I should've done in the first place." Reaching over to the nightstand, she grabbed her tote bag. She fished out her phone and dialed a number.

Who in the world was she calling?

Kelly put the phone on speaker.

The line rang and rang as Hunter sat up, wondering if anyone would answer at this hour.

On the eighth ring someone picked up. "Hello," a woman said. The voice was strong, alert, familiar.

"Hi, Judith. It's me." Hunter met Kelly's gaze as she spoke.

"Oh, my dear. I've been so worried about you since I saw the news. I went to your house last night to check on you and to take you somewhere safe, but you weren't home. I was reluctant to call. For obvious reasons."

Judith was worried about the line being monitored, as well she should be.

"I'm fine. No need to worry," Kelly said. "Can you make some time for me in your schedule today? I could still use your help."

"I won't be in the office. I'll be working remotely for the rest of the week. I felt it best to get away from it all. I wish I could help you, my dear, but that won't be possible. Do you understand *the point*?"

"I do. I understand. I'm sorry to have troubled you." Kelly hung up and grinned as though she'd gotten a completely different response from the one he'd heard.

"Why are you smiling?" he asked. "She just refused to help. Although I am surprised that you'd take the chance of asking her after what happened to Freddie."

"Judith has access to everything. She can help us, and once she does, we can keep her safe. I won't leave her side."

"But she won't help. Not that I blame her."

"I'm smiling because she just agreed to."

"Were we listening to the same responses she gave?"

"All that business about it not being possible was for Price's sake. Judith isn't going into the office, and she isn't at home. She has the same app on her phone as I do that prevents anyone from pinpointing her geolocation, but she told me exactly where to find her."

They'd been speaking in code. "And where is that?"

"The Point. It's the location where the Potomac and Shenandoah Rivers meet. Harpers Ferry."

"Her house in West Virginia?"

"Yes, but in the divorce, the house was donated to an LLC."

"Owned by Judith, I take it."

"Yes. She set it up to be able to pass her assets to her son to avoid taxes."

"Savvy woman."

"Since she's working remotely, she'll have a classified laptop with her. She can give me the documentation we need without endangering her."

Sounded lovely in theory, but things rarely worked out so simply. "She'll want to know why you need it. Once she realizes it's related to Topaz, a rogue team, one that I led, she'll refuse."

Judith never did care for him. Whenever they'd been in the same room, she'd always been brusque and cold toward him. Arctic-level deep freeze. Sometimes he wondered if that was the reason Kelly had never given a relationship between them serious consideration.

Kelly pinched her lips. "No, she won't."

"Judith will think she's protecting you by not doing it. The odds of her going against her motherly instinct toward you are slim."

"Which means it's possible," Kelly said brightly, clinging to hope, no matter how small. She jumped out of bed and padded toward the bathroom. "I'll have to turn on the daughterly charm and persuade her. Failing that, I'll beg." She blew him a kiss and disappeared into the bathroom.

He'd never thought he'd see the day when Kelly Russell would be willing to beg, much less enthusiastic to do so. When she'd told the team that she'd fight for them, she'd meant it.

Still, he doubted Judith would be persuaded. She wasn't the type who would bend to anyone else's will. A real mama bear. Judith was more likely to turn his team over to Price than she was to give Kelly any documentation that would pit her goddaughter against the head of the CIA.

The situation was a tinderbox. The wrong move a lit match.

But he knew better than to try talking her out of this. She was headstrong, tenacious, and once she set her mind to a task, there was no stopping her.

Kelly came out of the bathroom, dressed, her long red hair, vibrant as flames, up in a messy twist. She leaned over and kissed him. The surveillance necklace slipped out of her sweater, dangling between them.

With her porcelain-grained skin, high cheekbones, those cobalt blue eyes and a delicate nose, she had the most arresting face. One he wanted to look at for the rest of his life.

"Let me send someone with you," he said.

Kelly pulled away, her eyes narrowing. "You're still going to see Price, aren't you? It's the only reason you wouldn't offer to come with me yourself."

"We need to be prepared in case your way doesn't work."

"You're unbelievably stubborn."

"It takes one to know one, *Red*."

She pursed her lips with a hint of a smile. "Kicking a hornet's nest isn't a good contingency plan."

He ignored the comment. "Who are you going to take? Gage or Dean. Or both." He was worried about her and would be until they had stopped Price. There was no telling what proverbial traps the master spy had in store for them. Getting caught unawares terrified him when it came to Kelly.

"None of the above. If Judith spots anyone with me, our chance will go right out the window. She trusts me, but she'll be suspicious of anyone who tags along, especially Gage or Dean. A total stranger might make things complicated." She put on her coat and slipped the straps of her tote bag over her shoulder. "Don't underestimate Price."

"I won't."

"Take your guys with you. The SEALs, too."

That was already his plan. "You can't resist being in charge, can you?"

They were both alphas, but this would work between them, if fate gave them a real chance. He felt it in his bones.

She grinned. "You didn't seem to mind yesterday afternoon when we were in the other motel room."

Hunter visualized Kelly straddling him and having her way. Nope, he hadn't minded one little bit. "You're quite right."

He wanted to get up, cross the room and haul her into his arms. But he forced himself not to move, knowing if he touched her, he'd kiss her sweet mouth again with its bow-shaped full lips. Then one thing would lead to another, and they didn't have time to enjoy each other.

Kelly gave him one last smile and left.

He rested his head back against the wooden frame of the bed.

Going to see Price was a big gamble. He was the director of the CIA, with his guard up. Hell, he might've even contracted bodyguards to keep him safe until this was done. The man was dangerous and powerful—and totally paranoid.

None of their options were risk-free, and this one had the potential to pay off.

But Kelly was right.

Anyone who would set them up, send Kelly to a black

site and endeavor to silence his unit with a bullet would cross any line, go to any extreme to see this through to the end.

Hunter would take Gage, Dean and the SEALs, to be prepared for anything.

He knew all too well that there was no greater danger than underestimating one's opponent.

Chapter Fourteen

It had started snowing as soon as she'd gotten on the road. This was probably the last snowfall of the season. The music from the radio washed out the drone of the wipers that kept the windshield clear.

Hopefully, they'd all be alive to see spring.

Despite her worries and fears and regrets, she'd gotten the best sleep this morning. Thanks to Hunter. With him beside her in the bed, she had been able to let it all go for a little while, comforted by his presence, his warmth and the knowledge that she wasn't alone anymore. She only wished he had rested longer.

He would need his wits about him with Price.

The drive to Harpers Ferry had taken over an hour since she'd stopped at a local café that Judith loved and picked up breakfast. One thing her godmother had taught her was never to show up at someone's house empty-handed, family, friend or otherwise. Good manners aside, she'd use anything to win Judith over to her cause. Even a crust-less mini rainbow quiche loaded with veggies and cheese.

She forced herself to breathe through the pressure mounting in her chest. The last thing she wanted was to endanger Judith the way she had Freddie. This time would be different.

This time she would keep her godmother safe, she vowed to herself.

Kelly made a right, turning onto the less traveled single lane that led to the house. A white waterfall of flurries cascaded down and blanketed the road. The two-story house that sat on eight acres of paradise close to the river and tucked back in the woods came into view along with the old stable. Judith used to own horses until one day Zach had lost his love for riding.

She parked her car in the driveway alongside Judith's SUV and shouldered out of the vehicle, holding the bag from the café.

It was serene. Picturesque. Everything swathed in white, the stillness, the woods, the rush of the river not far away. The air smelled clean with a hint of pine. She'd spent more than one summer and Christmas here. The place held special memories for her, some magical and some she'd rather forget. When she was five, it was here they'd gathered around her and told her that her mother was sick, dying from cancer, and they'd explained what a godmother was. It was here that her father had died from a heart attack as she'd watched Judith perform CPR until the ambulance arrived.

It was here, in this place, she'd decided to join the CIA the way her father had always wanted.

And it was here that she needed to right her greatest sins against Topaz.

She marched up to the front walkway, determined, focused, and knocked.

A minute later, Judith opened the door and beckoned her inside out of the cold. After Kelly crossed the threshold, Judith scanned the surroundings before closing the door.

"Are you all right?" Judith wrapped her in a big hug.

"Yes, fine."

"You weren't followed, were you?"

"Of course not. I took my time. I was careful." She handed Judith the bag.

"You stopped at the Rainbow Café?"

"I figured you'd only had black coffee for breakfast."

Judith kissed her cheek. "Thank you, my dear." She gestured to the wall with a pointed finger.

Kelly hung her coat up, placing her tote bag on the hook. Then she followed the rule of the house, dropping her phone in the Faraday pouch on a shelf. It clinked against Judith's.

Faraday pouches blocked incoming and outgoing signals from smartphones, tablets and laptop computers. Judith always kept one by the front door and insisted everyone who entered her home put any smart devices inside.

"Let's get you a cup of coffee." Judith led the way to the kitchen.

Kelly sat on a stool at the expansive Carrara marble island.

Judith took a mug from the cabinet, filled it with piping-hot coffee, handed it to Kelly and refreshed her own cup. She opened the bag from the café and took a whiff. "This smells so good." She put one quiche on a plate and set it on the counter in front of Kelly with a fork.

"Aren't you having the other one?"

"I'm tempted. I wish I could, but there's so much cheese." Judith frowned. "Once you reach my age, you've got to watch your dairy intake. The inflammation can be hard on the body."

Was that her future? No carbs, no dairy. What was next? No wine, no meat?

Kelly was drawing a firm wine-and-meat line. She was not going to give up all life's pleasures.

"You eat up. You're so young, with a robust immune system. Let me live vicariously through you."

Kelly looked around, noticing Judith's laptop wasn't in the kitchen. "Do you mind if we go to your office and talk?"

"Why the office?"

Kelly shrugged and cut into the quiche with the fork. "Every important conversation I've had in this house has been in the office."

Judith sighed. "Can we save the serious talk until tomorrow? Or at the very latest until dinner? I just want to enjoy having you here, knowing that you're safe." She reached across the counter and patted Kelly's cheek. "Please. For me, let's spend the next few hours remembering what it's like to be here together. Enjoying each other's company."

She wished she could, but Hunter and the others were counting on her. Their lives had been on pause for almost year. She wasn't going to force them to wait any longer than necessary. If she could get the documents from Judith, she could be in the DNI's office before the end of the day.

"I'd like that, but there isn't time." Kelly set the fork down. "It's too important."

Judith sagged with disappointment, slumping over the counter. "I was afraid you were going to say that. You didn't come here to check on me, or because you needed somewhere safe to go. You only came because you need me to do something for you. Right?"

An acrid taste filled Kelly's mouth. She hadn't come for any of the reasons Judith had wanted. But her motives weren't selfish.

Still, her throat clenched from the burn of guilt. "I do need your help. I promise I'll come back and spend a week here with you over the summer. We'll be able to catch up properly."

"I'm not asking for a week. Our jobs are nonstop. There's always a fire to put out. I'm asking you to spend the day with me, like we used to. I've been watching the news all night about the drive-by shooting in Pentagon City. Gang-related." She tsked. "And the horrible accident with poor Freddie at a Metro station nearby. I've been worried sick about you. Life is so precious, and time goes by faster than you think. Just give me until dinner before you ask for any favors."

Shame speared through her chest. Kelly lowered her head. She didn't want to hurt her godmother. Once this was resolved, she'd make it up to her. But right now, Topaz didn't have the luxury of her wasting that kind of time. "If I could, I would, but it can't wait." She met Judith's brown eyes. "Can we discuss this in your office?"

With a defeated look on her face, Judith nodded. "If you insist."

HUNTER HAD TAKEN his time feeling out the SEALs John had brought in to help them out. They didn't use their real names. Instead, they went by the capitals of states—Austin, Denver, Jackson, Nashville. Austin was the one who had some talent with computers.

They didn't question Hunter's authority or doubt the importance of why they were there. Brothers-in-arms, giving up their precious free time, willing to fight on John's behalf, ready to put themselves in harm's way. All because a fellow SEAL had asked them to.

Hunter was committed to getting these boys back home, breathing and in one piece.

They'd made their way to Price's house in McLean. The back of the property butted up against Scott's Run Nature Preserve, a slice of wilderness in an urban sprawl. They'd parked at the preserve and cut through it, approaching the rear of the house.

Nashville was out front on point, conducting recon. With the snowfall painting everything white and the sun climbing higher in the sky, it made subterfuge harder. It was smarter to send one man ahead to scout things out and give them the all clear rather than have one of the neighbor's dogs catch them unawareness and alert the whole block to their presence.

They all wore balaclavas and gloves so that on the off chance they were spotted, no one would be able to identify them.

Hunter had called Price's office once they'd arrived at the preserve, to make sure he hadn't gone into the office early, though it was possible he was en route and they had missed him entirely.

Pale sunshine glinted off the snow on the ground, on the trees, on everything except the matte-black weaponry in their hands. Waiting for the cover of darkness would've been optimal, but the longer they delayed, the higher the odds of Quinlan finding them. Not to mention Hunter had no idea what kind of fallout to expect from Kelly's visit to Judith.

Staying low, they made their way through the woods. A knot of dread and uncertainty tightened in his gut. He had no idea what they were walking into. If he'd be able to rattle Price enough to get him to crack and give them the final piece of the puzzle they needed.

"You guys should come see this," Nashville said over the Bluetooth comms in their ears.

Hunter exchanged a questioning glance with Dean, who was closest to him.

They hustled through the rest of the preserve, getting to the tree line that faced the back of Price's house, and took a knee in the snow. Hunter glanced around, half expecting the house to be surrounded by armed guards, but there was no one in the immediate area.

"See what?" Hunter asked.

Nashville hand him a pair of binoculars. "The garage. Right side of the house."

Hunter peered through the lenses, focused where Nashville pointed.

Wisps of smoke wafted under the doors of the two-car garage. The hairs on the back of his neck rose on end. *What in the hell?*

Something was wrong.

He scanned the rest of the house for movement or signs of smoke or a possible fire anywhere else.

Nothing.

That knot in his gut grew bigger, tighter. "Let's check it out," Hunter said.

They burst from the tree line and swept up to the back door in formation like a coordinated unit that had worked together for a long time.

Nashville tried the knob. It turned. Unlocked. He opened the door, pushing it wide.

No alarm pinged.

If the security system had gone off, Austin had been prepared to use one of Zee's tricks to take care of it. The fact the system hadn't been armed was another bad sign.

They moved into the house soundlessly, spreading out in different directions. Silence descended around them as the sickening feeling he had ballooned inside him.

Hunter made a beeline through the kitchen to the garage. Exhaust fumes penetrated the space, prickling his senses. He reached for the knob.

Gage tapped him on the shoulder, stopping him. "Hold on." He unzipped a small backpack he'd brought with him and pulled out a couple of half face-piece respirators. As the team fixer, he was always prepared to stage a scene, make a body disappear. Ready to deal with the unexpected, including handling dangerous chemicals.

They removed their balaclavas to keep smoke from permeating the cloth and each put on a mask. Hurrying into the garage, Hunter shut the door quickly behind them.

Toxic exhaust fumes clouded the air gray. The bitter taste filled his mouth.

A Mercedes parked in the right bay, close to the door, was running. Based on the amount of smoke filling the space, he estimated the engine had been on at least a couple of hours. Maybe longer.

They drew closer to the vehicle.

"Do you see that?" Gage pointed to the tube stuffed through the cracked window into the car from the exhaust pipe.

Hunter's stomach clenched. He opened the door, letting out a noxious wave of smoke. Even with the masks, they both coughed as Hunter's eyes watered.

Wayne Price was in the front behind the wheel. His head was tipped to the side toward them. Blood and brain matter were splattered across the back of the seat. A gun lay near his right hand.

Hunter slammed the door shut, and they went back into the house.

They removed their masks and headed outside through the patio door for fresh air.

His eyes stung. His throat burned. His mind spun. Wayne Price was dead.

He handed Gage the mask and pulled the black balaclava on his face in case a neighbor was watching from behind curtains in a window.

Dean poked his head out the door. "Austin found something."

With a nod, Hunter followed Dean down a hallway to

the other side of the house. They entered an office. Austin was seated behind the desk and waved them over.

Hunter came around to the side of the chair. Austin moved the mouse, and the monitor woke up, but the screen hadn't been locked.

"It wasn't password protected?" Hunter asked.

"Nope. Either that's how the man in charge of one of the most clandestine organizations in the world operates or someone had him remove it. There's also this." He gestured to a Word document on the screen that read, *I'm sorry for the pain I caused. Forgive me.*

"That's convenient," Gage said, looking at the screen from the other side of the chair.

"I think it's safe to assume we agree this wasn't a suicide, but the work of a professional," Jackson said. "My question is, who has the guts, the power and the money to have the director of the CIA killed?"

Dean pulled his mask up, uncovering his face. "Andrew Clark?"

"Let's say it was him," Gage said. "*Why* would he do it? The odds are stacked against us, not them. Honestly, he didn't need to do this. He certainly didn't need to shoot him in the head and flood the garage with exhaust fumes."

"Wow," Nashville said. "That's some serious overkill."

It bugged Hunter, because it wasn't overkill. It had been deliberate, but he couldn't figure out the point. The gunshot had done the job—the exhaust fumes would only draw unwanted attention.

"Andrew is capable of a lot. But cold-blooded murder?" Hunter shook his head. "He doesn't have the spine for it, and how does eliminating Price help get him any closer to catching us?" This came back to the *why* at the heart of this. The one question they'd been trying to answer. "We were set up to protect a surveillance program the CIA needs in order to continue operating successfully over-seas," Hunter said, thinking aloud, still not certain about which one—Arcane or Silent Shadow. Both were vital, and public criticism of either would be devastating for the CIA. "A program that Price was willing to do anything to pro-tect, including kill our team." Now Price was the one dead.

"Who else would kill to protect it?" Denver asked.

An icy chill splashed over Hunter.

No, no, no. He didn't want to think it was possible.

But only one other person had the guts, the power, the resources, the hardness, the motive to go this far.

"The head of the NSA." *Judith.* "Anything or anyone that threatens one of her surveillance programs is a threat to her professionally." And the woman he loved had just gone running straight to the real enemy. "Kelly is in dan-ger. We've got to get to Harpers Ferry."

Chapter Fifteen

Judith sat behind her desk with her back to the windows that overlooked the snow-covered backyard. The second door in the office led to a private patio where Kelly had had countless heart-to-hearts with her godmother over the years.

"What is so pressing that couldn't wait a few hours?" Judith asked.

Kelly shifted her gaze from the classified laptop to her godmother. "I still need the documents that Freddie found for me."

"Freddie's death wasn't an accident, was it?"

"I don't think so."

"Were you somehow involved in the drive-by shooting?"

"I was the target."

Judith squeezed her eyes shut, clutching the arm of her chair as though she'd gotten dizzy for a moment. Then she looked at Kelly. "What is this about? And why is Price on the warpath?"

Kelly cleared her throat. "I need to know the truth about Ashref Saleh and why he was really killed."

Judith straightened in her chair with that laser-focused, command-the-room way she had about her. All vestiges of a loving godmother vanished in a blink. "Ashref Saleh? Is all this about the rogue Topaz unit?"

Sweat rolled down Kelly's spine. "Yes. It is."

"I'm confused." Her eyes narrowed as her tone turned cold and hard. "I was under the impression you already knew why and were in the process of hunting down those traitors."

"It turns out things are more complicated than I was led to believe." Less was always more when it came to Judith, but she didn't see a way around telling her the whole story.

Her godmother's jaw clenched, her gaze raking over Kelly with a look that could strip the paint off the walls. "I don't think it's complicated at all. I think it's about one man. Hunter Wright."

"No." Kelly scooted to the edge of her chair and leaned forward. "This concerns the entire team."

"Have you seen him?" When Kelly didn't immediately respond, Judith continued, "You better tell me you have more common sense than to let that man get into your head, filling it with garbage, ridiculous theories that'll ruin your career."

Kelly's stomach rolled as she replayed the things Hunter had said in the motel room about how this conversation would go. "I haven't seen him. I've done some digging into—"

"Now you're lying to me?" Judith shook her head. "You have a love bite on your neck, and the smell of a man is all over you. Did you even bother to shower after you crawled out of his bed and came rushing to me to help him, an enemy of the state?"

Shame and guilt bubbled up in her throat, choking her. Before she could gather her thoughts for a worthy response, a car door slammed closed outside.

They both looked toward the hall.

"Who's here?" Kelly asked.

"It must be Zach. He was the one who suggested I come up here to avoid the news frenzy that would be outside Fort Meade this morning because of Freddie Herschel. We have to draft a statement to release to the media." She leaned back in her chair. "He was also the one who told me you were only coming here to get something out of me." A hint of pain flashed across her face. A second later, she'd wiped her expression clean.

"You told him I was coming?" *Why would she do that?*

"He predicted it last night, and I confirmed it this morning. You show up at my office, wanting to tap an analyst because you've been locked out of certain files at Langley. Then one of my senior guys turns up dead. Zach put two and two together. He figured you didn't get what you needed and would have no qualms endangering me in whatever you've gotten yourself involved in. Apparently, that's Hunter Wright."

The front door opened. A cold draft blew through the house, reaching the office. Footsteps came down the hall.

Kelly turned, glancing over her shoulder as Zach appeared in the doorway.

"You were right," Judith said to him. "She doesn't care about me. The only thing she's concerned about is Hunter. Can you believe she wants me to help a traitor to this country, a fugitive on the most-wanted list of every law enforcement agency and Interpol?"

"I can believe it." Zach strode into the room, up to his mother, and put a hand on her shoulder. "Did you give any thought to how this could hurt her?" he asked Kelly. "What the possible impact would be to her career?"

She stared at her godmother. "I don't want to put you in this impossible position." If there were another way, a better way...

"Then don't." Judith's voice softened along with the look in her eyes. "Think about my life and your own. You already got Freddie killed. How many more need to die?"

"I'm here trying to prevent that. I'm trying to save lives. Those of the Topaz unit. They were set up to assassinate Ashref, and I won't stop until I prove it. With proof of a motive, I can take the rest of the evidence we have and go to the director of national intelligence. Make sure that Price pays for what he did. I'm begging you to help me. I promise I'll keep you safe. Topaz will protect you."

Judith scowled at her, a look she knew too well, telegraphing disappointment. "Oh, my dear, I'm not the one who needs protection. I've been the one protecting you."

Kelly recoiled in her chair, not understanding what she was talking about.

"Ashref Saleh found out about Arcane," Judith said slowly, but the words plowed into Kelly like a high-speed train. "We intercepted a conversation of his where he was planning to hold a press conference to tell the world about how we spy on our allies, which wouldn't have been too detrimental by itself, but somehow, he'd learned about our methods and how to circumvent them. Now that would've been damaging."

That was the understatement of a century. It would've sent shock waves through the intelligence community, crippled CIA operations abroad and ended Judith's career.

It was the kind of thing you had buried by any means necessary before it buried you.

"When I approached Wayne Price about a solution to our mutual problem, he was unwilling to cooperate with my proposed methods, which left me one option. Blackmail. I had unsavory information about him. Something he never wanted disclosed to the public. Once he was on

board with my plan to have Ashref assassinated, I chose
Topaz for the mission."

The declaration unhinged Kelly's jaw. She shook her
head, not wanting to believe her godmother was capable
of this. "Wh-what? Why them?" Not that any team should
have been set up and painted as traitors, but this felt deeply
personal. A direct attack against her.

"Because your relationship with Hunter Wright needed
to end," Zach said.

"He was a distraction," Judith said. "An impediment
to you reaching your full potential. I even had my private
IT expert create the video of Hunter outside the bank in
the Cayman Islands. He altered real footage of him in
Miami. From what Wayne told me, after you watched the
clip, it sealed the deal. You believed the story hook, line
and sinker."

It was true. Kelly had swallowed the lie they'd spoon-
fed her and had presumed them guilty. "You had no right.
To meddle in my life. To destroy theirs."

"I was doing you a favor," Judith said, anger festering
just beneath the surface.

Kelly sat stunned and reeling, trying to wrap her mind
around what this meant. "The black site, where I was
taken? Were you behind that, too?"

"Of course. I knew you wouldn't let this go. Not unless I gave you something else to focus on. Like your own
survival."

Something inside Kelly withered. "So you had me and
Andrew tortured?"

Judith made an amused sound, almost a snort. "You
still haven't put it together?" She cackled. "Andrew works
for me. He's my inside man who was keeping an eye on
Wayne and you. For the record, he was never interrogated."

"But he had bruises. I saw them."

"He was roughed up a little to make it convincing. To sell you the idea that you two were in it together. But he was the one who oversaw your torture."

The more Judith confessed, the more a sickening anxiety churned inside Kelly. The last bit of hope for a misunderstanding died. This was the demon she'd been battling for almost a year. Her godmother. "How could you do that to me? How could you let him… Andrew…" Her heart crumbled. The pain swamping her was so intense, so brutal, it stole her voice. There were no words for this. The magnitude of such a betrayal was unfathomable.

Unconscionable.

"In addition to more money, it was a nonnegotiable for him. I had your predecessor eliminated in the 'avalanche,'" she said, using air quotes, "to clear the way for you to be promoted over Andrew. How could I not give him the one thing he asked for?"

Horrified, she stared at the woman who had helped raise her. The same one who she always thought of as too perfect to measure up to her example. Of how to be a woman. A leader. A mother. "Do you have any idea how I suffered? The nightmares I still have about that place. The anxiety. The paranoia. The psychological scars it left. How dare you?" The words left her mouth like a barrage of bullets.

"It was for your own good. Temporary trauma to keep you from digging where your nose didn't belong. And it worked, too. Better than I expected." Judith sounded so pleased with herself, so smug. "It had you chomping at the bit to tear Topaz to pieces. Then Hunter Wright got to you and set this whole disaster in motion. I warned Wayne to keep you focused and from stirring up any trouble. Since he couldn't even do that right and had the nerve to let Andrew run the op that almost got you killed in Pentagon City, I had him taken care of earlier this morning. *For you.*"

The last two words seared through her.

One heartrending blow after another. She couldn't take much more. "Price? He's dead?"

"I had the whole thing worked out once I realized Zach was right and that you'd come to me again for help. If you had only waited until dinner, not even that long. I made sure Wayne's body will be found soon, if it hasn't already. A neighbor walking their dog will see smoke coming from his garage and report it. Then I was going to convince you that Hunter was responsible. The police will find his fingerprints on the scene."

Hunter.

Thinking of how Judith had manipulated this tragedy into something even more devastating sent an ache through every cell of her body. Hunter and his team had been set up because of Kelly's attachment to them. Her love for them. For Hunter.

"The situation would've been resolved," Judith said, "with you back on the right side of things. On my side. But you had to go and ruin it. By sleeping with him."

"What?" Zach said, his gaze bouncing between them.

"Yes." His mother patted his hand. "She's been with him instead of recognizing the perfect partner she could have in you. It's the reason she's hell-bent on helping that man."

Rage burst through Kelly like a strip of firecrackers exploding. "You're going pay for this. For all of it. You're going to rot in prison."

"No, I don't think I will." Judith slipped her hand in her pocket and held up a fob. A sad smile tightened across her mouth as she hit the button. "I'm sorry about this. After your father tried to stand in the way of my appointment to director of the NSA because he thought I was unfit, unstable, I poisoned him, but I promised myself I would look after you," she said, and bile rushed up Kelly's throat, making her want to heave. "Ensure you got to the very top of the CIA and that nothing would stand in your way. Unfortunately, now it comes to this."

Zach's gaze lifted to something behind Kelly.

In the reflection of the window, she caught a glimpse of a man. Six-two. Muscular. Bald.

Quinlan.

Fear crystallized her blood.

A flash of wire swept past her face. Without thinking, she reacted, thrusting a hand up. Her wrist caught the garrote meant for her throat. The wire of the strangulation device bit into her skin, locking her arm in front of her neck. She flailed, trying to break free.

"Mother! What are you doing?" Zach lunged to help her.

Judith snatched his arm and dragged him backward. "What does it look like I'm doing?"

Kelly's heart thudded against her rib cage as she struggled to get loose from Quinlan's vicious hold. The wire dug savagely into her wrist, breaking the skin, drawing blood as the pressure on her arm lodged against her windpipe and cut off her oxygen.

If she lost consciousness, it was game over.

She slammed her foot up onto the edge of the desk and pushed with all her might as she thrust her body back, sending the chair flying down to the floor.

The swift change in angle forced Quinlan to adjust and lower himself in response, but he didn't let go.

She threw her other foot up and back, kicking him in the head. Once. Twice.

His hands opened, dropping the garrote as he instinctively clutched his face. She flung the wire away, rolled onto all fours and spun with her leg extended, plowing a boot heel into his knee.

An *oof* left his mouth, but he didn't fall as she had hoped.

Kelly scrambled backward and climbed to her feet. A quick glance over her shoulder at the door that led to the patio told her there was no escape. Another man from Beta team was standing outside. She was trapped.

Breath tight in her lungs, her heart a jackhammer, nerves jangled, she welcomed the adrenaline flooding her body. She'd need every drop of it.

Zach yanked loose of his mother's grasp. "You're not supposed to kill her! She's mine! You promised."

Judith slapped him hard across the face, the sharp sound bouncing off the walls. "Pull yourself together. Remember who you are. A Farren! We don't fall to pieces." She turned to someone else entering the room. "Get him out of here."

Two more men from Beta team entered. One grabbed Zach and hauled him out. The other came up alongside Quinlan, helping him block the other door.

"Don't kill her just yet," Judith said. "First, we need to find out where Topaz is so you can finally take care of them once and for all. Then you can dispose of her." Judith's gaze slid to Kelly. "You could've had everything. Led the CIA. Had Zach for a husband. Me, not only as an ally in the intelligence community, but as your mother-in-law, too. If only you'd heeded the warnings. If only you had been loyal, to me." She spat the words through gritted teeth. "Now instead of punishing Andrew and this beast," she said, waving a hand at Quinlan, "for targeting you, Andrew will get to wear the crown." With a heavy sigh and a distressed shake of her head, Judith strode out of the room.

Quinlan smiled, his teeth bloody from her blows to his

face. "I bet you're wishing I had tossed Andrew Clark out of that helicopter now, aren't you?"

"As a matter of fact, I am." Widening her stance and raising her fists, she braced herself for what was to come.

AFTER RUNNING THROUGH the woods alone, Hunter came to a sliding stop and took up a position, lying prone, concealed by trees in the rear of Judith's house. Out of the group, they'd agreed he was most likely the best shot at a distance. The others were surrounding the house, preparing to breach.

A ball of dread had lodged in his chest as they'd sped to Harpers Ferry. Now his heart was racing, and he was anxious to find Kelly. To get her out of the house. The place was crawling with mercenaries. There had been additional vehicles parked on the far side of the old stable, hidden out of sight.

Looking through the scope of his sniper rifle, he spotted a man posted outside a patio door.

Past him in the office, Hunter saw Kelly. She was in a chair with her arms behind her back at an awkward angle, and it seemed her wrists were bound. Her bottom lip was bloody. Her hair was disheveled. The office was a wreck, as if there'd been a knock-down, drag-out fight. His heart squeezed like a fist at the thought of what she must've been through.

Quinlan stood in front of her, his mouth moving—he was talking to her.

Kelly shook her head, saying something in response.

Quinlan slapped her backhanded, so hard that her head twisted, and she nearly fell from the chair, but before she could, he grabbed her chin and wrenched her up in the seat.

A surge of rage rushed through Hunter, faster and hotter than anything he'd ever known. He wanted to kill that man. Storm inside the house and do it with his bare hands. But to help Kelly get out of this alive, he had to remain calm and calculated.

He sighted back through the scope and waited for his team to make their move. Opening fire now on Quinlan or the guy standing outside would be premature. He didn't have a full view of the office. Another man, armed, could be standing in a corner or near the doorway out of his line of sight.

Quinlan drew close to Kelly. The bastard smiled, laughed in her face.

She threw a forward headbutt into the man's skull.

He staggered backward, only a step or two, blood gushing from his nose. As he wiped at it with his hand, anger radiated from him in waves. His face twisted into a dark scowl. Raising a fist, he punched her in the stomach.

Hunter's whole body clenched.

Kelly doubled over, coughing and trembling as though she'd felt the blow down to the bone. Quinlan yelled at her. Then he reached behind her back and did something that made Kelly rear back and scream in agony.

What was he doing to her?

Had he broken her hand and was applying pressure to a fracture?

Whatever he did to her, the pain had been instantaneous and horrific.

Fury spiked through Hunter, kicking up a revving sensation in his chest. Gritting his teeth, he caressed the trigger. An inner voice cautioned him to wait, to remain steadfast, but he couldn't stand by and watch Kelly get beaten. He wasn't equipped to do it.

He tapped the comms in his ear. "You need to hurry up before I do something rash."

"Hold position," Nashville whispered in a detached tone. "Preparing to enter on my count."

Hang on, Red. We're coming for you.

Hunter took comfort in the sound of the countdown in his ear.

"Three," Nashville said. "Two. One. Breach!"

The din of percussive bangs, thuds, shouts and gunfire erupted in rapid succession, blending in a blur.

SEALs were experts at combat in close quarters. Hunter was relying on their experience, combined with the skill sets of Gage and Dean, to squash the other mercs and drive Quinlan out through the back door into the open.

As the others took out targets and cleared the house, Hunter held his position, peering through his scope. Finger on the trigger. Ready to pull it.

The man posted outside the door had drawn his weapon, his head on a swivel looking for incoming targets. As Hunter had suspected, a third man emerged from a corner in the office that had been beyond his line of sight and hustled toward the inner door, heading for the hall.

Now. This was his chance.

But before he could get Quinlan in his crosshairs, the man grabbed Kelly by the hair and yanked her up onto her feet.

Come to me. Don't go deeper into the house. Come to me. Hunter repeated the words, over and over.

A prayer.

A mantra.

A war cry.

Quinlan held a gun to Kelly's head and locked his free arm around her neck, pulling her back against him. He steered her toward the patio door.

That's it. Keep coming.

The second man scanned the perimeter, providing cover

for Quinlan. Gunfire continued inside the house along with the thunderous sound of flash-bang grenades designed to stun and temporarily disable a person's senses.

Quinlan shoved his way outside, using Kelly as a human shield. Her hands were restrained behind her, but her feet were unbound. He shuffled her forward, keeping his head behind hers like he was prepared for a sniper.

The second guy changed position, moving to cover Quinlan's back in case anyone came through the house and attacked them from behind.

With the gun to Kelly's head, Hunter was reluctant the pull the trigger. But he couldn't let them get around the side of the house to a vehicle. He had to take action before that happened.

He thought about what to do as he weighed his options. They were limited. He was too far away to rush either man and hope for the best.

Taking out the second man first might work, since he was positioned behind them, closer to the door.

Quinlan would have to turn around to see what happened to him, leaving his back exposed for Hunter to take a shot.

Hunter adjusted the side knob for windage and put the other guy in his crosshairs. He took a breath, his finger on the trigger. On the exhale, he squeezed. The attached silencer swallowed the sound, and the man dropped.

Quinlan must've heard the body fall, because he froze. But he didn't turn around as Hunter had needed him to. Instead, Quinlan kept the muzzle of the gun pressed to Kelly's temple with her still trapped in front of him and stared at the tree line, searching for the shooter.

For Hunter.

What he feared by holding the position was that one

of his men would make it to the office and that Quinlan would panic. Possibly shoot Kelly.

"Come out!" Quinlan said. "Or she's as good as dead!"

Hunter removed the safety from the nine-millimeter with attached sound suppressor that he had in his shoulder holster under his jacket. "Okay. Just don't hurt her." He got up from his position, exposing himself. With both hands raised, holding the rifle out in the air, he stepped out from between the trees.

Quinlan tightened his hold on her. "Drop the rifle."

Still walking forward, Hunter kept drawing closer to them. "Let her go first."

"This isn't a negotiation. Drop it or I'll kill her right now," Quinlan ordered.

The fear on Kelly's face was palpable, but he knew that it was more for him than herself. She shook her head as her busted bottom lip began to tremble. "Don't. He'll kill us both."

"Shut up!" Quinlan jerked back the arm locked around her throat, choking her.

Hunter took another step and another. "All right. Please, don't hurt her anymore."

There was desperation in Quinlan's cruel eyes, and that made him even more dangerous. Because he'd do absolutely anything to get out of this and save his own skin.

"Stop where you are," Quinlan demanded, jabbing the muzzle of his gun into her temple so hard that she winced. "Not another step."

Hunter's throat went bone-dry. "No one else needs to die." He slowly lowered the rifle to the ground, but he was still too far to lunge for the man. A few more feet and it would've been possible.

Now there was nothing stopping Quinlan from shooting him.

He was counting on the merc to seize the opportunity. Hunter was ready, but he'd have to move fast the second Quinlan pulled the gun away from Kelly's head. The probability was high Hunter would be shot, but it was a risk worth taking if it meant he could save Kelly.

Quinlan moved the muzzle, swinging the gun in his direction as Hunter drew the nine-millimeter from his holster.

Kelly rammed her elbow back into Quinlan's ribs, throwing off his aim. Giving Hunter the clean shot he needed.

He pulled the trigger twice. Bullets whispered through the air, putting Quinlan down with two in his chest.

A flash of movement registered in the patio door. Judith. She was holding a gun, pointed at Kelly.

His heart seized. Hunter whirled and raised his weapon. Too late.

A gunshot rent the air, sounding like an explosion.

Kelly spun and fell to the ground. The snow was splattered red with her blood.

Hunter was about to fire at the woman responsible for this entire mess, sending Judith straight to hell where she belonged, when Gage charged out of the patio door, tackling the older woman to the cold earth.

Instantly, Hunter was moving.

"Kelly!" he cried as he ran to her. His legs weren't moving fast enough, as though he was treading through quicksand.

She was facedown.

Dropping to his knees, he pulled a butterfly knife from his pocket and cut the zip tie binding her. He noticed the deep gash on her wrist but was frantic with worry, terrified she'd been badly injured, and turned her over onto her back.

She blinked up at him. *Alive.* She was alive. The snow around her was red, blood splattered across her sweater. He couldn't be sure where she'd been shot.

"Hunter." Face bruised, she clutched her left arm and sat up, groaning.

The bullet had hit her in the shoulder.

He sat on the ground and gently tugged her into his chest. A flood of relief nearly brought tears to his eyes. Gratitude clogged his throat. "You're going to be all right."

She rested her head against him. "I can't believe you're here."

Stroking her hair, he kissed her forehead, her cheek. She was alive, safe and in his arms, and he was never letting her go.

Kelly turned her head toward Judith, who had been restrained and was being hauled up off the ground by Gage.

"Why couldn't you be loyal?" Judith screamed at her. "Why! After everything I've done for you. Ungrateful. Selfish. Brat."

Gage dragged the raving woman into the house.

"Oh, no," Kelly muttered.

"What's wrong?" He looked her over once more to be sure he hadn't missed an injury. "What is it?"

"Judith killed Price and planted your fingerprints at his house for the authorities to find. It'll be her word and Zach's against ours. She'll twist and manipulate everything." Kelly looked at him, her eyes glassy, exhaustion stamped all over her. "The police may not believe us about what happened. I can't lose you. Not again."

"It's going to be okay, Red." He smiled. "We've got Judith's confession recorded."

"But how?"

He took the pendant of the necklace between his fingers and held it up. "As soon as you left the motel alone,

I activated it because I was worried about you. I left the computer with Hope and Kate. Asked them to watch out for you and if you ran into any trouble to call me. Sure enough, they did, but we were already on the way here."

"You knew? About Judith?"

"I suspected after we found Price dead at his house."

Pressing her mouth to his, she gave him a tender kiss and hissed in pain at the pressure to the cut on her lip.

"I'm sorry I didn't get here sooner," he said, staring at her bruises, hating that she'd been hurt.

She leaned against him. "Thank you."

He put his arm around her. "For what?"

"For being you. For following your instincts. For coming here for me."

He smiled, even though she couldn't see it. "I'll always be here for you. You can count on that."

Epilogue

Four months later

The sun was low on the horizon over the water of Jamaica Bay, painting the sky dusky orange and purple. With her arms entwined around Hunter's neck, Kelly stared in his crystal-blue eyes, swaying with him on the dance floor of the Bay Resort on Breezy Point in New York.

"The wedding was so beautiful," she said. "Zee is such a gorgeous bride." She glanced over at the couple, who were also dancing.

The bride wore a formfitting gown of champagne silk with a deep V neckline that was sexy yet tasteful. The fabric artfully gathered in all the right places to ensure flattering lines all over her body. Her long hair was in a chic updo with loose spiral curls framing her face.

John wore an impeccable tux. Classic. Debonair.

They'd gotten married at sunset on the beach outside the Bay Resort.

"One of the sweetest parts of the ceremony," Hunter said, "was when John gave Olivia a ring, too, and vowed to be the best father that he could."

Kelly had gotten choked up by it. The heartfelt declaration had even made Zee's parents teary-eyed. "This has been a perfect day." She felt lucky to be a part of it.

She glanced around the reception hall. It was packed

with SEALs from John's side, cops from Zee's and operatives who were thrilled to see them tie the knot. Only at a Topaz unit wedding.

Judith was behind bars, awaiting a trial that would never be held in the public eye. Andrew was also locked up, but he had copped a plea deal and provided a sworn statement against Judith. Zach had been fired from the NSA. No charges had been brought against him due to the lack of incriminating evidence.

The Topaz unit had been exonerated, fully cleared of any wrongdoing and reinstated to the CIA with commendations for meritorious service and back pay for the time they had spent on the run, trying to clear their names.

Kelly was allowed to keep the position of deputy director, and the president had appointed a new director of the agency. Only Hunter had resigned, choosing to take a job as a contractor, working for a private security firm to prevent any future conflicts of interest.

Things were as they should be.

Gage sat beside Hope with a hand on her growing belly. They'd made plans to get married right after the baby was born.

Dean, his brother, Lucas, and Kate toasted to something with bubbly. The trio talked and laughed, inseparable. It warmed Kelly's heart to see the two brothers patch things up and have a fresh start together after everything they'd been through.

"Have I told you how spectacular you look?" Hunter twirled her around, letting her spin in the sapphire dress that matched her eyes, and brought her back flush against his solid body.

"Yes, you have, but feel free to do so again."

They both chuckled.

"Having you in my arms, living together, I feel like I won the lottery."

"I'm definitely the winner. You cook. You change Coco's litter box. You're great in bed and easy on the eyes," she said, and he patted her backside. "Easy, tiger. Don't start something you can't finish." More laughter flowed between them. "Seriously, I am the winner. I learned very early on not to show anybody who I really am because I thought nobody would see me and love me for it. That I wouldn't be good enough. But then you made me feel like I was everything you ever wanted."

"You are." Sincerity gleamed in his eyes.

"Your heart is so strong, and your belief in me surprises me every day. You taught me how to feel safe in a world where tomorrow isn't guaranteed. You showed me what a family is supposed to be. I don't ever want to be without you. I love you so much."

"I love you, too." He cupped her face in his hands and kissed her. "You just stole my thunder."

"What do you mean?"

"I was going take you outside, pull out the diamond ring I have in my pocket and propose, but I don't think I can top that."

Her heart fluttered in her throat, and she tensed. "You were?"

"I was." A devastating grin spread across his lips. "I guess I'll have to keep the ring."

"I don't need a ring." Slipping her arms around his neck, she pulled him close. "All I'll ever need is you."

He kissed her again, running his hand up and down her back, making her entire body tingle. "So does that mean I can return it and get a refund?" He raised an eyebrow.

"No, I'll still take the diamond."

He laughed, and she grinned up at him as her heart swelled to overflowing.

A perfect day indeed.

* * * * *

COMING SOON!

We really hope you enjoyed reading this book.
If you're looking for more romance, be sure to
head to the shops when new books are
available on

Thursday 3rd February

MILLS & BOON

THE HEART OF ROMANCE

A ROMANCE FOR EVERY READER

MODERN

Prepare to be swept off your feet by sophisticated, sexy and seductive heroes, in some of the world's most glamourous and romantic locations, where power and passion collide.

HISTORICAL

Escape with historical heroes from time gone by. Whether your passion is for wicked Regency Rakes, muscled Vikings or rugged Highlanders, awaken the romance of the past.

MEDICAL

Set your pulse racing with dedicated, delectable doctors in the high-pressure world of medicine, where emotions run high and passion, comfort and love are the best medicine.

True Love

Celebrate true love with tender stories of heartfelt romance, from the rush of falling in love to the joy a new baby can bring, and a focus on the emotional heart of a relationship.

Desire

Indulge in secrets and scandal, intense drama and plenty of sizzling hot action with powerful and passionate heroes who have it all: wealth, status, good looks…everything but the right woman.

HEROES

Experience all the excitement of a gripping thriller, with an intense romance at its heart. Resourceful, true-to-life women and strong, fearless men face danger and desire - a killer combination!

To see which titles are coming soon, please visit

millsandboon.co.uk/nextmonth

LET'S TALK
Romance

For exclusive extracts, competitions
and special offers, find us online:

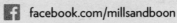 facebook.com/millsandboon

@MillsandBoon

@MillsandBoonUK

Get in touch on 01413 063232

For all the latest titles coming soon, visit
millsandboon.co.uk/nextmonth

MILLS & BOON
MODERN
Power and Passion

Prepare to be swept off your feet by sophisticated, sexy and seductive heroes, in some of the world's most glamourous and romantic locations, where power and passion collide.

Julia James

Heiress's
PREGNANCY SCANDAL

MILLS & BOON
MODERN

Jennie Lucas

Chosen as the
SHEIKH'S ROYAL BRIDE

MILLS & BOON

Kim Lawrence

A WEDDING
at the
ITALIAN'S DEMAND

Sharon Kendrick

The
SHEIKH'S SECRET BABY

MILLS & BOON
MODERN

MILLS & BOON
MEDICAL
Pulse-Racing Passion

Set your pulse racing with dedicated, delectable doctors in the high-pressure world of medicine, where emotions run high and passion, comfort and love are the best medicine.

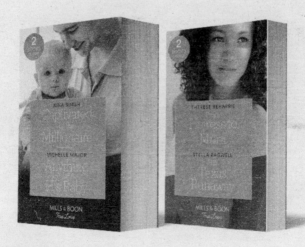